DEATH
RATTLE

DAVID JEWELL

A Wild Wolf Publication

Published by Wild Wolf Publishing in 2020
Copyright © 2020 David Jewell

HB ISBN: 978-1-907954-76-4
PB ISBN: 978-1-907954-75-7
Also available as an E-Book

www.wildwolfpublishing.com

Cover photographer: Phil Punton
Cover Model: Matthew Jackson

*To Alistair for almost fifty years of friendship
and sage advice.*

Thanks to The Cramlington Writer's Group and, in particular, former Detective Chief Superintendent Barry Stewart for his sage advice.

My thanks to the acclaimed author Mari Hannah and her partner, my former boss, Mo for their encouragement from the very start. I must thank all my author friends, who had confidence in me when the going got tough.

Thanks to award-winning screenwriter, Elliott Kerrigan and John Cowton of No Quibble Scribble for their constant encouragement and faith in me.

Thank you to all my family and friends, too numerous to name, who have constantly been there, backing, supporting and putting up with me through the long and difficult process of writing.

A special thank you goes to Rod Glenn and Wild Wolf Publishing for all the assistance and for bringing this book to fruition.

A special thanks to my good friend, Philip of Phil Punton Photography, whose skill and professionalism brought the cover images to life, and also to cover model, Mathew Jackson and mum Corina for their invaluable input.

The *Death Rattle* is a common term used for Terminal Respiratory Secretions: It occurs when a person loses the ability to clear their throat or swallow, and is the wet, rattling sound as the person breathes in and out through the resultant blockages. It signals that the person is transitioning to the final stage of the dying process.

i

CHAPTER 1

Darren Wilson was dying.

The crimson stain rapidly spreading across his white shirt, confirmed it.

He stared up at the night sky and felt his body shutting down.

He could hear an unfamiliar gurgling sound.

It was the sound made by someone as they take their last breath.

The sound just before the silence.

The death rattle.

Alex Morton had been standing still in the shadows of the twelfth century Castle Keep for almost twenty minutes. The Keep and its fortified gatehouse, The Black Gate, were all that remained of an ancient city fortress.

Originally, a Roman settlement, Pons Aelius, had guarded a bridge across the River Tyne, but over the years, the wooden motte and bailey style fortress had been replaced by a new castle upon the Tyne, from which the modern city had derived its name.

At eleven thirty at night, Alex was not on a historic tour of the city. The reason for his night time expedition to the area was moored firmly in the present.

Below The Keep, an ancient stone stairway, weathered and worn, concave from centuries of human footfall, meanders down towards the Quayside area of the River Tyne, which marked the southern boundary of the city.

Slipping out from the shadows and treading softly on the granite steps, Alex made his way down and under a stone arch, and quietly took a right turn into the area known as the Gardens. In that isolated and poorly lit area, lurks a secret world hidden from the lights of the nearby bars. To those in the know, it is the busiest of the city's gay cruising areas, where amongst the overgrown walkways, barristers and builders, professionals and prostitutes, meet as equals on the level playing field of anonymous sex.

DEATH RATTLE

Alex paused and listened. In the distance, he could hear the sounds of revellers from one of the city centre bars but, from the Gardens, there was silence.

To Alex, traditional gay bars were dying a slow lingering death; now populated by old men, sitting silently at the bar and swivelling on their stools to peek at the door whenever anyone entered.

They were all hoping that it might be some handsome young man, who would saunter across to them and begin a conversation, before heading home with them, to the envy of all the other old men clutching their warm beer.

It never happened.

Alex was well aware that at forty-five, the blush had already left his rose. The expanding midriff and thinning hair made it near impossible to pick up in bars the sort of young man who could set his heart thumping.

These days, the young good looking ones used apps or gay chat sites, where they sought other young *twinks* for *right now* sex. On their profiles, they would include categorical disclaimers, such as 'No-one over twenty five' and 'Don't be older than my dad'.

Bastards! One day, they too would be in their forties with fading looks.

Alex sullenly referred to these apps and sites as *dial a fuck*.

Instead, Alex resorted to regular visits to this, his favourite cruising spot. Here, he could find his release from more readily available partners. Sometime he would score lucky with some wanderer, too far in the closet to go on the scene, in case someone saw them. Usually they were married. Very occasionally, he would spot a teenager, too young to get into the bars without fake ID, but guys that young held no appeal to Alex. He had never regarded himself as a *chicken hawk*.

Moving cautiously along the path, bordered on both sides by shrubbery, he strained to catch any sound that might indicate he was not alone. Taking out his mobile phone, he glanced down at the display.

Almost midnight on a freezing Sunday night in early December, a frost was forming on the ground.

He decided to hang on another fifteen minutes, before

3

giving it up as a bad cause and retreating to the isolation of his one bedroom flat.

Suddenly, he could make out the faint sound of footsteps coming from further along the path and spotted a shadowy figure skulking in the darkness. As he watched, the figure slipped off the path and into the gloom.

Was his patience about to pay off?

His heart began to beat faster.

It could be a possible conquest, but equally it could be someone wanting to rob or beat up those who cruised the area. How much of the excitement was expectation and how much fear, Alex couldn't decide.

Advancing towards the area that the sound had come from, Alex warily approached a gap in the bushes, where the figure had melted into the darkness

Ahead of him, he could see a vague shape, barely visible against the thick dark mass of foliage.

Alex hesitated. Unsure whether to step further into the gloom.

The figure slowly moved towards him, until close enough for Alex to make out the stranger's features.

The face looking back was quite a few years younger than Alex, possibly in his early twenties, but that hardly registered, as Alex gave what he hoped was his best seductive smile.

There was the briefest exchange of glances, an unspoken agreement, and seconds later, both were making their way deeper into the thick undergrowth to a small deserted clearing shrouded by bushes.

They turned and faced each other.

Wordlessly, Alex dropped to his knees.

The younger man glanced around nervously, before reaching down and quickly unzipping his jeans.

It was then that Alex sensed that they were not alone.

Glancing into the dense vegetation, no more than three feet away from where he knelt, eyes were staring out at him.

With trousers open and unaware of the third person in their unholy trinity, the stranger hissed an impatient, 'Hurry up!'

But Alex didn't hear him.

Instead, he gazed transfixed at the figure lying on the

nearby ground.

At first, he had thought it was one of the voyeurs who come to the area, not to meet sexual partners, but to watch others indulge; getting their erotic thrills through a sort of sexual encounter by proxy.

However, the eyes that stared back were not wide with interest, but with shock.

The same shock Darren Wilson had expressed thirty minutes earlier, as the point of the blade had slid between his ribs, slicing upwards through the vital organs and penetrating deep within his chest.

DAVID JEWELL

CHAPTER 2

The caterwauling wail of the police siren forced several drunken revellers to sprint for the kerb, as the marked patrol car, blue lights flashing, scythed through the crowded Bigg Market and down towards the High Level Bridge.

The anonymous caller had telephoned from a nearby phone box, claiming to have seen a dead body in the Gardens. The two police officers didn't think so. With almost all calls coming from mobiles these days, anything from a public phone usually spelled hoax.

Any misgivings had to take second place to force performance indicators; that detailed the requirement to attend the scene of any treble nine call within set timed guidelines. Even as the patrol car slid to a stop on the cobbled stones below the Castle Keep, the passenger was calling in the *at scene status* to Control Room.

Climbing out, the two officers made their way across the glistening cobblestones to the top of the steps, leading into the Gardens. Gingerly descending the worn steps and through the ancient stone arch, they turned right and into the murky darkness.

Together, they began rummaging in the bushes on either side of the main pathway, using their extendable batons to part the undergrowth.

They were going through the motions of searching, but both had already decided that the incident had all the makings of a wasted journey.

'Dirty bastards,' the older of the two officers muttered under his breath as, twisting his face, he avoided a used condom hanging limply from a lower branch of a bush.

Parting some branches, his eyes becoming accustomed to the gloom, he noticed what appeared to be a bag of abandoned clothing. Being careful to avoid the obscene decoration dangling to his left, he leaned further into the undergrowth.

A sharp cry escaped his lips and he jerked back, causing his partner to hurry to his side. Together, they took in the scene before them.

Lying on his back, wide eyed, with face frozen in

6

horror, was the body of a man. His shirt and leather jacket were soaked with fresh blood, which ran in rivulets across his chest and pooled on the frozen soil, forming a dark stain.

A cold corpse on even colder ground.

The phone on Jack Slade's bedside table rattled him awake.

Glancing over at the display through bleary eyes, he gave an involuntary wince. He had no doubt who was on the other end.

If the on-call Detective Inspector was being woken at one o'clock in the morning it was never good news. Usually, it meant one of two things; some poor sod was either lying in a hospital fighting for his life - or more often than not, had already lost the battle.

Jack reached out for the phone.

Less than fifteen minutes and a quick shower later, he felt human again. Pulling on a white shirt, he selected a dark blue tie, which he tied into a double Windsor. Finishing the knot, he stared at his reflection in the mirror.

At thirty-five, his dark brown hair had not yet started greying and at six foot two and eighty-five kilos, he could not be accused of letting himself go to seed. But, it was the deepening lines around his pale blue eyes that betrayed his age. They bore testament to a police career in which he had dealt with the incidents that most reasonable people only got to see in horror movies.

In the past thirteen years since joining Northumbria Police, Jack had seen more than his fair share of bloodshed and violence, ranging from tragic accident to vicious murder.

Now, as Detective Inspector on H.MET, the Homicide Major Enquiry Team, Jack and Death had become more than nodding acquaintances.

Add to the mix, a failed marriage that had barely lasted eighteen months, and he was lucky to still have any hair left at all.

The marriage had been doomed from the start and the only decent thing that came out of it was his son. Not that he got to see much of him since Elaine had moved away. How old would he be now? Ten? No, eleven.

To help mask the pain of his son moving away, Jack

had become utterly consumed by his work.

Shaking off the dark thoughts, he checked in the mirror that his tie was straight and his jacket collar down. Even at stupid o'clock in the morning, the dead deserve some respect; and from what he had been told in the brief telephone call, it was one of the dead he was about to call on.

Moving through to the living area of his seventh-floor apartment, he paused at the large window and looked out across the lights of the city towards Castle Keep. The scene of the suspicious death was only about a quarter of a mile away on the other side of the River Tyne below.

Glancing at his watch, he considered whether or not just to cut across the Millennium Bridge and walk to the murder scene. It would probably take a shorter time than it did to drive.

It was the icy streets below that made up his mind, and dismissing the thought, he snatched up his keys and headed down to the car park.

After a ten-minute drive across the iconic Tyne Bridge and a meandering route through the early morning traffic to Castle Garth, he parked his BMW next to a white Crime Scene Investigation van, displaying the Northumbria Police insignia.

The young probationer standing next to the blue and white police tape recognised Slade immediately and greeted him with a nod and 'Sir', as he scribbled down Jack's details in the crime scene attendance log.

Slade was handed a white forensic suit, blue gloves and shoe coverings, which he pulled over his clothes with practiced ease, before crossing under the tape and walking, with echoing footfalls, down stone steps and along a walkway to where he could make out the tall slim figure of Sergeant Dave Armstrong.

Five years younger than Jack, with a boyish face and a thick mop of dark hair, Armstrong gave the impression of an easy going overgrown teenager, but Slade knew that appearances could be deceptive. Beneath the college boy exterior was a tough and seasoned copper, who possessed a detective's insight as sharp as a box cutter.

Armstrong had passed up what could have been a

promising career in Information Technology to join the police and had attended the Police Training College at Durham, which was where he and Jack had first met. From their first encounter, the two rookie officers had hit it off, sharing a similar gallows sense of humour. They had very quickly become good friends, so Jack had been pleased when Armstrong had requested, and been given, a transfer to the Homicide Major Enquiry Team.

As he got closer, Jack's smile at seeing his friend and fellow detective, was replaced with a frown, as he caught sight of the older man standing with him.

Detective Superintendent Thomas Charles Parker was a dour faced, humourless man, with few friends outside the job... and even fewer in. As Jack appeared, he looked up, but other than a curt nod, barely acknowledged the Inspector's arrival.

In his mid-fifties, what hair he had left surrounding his bald pate was grey. Shirt buttons strained to contain an ever-expanding stomach hanging out over ill-fitting trousers. Someone once described his belly as like a cow catcher on one of those old Wild West locomotives. At times, Parker could blow off enough steam to match.

Slade didn't like the man and suspected that the feeling was mutual. Parker had a reputation as an old school bully type and who used his rank as a weapon with which to intimidate and oppress junior officers.

Slade was not alone in his opinion and Parker had acquired a nickname of T.C.P. which Jack felt was well deserved.

Parker was required to note reports that passed over his desk and did so by jotting down his three initials, so thought nothing of it, should he occasionally overhear himself referred to by others as such. What he didn't know was that, to those in on the joke, T.C.P. stood for That Cunt Parker.

Parker had turned back to look at something lying in the bushes and, as he neared, Jack was able to take in the crime scene for the first time.

Some heavy duty portable lights had been erected, illuminating the pathway and adjacent shrubbery, with plastic tread boards carefully set down, marking a single access/egress track to and from the location of a grey corpse, lying crumpled on the frozen ground.

Jack noted the victim as male, mid-twenties and casually dressed in jeans, a white shirt and a black leather blouson jacket. From a once handsome clean-shaven face, dead sightless eyes stared out and up at the dark night sky.

Two Crime Scene Officers in blue hooded coveralls were carefully sifting through various discarded bottles, cans and assorted rubbish surrounding the body, meticulously preserving any item that might later prove to be evidential.

Jack saw one of the officers use plastic forceps to pick a used condom from the branch of a bush, drop it into a forensic bag, seal and label it, and then place it carefully on top of a pile of other similar exhibits. Armstrong looked across at Jack and smiled a warm welcome, strangely at odds with the death in close proximity.

'Good morning, Inspector,' he said, giving his friend his official title for the benefit of the senior officer present. 'Detective Superintendent Parker is the S.I.O. on this one.'

S.I.O. was police speak for Senior Investigating Officer and Jack inwardly groaned that Parker had somehow arrived at the crime scene before him. How had that happened?

Armstrong seemed to read his mind. 'The Superintendent was duty officer and at the nick for a custody extension when the call came in.'

The Superintendent again only offered a nod. Apparently, the higher in rank you got the less you were obliged to make small talk with lesser mortals.

'Sir,' Jack said, shifting his gaze back to the blood-stained corpse. 'Stabbed?'

Armstrong nodded. 'Judging from the way he bled out, it looks like this is the primary scene. As you can see, male, early twenties. There's a puncture wound through the chest, from what appears to be a large blade.' Glancing at the clutter around them, he continued, 'We haven't found the murder weapon yet, but the forensic lads are searching, before they start on the actual body.'

Jack nodded, assimilating the facts. 'What about any ID?'

'Nothing yet,' Armstrong said. 'SOCO are doing their stuff, before he gets bussed off to the hospital for the P.M. No sign of rigour yet, so we're talking less than two hours since death.'

Jack turned and, catching his friend's eye, posed the silent question.

Armstrong shook his head. 'There's no way the wound could be self-inflicted. We're definitely looking at a murder.'

Jack glanced across at the pile of forensic bags. He noticed some sort of lubricant, as well as several condoms.

'From what I hear, this place is not part of the usual night time tourist trail.'

Armstrong allowed himself a wry smile.

'Maybe for a select type of tourist. It's widely known as a gay cruising area, so we're most likely looking at a knife point robbery gone wrong. This place at night is easy pickings for thieves and homophobic attacks.'

Jack knew from previous incidents that those who frequented the area were often targeted by the local low life, safe in the knowledge that their victims were unlikely to report a crime. Most victims would prefer to write off their cash, rather than face intrusive police questioning about why they had been in the area in the first place. It was suspected that ninety-five per cent of robberies in the Gardens never came to police attention.

He wondered if the man had been a regular visitor. Or perhaps he had come down to the area for the first time and was not aware of cruising conventions. He may not have known to leave his wallet behind and only carry as much cash as he could afford to lose. Perhaps he had fought back to protect his credit cards and whatever ID was in his wallet. That could often prove a bad decision.

On this occasion, a fatal one.

As Jack stared at the body partially obscured by the undergrowth, his thoughts turned to what the dead man's family and friends would make of the location and its reputation. It was bound to come out, potentially adding further distress to relatives' grief.

Then there would be the gutter press. They thrived on crimes in these circumstances, knowing their readers, like chair bound vampires, lapped up blood and gore stories of the seedy side of life... and death.

One of the forensic officers emerged from the darkness and strode towards the small group, breaking Jack's train of

11

DAVID JEWELL

thought. In his right hand, clamped in plastic forceps, he held a small black leather wallet. 'Sir, you need to see this,' he said, directing his statement at Jack.

Slade reached out a gloved hand and took the proffered wallet but, even before he opened it, they all knew what he would find. Taking it by one corner and allowing the flap to drop down, he revealed the silver badge and photograph of a police warrant card.

The man lying dead amongst the dirt and detritus of the gay cruising area, was a serving police officer.

DEATH RATTLE

CHAPTER 3

Slade and Armstrong left Parker with the forensic officers and their search, and climbed the stairs, back to the dimly lit car park beneath the castle, where they gave their names to the probationer, who dutifully recorded their time of leaving.

Slade noticed off to his left, a forensic officer kneeling on the frost covered ground beside a public phone box.

The telephone receiver was covered in aluminium fingerprint powder and the officer was lifting a cellophane square from it and carefully fixing it to a piece of card.

Armstrong followed his gaze. 'It's where the call came from,' he explained. 'I asked them to dust it in case the caller wasn't wearing gloves.'

Jack nodded to himself as Armstrong indicated to an unmarked police car. 'Want a lift, Jack?'

'No thanks. I brought my own.'

'Bet it smells better than this one. It's the spare C.I.D. car from the back yard. I don't know who they've had in the back on late shift, but it smells like the inside of a Turkish wrestler's jockstrap.'

'I'll see you back at the fun factory,' Jack replied with a smile as he climbed into the BMW. He silently thanked God he didn't have to travel in the police car.

He recalled one time someone had spilled a bottle of milk inside a patrol car. In just a few days the smell was so bad that the car had to be taken out of service until the carpets could be decontaminated.

Despite extensive enquiries, no-one would admit responsibility and the culprit was never traced. They had more chance of getting the Whitechapel Jack the Ripper on a charge sheet than having anyone cough to that particular offence.

As Jack eased out from the car park, he ran over in his mind an update for the night shift uniform Inspector. It would be uniform's task to provide suitable cops to maintain the sterile area around the crime scene, until a full fingertip search could be carried out in daylight.

In the good old bad old days, it was the newest probationer who would be handed the poison chalice of standing in the cold all night, preventing any curious passers-by from contaminating the crime scene. In recent years, the introduction of Police Community Support Officers meant there was an additional tier of personnel to shuffle the role to, but with none on duty at this time of night, nightshift would have to provide.

It's a fact of life; those at the bottom of the pecking order get the shittiest jobs.

Forth Bank police station was a short drive from the crime scene and the part of Northumbria Central Area Command that covered Newcastle upon Tyne city centre. Jack still missed what he referred to as *the proper Nick* on Market Street, which had been in the very heart of the city.

Constructed from ashlar Portland Stone, with an entrance framed by two large torch-like blue globes and surmounted by a carved ancient heraldic Newcastle City crest, it had dominated the surroundings, looking more like the entrance to a castle than that of a local nick.

By comparison, the new station looked exactly what it was; a modern office building contained in a former warehouse.

Parking up and striding up the stairs to his office Jack telephoned the Control Room Inspector, provided details of the dead officer, and requested notification of next of kin. With the victim being a dead cop and the location of the body in a cruising area, he felt sure that the Chief was also about to get an early morning call to inform him of the situation.

'I'm up... why shouldn't he be?'

When the body was removed to the mortuary in the morning, there would be the identification to consider, but having checked the victim facial features against the recovered warrant card, Jack knew this would be a formality.

He had just put the phone down, when Parker arrived back from the crime scene. On seeing Jack, the Superintendent immediately asked for enquiries to be made with the next of kin, to get some initial background, and to perhaps establish what their murder victim, Wilson, had been doing in the area.

Slade was pleased to be able to tell him that it was already underway.

Parker instructed that both Slade and Armstrong should

14

attend a meeting at eight in the morning, where the H.M.E.T. would be briefed on the circumstances. Parker went on to say that he was off home, but would return in the morning to check on any developments.

As Jack watched his senior officer leave the office, he glanced at his watch. Twenty to four. He grimaced as the Beatle's song 'Hard Day's Night' popped into his head and wondered when he too would get back to his bed.

The next few hours flew by, as Slade and Armstrong collated the results of the various initial enquiries. Two night shift detectives, one from the East End of the city and one from the deceased officer's station, the West End, had driven across to assist.

Day shift C.I.D. officers began arriving from just after half past seven, and were joined by regulars from the H.M.E.T, so that by eight o'clock, a makeshift Murder Incident Room had been prepared in a large room on the top floor of the station.

On one wall, a six foot long whiteboard displayed a photograph of the victim, clearly taken from the deceased officer's headquarters personnel file and identical to the one Jack had seen on the warrant card.

The smiling face on the wall was a world away from the blood and mud stained corpse that was now all that remained of the young cop.

Below the enlarged image, was the name Darren Wilson P.C. 340. Radiating out to the right of this, were several photographs showing the crime scene, and below that, drawn in black marker pen, was a rough hand drawn map of the surrounding area. Someone with a bit of foresight had contacted control room and obtained a blown-up Google earth photograph of the Gardens area.

In one corner of the room was a set of trays marked 'Actions In' and 'Actions Out'. Each morning, after the briefing update, officers would be allocated one or more actions, which were particular lines of enquiry thrown up from the previous day's investigations, or some additional task requested by the S.I.O.

The action might be to trace a potential witness, or to follow up on a telephone tip off. Each one had to be completed and returned, before the data was updated onto the Home

Office Large Major Enquiry System computer, known by the acronym H.O.L.M.E.S.

First introduced in 1985, following difficulties revealed by the overwhelming complexities of the Yorkshire Ripper murders, H.O.L.M.E.S. and the subsequent H.O.L.M.E.S. 2 process the mass of information accumulated in a murder investigation, to ensure that no vital clues were overlooked.

The role of Exhibits Officer had been allocated to Jim Jackson, an experienced detective, with over twenty-five years in the job, eighteen of which were C.I.D.

Jackson was an old hand at the task, logging in any piece of evidence and recording where it was stored or had been sent. It was a vital job in any investigation, but one that most detectives dreaded, because of the number of items that required tracking, and the shit storm that would rain down upon them if any one item should go astray.

There was a tangible air of sadness in the room, and a noticeable lack of the usual banter, as if each of the assembled murder team had a heavy weight upon their shoulders.

They were all aware that this was not just any murder; this was the murder of one of their own.

Unspoken, but adding to the gloom, was the knowledge of the location in which the murder had occurred. They all knew of the areas reputation and sensed that it was going to have implications for the investigation. Once the press got wind of the circumstances, they would strive to find a story to weave and the gay angle was the one they would most likely go for.

Liz Harmon heard the gossip as soon as she got to her desk in the newsroom of the local daily that morning. The murder scene was only a short distance away from the newspaper offices and several of her colleagues had spotted the cordoned off area and had watched police officers turning away the curious and the downright nosey.

Nursing a hangover from the night before, Harmon poured herself a strong black coffee and headed for her desk. As she sipped her coffee, she checked for any messages or voicemails.

She had been running late, so had skipped breakfast. To

help fight the hangover from last night's drink, she had bought a packet of doughnuts. She stared at them, sitting innocently on her desk. It took a moment, but resisting temptation, she shoved them in a desk drawer, out of sight, out of mind. They would probably resurface for mid-morning coffee break.

She knew she had to lose some pounds. Her doctor had told her as much during the last check-up. She had tried to excuse away the weight gain as being the work related junk food diet; the result of the anti-social hours required of a reporter.

When he had asked about alcohol consumption, she had lied like a cheap watch. She reduced her true consumption by about seventy per cent.

Apparently, that was still too high.

She tried not to appear too shocked when the doctor solemnly told her that she was consuming several times the recommended units for an adult female, as the government had recently reduced their guidelines.

Alcohol was as important to getting her stories featured as the laptop she typed them on. It loosened tongues, and drinking with people in the know was a sure-fire way to glean information. Excessive drinking came with the journalistic lifestyle, and many of her fellow reporters were, if not already alcoholics, then on the way.

Liz Harmon prided herself on an ability to sniff out a good story and it was by listening to throwaway comments fuelled by too many drinks, that she had acquired some of her most memorable headlines.

She had always been a dab hand at developing a lead article from rumour and innuendo, and was never one to allow the facts to get in the way of a good story.

That, combined with her close contacts within the police, had enabled her to step over others in the office to land the job as the newspaper's Chief Crime Reporter.

Harmon always hoped to one day get a foothold in one of the nationals, but here in Newcastle, she understood that she was a big fish in a small pond.

Over the years on Tyneside, she had built up an impressive list of contacts, quite a few of whom owed her favours... and she made damned sure that they never forgot it.

As soon as had she got wind of the possible serious

crime incident overnight in the city centre, she had telephoned the Northumbria Police Press Office. Some woman she hadn't spoken to before answered, but wouldn't give any details of the incident, stating haughtily that a press release would follow in due course.

Unperturbed by the minor setback, she rang the switchboard again, this time asking for a particular extension at Headquarters. She knew the department number off by heart and, after a couple of rings, a voice answered. She hadn't realised until quite recently how whiny the voice sounded. It was starting to get on her nerves.

Mick Spence was her best contact within the police. It helped that he was going through a rough patch in his marriage and, to keep him co-operative, Harmon was giving him more than just the usual free drinks.

The previous Valentine's Day, in an effort to improve the situation in his crumbling marriage, Spence had asked his wife over breakfast what she would most like for a present.

Without drawing breath, she replied, 'A divorce.'

Turns out he hadn't been intending to spend that much.

Since then, Harmon had become painfully bored of listening to the short and balding Chief Inspector's constant complaints about his bitch of a wife and how, if they divorced, she would bleed him dry and claim half of his imminent pension.

However, she had seen an opportunity. When it came to sex, Spence was pretty low on the Richter scale, but his position within the force Intelligence Unit was too good to pass up, and he was always guaranteed to furnish the ambitious crime reporter with as much inside gossip as she required. She intended that today would be no exception.

In hushed tones, he confirmed that the overnight incident was, as she guessed, a suspected murder, but admitted that the usual channels of communication were strangely subdued about this one. What he did know was that Headquarters was buzzing, and that there was unconfirmed gossip that the victim might be a police officer.

Harmon had long ago learned that all it took was the tiniest bit of loose talk from one of her police contacts and she could put a story together. She was already planning how to present this one.

Firstly, she would ring back that tight lipped bitch in the press office, who had so condescendingly given her the brush off earlier, to ask her outright whether the victim was a police officer. It really didn't matter a damn what reply she got. If they confirmed it... Bingo. She had the story before any other reporters.

If they denied it then she would run her article as, 'Police today denied rumours that a body found in the centre of Newcastle was that of a police officer'.

If they refused to comment then, 'Police refused to comment that a body found was that of a police officer', would suffice.

Either way... fuck them, she would have her story.

CHAPTER 4

It wasn't just Liz Harmon who was wondering how the story would run.

At Forth Banks, in an office along from the incident room, Jack was sitting opposite Parker. The morning briefing had been a sombre affair, and the assembled detectives had been wary about speculating why Police Constable Darren Wilson had been in such a notorious gay cruising area.

Now, sitting silently in Parker's room, Jack could hear the steady hum of detectives answering phones and discussing the various actions.

A large amount of forensics had been packaged and sent off to the lab for DNA and fingerprint testing. In the modern police force, it was usually the scientific results that pointed detectives in the direction of the offender, rather than relying on a confession during an interview. As soon as a solicitor was involved, they usually advised their clients to say very little, even if caught in the act.

Darren Wilson's mother had been informed of his death, although the exact circumstances were being kept vague; partly to avoid further distress and partly to avoid any leaks which might cause complications in the subsequent investigation.

A family liaison officer had been allocated to support her through, what were clearly going to be the traumatic weeks to come, and to keep any press at bay.

Two of the community beat officers and a couple of PCSOs had been roped in to do house to house enquiries at all of the premises around the crime scene and to check if there was anything useful to be found from any nearby CCTV cameras.

One of the Murder Incident Team had been instructed to check through the police's own CCTV recordings, and to painstakingly interrogate all of the incident logs from the previous evening for any calls that may, with the benefit of hindsight, turn out to be relevant to the enquiry.

Sitting in the quiet of his office, Slade was suddenly very weary. Whilst the Superintendent had the benefit of at least a few hours' sleep, Jack was feeling the effects of the long night. His eyes were red and it felt like small pieces of grit were gouging into then.

His phone extension rang. To Jack, it felt like a circular saw starting up in his head.

Jack stepped into Parker's office and quietly closed the door, saying, 'Boss.'

At first, Parker seemed lost in the paperwork on his desk, but then the silence was broken as he looked up and stared at Jack. 'Just what the hell was he doing there in the first place?'

'He was stationed at the West End, boss, so we don't know why he should be on our patch. Particularly there in the Gardens area. There is of course the obvious conclusion.' Jack paused, before continuing. 'He's single and no sign of a current girlfriend.'

The unsaid suggestion hung in the air. It was a vacuum that neither man wanted to fill.

'Have we ruled out robbery as the motive?' asked Parker, breaking the awkward silence.

'His wallet was still in his jacket, so that suggests robbery as a motive is unlikely. It's not ruled out. The murderer might have panicked when he realised how seriously Darren was injured and ran off without grabbing his cash.'

'I somehow doubt that. Any of the cops at his nick able to fill in some back story? Who he drinks with? That sort of thing.'

'I've actioned detectives to interview all the officers on his shift,' Jack said, having anticipated the question. 'He's been in the job just over four years. A panda pilot at the West. He went to all the usual promotion and retirement dos, but other than that, kept himself to himself.'

'Family?' Parker said, who didn't like to use two words when one would do.

'Father's dead. Mother in her sixties. Family liaison is with her, but she's not adding anything we didn't already know.'

'Christ. I can see the headlines already,' Parker said, getting out of his chair to pace the room.

'Cop Murdered in Gay Cruising Area. The papers will

have a bloody field day. This could turn out bad for us.'

Jack glanced across at his boss, but kept his thoughts to himself.

It's not turned out so good for PC Wilson.

'We could ask the press office to pull in some favours. Maybe, see if they can get their contacts to tone it down a bit,' Jack suggested.

The senior officer turned to him, his glare incredulous. Jack took a wild guess, and surmised that Parker was unconvinced. *I wonder if he practices that look in the mirror.*

'This won't just be local news, Jack. It'll hit the Nationals. Before they went to the wall, it would have made front page of the News of The Screws, for Christ's sake.'

'I know it seems the obvious conclusion, but at this time, there's no actual evidence that Wilson was gay or cruising there. There might turn out to be a legitimate reason why he was in the area.'

Even as he said it, Jack thought, *I'm not convincing myself, so I've no chance in hell of convincing Parker.*

'Knowing my luck, he's bound to turn out to be a shirt lifter,' Parker snapped back, who clearly must have been busy the week of his Equal Opportunities course. 'No, the press will dine out on this story for weeks.' Parker rubbed at the bridge of his nose. 'And what the bastards don't know, they'll just make up. Let's just hope we uncover any dirt to be found before the papers do. Give us a fighting chance of damage limitation.'

He stood in the middle of the room, seemingly lost. Finally, he turned back to Slade. 'This is going to be a political one, Jack. The death of a cop. The circumstances and all that. I'm going to be liaising direct with the A.C.C. Crime and the Chief on it.'

Parker dropped back into his chair. 'I want you to take the lead with the day to day enquiries. Use Armstrong, if you need him.'

Jack nodded, but in the back of his mind knew what that meant. *I do all the work and take the grief if it turns to rat shit.*

'Go home, Jack. Get some shut eye, but I need you back here for the eight o'clock briefing tomorrow.'

It felt like Slade had been running on adrenalin for

days, but in reality, it was only nine hours since that first phone call had dragged him out of bed. The countless cups of strong coffee had done little to prevent fatigue taking its toll. His clothes were crumpled and his unshaven face was starting to itch. He not only felt like shit, but more than likely looked like it too.

Jack heaved himself up from his chair and started to leave, when Parker's phone began to ring. He was already imagining climbing into his warm bed, when Parker hung up the phone and stopped him in his tracks.

'Oh, Jack, there's just one thing I need you to do before you get away.'

CHAPTER 5

Jack hated Post Mortems. He hated the sight. He hated the way some pathologists acted like caricatures from a cheap B movie, making jokes at the expense of whichever poor bastard they were eviscerating at the time.

What he hated most of all was the smell.

The putrid smell of a dissected corpse was something once experienced, never forgotten.

Some cops took along handkerchiefs, soaked with menthol or aftershave, clutching them to their noses, like oxygen masks on a doomed airliner. Jack preferred the extra strong mints solution. Since his first visit to a P.M. nearly thirteen years ago, he had always taken them to suck on during autopsies, the stronger the better.

A noise behind him made Jack turn and he saw two apprehensive probationer constables slipping through the door and making their way across to the group, their boots echoing on the white tiled floor.

Jack smiled to himself. *Just out of their wrapping paper.*

The recruits had been sent along to experience the macabre spectacle as part of their training and development. How senior officers considered it officer development to view a dead man's intestines slopped into a plastic bucket and his brain deposited onto a set of medical scales, Jack hadn't yet fathomed.

Maybe they believed it would somehow immunise rookies against the sight of blood and guts, so that when they encountered it on the streets, they wouldn't faint.

Bollocks.

In Thirteen years of police work, Slade had never heard of a police officer fainting at the sight of some dismembered body. It was only in the realm of TV and movies that such clichéd incidents occurred. Whatever sights greeted cops, and Jack had seen more than his fair share, they just got on and dealt with them. It came with the job. Maybe in the nights that followed, they'd relive the incident, but at the time, professional training always kicked in.

But that smell...

24

The stench was something else, Jack thought, as he silently handed out mints to the two probies, who gratefully accepted.

The room they were standing in was one Jack was familiar with, having visited it more times than he cared to remember. The clinical white tiles on the wall and the scrubbed floor could have been any hospital room, were it not for the polished stainless-steel dissecting table in the middle, upon which lay the pallid corpse of what had once been Police Constable Wilson.

Towering over the table, was the angular frame of Doctor Paul Clifford, the Home Office Pathologist, one of several called in by the police for high profile or suspicious deaths. Tall and slim, with a thick head of salt and pepper hair, he was considered one of the best.

In over thirty years as a pathologist, he had encountered death in all its guises, yet Clifford had never ceased to be amazed by man's cruelty to man. Bullet wounds, stabbings, beatings and strangulation were all part of his stock in trade, and over the years he had become immune to the mortality around him.

'It would be a sad day if pathologists fainted at the sight of blood,' he had once said to Jack.

The only time Clifford showed any signs of emotion, was when dealing with dead children, and even then, he would go about his grisly task in a professional and detached manner that astonished Slade.

The laughter lines around his eyes were a stark contrast to his serious demeanour. Expert and thorough, he kept any wisecracks to a minimum, unlike some of the other pathologists.

Jack, however, knew that when Doctor Clifford was not on duty, he was more laid back than most of his customers.

To one side of the doctor, was the silent figure of the exhibits officer, Jim Jackson. With an assortment of see through plastic tubes and exhibit bags, he stood ready to receive any fingernail clippings, hair or piece of body matter that Clifford indicated could possibly be evidence.

Turning to the table, Slade watched as Clifford spoke into a small microphone suspended from the ceiling and began his grim task.

'Post mortem lividity shows a large concentration of blood to the posterior region, including the lumbosacral area. It isn't subcutaneous haemorrhage, so indicates that he likely died in the position he was found.'

The pathologist looked thoughtful. 'There's a deep entry wound to the front of the chest, made by a one inch wide double edged bladed instrument. My guess is a large knife.'

Taking a scalpel, Clifford began the dissection with two cuts behind each ear, making a deep Y-shaped incision to the torso of the corpse. Then, descending at a forty-five-degree angle along the neck, the cuts met at the top of the chest, before continuing vertically down the front of the chest to the pelvic region.

Jack had long ago stopped thinking of bodies on slabs as real people. Whatever personality had previously inhabited the lifeless form on the mortuary slab, no longer existed. What was left was an empty shell, a hunk of meat.

To Slade, the bodies became potential exhibits.

Jack heard the brisk tone of Clifford, as he went about his work. 'The blade missed the bone and entered below the fourth rib, causing some small damage to the rib cartilage.' Prodding around with the finger of a bloodied glove, he continued. 'The front of the heart shows a wound corresponding to the wound in the chest.'

He rummaged about inside the exposed innards, like a picky shopper in the fruit aisle.

'The blade entered the anterior wall of the left ventricle, before penetrating the septum, and emerging through the posterior wall of the heart.'

The pathologist looked up from his handiwork and fixed Slade with a steady gaze. 'Your officer was dead or dying before he hit the ground. Even if he'd had a paramedic standing next to him, I doubt he would have survived the ten minutes to the nearest A & E.'

He turned grim faced back to the task in hand. 'You're looking for a knife at least six to eight inches long and an inch wide. The angle of entry suggests the attacker to be right handed.'

Well, that narrows it down to about 90% of the population, Jack though.

Dismissing his thoughts, he watched Clifford pass to

Jackson, a large piece of flesh, which he plopped into a tube, sealing it with a twist of the plastic lid.

Clifford then took hold of the corpse's head and, with a practised action, born from years of experience, he peeled the whole of the scalp away, as if removing a mask. Then, with the flourish of a magician, he turned the whole face inside out, revealing the blood stained skull underneath.

With one deft movement, he slid down the Perspex visor perched on his head to shield his face and leant over the exposed skull.

From the corner of his eye, Jack noticed the two probationers inch forward to better hear the pathologist, his words now muffled by the mask.

As Clifford picked up the small electric circular saw, Jack realised that the two young cops at their first P.M. were unaware of what was about to happen.

He deftly stepped behind them and, with a sharp tug at each of their collars, dragged them backwards.

At first startled by the sudden jerk, within seconds all became clear, as the high-pitched whine of the circular saw bit through the skull, sending splatters of blood and tiny splinters of bone up in the air to where they had been standing seconds before.

That's my good deed of the day, thought Jack wryly.

CHAPTER 6

Liz Harmon's story was all over the front page of the local paper that afternoon and had been rapidly taken up by the local television stations, so that by the six thirty news that evening, everyone would know about the murder, and that the victim was believed to be an off-duty police officer.

So far, there had been no public speculation on any gay angle, but anyone aware of the dubious reputation of the Gardens area would already be making assumptions. It was only a matter of time before the press started mentioning cruising areas and questioning the officer's sexuality.

At Wallsend Police Headquarters, there was a lot of slamming of doors.

Staff in the Press Liaison Department were keeping their heads low and ensuring that they avoided eye contact with anyone above the rank of inspector. Word was out that someone within the force had leaked information on the murder victim being a serving officer.

If the culprit was discovered he or she would likely be collecting their P45 forms.

Not far away from the press office, was a suite of offices occupied by the Chief and his senior officers.

Despite being in a new office building, the suite was still called by most cops, Command Block, which was a reference to when it had been a separate building during the old Ponteland headquarters days.

It is an accepted fact within the police force that shit rolls downhill.

In his plush office, Assistant Chief Constable William Curtis was looking for someone to aim this particular pile at.

Six foot three with a guardsman like stature, he was a powerfully built man. At thirty-five he was one of the youngest A.C.C.s in the country and tipped to be a future Met Commissioner. His good looks and crew cut fair hair made him look more of a Hollywood leading man than a cop, and wherever he moved, he attracted glances of admiration from the female staff.

The male staff were more wary.

Curtis had a reputation for a quick temper and didn't

suffer fools gladly. As the ACC in charge of crime, he was known for being totally ruthless if he felt that any officer wasn't up to the mark.

More than one detective who crossed him had found themselves the following week plodding the beat, dressed in black and sporting a pointy hat. William Curtis was definitely not a man to upset.

This particular afternoon, even with the office door closed, his voice had been echoing around Command Block, demanding to know from his Staff Officer how the press had got hold of their information so quickly.

An extremely harassed control room Inspector was running around as if he had a rocket up his backside, scanning data trails on the force computer and listing everyone who had viewed the incident log in his desperate effort to trace the leak.

In any twenty-four hour period, there were usually about two thousand reported incidents for the Northumbria Police area, each allocated an individual FWIN or Force Wide Incident Number. The date and FWIN provided a unique computer link to any individual incident. Although some information was restricted to different levels, all officers had access to the FWINs as they were a necessary part of daily routine.

To view a FWIN, an officer simply inserted his warrant card into any of the hundreds of terminals accessing the force network and typed in his personal password. The computer then granted a level of access in accordance with the officer's level of security authorisation.

This had the benefit of providing a data trail for each and every single viewing.

However, no matter how much Curtis ranted and cursed, everyone knew that following the data trail would prove a waste of time. Several hundred officers had already viewed the FWIN, and the subsequent gossip was widespread. Within hours, it seemed like everyone in the force knew about the murder.

It was pretty certain, but not conclusive, that someone amongst those hundreds *had* provided the press with information, but uncovering the culprit was like looking for an MP in Westminster with scruples.

Everyone, especially those in the press department, was

giving Command Block a wide berth. Nobody wanted to have the finger of suspicion pointed in their direction.

Eventually, because of the press furore, the decision was made to release some details of the incident, and to confirm that the deceased victim was a serving officer. No details would be released of his identity at this stage, until all next of kin had been informed. A full press conference would be arranged for the following day, when further details would be given and a photograph of the victim provided, along with an appeal for any witnesses to come forward.

The powers that be didn't have much choice. Liz Harmon seemed to know most of the facts already, and other than the victim's name, any information that the police were intending to release had been already published.

Liz Harmon sat at her desk in the newsroom and basked in the glory of her latest scoop. She especially enjoyed it when her stories headlined on the front page... and given her nose for any kind of scandal, that was frequently.

She knew that everyone in the newsroom was shooting glances in her direction; jealous of her success. She reached for her coffee and eased back in her chair, pretending not to notice or care.

The editor had come into the newsroom earlier, and in front of the other reporters, had complimented her on the exclusive. She could almost feel the burning envy from the others in the room, as she feigned modesty.

Underneath, she knew that she was better than the rest of the rabble in the office put together.

When younger, she had considered pursuing a career in television news; maybe starting in the North East and progressing to ITN or Sky News. She had even once applied for a newsreader position with Tyne Tees Television, but didn't get the job.

One day, she had casually mentioned her aspirations to a couple of the other reporters.

Afterwards, in the pub, she had overheard the paper's arts reporter sniggering and saying, 'Not sure about TV... but she has a good face for radio.'

Harmon had pretended not to hear and didn't respond, but that single remark cut her deeply, and, in time, hardened her. Like an elephant, she would never forget. She would bide her time.

Three weeks later, that same reporter had just finished writing up a two-page exclusive interview with a huge pop star, which had taken hours to transcribe and edit in time for the weekend special report. Returning from lunch, he discovered that it had mysteriously been deleted. Nobody had seen anyone near his computer.

That wiped the sneer off his face.

Yes, as long as she kept the exclusives coming, her position was secure.

It's only a matter of time before one of the nationals makes me an offer.

CHAPTER 7

The next morning, Jack got up before five. Exhausted, following the long night and subsequent Post Mortem, he had returned to his apartment just after two in the afternoon, and without showering had fallen straight into bed and passed out.

His slumbers had been restless; filled with images of bodies in various locations and states of decomposition.

At one point, he was back in the autopsy room, fearful, apprehensive. Clifford appeared to take an age to draw back the bloodied sheet, covering the corpse on the slab. Dark brown hair came into view and Slade saw his own dead face staring up at him.

He awoke with a start and, not feeling any urge to try to go back to sleep, dragged himself out of bed and through to the bathroom for a quick shower and shave.

The shower managed to revive him somewhat and so, after a light breakfast of scrambled eggs and a pot of strong coffee, he almost felt himself again.

He checked his watch. *Not yet six o'clock.*

Sod jet lag. It's shift work that can really screw up your biological clock.

Outside, the moon was still up and sparkled on the frost covered pavements. Below his apartment, the river was flat and calm, the water like a mirror, reflecting the Crown Court and other buildings to the north side of the Tyne.

Looking out, Jack could see all of Newcastle's bridges, including the most famous, Tyne Bridge, and his favourite, the lowly Swing Bridge. Made to carry vehicles between Newcastle and Gateshead, it had been designed and paid for by the industrialist, Sir William Armstrong.

Hydraulically operated, when required it could pivot on a central axis to allow large ships to pass either side. A marvel of Victorian engineering, opened in 1876, it was still in perfect working order.

The view from Jack's balcony was beautiful and in stark contrast to the old quayside that he could still remember. The derelict buildings and slum properties of his childhood had given way to up market apartments, expensive wine bars and the ultra-modern structure of the Sage Arts Centre.

DEATH RATTLE

When Jack had been young, growing up in the suburbs of Newcastle, his father, Charlie Slade, had been a police officer, based in the West End, but had later transferred to the City Centre.

Charlie Slade loved working the city. In his day, there had still been an aura about being a city cop; a hangover from the early seventies, when the separate Newcastle City Police Force was considered a cut above their country cousins in Northumberland. To be a Newcastle cop still had a certain cachet.

By contrast, he had hated his time at the West End; working the rough Scotswood area, where every night brought the usual round of drunken domestics and pub violence.

Charlie Slade used to say that if God was going to give the world an enema, he'd shove the tube up the Scotswood Road.

In retirement, Slade Senior had at first maintained his links to the force. Frequent visits to the police club and the many invitations to promotion or leaving do parties had managed to partly assuage the feeling of detachment from The Job. However, he soon grew tired of hearing the mantra, 'Aye, Charlie, but it was different in our day', and knew that it was time to move on.

It had always been the dream of Jack's parents to live on the North Northumberland coastline. Only a few months into Charlie's retirement, they sold the family home and bought a country cottage in the small picturesque village of Belford, just a few miles outside Bamburgh, where they looked forward to many years in a rural idyll far from rising crime rates.

Six months after moving in, Jack's mum was diagnosed with cancer and within three more, was dead.

Towards the end, she had mentioned her regrets at not getting to see her grandson. That wasn't Jack's fault. Elaine was living on the east coast of Scotland and said that it was too difficult to arrange. Jack couldn't help but feel that was one of the things that had driven a wedge between him and his father.

It had only been mentioned once, but it always seemed to be present, lurking in the background.

The elephant in the room.

Following the death of his wife, Slade Senior became more introverted. Bitter at the cards that fate had dealt him, he lost interest in everything that his life had once revolved around. Cutting off contact with many of his old friends, he rarely visited Newcastle, claiming that it was too far to travel at his age. When pressed, he claimed that nowadays there seemed to be more funerals than promotions to attend.

Refusing to sell up and move back to the city, he became more and more withdrawn and, with his son's busy schedule, what contact they maintained was usually by telephone... and infrequent.

It was undoubtedly his father's stories of police life in the sixties and seventies that had instilled in Jack the desire to join the job. His dad once told him of how the notorious Kray twins had come to Newcastle, hoping to infiltrate the growing night club trade and forge links with the Tyneside gangsters of the day.

Two of the biggest and ugliest detectives that could be found, had been sent down from Market Street nick to the Kray's hotel, brandishing a couple of one way tickets back to Kings Cross... and a strong suggestion that the brothers should make use of them at their earliest convenience.

They took the advice.

Regaled with anecdotes about characters of the time, both cops and villains, Jack had envisioned a life of thrills and daring exploits, and couldn't wait to be old enough to join in the adventure.

When he had first joined the job, he had thought there couldn't be a better job in the world. He looked forward to exploits similar to those his father had described. But, the past is a foreign country. They do things different there.

Now, thirteen years later, every day began with a mountain of paperwork rising from his desk. Staff appraisals, minor complaints against cops and a weekly return of Home Office statistics on crime and detection rates.

So much for sodding adventure.

Performance targets and political correctness had robbed the force of many of its colourful characters... and along with them, its heart.

Now, on top of all the crap, he had been landed with the murder of a cop to investigate. A cop who was likely to turn

34

out to be gay. Although institutional homophobia was no longer open within the force, it still bubbled under the surface. He knew that he was about to take his first steps into a politically correct minefield.

And the slightest wrong step could blow his career at any minute.

CHAPTER 8

Jack decided to walk in to work and, crossing the Millennium Bridge, he made his way along the deserted Quayside.

The futuristic design of the bridge allowed the walkway to tilt, so that taller vessels could pass. It gave the image of an eye opening and closing and so was known to the locals as the *Blinking Eye*.

The air was crisp and icy and, with every step, Jack's breath clung to the pre-dawn chill and his shoes crunched on the frosty ground of the empty streets as he turned up the steep bank to the nick.

Arriving at the station, Jack let himself in with his box key. Everyone in the job referred to the police station key as the box key; a throwback from a time before police radios, when the only contact with the station was via old fashioned police boxes, accessed by a common key.

These little factoids constantly reminded Slade that the police force of today, despite all the computers, helicopters and modern gadgets, still refused to let go of some of its traditional past.

Taking the stairs to his first floor office, he entered, only to be greeted by an ever increasing pile of paperwork.

I swear this pile is half as much again since yesterday.

He decided to prioritise.

He went straight to the coffee machine.

For many cops, the first two goals of the day were to make it into work early... and have a coffee. That way, they always felt they were already having a successful day.

Sipping his coffee, he sat down in front of the imposing stack of routine reports and began to work through them.

An hour later, the pile had dropped considerably, so he headed for the incident room. On the way, he clocked a bleary-eyed night shift detective watching the hands of the clock and counting down the minutes until the arrival of day shift signalled his freedom.

Ascertaining that there had been no new leads during the night, Jack was handed the results of the previous day's actions. Yet more paperwork to be sifted through in order to get up to speed.

The phone box had been fingerprinted, but despite over a dozen different usable prints being found, none had as yet been identified. That meant that nobody who had recently used the phone had been previously fingerprinted and had their prints recorded on file.

An appeal for any witnesses to come forward had produced nothing and there was to be a press conference later in the day, when a further request would be made.

Jack recalled that the last thing he had done before leaving for home the previous afternoon was to request a full search of PC Wilsons flat.

A team of Area Support Group officers, who had all completed a search training course, had been allocated the task.

Anything considered as possibly relevant to the murder enquiry was to be seized and stored in the evidence store for detailed forensic examination.

Slade picked up several sheets of the search record and began to work his way through them.

Liz Harmon sat at her desk, sifting through sheets of her notes and typing away at her laptop. Her latest article was, in general, a rehash of the previous day's story, along with some additional information that she had been able to glean from minor contacts.

It seemed that there had been several reports of people being attacked in the Gardens area over the past few months, with the motive either being homophobic or just straightforward robbery. Usually, it was a mixture of the two.

The gay angle to the story was the one that would quickly hook her readers. Everyone loved a bit of scandal, especially if it involved the police.

Unfortunately, despite her wide network of contacts, she knew of no-one on the gay scene that might be able to give her an inside line. Contacting a couple of gay organisations, she had feigned concern about the spate of recent attacks. Although none of the victims was prepared to come forward and speak on the record, she had managed to obtain a few quotes that she could use in her article.

It was apparent that there had been numerous incidents

passed on to various gay organisations, but many victims were unwilling to report matters to the police. Of those reported to the cops, there had been no arrests.

Were the attacks being ignored by the police because of institutionalised homophobia? It was an interesting angle to her article, which might cause the investigation some embarrassment, but then it was her duty to call out such disgraceful behaviour in public services.

The press office had confirmed that a conference had been scheduled at Police Headquarters in a few hours and she knew that, if she got most of the story written before then, she could just pad it out with any new information that was released and still make the late edition.

Harmon made a mental note to also contact Spence and see what else he might've heard on the grapevine. Sometimes he was wary about speaking on the phone, but if the worst came to the worst, she could meet up with him. She was even prepared to put up with a grope if there was a juicy bit of inside information to be had.

True, he was a balding, boring, inadequate lover... but had his uses.

Until something better came along.

Detective Superintendent Parker's office was just along the corridor from the incident room. Jack knocked and heard a curt, 'Enter' uttered from inside.

Jack glanced at the wall behind Parker's imposing desk. There were several photographs of the superintendent in uniform at various events, and one black and white group photograph, which Jack assumed was of his class at training school.

Other than a silver-framed photo of Parker's rather dour-looking wife, the imposing desk was rather sparse. The IN tray held only a couple of crime circulations and the latest edition of The Police Review. Jack couldn't suppress a frown, when he thought of the stark contrast to his own overflowing tray.

Parker didn't look happy, but then again, he never did. A camel sucking a lemon, sprung to mind. Maybe that was why his wife looked so pissed off.

'Boss, here's the preliminary report on the P.M,' Slade said, handing over several pages from the file he was holding. 'It confirms death from a single stab wound to the heart. He bled out where he fell.'

Parker studied the pathologist's report for several minutes. 'Any sign of the murder weapon yet?'

'An Area Support Group team is doing a fingertip search of the Gardens as we speak. If it's there, we'll find it, but my guess is it's somewhere at the bottom of the Tyne by now."

'What about the Underwater Search Unit?'

'Steve Maitland from Marine is sending a search adviser up this afternoon. By that time, ASG will have finished in the Gardens, so we'll know if we need to extend the search parameters.'

Parker nodded. 'Is there anything in the P.M. that's going to bite us on the backside if the press get hold?'

'There's no sign of any recent sexual activity, if that's what you mean. Preliminary forensics report shows no traces of semen on the body or clothes.'

'Small mercies,' muttered Parker, dropping the report onto the desk. 'What did we get from the house search?'

Jack separated some papers and handed them across.

'This is the search record from Wilson's flat.'

Parker glanced through the document without speaking.

After some time, without looking up at Jack, he finally broke the silence. 'You'd better make yourself available at the press conference. Just in case we need to action something as a result.'

Jack nodded.

After a few moments, Parker looked up, with an expression that seemed to say, *Why are you still here?*

Jack said, 'I'll let you know if there are any developments,' and made his way back to the chatter of the incident room.

CHAPTER 9

The press conference was scheduled for mid-day to maximise coverage from local media, and was to be held in one of the large rooms at the modern purpose built Police Headquarters in Wallsend to the East of the city.

At one end, a stage took up almost the full width of the room and in front of a backdrop of blue boards emblazoned with the force logo, stood a long trellis table with three chairs. The rest of the room was taken up with several rows of seating and a number of television and press cameras mounted on tripods focused on the stage, waiting for the anticipated briefing to start.

A steady buzz of conversation gave the air of a social gathering, as reporters from various media agencies chatted amongst themselves; catching up with friends and acquaintants not seen since the last press conference.

Jack had met up again with Parker prior to the conference. Even at this stage the Superintendent was complaining to him about how the media would portray the circumstances. He was hoping that by feeding them some titbits it might satisfy them enough to limit further speculation.

As Slade watched Parker enter the room, nervously straightening his tie, he thought to himself, *you haven't got a snowballs chance in Hell.*

Glancing around the room, Slade had spotted the familiar face of Liz Harmon sitting several rows back from the stage.

Dressed in a black skirt and a pink blouse that would have better suited someone twenty years short of her forty five, her dyed blonde shoulder length hair framed a face plastered with too much make up. With over a dozen years as a crime reporter she wore her prune faced expression like a badge of honour. Although she might not be physically fast, mentally she was as quick as a fox... and twice as sly.

As Jack watched, he noted Harmon's eyes darting around the room, checking who was present and noting any new faces. She appeared to be frequently twisting her head like an owl, as if to catch any unguarded snippet of gossip she might later be able to weave into a story.

Jack knew from her reputation that Liz Harmon was someone to be wary of. She could be cloyingly sweet when chatting away to cops, but all that mattered was her name on the by line, and she didn't mind who she pissed off to get it there.

All the senior cops in Northumbria had clashed swords with the investigative crime reporter at some time in their service.

Yet Harmon had an uncanny knack of getting information about investigations, no matter how close officers kept their cards. It was said that previously she had more than passing friendships with a number of police officers, and an unconfirmed rumour was going around that she had been spotted recently in a pub with a married chief inspector from Headquarters.

Jack knew the officer concerned. Spence was a small moustached man, who had built his career on a series of desk jobs. He had spent so little time on the streets doing proper police work that he wouldn't recognise an angry man if one sneaked up and bit him on the arse.

Slade half laughed at the thought of the journalist being some sort of sex siren, drawing in her prey and extracting confidential information by way of pillow talk. The image of Harmon and the little Chief Inspector as possible lovers caused him to shudder.

A particularly unkind detective had likened the possible scenario to a ferret on a spacehopper.

As he tried to banish the uncomfortable vision from his brain, he felt Harmon's eyes boring into him, and glancing across at her. He hoped that her knack of information gathering was only through her sexual liaisons. If it was as the result of mind reading, he was busted. A door opened and in walked Superintendent Parker, followed by the tall figure of A.C.C. Curtis.

Curtis was taller than most around him. He seemed every inch the senior officer and Jack was aware of his rapid rise through the ranks, having first encountered him at the long defunct, Newburn nick. At that time, Curtis was still a uniform sergeant and Jack was a temporary detective. Even then everyone knew he was going places.

As Parker made his way to the stage, Curtis hesitated

for a time at the side of the hall, taking everything in. As he surveyed the gathered press, he reminded Jack of a periscope from a submarine scanning the room. After a moment, he followed Parker onto the stage.

The hubbub began to dispel as Curtis took his seat centre stage, to one side of Parker, whilst seated on the other side was Sandra Briggs, the Force's Senior Press Officer. Slim, mid-thirties, with neat shoulder length brown hair and wearing a well cut trouser suit, Sandra Briggs looked every inch the professional. Many of the reporters had tried their charms on her, hoping to elicit some juicy gossip. None had succeeded. Parker tapped the microphone twice, before clearing his throat and all eyes turned to him as the conversation dissipated.

'Firstly, can I thank you all for coming here today? We've asked you here to give you the latest news on the details surrounding the death of Police Constable Darren Wilson, and also to appeal to the public for any information that they feel might be relevant to the on-going investigation.'

The room remained silent as he continued. 'After I have outlined the progress of the enquiry, I will take some questions from the floor.'

He went on to give brief details of when and where the body had been found and that Police had been alerted by an anonymous caller. He appealed for the person who had made the initial telephone call to come forward.

'We need to eliminate him from our enquiries. All information of course will be treated in the strictest confidence. Are there any questions?'

A reporter from towards the back shouted out, 'What was the victim doing in the area at that time of night?'

Parker avoided answering, adding a caveat that he hoped that there would be no wild speculation about the motive for the murder.

That of course began the wild speculation.

In the melee that followed, Parker indicated to take a question from one reporter in the second row, whose arm kept going up and down like a one armed weightlifter.

'Was the officer on duty at the time of his murder? And if so what was he investigating?'

'PC Wilson was not on duty and there is no information

to hand on whether his death was linked to any enquiry he may have been involved in.'

Liz Harmon slowly raised her hand in the air. Parker tried to ignore it and answered a couple of questions from other reporters dotted around the room.

'How long had the officer been in the police and did he have any family?'

'PC Wilson joined four years ago and had an exemplary record. He was unmarried and is survived by his mother.' He fixed them with what he believed was a hard stare. 'I hope at this distressing time you will respect her privacy.'

Some bloody hope.

As Parker answered questions he kept glancing surreptitiously in Harmon's direction. If he answered other reporters perhaps she might get tired and put her hand down.

No chance!

Harmon's hand hung in the air like a bad smell in a small lift. To ignore it any longer would start to look obvious. He bit the bullet.

'Miss Harmon. You have a question?'

Everyone knew her reputation for ferreting out a story and the room once again fell silent; waiting to hear what she might know about the case that they hadn't yet been told.

'Is it correct that the area in which the officer's body was found is known to be frequented by perverts, and do you believe that this will have any bearing on the enquiry?'

One reporter from a rival newspaper muttered, 'The elephant in the room,' and there were sniggers, when another whispered, 'Who, Harmon?'

Every stare fixed on Parker. Like the sharks they were, they scented blood and looked for the slightest indication that Harmon had delivered a wound.

'There have been occasional reports of incidents in the area.' He cleared his throat and glanced down at some notes. 'But at this stage, we are not linking any of these to the officer's death.'

He was lying and every hard-nosed cynical journalist in the room knew it.

CHAPTER 10

In a Tyneside flat in the run down area of Benwell to the west of the city centre, eighteen year old Drew Sterling was sitting alone, channel hopping through the television news stations.

He was a worried young man. His heart was thumping with each channel change as he searched for any further information about the city centre death.

A newspaper lying on the table beside him had the headline, 'Off Duty Police Officer Found Dead in Suspicious Circumstances'. Drew rarely bought a newspaper. He liked reading them, but when it came to *buying* them, there were always other essentials that he needed more.

Today had been an exception after he had seen the photograph on the local television news, showing the face of the dead police officer. It was a face that he knew well and, no matter how much he screwed up his eyes, he couldn't erase the image from his brain.

After seeing the newsflash, he had hurried to the local corner shop, where the same photograph stared out at him from the regional daily. It seemed to be some kind of official photograph released by the police. The features seemed a little younger and fresh faced, but there was no doubting who it was.

Drew hurried back to his flat and watched the live feed of a news conference through red eyes that stung from a mixture of crying and lack of sleep. The old detective on the television had appealed for anyone with information to come forward and Drew glanced towards his mobile phone, face up on the small coffee table, surrounded by empty cups. It was drawing him, urging him to ring the number he had seen on the screen.

He stood up and glanced out of the window. A group of teenagers were kicking a football in the street outside. Broken half bricks had been placed on the road as makeshift goalposts. The boys all wore trainers, tracksuit bottoms and sports branded sweat tops.

Probably all fake.

Despite the weather, they seemed impervious to the cold, as they chased each other for possession of the scuffed football.

Drew was only a few years older and envied their lack of concerns, when at that moment, he felt that his shoulders carried the weight of the world. He had information the police wanted. But there was no way that he could come forward.

Drew probably knew more about the murder than anything mentioned on the TV or in the newspaper.

He knew that he was responsible for Darren Wilson's death.

CHAPTER 11

The press had packed up and headed back to file their copy or edit their reports for the evening news. There was a steady clamour as they called out farewells to friends and colleagues and hurried towards the car park and waiting cars.

Slade walked across the foyer outside the hall and into the secure area out of earshot of the departing press. He spotted A.C.C. Curtis talking to a red faced Parker. One of the senior Press officers hovered to one side.

Parker spotted Jack and muttering something to Curtis broke away and strode across to cut off Jack's approach. He didn't look happy.

'That bitch Harmon! If I ever find out anyone on the team passing her information I'm going to chop some bastard's balls off.'

'Assuming the person leaking stuff has balls,' Jack answered.

Parker ignored the remark. 'I'm staying here. The A.C.C has asked me to talk through the case with him. You head back to Forth Bank and take the reins. I'll catch up with you later.'

With that he turned and re-joined Curtis and the press officer.

Slade was pleased to be leaving T.C.P. behind. His constant grouchy mood was beginning to grate.

If complaining was a sport he could moan for England.

Slade accepted that the involvement of a murdered police officer made things very political, but the involvement of ACPO rank always unnerved investigators. All major enquiries were like a vast jigsaw puzzle and cops had to sort the various pieces, before putting them together to form the final picture.

If cops were too distracted by Command Block micro management it could stifle them and they might miss some small, but vital, piece of the bigger picture. Just like a jigsaw puzzle, where you might sort the pieces into foreground, subject and sky, experienced detectives tried to arrange their investigation around Motive, Method and Opportunity.

The unwanted scrutiny of someone as senior as A.C.C.

Curtis could prove a hindrance.

Engaged to the daughter of a local M.P. William Curtis was never going to spend his career pounding the streets like his colleagues. His destiny was to be theatres and dinner parties, not pubs and police piss ups.

As he had slithered his way up the ranks he was always cautious to avoid anything that could possibly hamper his carefully structured progress. He led a charmed career and anything negative always seemed to slip by him without leaving a taint.

Like shit off a shiny shovel, as Jack's dad used to say.

Last Jack heard he was being tipped as a future Chief Constable in one of the smaller forces.

As he watched, he noticed T.C.P. lean in close to Curtis and whisper into the A.C.C.s ear. Unnervingly, Slade spotted a surreptitious glance across in his direction.

Is that why I'm being given the lead? It was a poison chalice.

If the investigation upset the wrong people they would be accused of homophobia. If Wilson turned out to be involved in some sexual misconduct the press would plaster it all over the front page linking Northumbria forever with a sex scandal.

If the force tried to tone it down they would get accused of a cover up.

Jack looked across at Parker and Curtis and noticed them give a second glance across at him before quickly turning away. Was Jack being set up as the fall guy should the enquiry turn to rat shit.

Will I be the one left without a chair when the music stops?

CHAPTER 12

This was the third telephone box Drew had tried. The first had been vandalised and the second was missing the handset completely. He must have walked almost into the city before he found one that worked.

Telephone boxes were rapidly being consigned to history with the increasing use of mobile phones. Drew had no intention of using his mobile phone knowing that to do so would trace the call directly back to him. Using his debit card would have similar consequences.

In the films he saw on TV people had throwaway phones that they discarded after making their untraceable calls. Unfortunately they cost money and Drew's budget didn't extend to that. It would have to be the old fashioned call box and one that was not overlooked by CCTV would be difficult to find. When he did find one that was intact, it smelled of stale urine and someone had written *Fuck the law* several times in black permanent marker pen on the Perspex covering. Drew hesitated several minutes before picking up the handset and then putting it back down again.

Should he forget the whole thing and hurry back to the safety of his flat, bolt the door and shut the world out. Pretend all of this had never happened.

Gathering up all his remaining will power he picked up the telephone and dialled the number for Northumbria Police.

After only a few seconds the telephone was answered by a friendly female voice.

'Hello. You're through to Northumbria Police. How may I help you?'

There was a slight pause before Drew found his voice. 'I want to speak to someone about the murder of Darren Wilson.'

'Yes. Can I take your name and contact number?'

'I don't want to say. I just want to speak to someone. I think I have some information.'

'Alright but if you could just give me your name it would…'

'I'm not leaving my name,' he interrupted, 'I just want to tell someone that I think I know why he was killed.'

Nine miles away in the Northumbria Police Control Room the telephone operator glanced down at the digital display. She already had the number from which Drew was calling, but her training was to fill as many details onto the computer as she could obtain, before routing the call or despatching any units to an incident.

'Listen. I'll get someone to come down and talk to you. You just need to...'

The line went dead.

The operator filled in the scant details she had about the call and then switched the log across to the Control Room Inspector to bring it to his attention.

It would be up to him whether he despatched any unit to the location of the call or merely switched it across for the information of the incident room. Decisions like that were above her pay scale.

Drew stood still for several minutes staring at the handset swinging on the black plastic cord, wondering whether or not he should ring back.

Reaching into his pocket he used a tissue to wipe any fingerprints off the phone.

By the time the police car pulled up at the abandoned telephone box Drew was long gone.

CHAPTER 13

Back at Forth Bank Jack was sifting through his paperwork tray checking for any new information and 'actioning' any follow up enquiries.

He left messages on answer machines for two of his Confidential Informants and before he knew it the bright winter day had given way to a dark December afternoon with streetlights fighting against the gathering darkness outside.

Rubbing tired eyes, he checked his tray one last time and made a short 'to do' list for the following day.

Two detectives were staying on duty until eleven o'clock to field any enquiries and log any information that came in. After that calls would be diverted through to the police station front office until the Murder Investigation Team met at eight o'clock the following morning. Anything deemed urgent could be referred to the night shift detective or on call Detective Inspector.

Jack was reaching for his jacket when Dave Armstrong came into the office with several members of the team. As they began to tidy away papers from their desks, Dave sauntered over to him.

'I watched the press conference on the box. When Harmon asked about the gay angle T.C.P. looked like he was about to burst.'

'I left him brown nosing Curtis,' Jack said, glancing at his friend.

Armstrong lowered his voice. 'Jack. Don't mind me saying, but you look like shit warmed up. The lads and me are going for a pint. You coming?'

Slade was tired and starting to feel hungry. Other than a supermarket cheese sandwich he hadn't had anything since breakfast and it was now well after five. Drinking on an empty stomach was never a good idea, but the thought of going straight home with his brain still whirring over the day's events held little appeal.

In the end the thought of a refreshing pint won the argument. 'Sod it! I could do with a beer,' he relented, grabbing his jacket and following Dave and the others as they headed for the door.

DEATH RATTLE

A ten minute walk from the station, tucked discretely away above an Italian restaurant, was 'The Police Club.'

Dave placed his plastic door key next to the security fob and the lock disengaged with a loud metallic click.

Groups of off duty police officers drinking in local public bars could prove problematic, especially if they were in part uniform under their jackets. Police clubs had always been safe environments where cops could sink a pint after work, unwind after a stressful day, or just chat with colleagues and try to make some sense of the crazy often violent world they all inhabited.

Several years earlier in a move guaranteed to undermine morale, a Home Office directive instructed all Chief Constables to make better use of any available space, with the result that all clubs on police premises were closed down.

A few disgruntled officers upset at the loss of their sheltered surroundings decided to form their own club, leased and run by the cops themselves. Newcastle Police Club was the result. As Slade and his group entered, he spotted the familiar face of Paul Brunton serving behind the bar. Paul, now retired was one of the founding members of the club and most nights helped out behind the bar to keep the costs down.

At over six feet tall and well-built he looked every inch the no nonsense barman, but this was probably the one bar in the city where there was never any problems from unruly patrons.

Every member was a cop, ex-cop, or worked for the police.

'Watch out lads. Here comes the Serious Drinking squad,' Brunton called out by way of greeting, causing several pairs of eyes to swivel in their direction.

'Never mind the lip. Just do your job and pour the beer, Brunton,' Armstrong retorted, making his way up to the counter.

The room was large with a bar running half the length of the room. At either end were assorted tables and chairs at which several serving and retired officers sat chatting and drinking pints.

In one corner were seated two young cops each sipping from half-finished pints of lager. Jack recognised them as the two 'autopsy virgins' from the Post Mortem the previous day and nodded an acknowledgement towards them.

Slade knew he wouldn't be staying too late so offered to get in the first round and everyone having ordered their drinks, they pushed a couple of tables together in a part of the room furthest from the bar and settled down in a group.

Armstrong eased onto a chair seat next to Jack whilst opposite sat Jim Jackson and next to him Mick Henderson.

Henderson, fifteen years on C.I.D, had a round face and a bulbous nose from too many late night drinking sessions. The lethal combination of a lack of exercise, poor diet and excess of booze had taken effect. He was more than a little overweight.

He regarded himself as an old school detective for whom crime detection was the only force target that mattered and considered himself a no nonsense straight talking cop. Others thought him a boorish loud-mouthed pain in the arse, who thought any form of political correctness was the thin end of the wedge for all the lefties and 'do gooders'.

Although a very competent detective, how he survived in the modern police force was the biggest mystery and one that couldn't be solved by any of the other detectives. Jack supposed Henderson had a keen sense of when he could rant, and when to keep his views to himself.

Jim Jackson was the polar opposite. Approaching twenty nine years' service, he was content to be a small cog in the workings of the force. He had been a detective for longer than anyone could remember, but never expressed any interest in promotion or working in any other department but C.I.D. Over the years he had been involved in many of the higher profile criminal investigations. Lately he was being seen as the first choice as exhibits officer because of his reputation for always going about the task in a cool, calm and methodical way.

Everyone with pint in hand, it wasn't long before the alcohol steered the conversation towards the current investigation.

'If we're going to detect this one we need to clear up exactly what Wilson was doing down there, boss.' Jackson said, between sips of his bitter.

'There's a lot of speculation, but I want everyone to keep an open mind. He might have spotted something and been following someone. He might even have been meeting an informant,' Jack replied.

Henderson grunted and looked unconvinced. 'He was a woodentop. Unlikely a plod would be meeting a snout in the middle of the night. If that's what he was doing he should've maybe stuck to traffic and domestics. He might still be walking his beat.'

To Henderson any cop who didn't aspire to be in C.I.D. was to be regarded as slightly suspect. Always dressed in a collar and tie, he thought he looked the epitome of the professional 'tec but everyone knew he had worn the same dark blue suit for the last ten or more years.

He was probably hoping it will come back into fashion one day.

He had his own fixed ideas about what police work should be about and harboured a deep distrust of anything that lay outside those strict parameters.

A particular hate had been the introduction of Police Community Support Officers to patrol the streets and give public reassurance.

'Plastic Polis. They're bloody useless! They can't go out by themselves and can't even arrest anybody. If they do come across anything that needs a proper copper they have to call one in. They create more problems than they solve.'

This particular hatred had taken over from his previous abhorrence, which had been the Special Constabulary. 'Sodding hobby bobbies. Don't get me started on them.'

PCSOs, Specials, Graduate entries, woodentops, local crime teams, probationers and anyone above the rank of Detective Inspector, Henderson was a true equal opportunities misanthrope.

He was however, a good detective and could read a suspect like an open book.

Slade had suggested that next time there was a crime scene that needed preserving he might like to undertake the task himself instead of using a Special or PCSO. This had shut him up for a while, but once he'd had a few beers he always reverted to form.

'There's more to being a cop than fiddling your crime figures,' Armstrong said, clearly annoyed by his arrogance and prepared to wind him up.

'It's what we all joined the police for, isn't it?' Henderson was fond of telling anyone who would listen. 'Detecting crime and locking up the villains.'

'I think you'll find the primary duty is the protection of life followed by the *prevention* of crime,' Armstrong countered.

'Crime prevention! If you're talking mascots like that poor sod who the Chief had walking around Headquarters in a dog costume a few years ago you're talking bollocks.'

He was referring to a scheme some years previously that had involved a police officer donning an animal outfit to promote a cartoon character; part of a launch of a new crime reduction strategy.

'I say our job is locking the shite up and keeping them locked up for as long as possible.'

Henderson had already almost finished his drink, and the alcohol had gone straight to his vocal cords.

'Do gooders who reckon prison doesn't reform criminals are talking crap. I'll tell you this. Long sentences might not reform the bastards, but at least it gives the rest of us some peace.'

Getting to his feet he drained his glass and nodding in the direction of everyone else's half empty glasses, slouched off to the bar to place the order.

He had a point, thought Jack, but in this modern world of political correctness and equal opportunities, cops had to mind their opinions and how they expressed them. The current investigation was a case in point.

Already Harmon and her ilk were sniffing around for some tittle-tattle. Any unguarded comment might find itself on the front page the following day.

The press eager for any whiff of scandal were going to lap up the death of a police officer in a notorious gay cruising area.

Jack had much to be worried about.

Over the next hour the bar banter touched on several subjects, but the conversation regularly slipped back to the current investigation.

'Owt recovered from Wilson's flat that identified him as a shirtlifter?' Henderson directed his question at Jim Jackson, who had been sitting quietly listening to the banter, but rarely contributing to it.

Ignoring the homophobic jibe, Jackson replied quietly, 'His laptop's been seized for the lab and DVDs taken for examination. Apart from that just the usual electric gadgets, music CDs and family photos. Nothing that gives any reason for his being at the Gardens or why anyone would want to kill him.'

'It's the computer that'll prove it one way or another,' Henderson said with a knowing nod. 'That's what knackers Glitter and his sort.'

The conversation then went off at a tangent via glam rock to what it had really been like policing in the golden years of the eighties and nineties.

After a couple of pints the lack of sleep was catching up and Slade decided to call it a night. Taking his leave from the others, who looked set for a long session, he made his excuses and headed out the club, picking up a takeaway pizza from the Italian restaurant, before wending his way past the crowds of partygoers down towards The Quayside. A short stroll along the river and he could see his apartment just over the Millennium Bridge.

He was well aware that this enquiry was going to be difficult. The fact that it involved one of their own was a major factor but the link with the gay scene was adding a whole new dimension.

As he took the lift to his apartment the alcohol and lack of sleep were having their effect.

His brain was still processing the day's events as he threw off his jacket and tie, took the pizza out the box and poured himself a large glass of Malbec.

He only managed one slice and about half the glass of wine, before he gave up and, staggering from the lounge, pulled off his remaining clothes and fell into his bed, exhausted.

Within seconds he was asleep.

It was only nine thirty.

Liz Harmon glanced at her watch: It was nine thirty. She had left her office over three hours earlier and, although it might not look like it to the others sitting around in the small country pub on the outskirts of Morpeth, she was still working.

When she had met up with her Chief Inspector lover at the pub, there were only a handful of people, and apart from the few old regulars propping up the bar, the rest consisted of middle aged couples dotted around the lounge in hushed conversation.

It was the sort of discrete place where husbands meet up with wives. So long as it wasn't their own wife that they were meeting.

Spence insisted in sitting in the farthest corner where he could have a view of the door and spot who was entering.

He had seemed more than a little on edge, whispering that there were intensive enquiries at Control Room to track down the source of the press leak. Although he was only one of several hundred who had accessed the log, Professional Standards department were checking times of access to narrow down the investigation. Everyone who had viewed the incident on the computer was getting an email request asking them to explain their reasons for access.

Spence knew he had a perfectly reasonable explanation as to why he had downloaded the log; intelligence gathering and distribution was part of his job. Still if anyone was to see him sitting with the writer of the article it wouldn't take a top detective to work out who might have been her source.

He leant in close so as not to be overheard and suggested that maybe they should avoid meeting up and cool it for a while so as not to risk drawing attention.

Who the fuck was he kidding? There was a murder investigation going on that involved a cop and he was her best source.

She suppressed her anger, smiled at him reassuring him as she would a little boy and persuaded him to come back to her flat for a nightcap. Despite his fears of being spotted Spence's little piggy eyes lit up at the prospect of a shag so he hesitantly agreed.

Back at her apartment in the Gosforth area of the city he had still seemed tense so it took him a while to get a hard on, but once he had managed she had given him a good seeing to, which fortunately for her hadn't taken him very long.

Poor bugger's obviously getting sod all at home.

As Liz lay back noting that the crack in the ceiling seemed to be getting longer and she really should have it fixed, she was increasingly aware of just how bored she had become with him. However, needs must, and the last thing she wanted was lose her best source at this crucial time.

When he had finished she managed to wheedle out of him that although the S.I.O. was that grumpy bastard Superintendent Parker, it was actually a Detective Inspector Jack Slade who was running the show day to day.

So as soon as he had cleared off back to his wife she had noted down the name.

The next morning Inspector Jack Slade would be getting a call.

CHAPTER 14

Jack was up early the next morning. He hoped that it was a sign that his body clock was getting used to the early shifts.

More likely he couldn't sleep properly because of everything running through his mind.

The bedside clock said six o'clock and pulling back the blinds he looked out onto the silent city. The night time revellers had long since wound there way off to their bed... or if they'd been lucky someone else's.

The only movement outside appeared to be a scruffy council gritting lorry trundling along the street below, flashing yellow light bouncing off the deserted buildings.

Jack couldn't face cooking breakfast so made do with a piece of re-heated pizza from the microwave, and a cup of coffee. With a diet like that it was no wonder so many cops were overweight and a heart attack waiting to happen.

Twenty minutes later he was grabbing his coat and heading out for the lift.

Car parking in the yard at the nick was at a premium so deciding to take his usual walking route he crossed the Millennium Bridge onto the north side of the river. Crossing the fast moving black waters below Jack turned to his left passed the Pitcher and Piano bar, wandering past shuttered bar fronts which a few hours before had been teeming with late night drinkers.

The streets were silent and deserted with a thin coating of powdery snow covering the pavements. Jack smiled recalling that every year without fail at least one young burglar was caught by a cop simply following footprints in fresh snow from the crime scene back to the offender's home.

Each year there must be a new generation of 'numptys' who thanks to their incompetence helped local cops to bring about their own incarceration. It certainly helped the crime figures.

When it came to the gene pool, many of the people they dealt with seemed to be paddling in the shallow end.

Pulling the collar of his coat against the biting wind rushing along the river valley, he followed the north bank along the quayside and up Forth bank. Quickening his pace against the cold he soon arrived at the nick and the warmth of the station.

Entering the secure front office area he passed a bleary-eyed nightshift constable on the desk and made his way to his office. His eyes avoiding the ever increasing stack of paperwork he made a beeline for the coffee machine. A decent coffee always helped to prepare for whatever the day would throw at him, and drink in hand he ambled through to the incident room.

The room was more cluttered than the previous morning as detectives had begun to settle into their new work space and make each desk their own. After only a day some personal photographs had already appeared on a couple of the desks It was a subtle indication that some of them believed the investigation was going to take some time and they were in it for the long haul.

Glancing up at the display board a blown-up A4 size photograph of Darren Wilson stared down at him, with lines radiating off from it linking to various actions.

Jack sipped his coffee and stared silently at the board.

There was a constant voice at the back of his mind telling him that he had missed some link, and his copper's instinct told him something was not quite right. He thought back to his restless night wondering if it had been some subconscious nagging feeling that had caused sleep to evade him.

He turned to study the rest of the murder wall. Lined along the bottom were a series of photographs showing the interior of Darren's flat and others the murder scene. Arrows in marker pen pointed hither and thither linking enquiries and locations… but so far no arrows were pointing to suspects.

What was he missing?

Jack moved across to the exhibit officer's desk and sifted through various papers until he found what he was looking for. The search record for potential exhibits removed during the search of Darren Wilson's flat.

Wilson apartment was a compact two-bedroom apartment in South Gosforth; an up-market suburb of the city. C.S.I. Photographs of the interior showed a very modern looking flat with laminate flooring and trendy furniture from some Swedish supplier. The lounge area was dominated by an over-sized flat screen TV. Blinds rather than curtains, screened the windows from passers-by and added to the minimalistic style.

The search had resulted in the recovery of several items, some of which might prove important, and others which would prove valueless to the enquiry. Jack slowly ran his finger down the list scrutinising each individual article.

First recorded was a computer recovered from one of the bedrooms and packaged for the I.T. Forensic Lab. It had now become standard practice to recover any data storage devices from the homes of both suspects and victims. Although it would take a few days for the hard drives to be examined by the lab, computers, ipads and mobile phones could turn up invaluable evidence or clues in serious cases.

Moving down the list there was an assortment of typed and handwritten papers, and letters itemised in the report, but nothing that immediately jumped out at him.

It wasn't until he reached the last couple of entries that something caught his eye.

Jack made a mental note of the property exhibit number and made his way quickly to the see the custody sergeant.

The Custody office was a grim cold room with cream walls and lit by harsh fluorescent lights. It was still dark outside but even during the day the only natural light came from a translucent window overlooking the station yard where prisoners arrived for processing.

On one wall was a white board listing the numbers of cells and written on it in black semi-permanent marker were brief details of detainees; showing time of arrest and alongside in red the relevant 'Review Time'.

The time any person can be kept in police custody is governed by strict legislation and the 'Review Time' dictates when an official assessment of the facts must be undertaken to see if further detention is still justified.

The only other decoration in the room was a variety of faded crime prevention posters and a list of extension numbers for various departments.

Jack smiled when he saw a small obviously unofficial poster that had been laminated and pinned to the wall behind the custody desk. Evidence of police black humour it announced in bold black letters, 'Please Do Not Ask For Bail

DEATH RATTLE

As Refusal Often Offends.'

The room was dominated by the custody desk, behind which perched the custody officer, Sergeant Bob Clarke, who was busy updating custody records.

Bob Clarke was fifty two years old, overweight and with a bald pate framed by a ring of silver hair. As he scribbled notes onto custody records he looked like a medieval monk illustrating a manuscript. No-one could ever have described Bob as a dynamic officer and when after promotion he had found himself in the role of custody sergeant he had found his niche. This for Sergeant Clarke was his 'raison d'etre.'

Not for him the violence and increasing complications of mounds of paperwork generated by street work. He much preferred the warmth and endless cups of tea of his cosy custody suite.

Clarke's reluctance to leave the confines of the warm station had over the years earned him the nickname of 'The Olympic Torch.'

When Slade had asked why, a smirking cop explained, 'It's 'cause he never fucking goes out.'

Clarke looked up as Slade entered. 'You're in early, Jack. What's up? Shit the bed?'

'Work to do, Bob. Work! You remember that, don't you?'

'I wouldn't have thought we had anything in here tonight for you, Jack. There's just a couple of drunks and a domestic assault. Nowt to interest the likes of a Detective Inspector.'

'I'm after the keys to the H.MET. exhibits store, Bob. There's something in there I want to check out.'

'You landed the PC Wilson murder? I thought that was going to be T.C.P.'s?'

'You know how it is. We do the graft. He takes the glory.'

Clarke gave a knowing nod.

'Aye. Still, a nasty business there, Jack. Let's hope you get the bastard.'

The sergeant sorted through a large selection of keys on a ring and selected one.

'There you go. Bring it back as soon as you're

finished.'

Taking the key, Jack walked down the corridor to a large walk in cupboard and opening the door stepped inside. Each shelf was stacked with a variety of packaged exhibits both small and large.

On one shelf he saw a laptop computer wrapped in a Police exhibits bag and beside it a number of computer discs and memory sticks all similarly packaged. The computer was to be taken down to the lab later that day by Jim Jackson the exhibits officer to ensure continuity of evidence.

A nice day trip out for him.

Looking around he glanced at the top shelf and spotting the item he was after, reached up and took it down. Checking the exhibit number and careful not to damage the seal in any way Jack stared through the polythene wrapping at the item inside.

In the club Jim Jackson had mentioned the recovery of some family photographs. Jack held one such framed photograph that had been recovered from Wilson's bedside table.

In the photograph, a casually dressed Wilson was standing on a sunny beach and had his arm around the shoulders of a slightly younger guy.

The other man looked to be about eighteen, slim, shirtless and dressed in a pair of dark blue shorts. A wide grin beamed out from the youthful face under a mop of unkempt blond hair.

Jack was drawn to the way Wilson's arm was casually draped over the teenager's shoulder in a relaxed, very familiar way.

By your bedside you might keep a photograph of your wife or girlfriend... maybe even your mother.

So who was this? A relative? Maybe a friend?

Or was he something more?

CHAPTER 15

When Parker arrived at the office just after seven thirty Jack was waiting. Although it was just a hunch at this stage, he knew that the slightest suggestion that the victim may have been in a relationship with a teenage boy was not about to go down well with his boss.

He wasn't wrong.

'Fucking marvellous. I knew from the start that this case was going to turn to shit.'

I'm sure you did! Which is why I'm being lined up as the fall guy, thought Jack.

'I'm going to have to tell Command Block about this. They're already shitting bricks wondering what will turn up on Wilson's computer. He's going to turn out to be a kiddie fiddler, I'm fucking certain of it.'

'The lad in the photograph is at least eighteen. He's hardly a kid. In fact just a couple of years younger than Darren Wilson. This is the twenty first century and even if they are more than just friends, there's no suggestion of anything illegal.'

Parker looked up and glared at Jack. 'That won't matter to the press. He's a copper, for God's sake.'

'Still, boss, we might be getting ahead of ourselves. Let's cross that bridge when we come to it.'

Parker replied by way of a grunt, which doubled for a dismissal, so Jack headed back to the incident room. Before he was out the door, his boss was already reaching for the telephone.

The update for Headquarters was likely to be lively this morning.

The Superintendent had scheduled the murder squad briefing for eight o'clock and there was an expectant hush as he came through from his office. All mobiles were switched to silent and the office telephones taken off the hook.

Parker straightened his tie, and standing in front of the 'Murder Wall' which dominated one end of the room addressed the squad about progress to date.

There was little to follow up as the result of the television coverage. A few crank calls from the usual 'nutters' and several from people informing the police that the Gardens were a gay cruising area.

Like half of the City didn't already know that.

Amongst the calls one had been highlighted. Some young sounding male had telephoned claiming he had information about the murder, but had hung up before he could be properly questioned. The call had been made from a phone booth in the city centre, and although probably another hoax call, the voice had been recorded digitally, and would have to be followed up with an 'action'.

Officers working the beat that encompassed any of the gay bars were sent to make visits to the premises, gathering what information they could. Armed with a photograph of Darren Wilson they were tasked with trying to get any sightings of him, either in the bars, or in cruising areas.

They needn't have bothered with the photograph. It had already been emblazoned across the front page of the local newspaper. The gay scene would be buzzing with gossip of a murder in the Gardens.

Unfortunately, the almost traditional distrust of the police meant that very little of the gossip was likely to come the way of the cops. Despite that, every angle had to be explored.

Jack had been hoping that some snippets of information to the incident room would result in further actions being raised but it seemed this wasn't to be the case. With fewer and fewer new leads coming in there were less lines of enquiry. Already there was the impression of an investigation slowly grinding to a halt.

Community Services department had provided a couple of contacts in local gay groups, and one of the detectives was to be allocated a visit to something called M.E.S.M.A.C. The organisation apparently had an office in the city centre and was an outreach group for gay and bisexual people.

Neither Jack nor any of the other detectives had heard of it and nobody had a clue what the acronym stood for.

Armstrong had discovered that there was a national association for gay and lesbian police officers run by serving officers. He had telephoned the contact number asking for details of any locally based members but complained to Slade that getting any information was like pulling teeth.

Even a simple request as to whether the dead officer had been a member had met with short shrift; with frequent references to data protection issues and that membership lists were strictly confidential.

At first Armstrong had been annoyed telling Jack, 'For fucks sake we're on the same side aren't we?'

But when he calmed down he accepted the need for discretion.

On the surface the police promoted an equal opportunity policy including sexual orientation with any openly homophobic conduct leading to disciplinary action or even dismissal. But Jack knew from listening to the likes of Henderson that long held attitudes run deep. Scratch the surface of some older cops, especially C.I.D. officers and like a stick of rock they read bigot throughout their length.

In the end the voice on the other end had promised Armstrong that they would contact any Northumbria officers who were gay asking if they were prepared to come forward to assist.

Neither Dave nor Jack were holding their breath on that one.

Briefing over, Parker strode off back to his office and Jack began the task of allocating the actions to be followed up that day.

There was a sombre mood in the incident room as everyone realised that despite their efforts they appeared no further forward in tracing the murderer of one of their own. It felt as if at every turn the investigation was coming up against a brick wall. Jack was thinking that if things continued this way, simply keeping up morale would be a task in itself.

Returning to his desk to he found a yellow post it note asking him to ring Liz Harmon at the crime desk of the local rag. He read it over twice before dropping it into the bin.

The enquiry was already dragging. The red herring false calls were starting to come through. It was looking increasingly like there would be a gay angle to the case and now bloody Liz Harmon was sniffing about like a truffle hound.

Could it get any more difficult?

A couple of hours later and Jack got his answer.

CHAPTER 16

'Come in, Jack. Sit down.'

Parker was sitting behind his desk and quietly perched like a vulture at the side of the room was a second man, head down pretending to be engrossed in a file of papers.

'You know Inspector Mark Burton? He's currently at Professional Standards.'

Jack knew him well.

Parker continued. 'Following our discussion this morning concerning the photograph found in Wilson's flat the ACC thinks that in the circumstances the department should assist us. In case the investigation throws up any…' Glancing across at Burton, he cleared his throat, '…problems.'

Jack looked across at the seated man who lifted his head from his reading, as if noticing Jack for the first time.

'We've met,' said Jack coldly.

'Good to see you again, Jack,' Burton said, with as much sincerity as he could muster. A smile flicked on like a light bulb and just as quickly switched off again.

Mark Burton smelled of cheap after shave. The neatly pressed grey suit and dark blue tie with a plain white shirt was clearly meant to look the part given his headquarters position. Jack noted the well-polished shoes that were more used to walking the corridors of power than policing the streets.

About thirty five and medium build, Burton had swarthy skin, and straight black hair combed to the side. With his beady eyes and angular nose, he had always reminded Jack of a plague carrying rat… just not as endearing.

A cold fish, Burton was one of those cops who didn't mind who they stepped on or whose backside they shoved their tongue up in order to continue slithering up the ladder of promotion. Their goal would be achieved through fair means or foul.

Posts at headquarters could get you noticed and Burton had found his niche in Professional Standard Department; formerly known as Complaints and Discipline and tasked to investigate internal discipline matters.

The department, based in headquarters had offices close to the Command Block. The officers who worked there were viewed with suspicion by their fellow officers and referred to by most cops as 'the rubber heel squad.'

Jack knew that they were a necessary evil. The police force was a microcosm of society and as such had some bad apples that needed wheedling out; though not a fraction of the number the press and media would have the public believe.

There were many cops who transferred to the department for all the right reasons to weed out the occasional corrupt officer, but there were some who regarded it as a promotion prospect. Burton was definitely one of the latter. Jack had some dealings with him in the past and made no effort to disguise his distrust of the man.

He had, Slade thought, *the sort of face you could never tire of punching.*

Jack ignored Burton and directed his question at Parker.

'What sort of problems is Command Block expecting that might require Professional Standards to be involved at this stage?'

'Stop pissing around, Jack. You know as well as I do. We don't know where this investigation will take us. Cops and gay cruising areas. Might as well have input from Professional Standards right from the start.'

'So we're assuming that simply because there is a gay connection that Wilson was up to something illegal?'

'Wilson being queer...' Burton looked up for a second, and Parker stopped himself abruptly, shooting a quick aside towards him.

Burton looked back down once again, appearing to be engrossed in his notes.

Where senior officers were concerned, Burton clearly chose to be discerning in what he overheard. A political trait to be perfected if you want to get on in the police force.

'Wilson being... gay... does not mean we're assuming anything!' Parker snapped, clearly irritated by where the conversation was heading. 'We're just covering bases.'

Covering arses more like.

Political incorrectness having been narrowly avoided by Parker, Burton put down his papers and, looking at Jack, spoke softly, as if to a child.

'The ACC, Mister Curtis clearly feels that early intervention by our department may perhaps avoid any problems at a later stage, should Wilson be found to have involvement in anything...' He paused for effect, before emphasising the next word, '...*questionable*. We of course will simply oversee the investigation. All operational matters will be down to the Homicide Investigation Team.'

Burton smiled at Parker, who was happy they were now back on script.

'Quite,' agreed Parker. 'So, I'm sure that you will give Detective Inspector Burton any cooperation he requires.' He paused and then emphasised, 'It's what the ACC wants.'

The subtext being that what the ACC wants the ACC gets.

Burton gave what he felt must be his best false smile. 'I'm sure we'll get along.'

Jack's face indicated otherwise.

There was a short silence before Parker gave a slight cough and continued. 'So, Jack, the end of shift briefing is at six. I want Mark here to sit in on it. If there are any urgent developments in between now and then keep him up to speed and I will act as liaison with the ACC. Now, if there's nothing further, I'll let you get back to the incident room.'

There wasn't, so Jack got up and, nodding to Parker, gave a brief, 'Sir' and made for the door. He had his hand on the door handle when he was stopped abruptly by Burton.

'Just one thing, Jack,' Burton said, looking up from his notes, 'the computer found in Wilson's apartment... it's already been sent for analysis?'

'It went down this morning.'

'Let me know as soon as we get a result on the contents. We... that is the Command Block are interested to know the contents as soon as possible, so if you could chase it up, Jack.'

'Will do. Is that all?'

'For now.' Burton returned his attention to scribbling something in his notes.

Jack made his way out of the office, but noticed that Burton was in no rush to leave.

The interest of the Command Block was no surprise but such a sudden involvement of Professional Standards was a little unusual.

What can of worms were they worried he might be

about to open?

DEATH RATTLE

CHAPTER 17

That night, the end of shift briefing only emphasised the lack of progress in the investigation.

There were no new strong leads. The anonymous caller who had been recorded on tape had not telephoned back, and although the action had been allocated to a detective to chase up, most of the squad felt that it was a hoax and would lead to a dead end.

Wilson's mother had been shown a copy of the photograph from Darren's bedroom. She was unable to identify the teenager shown with her son, but confirmed that he was not a relative. Until all other avenues of enquiry were exhausted the photograph was not being circulated to the press. Although nothing in the photo suggested any sexual relationship it was considered that it could just cause further speculation as to Darren Wilson's possible sexuality.

No-one had yet been tasked to attend the gay group, MESMAC and Parker asked Jack to personally handle the visit the following day. Liaison with a gay agency was considered by HQ as a hot potato in the circumstances. The last thing the bosses wanted was some detective to make a non-politically correct comment that would end up plastered over the front page of the local rag.

Jack detailed the nightshift detective to monitor any leads that might come in during the night, and declining an invitation to go for a pint to the club, elected to spend an hour clearing some of the mounting paperwork in his tray, before heading home to the quiet of his apartment.

Later that evening Jack poured himself a glass of whisky and swirling the amber liquid around his glass took in the rich aromas as if it was a vintage wine. Settling down in a leather chair he gazed out of the window at the dark river below. On the quayside Jack could see the to and fro of people visiting the bars, and was amazed to see that despite the ice cold many of the younger ones were dressed in little more than thin shirts.

Jack recalled the days when he used to play on the quayside as a child and his thoughts drifted back to his father.

The smell of the whisky was stirring memories of the

last time that he had visited him at his home in North Northumberland and they had shared a couple of glasses. That journey up through Northumberland had been long with the rain lashing down onto the windscreen making visibility poor and driving difficult. It had been a tiring trek and things hadn't improved when he eventually arrived at the cottage near the centre of the village.

His father seemed to have lost weight and the once jet black hair was now almost white. He had a slight stoop which Jack hadn't noticed before and when he walked it was slow and laboured.

Jack had offered to help with any jobs there might be that needed heavy lifting but his father seemed to take it as a slight, making a conscious effort to stand up straighter.

'I'm not ready for the knacker's yard just yet.'

After that the conversation became strained, as they sat down to a couple of ready meals that Jack had brought up from the city.

Later father and son had sat together in the lounge of the cottage trying to make light conversation, as his father brought out a bottle of J&B whisky.

Jack considered it one of the best of the blended varieties and would under different circumstances have enjoyed savouring the drink, but having no intention of staying overnight protested that he had to drive back to the city.

His father had been insistent.

'One glass won't hurt you. It's the anniversary of the day I left the job. That's got to be something to celebrate.'

'The last thing I need is to be stopped by traffic on the way home.'

'Not much chance of that. From what I hear with all the cuts there's no bloody traffic cops left. They've been replaced with speed cameras to hit the ordinary motorist. It's just a revenue making exercise.'

He had reluctantly accepted the proffered glass, but whilst his father finished half his drink in one gulp, Jack sipped it slowly, concerned by what would be a long drive back to the apartment in poor weather.

Sometimes his father could be chatty and amiable; asking about people in the force that he had worked with.

Although most were retired and others dead, now and again Jack had bumped into the odd one who had been a lot younger than his father and they would pass on their regards.

At other times, his father could get moody and angry. On these occasions he would usually bring up the subject of the police and how changes had destroyed the job as he had known it.

Cops had never relished changes. During major restructuring of force boundaries in the early seventies there had been a great bitterness between the elite Newcastle City Police who were forced into merging with those in Northumberland, who they looked down on as their 'country cousins.'

Graffiti had appeared around the city centre police station, scribbled on walls, on posters, and on one occasion painted in whitewash on the rear entrance to the police car park.

It was just three letters. T.J.F.

It had stood for 'The Job's Fucked.'

Jack was concerned that this visit was going to develop into one of his father's diatribes, but resisted the temptation to swig off his drink and make his excuses.

'A top up?' His father's voice cut into his thoughts, and looking up he saw that he had already refilled his own empty glass.

'No thanks. I can't stop long. I have to get back.'

Jack was a little taken aback that his father had drained the first glass so soon.

Earlier, when looking for something in the kitchen, he had noticed a couple of unopened bottles in the back of a cupboard, and when he checked out the recycling bin spotted an empty bottle of Grants.

Jack had felt like he was snooping on his own father, and had guiltily looked around to make sure he wasn't being watched.

Whilst in the job, and later when first retired, Slade senior had always enjoyed his pint of beer in the pub or police club. He had never really been a spirit drinker, often making fun of Jack's preference for wine and whisky.

His father's sudden liking for whisky was a little disconcerting.

Then again, was it a sudden change of taste? Had it been a gradual increase in drinking over the past year or two? Jack knew that he didn't call up to see his father as often as he should. Constraints of work and the hundred mile round trip were the reasons.

At least that was what he told himself.

The truth was, that since his mother's death, he had never found himself too comfortable in his father's company. Neither wanted to mention Jack's mother, or talk of the pain of those last couple of months, watching someone that they both loved being eaten away by that vile illness.

Even now, several years later the hurt and loss was still acute.

At the time Jack had thrown himself into work in order to put the memories to the back of his mind and cope with the grief.

However, without any work to distract him, it was possible that his father was trying to find sanctuary at the bottom of a glass.

Jack subconsciously glanced at his watch.

Charlie Slade caught the movement.

'Well, I suppose you'd best be going then, son,' he said triggering those familiar pangs of guilt again in Jack.

The whisky certainly hadn't dulled his father's powers of observation.

Jack had drained his glass and stood up. There was an awkward silence whilst he checked for his keys and made his way out to his car.

The rain had not abated and the small stream running through the centre of the village was starting to rise. Jack hurried to his car to escape the relentless downpour and quickly climbed inside.

His father gave a brief wave as Jack started the engine of the BMW. He wanted to wind down the window and suggest his father should come down to visit the city but by the time he looked back the door had already been closed.

That last visit was over a month ago and they had only spoken once on the phone since.

Jack looked down at his mobile phone lying on the glass coffee table beside him.

Instead of reaching for the phone, he drained his whisky

and topped up his glass.

CHAPTER 18

Eight o'clock the following day and the briefing started with a sermon from Parker about unauthorised leaks to the press. It was clear that he was still smarting from the press conference of a few days ago, which, although still in everyone's mind no-one dared to mention.

'If it turns out that anyone in this office is responsible for the leak they'll not only be off the squad... but if I get my way they'll be up in front of the chief and looking to collect their P45.'

Several pairs of eyes flickered in the direction of Mark Burton, sitting silently at the back of the room like the spectre at the feast.

Jack was certain that the presence of Professional Standards hovering in the background like a bad smell would do little to raise team morale.

Following the previous day's enquiries, there were still no solid leads and a leaflet drop on all the gay bars by PCSOs was scheduled for later that day.

Questions to Wilson's shift and supervision at the West End nick had drawn a blank, and the family liaison officer had been unable to ascertain from his mother whether he had any close friends outside the job.

Darren Wilson clearly compartmentalised sections of his life.

The photograph showing the young man on the beach had been cropped to remove Darren's figure and the image enlarged, with copies being circulated to the shifts to be shown at start of parades. It had been suggested that the resulting photograph should also be circulated in the gay bars, but this had been overruled by Parker who felt it would be unlikely to produce any lead, but probably cause more unwanted press innuendo.

Everywhere was a hive of activity. Still they were getting nowhere and the more they ran around in circles the more they were in danger of disappearing up their own backsides.

Jack tried to remain undeterred by the lack of progress to date.

DEATH RATTLE

Every cop knows that the job isn't all excitement and glamour like on the telly. It was a laborious process of gathering seemingly unconnected facts. A giant jigsaw with the pieces being each snippet of information gathered. Cover the basics and with perseverance and a little luck every piece would eventually fall into place.

As Jack left the briefing room Burton followed him out into the corridor.

'Jack. I just wanted to say that any problems we may have had between us in the past... I don't want them to hamper the investigation.'

Jack turned so that they were face to face. 'Why should it do that?'

'No reason. I'm just here to help. In my opinion...'

Jack interrupted, 'Just so there is no misunderstanding on this... you said yesterday in Parker's office that I'm still running the enquiry?'

'No argument there.'

'Well, in that case can I say that I regard you purely in a consultative role?'

They stared each other in the eyes each refusing to blink.

It was Burton that broke the silence. 'Which means?'

'Which means... if I want your opinion I'll ask for it'.

Jack turned and strode away into his office where he found a second note on his desk asking him to telephone Liz Harmon at her office. He screwed it up and in a practised throw got it into the bin at the first attempt.

A couple of minutes later Parker stuck his head in the door. 'I've got an appointment at headquarters, but I want you to contact me on my mobile should anything break.'

Jack was relieved to see him go but guessed the appointment was with Curtis. The gay angle to the case had the A.C.C. and Command Block getting nervous.

It felt like the bosses were becoming more concerned with protecting the force's reputation, as with finding the killer of a dead cop.

Curtis appeared to have his priorities in a different order to me thought Jack.

Maybe that's why I'm still an Inspector and he's an A.C.C.

Jack was wondering when and if they would get their first good lead, when Armstrong barged into his office without knocking. He seemed slightly out of breath, as if he had just run up the stairs.

'I've just had a call put through from the front office. A witness has come forward and is waiting at the desk.'

'Is it the young lad from the photograph?' Jack asked, daring to hope.

'No. But maybe the next best thing. It's the guy who made the telephone call on the night of the murder.'

Over the past couple of days since he had found the body and made the initial telephone call Alex Morgan had become increasingly worried about what he should do. He was extremely reluctant to speak to the police, as like most LGBT people he didn't have much confidence in their discretion.

Eventually he had confided his involvement to a friend, hoping to get some reassurance that he was doing the right thing by remaining anonymous.

Alex was clinging to the belief that a problem shared is a problem halved.

Slade could have told him the truth.

A problem shared is a problem that two people now have.

When Alex told his friend of his dilemma he wasn't thanked for sharing his little secret.

'If they find out you were there and you haven't rang in they might think it was you. You might end up getting charged with murder. I think you best give yourself up.'

In reality, what his friend meant was, '*When they do eventually trace you and you cough up telling me about it... then we're both in the shit.*'

So, Alex had reluctantly walked into the Forth Banks Police Station and asked to speak with someone from the Murder Incident Room.

Now, sitting in the small cream coloured interview room, he wished a thousand times he had stayed at home that fateful night. It had shaken him so much that he hadn't been out cruising since. He had hardly eaten since Sunday and was sure he must have lost over a stone in weight. Although he had been trying to lose a few pounds for the past eighteen months... this hadn't been a part of his diet plan.

Even sleep was evading him as, every time he closed his eyes, he was haunted by an image of the dead man's eyes staring up at him.

Sitting opposite the two smartly dressed detectives he could feel their eyes boring into him. In different circumstances he might have found the younger one quite attractive but Alex didn't feel very flirty at the moment.

He kept thinking of what his friend had said about them suspecting him of the murder and shifted uncomfortably on the plastic seat.

The younger police officer went to a tape recorder fitted in a niche in the wall and pressed down a switch. The recording machine clicked into life and a loud continuous tone filled the room for ten seconds before everything again became silent.

'This interview is being tape recorded,' the detective began and went on to give the time, date, which police station they were in and his name as Sergeant David Armstrong.

Alex was asked to identify himself, following which the other officer who had been sitting silently up until then, gave his name as Jack Slade.

Alex was cautioned that he didn't have to say anything, but was falling over himself to get his story told. Although he hated the idea of being a witness in a murder case, he hated the idea of being thought of as a suspect even more.

The older police officer began by asking where exactly Alex had been on Sunday night, starting long before his visit to the Gardens.

With a tremor in his voice he told of driving in to the city, making his way down to the Gardens, and described to them how he had discovered the body of Darren Wilson.

He explained all about the man whom he had followed into the Gardens.

'Of course, I'm not in the habit of doing that sort of thing,' he lied, not at all convincingly to the flint faced detectives.

When questioned further about the stranger he could only give a very vague description and was a little embarrassed to admit that he couldn't actually remember anything about his face.

Alex admitted being the anonymous caller from the public phone and when asked, agreed to provide a set of fingerprints and a DNA sample to be checked against anything found in the telephone box or at the crime scene.

More than a dozen prints had been taken from the telephone box by Scenes of Crime. Eventually all of them would have to be traced and eliminated. When they had finally got everything out of him that they could, Slade and Armstrong left him sitting alone in the room and went to Jack's office, where over two coffees they mulled over Alex's account.

'He's lying through his teeth about not going there often. Couldn't look at us when he got to that bit,' Dave said, taking a sip from his mug.

'Yeah, but I think he's basically telling the truth.'

'What about the other bloke he saw. Could he be the murderer?'

'Didn't sound like it to me. We'll get another press appeal out, but I wouldn't hold my breath on him coming forward. Especially if he's married. He won't want any chance of the missus finding out.'

Jack paused for a second. 'Still check CCTV for the time of the incident. Pull any stills of people matching his description in the near vicinity. Check images of anyone heading down towards the Castle Garth and the Gardens area. We might get lucky.'

'I'll get that followed up and ask one of the team to take his statement. Then what do you want doing, Jack?'

Jack closed his eyes and rubbed them wearily.

'Scrub him from the actions. Get his prints for elimination and kick his arse back onto the streets.'

Armstrong nodded and left Slade to his thoughts.

It hadn't been so much a lead, as another dead end.
Fuck it! Back to square one.

DEATH RATTLE

CHAPTER 19

As the days passed everything began to slip into a routine. Each morning the various leads were allocated for following up, and at every close of day, there would be a further briefing with results evaluated and sometimes new actions raised. All the while the figure of Burton was quietly sitting somewhere in the background.

Though no-one dared say it out loud, they were all aware that each day brought fewer and fewer new leads as the investigation slowly dried up.

The results of the interrogation of Darren's computer had come back from the lab. There was nothing incriminating and it hadn't even been password protected.

So much for Henderson's dire warnings about what they would find.

From Parker's reaction at hearing the news it was evident that Headquarters had also been expecting something more out of the computer... maybe kiddie porn or explicit photos of Darren with some boy.

Something that disturbed Slade was when one of the CSI officers let slip that he wasn't the first to get the lab I.T. results. Parker and Burton had got in first and afterwards Parker had been seen with what was for him a rare smile. A smile of relief perhaps?

Or maybe it was wind!

In any case there had been nothing on the computer that was going to cause any great panic in the Command Block.

The only thing in the least bit interesting, were several further digital images of the unknown young man from the bedside photo frame.

He was as yet still unidentified, but the bosses were maintaining their reluctance to release his image to the press; wary of fanning the flames of press speculation.

Jack was becoming more convinced that the person in the photographs would hold the key to the mystery. He decided that if they were no further forward in the next couple of days then he would push harder for the photo to be released, with a press release that, although not a suspect, the youth may hold vital evidence relating to the enquiry.

It might generate some further press interest in the case. The lack of any developments had meant that Darren Wilson's death was no longer treated as front page news and was now relegated to a couple of columns on page five.

Jack was all for the Press Office keeping the enquiry in people's minds so long as it didn't require him speaking to the press. In particular Harmon who Jack had always mistrusted.

Background enquiries had gone as far back as Darren's training school years and statements had been obtained from his class tutors and anyone from his intake who was still in the job.

Some had not yet been traced as they had resigned and moved on and one was in Perth where he worked for the Western Australian Police. Henderson had been angling for that action to follow up and rumour was he had been seen pricing sun cream. He was visibly upset when Armstrong had mentioned video conferencing.

Welcome to the twenty first century.

Despite all their leads they were no further forward and every day Burton would be sitting at the briefings, never speaking but making the occasional jottings in a small black book.

On the plus side Parker was keeping his distance, only turning up occasionally when some information or new lead looked promising. Slade noticed that he was spending a lot of time at headquarters and had heard that he was frequently in the company of bosses from Command Block.

Jack was reminded of old cowboy movies with the besieged circling their wagons against attack. The bosses were obviously preparing their defences in advance of press criticism.

As the days went on Jack wondered if there would ever be a breakthrough. The cloak of secrecy and distrust from the gay scene was hampering the enquiry and all they kept coming up against was brick walls.

Added to this, at the back of his mind, was always the feeling that he was being set up to be the scapegoat should the enquiry go tits up.

At end of shift Jack would sometimes accompany the detectives to the police club, not so much for the odd pint, but in order to better judge their mood and feelings on the progress of the case, their inhibitions dulled by alcohol.

It was becoming clear that he wasn't the only one who thought that the case was going nowhere fast.

'This bloody gay scene is more secretive than the Masons,' Jackson muttered. 'I'm starting to feel useless. Today I put through seven exhibits. On other enquiries, I would be putting through seventy a day.'

'I heard they're thinking of scaling down the enquiry if nothing turns up soon,' Norton, a young detective, who had been seconded from the West End C.I.D. as liaison, said. 'I was just getting used to the extra overtime and it looks like it's drying up.'

'Joe in the front office told me that a couple of nights ago they had uniforms on overtime down the Gardens trying to get information from the rent boys down there,' Jackson continued.

'Is that a sort of whore to whore enquiries?' Henderson chuckled, amused by his own joke.

'The problem was at the first sign of a uniform everyone buggered off and spread the word. The woodentops spent three hours in the pissing rain and never spoke to anyone. It's a bloody farce.'

'Buggered off isn't the best choice of phrase,' laughed one of the detectives.

'What have you heard, Jack? Is it being scaled down?' Armstrong asked.

'Not that I've heard, but you know the score with budgets and all that. However it's gone over the time limit, so it qualifies for central funding…and with a murdered cop I can't see them wanting to close it down for some time yet.'

'I think some of the bosses would be happy if it just faded out and went away,' Henderson said, draining his third pint of the evening. 'There's that bloody Burton hanging around – as welcome as a turd in a swimming pool. Every bugger knows he's only here to snoop in case we get a lead that might put the force and the big cheeses in a bad light. Trust me on this one. I think Command Block don't really want us to solve this. They're afraid what might come out if it ever gets to court.'

Jack didn't reply, but he had his own thoughts on Henderson's whinging.

DAVID JEWELL

He might actually be right on that one.

CHAPTER 20

The following day Jack turned in early again and found yet another note on his desk asking him to ring Liz Harmon. The cleaner had already been in so, with a careful aim, it was the first piece of paper of the day to land in his bin.

Once again Parker shied off from the morning briefing and it was left to Jack. He tried not to feed his own paranoia by thinking of Parker and senior command sitting over coffee and biscuits at HQ, plotting to make Slade the fall guy. Burton was in his usual spot at the back of the room, eyes darting around watching the assembled detectives and always listening, occasionally turning to catch some snippet of conversation.

Jack went through the results of the previous twenty-four hours enquiries and dished out the actions for the coming day. There weren't as many as on the previous day.

Posters and leaflets had been circulated around the gay bars, but so far there had been no feedback. They were struggling to advance the enquiry and little would help.

Notification came that, as the family intended burial and not cremation, the coroner had released the body, and a funeral was being arranged.

As macabre as it sounds with a burial the body was always still available should there be any future major disputes over the autopsy conclusions. It was easier to dig up a victim than to try to gather up his ashes.

A Police funeral was to be held and Jack was pleased that Darren's family would get some closure and his mother would be able to bury her son with some dignity. He knew that it was only a matter of time before the press would be probing his life and throwing whatever dirt they could find at Darren Wilson.

Sitting at her desk in the newsroom Liz Harmon was starting to get seriously pissed off. She had left several messages for Detective Inspector Slade but so far he had not returned any of her calls. The dead police officers name had been released to the press as Darren Wilson, but all requests from reporters to speak to his family were being rejected.

Harmon had used the electoral role to track down his mother's address and even tried to "doorstep" her for some comment. Her knock had been answered by a young stern faced policewoman who made it clear she was not welcome and referred her back to the press office.

The Press Office. They were as much use as a chocolate fireguard.

She had tried ringing Spence but his phone was continually going through to voicemail. Getting through to his office she was told by a receptionist that he was out on an enquiry but despite leaving a message he hadn't got back as yet. He seemed to be out of the office an awful lot recently.

The scrawny bastard better not be ignoring me.

She wondered about walking the few hundred yards to Forth Bank nick and seeing if she could get to speak with the elusive Inspector Slade, but suspected she would be told that he was also *out on an enquiry,* or in interview, or some such crap. He was definitely going to be hard to pin down.

Getting to the facts was proving more difficult than usual and the more dead ends she came to, the more she began to suspect a cover up.

Her editor was starting to get impatient, asking darkly what had happened to the famous Harmon informants.

She would try Inspector Slade again, leave yet another request and hope he got back to her.

There would also be another message left for Spence but Harmon was coming to the conclusion that she was being snubbed by both of them. Whilst that would be a mistake for Slade... it would be a much bigger one for Spence.

Jack was sitting at his desk processing the actions.

One of the actions that still had not yet been allocated was the visit to the gay outreach organisation MESMAC. Checking out the group's address Jack saw that it was on the other side of the city. Parking in the centre might prove a problem and feeling like some fresh air to clear his mind Jack decided to walk.

Grabbing his coat and a folder containing photographs of Darren and the mystery boy, he headed down the stairs and out into the cold. After a few minutes it started to drizzle and Jack wished he had opted to take a car, but increasing his stride he battled through the fine rain towards the Civic Centre and the offices of MESMAC.

Just over twenty minutes later he was sitting in warm office. Outside it was now raining heavily and the downpour was rattling against the windows.

He had telephoned ahead and been greeted at reception by a man who introduced himself as Jamie Hetherington.

Jamie led him to a cosy, warm and bright room with cream walls and a light blue carpet. There were two chairs and a glass topped coffee table on which lay back issues of a glossy magazine called Attitude. A light wood bookcase contained numerous paperback books and on the walls were posters proclaiming 'Safe Sex' with telephone numbers for confidential health advice lines.

If it wasn't for the comfy armchairs and a pottery bowl on the table filled with packets of condoms it could easily have been mistaken for a doctor's waiting room. Jamie handed him a business card that stated he was Regional Outreach Co-ordinator for MESMAC North East

Jack studied the card and glanced back at Jamie, a good looking twenty-two year old with short blonde hair and pale blue eyes. Dressed fashionably in designer jeans and a white short sleeved shirt he had an unblemished face that frequently broke into a ready and engaging smile displaying rows of even white teeth. He looked more like a first-year university student than a senior sexual health worker.

And they say that you know you're getting old when cops are looking younger.

'So what does MESMAC stand for?' Jack asked.

'It stands for "**ME**n who have **S**ex with **M**en. **A**ction in the **C**ommunity,"' Jamie said matter-of-factly. He had obviously been asked the same question hundreds of times.

'Seems a bit long winded. Why not something simpler? Gay Community Action or something?'

'In a way, you're right. Mesmac, doesn't exactly role off the tongue, but if we described it as a gay organisation we would lose about half of the clients we're trying to engage with.'

Jamie registered the quizzical look on Jack's face and, smiling, continued. 'Let me give you the sales pitch. MESMAC is a charity seeking to reduce STDs and A.I.D.S by promoting safe sex, giving out health advice and distributing free condoms in known gay cruising areas. Many people we deal with don't actually identify themselves as being gay as such, even though they do have sex with other men.'

'Now I am confused. Where I come from two blokes having sex makes them gay.'

'Now who's being naïve? What about the guy who for cultural reasons has to get married and has never come to terms with his sexuality? Or the guy who doesn't want his friends to know about him and puts on a façade. What about the married guys?'

Jack considered what Jamie was saying. 'Do many people access your services?'

'Of course. We distribute leaflets and free condoms around the bars. We even have a gay youth group strictly for people too young to go on the gay pub scene. Teenagers who want to just meet with people their own age in a safe environment. Here they can ask advice that they maybe feel unable to get anywhere else.'

Jack decided to get to the point of his visit and explained that he was working on the murder in the Gardens.

'Because of the location we're looking at the possibility of a gay connection.'

Jamie nodded. 'So how can MESMAC help you?'

'We're interested in tracing any possible witnesses. We've been told that your organisation does outreach work in the Gardens where the murder occurred.'

'That's right. It's a regular port of call for our staff and I'm often tasked down there myself. As I said, one of our key objectives is the promotion of safe sex, and that involves condom distribution to high risk groups. The Gardens is a meeting place for gay men, but also attracts sex workers, who, although they engage with gay men, may actually be straight. They just see it as a very simple way to make some easy money.'

'Well, we're hoping that you could assist the enquiry by providing us with some names of possible witnesses that might have been in the area at the time of the murder.'

Jamie sat back in his chair and stared at Slade, mouth open. After a moment, he said, 'You're not seriously suggesting that we should just provide you with details of our clients?'

'Well this is a murder investigation.'

'I understand that and I sympathise with your problem, but you have to see it from our point of view. I can tell you now there is no way we would ever give you client details, even if we had them. Often we just know first names... sometimes just nicknames, but even so we would never break client confidentiality. I'm sorry, Inspector Slade, but if that's what you're here for you've had a wasted journey. It's just not going to happen.'

From the look on his face it was clear that Jamie was not going to budge. Jack knew from past experience never to threaten anything he wasn't prepared to do. Trying to bluff by suggesting seeking a warrant was a none starter. They both knew that getting the private files of a health organisation was never going to happen.

Jack reached into a waterproof document folder and took out two photographs. The first was of Darren Wilson.

'Can you at least tell me if you recognize this man from your visits to the cruising areas and, in particular, the Gardens?'

Jamie hesitated but after a couple of seconds reached out for the proffered photos. He stared down at the file photograph of Darren Wilson.

'I saw this photograph in the paper. It didn't ring a bell. He certainly isn't one of our regulars, but I couldn't say for sure. One of the other workers may have come across him at some time or the other. I'll ask around, but you have to understand we deal with scores of people every month.'

Jack nodded and handed over the enlarged photograph taken from Darren's bedroom and showing the blonde youth.

'What about him?'

Jamie studied the image for a while. 'He's vaguely familiar. He's not one of the regulars from the Gardens or cruising areas... but I've seen him around before. I think he occasionally gets in the bars. I'm sorry that I can't be of any more help, but there really is no way that we can open up our client files to you.'

'I can understand your position, but would you please just ask around for me? See if anyone is prepared to come forward or just give us information anonymously? It would be a great help.'

Jamie offered a warm smile and replied, 'I'll do what I can... but don't hold your breath.'

Jack smiled back and, shaking his hand, allowed himself to be led back to the entrance where he bade farewell and pulling his jacket tighter, stepped back out into the rain.

Checking his watch he saw that he would just have enough time to head back to the de-briefing and maybe get an early finish for what had been yet another unproductive day.

He had cleared one more action but it was just one dead end after another.

Back at the station, he brought Armstrong up to date with his enquiries at MESMAC, before they went in to the late briefing.

'What about a bit of surveillance on their offices? Try to get a lead on the people that go there.'

'On what grounds would we get a surveillance authority? After that recent fiasco in Yorkshire everybody is keeping shy of R.I.P.A.'

Jack was referring to the Regulation of Investigatory Powers Act and a recent case where a police force had unlawfully used surveillance legislation to eavesdrop on retired officers and reporters.

'I'm afraid it's a nonstarter. In the current climate it would be political suicide to even think of doing something unofficial and would taint any evidence we gathered. No, I think we have to leave it and just pray that this Jamie Hetherington character gets back to us with some lead.'

'Do you trust him?'

'I don't have much choice... but, yes, I think he was being upfront and honest. He was certainly not backward in coming forward when I asked to see their files.'

'Well, I've just been chatting to the beat officers that cover the gay area. From what they say, I don't think many of the clientele are rushing forward to help with enquiries. In fact, the bar owners are complaining of a drop in takings since we started asking questions. Looks like many of their customers are finding somewhere else to drown their sorrows with so many uniform cops around.'

'Yeah, well shit happens. The bar owners will just have to put up with it until we get our murderer.' Jack glanced at his watch, before saying, 'Better get in to the briefing, but I'm guessing we're no further forward or I would have heard something.'

Jack wasn't wrong in his assumption. None of the day's actions had turned up any new leads, and after he had gone around the room Jack told them of his visit to MESMAC which had also so far been unproductive.

The funeral for Darren Wilson was scheduled for the following day. A number of his colleagues from the West End had volunteered as pall bearers and a couple of on duty officers had been allocated for traffic duty at the cemetery. Several other cops were tasked with trying to keep the inevitable press at bay, and stop the ceremony turning into a media scrum. The H.MET officers were being represented by Jack and Armstrong, whilst the rest of the team crewed the office and followed up enquiries.

Jack brought the briefing to a close and as the detectives meandered out of the incident room to go home or to the pub, he tried to ring Superintendent Parker. The phone just went through to answer machine.

Slade didn't leave a message and instead headed out of the building to make his way home. It had stopped raining as he set off but he had only managed to walk half way down Forth Bank before the heavens opened and rain fell like rods, running down his collar and soaking the back of his shirt. Jack cursed under his breath and made a mental note to bring the car to work the next day.

It was proving a perfect end to a shit day.

CHAPTER 21

One thing they get right in the movies... it always rains at funerals.

On this occasion, the rain mixed with snow to form a freezing sleet which, carried on an ice cold north east wind, sliced its way across the cemetery.

The West Road Crematorium about five miles outside the city centre consisted of two chapels linked by a cloister and had served the people of Newcastle upon Tyne for the best part of a century.

With rain forecast for most of the day and remembering the soaking he had endured the night before Jack had driven in to work that day. The car was now standing in the car park of the Crematorium which was packed with a mixture of private cars and police vehicles.

The funeral service had taken place in the West Chapel which was the larger of the two. Even that had been insufficient to seat the number of mourners who had turned out. Dozens of people were forced to cram in and stand at the back in order to escape the icy wind.

The coffin had been carried in by six police officers resplendent in dress tunics and each wearing a pristine pair of white cotton gloves. Numerous other officers in the congregation were wearing uniform with some sporting military medals and many wearing the gold coloured Queen's Jubilee Medal and the blue and white ribbon and medal denoting police long service.

The medal used to be called "The Long Service and Good Conduct Medal" but everyone now preferred to call it by the more honest "Long Service".

It seemed in many minds these days 'police' and 'good conduct' were considered mutually exclusive terms.

The ceremony had been different to what Slade had expected. The more traditional Hymns that he recalled from his childhood had been replaced by some modern ballads, usually about leaving behind loved ones. But the contemporary songs did nothing to alleviate the depressing atmosphere that pervaded the Gothic style chapel.

Darren's elderly mother stood in the front row flanked

by family and broke down several times during the service.

Outside, a short walk from the chapels was a large cemetery which made provision for those families who preferred a more traditional burial, as opposed to the scattering of ashes in the Garden of Remembrance. This was to be one such occasion.

Following the service Jack found himself standing by the edge of a neatly dug open grave bordered by a bright green matting. Two heavy leather straps lay to one side. They were to be used to lower the beech coffin the traditional six foot into the frozen ground.

Everything about the setting seemed sombre and to Jack it appeared as though even the nearby willow trees were bowing in respect.

As the casket descended Slade only vaguely heard the priest intone, 'Ashes to ashes. Dust to…'

As he had glanced around something else had caught his attention.

At the start of the graveside service a number of people could be seen gathered, standing at a discreet distance, silently observing the ritual. It wasn't often that members of the public got to see the spectacle of a police funeral. The inquisitive group were a mixture of elderly women and men with a couple of curious children who appeared more interested in the various marked patrol cars.

One person however was different. Some distance away from all the others, and partially concealed by an overgrown Willow tree standing bare in the winter frost, was a young man of about eighteen. Jack didn't know his name but knew his face.

It was the youth from the photograph.

Jack slowly edged away from the group of mourners, deliberately walking in a direction that took him away from where the young man was standing, and towards the twin chapels. Then once concealed behind the shrubs that bordered the main pathway and rows of gravestones, he altered his course edging his way towards the car park and the group of onlookers.

Unhurriedly in almost panther like movements, he circled around and moved towards his quarry who was transfixed by the graveside service, totally unaware that he was being stalked.

Suddenly, as if alerted by some sixth sense, the youth glanced to his left and spotted the approaching figure of Jack. Wheeling around he began to make his way towards the tall wrought iron gates at the entrance to the cemetery grounds. Slade quickened his pace and as he did so saw the teenager do the same, until they had both broken into a sprint.

Although the younger man had the advantage of age Jack was still fit, and managed to keep up with him as they ran past the granite gateposts and out onto the busy West Road beyond.

The strident blast of a car horn yelped out as the youth charged headlong in front of the busy traffic in an attempt to lose his pursuer.

Dodging in front of a battered car that had screeched to a halt, Jack bounded after his target who was now running wildly down the centre of the busy carriageway desperately seeking an escape route through the moving vehicles and onto the opposite pavement.

Seeing a gap in the traffic he dodged between two cars and started towards a bus which had come to a halt further down the bank.

Jack knew if the runaway made the bus before he got to him then he would be lost. Putting on an extra spurt and ignoring the burning pain in his muscles Jack made a last ditch attempt to catch up with him and did so, just as the youth reached the door to the bus.

In true police parlance, he felt his hand grip the lad's collar just as the latter managed to jump onto the platform of the bus. With a sharp tug the youth lost his footing, was unceremoniously yanked backwards and fell in a clumsy heap onto the damp pavement.

Whilst a number of passengers gawped at the sight of someone being dragged to the ground, no-one wanted to become involved in what was obviously none of their business. The bus driver pretending not to have noticed anything untoward quickly pressed the button to close the doors and pulled away into the busy traffic.

Jack, hand tightly gripping the collar of the teenager's jacket, looked down at him gasping on the ground. The face that stared back at him displayed a look that was no stranger to

DEATH RATTLE

Jack.
It was the look of fear.

Jack and the young man sat together in the corner of an almost deserted pub a short distance from the cemetery. Tucked away in a corner at the back of the room the boy stared out of the window at the empty car park as sleet splattered against the glass.

The bar was very quiet apart from two wizened old men sipping Newcastle Brown Ale out of half pint glasses, and a woman in the corner who looked like she might be asleep; a glass of cider going flat in front of her.

A bored barman who couldn't have been more than just legal drinking age himself sat on a stool. His lank dark brown hair fell down over an acne scarred face as he glared hypnotically at his phone. Stabbing away at the mobile with nicotine stained fingers he appeared far too engrossed in texting to care about the two mismatched customers; Jack in black suit and tie and the teenage boy in jeans and blue waterproof jacket.

The youth sitting with Jack had grudgingly given his name as Drew Sterling.

'Only my mam called me Andrew and she died last year.'

Though he attempted to hide it Jack suspected that he had been crying, and there was still that fear in his reddened eyes. It held Jack back from questioning him too harshly.

When Jack had suggested returning to his car back at the cemetery, the boy looked terrified and refused outright to get into any vehicle. Despite attempts at reassurance it was clear that he regarded Slade with extreme suspicion.

Drew agreed to talk to Jack only if they spoke in a public place and had rejected all attempts to persuade him to go to the police station. Jack had dozens of questions bouncing around in his head but knew that, with no grounds to actually arrest him, pushing the lad too soon would spook him into doing another runner.

He had reluctantly agreed to Drew's demands and now they sat together, Jack drinking coffee and the lad with an untouched glass of coke. The drinks formed a defensive barrier between them and the teenager stared down at his glass as if the liquid was an oracle that might provide solutions to all his current woes.

Experience had taught Slade that nature abhors a vacuum so they sat in silence, Jack waiting for the boy to begin to talk.

Breaking the stillness, Drew blurted out, 'I won't go to court!'

Jack merely nodded, knowing if he didn't speak, the boy would feel obliged to continue filling the silence.

After a time, Drew looked up at Jack and asked, 'Why did you come after me anyway?'

'I recognised you from the photograph at Darren's flat.'

The boy looked down and stirred his coffee as he contemplated this.

'The one on the beach?'

Slade nodded studying the boy's face as he mulled over how significant the photograph would prove.

'Darren loved that photograph, but never put it on display in the lounge. He was pretty closeted like that.'

The word 'closeted' jumped out at Jack. It seemed like Darren Wilson may have been gay after all, though clearly not open about the fact.

Slade took this as his opportunity to progress the conversation and went in for the kill.

'Drew…was Darren your partner?'

After what seemed an age, the boy finally looked up at Jack, and, holding his gaze for a few seconds, nodded silently.

Slade waited patiently allowing Drew to begin to tell his story. At first his speech was stilted but as he continued the words began to flow more freely and Slade knew that eventually it would become a deluge.

This young man opposite him had clearly been keeping secrets for a very long time and the opportunity to unburden was proving cathartic.

'It was taken on a beach near Silloth in Cumbria. We went there on a short holiday to celebrate my nineteenth birthday. Darren wanted us to go abroad, but I didn't have a passport, so we settled for a week camping in The Lakes. The further from Newcastle the better, so far as Darren was concerned.'

Slade looked at him quizzically.

'It meant less chance of us being spotted by anyone who knew him,' he explained, smiling for the first time since they had met.

Over the next hour Jack learned the answer to many of the questions he had about his victim. The answers just seemed to throw up additional queries about the circumstances of his death.

Drew told him that he and Darren had met at a party at the home of a mutual friend and although Darren was a couple of years older they had immediately hit it off.

The friendship had quickly developed and soon they had embarked on a deeper relationship. Drew had been aware of his sexuality since he had been twelve or thirteen but Darren had not had any kind of intimate relationship with either sex before meeting up with the younger man.

Even though they were doing nothing illegal, Darren had been very wary about anyone finding out about the relationship, so they met infrequently in public, keeping things secret from all but a very few close friends. Drew spent many nights at Darren's apartment but still maintained his own place in a small council flat in the Benwell area of Newcastle, where he had been living since his mother's death the year previously.

They had discussed moving in together but Darren's caution had overridden his desire to be with Drew as much as he could. Keeping separate places whilst spending most nights at Darren's Gosforth apartment was a compromise.

Occasionally when he mentioned Darren, Drew's eyes would fill up and Slade was concerned that he might begin sobbing as the young man strove to maintain his composure.

'It must've been hard for you to have a relationship, but keep it hidden from everyone, especially today at the funeral,' Slade said during a pause in the boy's story. 'It's going to make it doubly hard for you to get over it.'

Drew raised his face and looked directly at him, 'I'll never get over it.' Tears spilled down his cheeks.

'You see, I'm responsible for his death.'

CHAPTER 22

The words were like the chill wind outside and Jack felt a shiver down his spine. Was the boy confessing to Darren Wilson's murder?

In the ensuing silence Slade could hear the rain and sleet rattling against the window.

Drew was struggling to hold back the tears. Jack saw the barman looking over but when he caught Slade's eyes he quickly went back to his texting. In the West End it didn't pay to get too curious about other people's business.

It could seriously affect your health.

Jack spoke softly. 'Why do you say that you're responsible for his death?'

'I asked Darren to try to find a friend of mine who was missing. That's the reason why he was down the Gardens that night. He wasn't cruising like the papers are hinting. He was only there because I asked him.'

'Do you believe that he was the victim of a mugging or a homophobic attack?'

Drew paused, considering the suggestion.

'It's possible, but I think that his murder was something to do with my missing friend.'

'You're going to have to start from the beginning. Let's start with your friend who's gone missing. What's his name?'

'Johnny... Johnny Lee.'

Drew began to open up and as Jack had known it would, once started the words began to pour out. As a child Drew had grown up in the West End of the city where he lived with his mother.

His father had left when he was just five and he had no further contact with him.

In his early teens Drew made friends with a neighbour's son from a few doors away in the same street. It was a friendship that Drew's mother did not encourage.

Johnny Lee was the same age as Drew. Slim, with a shock of blonde hair, his fine features lent him an almost girlish look. The deep blue eyes had made him instantly attractive to Drew.

Johnny also came from a single parent family but there

the similarities ended and their home lives could not have been more different. Where Drew was cherished and cosseted by his mother, Johnny was the personification of the 'Latchkey Kid'. From the age of seven he had been often left by his single mother to forage for himself and he was not so much brought up as dragged up.

Numerous *'uncles'* over the years compounded the problems and as Johnny grew up he was often out late at night, alone on the streets whilst his mother entertained her many casual partners.

For a while Johnny's mother appeared to settle down with a man she had met one night whilst out drinking in a city centre pub.

George seemed a bit different from many of the others and for about three months moved into the small council house with Johnny and his mother. The first few weeks were good, with George making an effort to get on with the boy who was now aged twelve and had up until then never had a father figure living in. When his mother took a bar job for a couple of nights at the local pub for a while it looked like Johnny would finally have a little stability in his life.

That changed one night when, with his mother working late, George was drinking cans of cheap beer and watching TV, with Johnny curled up asleep next to him on the threadbare sofa. Johnny awoke to feel George's hands stroking his chest. As the hands worked down his body, Johnny, still half asleep, was unsure what was happening and felt his jeans being undone and hot breath on his body.

What happened next was Johnny's first real sex education lesson. He was a quick learner.

The *'lessons'* went on for several weeks until one night his mum returned home early from work and walked in on what George was doing. That night George left hurriedly and, although mother and son never discussed it, George was never seen again.

By the time he turned thirteen Johnny was a very streetwise kid and his experience with George had given him an appetite to repeat the experience. Being young and feminine, there was no shortage of eager sexual partners his own age, although he preferred it when one of the older boys took a shine to him.

Then one night when walking through a park near his home a chance encounter changed the way he viewed his sexual partners. He discovered that older men were not only prepared to relieve his adolescent sexual tensions, but were only too ready and willing to pay for the privilege.

That night a young entrepreneur was born.

Soon Johnny was earning almost as much as some of the teachers at the school that he no longer bothered to attend, and by the age of fourteen had become the family breadwinner.

His mother was taken care of financially with the strict condition that the introduction of numerous new uncles ceased. Although she strongly suspected what was going on, she knew better than to query the source of her young son's new-found wealth.

Much of his surplus cash was spent on clothes and the latest electronic gadgets and Johnny quickly noticed that the improvement in his personal appearance increased his earnings substantially.

With the increase in social networking sites Johnny found that meeting men over the internet avoided trawling cruising areas and any risk of contact with the police. His profile on the various "dating" sites always listed his age as eighteen.

Johnny had known since his time with George that he preferred his own sex. After meeting with Drew they had a couple of brief encounters together, but in truth Johnny preferred older people. However, although the sex dried up between them they became friends and on several occasions Johnny had suggested that Drew too could earn extra cash and that he 'knew someone who could help.'

Drew's mother didn't approve of her son's street wise friend and the thought of how she would react if she ever found out horrified Drew. He always declined Johnny's offers.

As time went on and they grew older Johnny changed. He developed a harder more cynical edge and, as the two boys began to move in different circles, they slowly drifted apart.

When Johnny was seventeen his mother died suddenly from a heart attack and he was forced to leave his home to be rehoused in a one bedroom council flat on the outskirts of the city.

DEATH RATTLE

Just after Drew turned eighteen he would occasionally bump into Johnny in a gay bar or café in town when they would exchange chat and maybe have the occasional drink together.

Whilst Johnny progressed in his lifestyle Drew made other friends and it was through one of these that at a party he met Darren Wilson.

Since Drew and Darren had become partners Drew only occasionally went on the gay scene because Darren refused to go in case he was spotted by someone he knew. However, when Darren was on late shifts Drew would, with his blessing, go out alone to catch up with friends.

About three weeks ago Drew and Johnny had met in one of the smaller bars in the gay quarter of the city and had exchanged greetings.

Johnny appeared high on something and Drew guessed that it was more than just drink that was fuelling his good spirits. It seemed that Johnny may be developing a 'habit'.

He was very talkative, flashing a wad of twenty pound notes and bragging that there was more where that came from. At one point, he leaned in and whispered to Drew that he was onto '*a good little earner*'. Something that was going to make him very rich. When Drew pressed him he just put his finger to his lips and laughed.

Johnny was clearly worse the wear, becoming loud and drawing attention, so when Drew spotted another friend of his passing the window he made his excuses and left. As he looked back through the bar window Johnny was propping himself against the bar and ordering another drink.

It was three days later and about eight o'clock at night. Darren was working a late shift and Drew was having a quiet night in at his own flat when there was a loud knock on the door. Checking through the spyhole in the door Drew was surprised to see Johnny standing outside.

Opening the door it was a very different Johnny from the one he had encountered a few nights before. His face was pale and drawn and he seemed to have aged in such a short time. Without waiting for an invitation, he squeezed past Drew and into the hallway.

He had a haunted look in his eyes, his clothes were crumpled and in places a little grubby. This was not the cocksure Johnny that Drew had come to know and he was shocked at the rapid change.

Johnny went through to the lounge and peeling back the blinds a little peered into the street outside as if checking for someone.

'What the hell's going on?' Drew asked uneasily.

Without replying Johnny moved to the couch where he collapsed in a heap. After a few moments he looked up with bloodshot eyes. 'I just need somewhere to crash. Can I stop here?'

Johnny had a strange frightened look in his eyes that Drew had not seen before and it made him anxious.

'What's wrong? Let me know. I might be able to help.'

'They're after me. They know and they've been down the bars looking for me.'

The voice was a little slurred and Drew wondered if his friend was drunk or had dropped some bad drugs to lead him to this state of paranoia. He had recently began to suspect that much of Johnny's proceeds from his entrepreneurial lifestyle was ending up his nose

'Who is after you? What have you done?'

'I need somewhere to stop. Just for a couple of days.'

'Look, I don't know. Why can't you tell me what…?'

'If they get me they're going to kill me!'

Whether real or drug fuelled paranoia, the look of terror in Johnny's eyes had been genuine and Drew knew that he had to let him stay. Maybe he would get better sense out of him in the morning.

He found a sleeping bag in a cupboard and threw it down onto the couch along with a spare pillow. Johnny forced a smile of thanks and Drew went to the kitchen to make a couple of coffees. By the time he returned Johnny was already fast asleep.

Drew switched the light off and left his friend asleep.

The next morning Drew got up about eight o'clock and went through to check on his unexpected house guest. The coffee was still on the table, cold and untouched.

Johnny was gone.

Drew never saw him again.

At first Drew thought that after a couple of days Johnny would turn up but when after more than a week he did not appear he checked with friends on the scene. No-one had seen Johnny at any of the bars or cafes and he had been noticeably absent at the gay nightclub which was his regular haunt. Drew became increasingly concerned and decided to confide in Darren Wilson to see if he could find anything out. Maybe Johnny had been arrested and was locked up somewhere.

Darren had agreed to check him out but reported back that there was no record of his having been arrested, and no missing person report. Because there were no relatives with whom Johnny might have contact it looked like there was little to go on in order to trace him.

Neither of them wanted to make a formal report as they were certain to do so would be inviting some very difficult questions from Darren's colleagues. However, after a long discussion it was agreed that rather than make anything official Darren would do a few discrete enquiries of his own and see if he could find Johnny's whereabouts.

Darren had found sightings on the police Information System data base linking Johnny to the Gardens area but none were recent and there was no further information as to where he might be now.

Darren was concerned about Johnny's claim that someone was out to kill him and they had discussed at length whether to make a formal report to the police. If so it would be up to Drew to make the report as Darren didn't want to be involved.

However, that in itself might cause some problems for Darren. Having done some discrete checks on the computer Darren was aware that any subsequent data trail of Johnny's records would reveal his interest. The fact that he had been going through Johnny's records prior to the missing person's report might raise some awkward questions.

Any breach of data protection could lead to Darren's dismissal.

Suddenly out of the blue a telephone message had been left for Darren at the station saying that Johnny was safe and well and would meet him at the Gardens that night. At first Darren was scared that the message was in some way the result of his unauthorised checking of Johnny's record on the force computer system.

How could Johnny be aware he was searching for him

and how had he known where to contact Darren? Was the message really from Johnny?

Drew wanted to go with him but Darren was concerned for him and refused to expose Drew to the chance that it was some kind of set up. No matter how much Drew protested Darren would go alone.

That night Darren went to the meeting with Johnny.

He never returned.

CHAPTER 23

Jack walked with Drew back to where the unmarked police car was parked in the crematorium car park. Although all the mourners had now left from Darren's service there was singing coming from the East side chapel and a hearse carrying a coffin was just pulling up outside the West side building.

Even processing death had become a conveyor belt in this go-faster modern age.

Shaking off the morbid thoughts, he swiped his mobile back on and saw several missed calls from Dave Armstrong.

He must be wondering what happened to me and where I suddenly disappeared to during the funeral.

Jack decided to wait until he got back to the station to update him about the real reason Darren Wilson had been in the Gardens that night.

He wasn't cruising as everyone had suspected, but working on an off the books police enquiry of his own to trace a missing teenager. A teenager that Jack was beginning to suspect might already have been dead.

And now Darren Wilson too was dead and no-one knew why or who had killed him.

This was going to add a whole new level to the murder enquiry and spin it off into a totally different direction.

Slade took Drew back to his flat which was in a run-down part of Benwell, and as he turned into the street he was forced to steer around broken bricks and assorted rubbish lying in the road.

Overgrown gardens and graffiti signalled that the area was in a steep decline from which it might never recover, and the shabby houses in the street reflected the urban decay.

Some years ago, the deprived council area of Scotswood adjacent to Benwell was in similar state, and for decades had been regarded as one of the worst areas of the city to live. Since the sixties it had been notorious for the grisly murders committed by the twelve-year old Mary Bell who had murdered two young boys leaving their bodies dumped on the estate.

Over the years various plans had been put forward to

improve the area. The joke was that in order to make Scotswood twice as good they should to knock half of it down. Comedy imitating life that was exactly what happened, with council workmen moving in to demolish what seemed like every alternate street.

Then, clearly flushed with success, a few years later the area had been improved one hundred per cent.

The rest was bulldozed to the ground.

All that was left was brown belt land which would probably be sold off at a knock down price to some property developer.

Drew's apartment was what Slade knew as a Tyneside Flat. From the outside, it had the appearance of a terraced house but a second front door led to a surprisingly spacious upstairs apartment.

Jack went inside and Drew confirmed that Johnny had left no clothes, possessions, or any kind of clue that would point to where he had gone.

Johnny had done a runner and seemed determined that no one would follow him.

Jack once again tried to persuade Drew to come with him to the police station but this proved as fruitless as before. He knew that he had nothing with which to actually arrest him and to force him in would possibly alienate him and lose Jack the only witness that he had.

Jack agreed that he would contact Drew after he had looked further into the background of Johnny. This time officially, as part of the current murder enquiry.

As he left, Jack promised Drew that all would be well. He was not telling the truth but it seemed to reassure Drew... if not himself.

Despite what he had said Drew would eventually have to give a statement. There was no way that Slade could withhold the information from the enquiry. Then, no matter what Drew wanted, it would be up to Parker what happened next.

This was a murder investigation and Drew was a crucial witness.

Jack was aware of what was likely to await Drew. Interrogation by the team and then, when the gay policeman and teenage boy angle leaked out, intrusive harassment from a press hungry for juicy scandal. With a pang of remorse Jack left Drew in his flat and went out into the street.

He was relieved to see that the wheels were still on his car and starting the engine pulled away and turned in the direction of the city centre.

Jack was seated in Parker's office with the door firmly shut. His sour faced boss was sitting behind his desk in front of a pile of reports. Jack wished that he was on the other side of the door. Parker was clearly not a happy man.

'What do you mean you took him home? He should be here in an interview room, for God's sake!'

'He's very frightened and doesn't trust the police.'

'I don't give a shit. Get back there and bring him in. Drag him in if you have to.'

Thomas Charles Parker appeared to puff up like a balloon and little flecks of spittle flew from the corners of his mouth. His face was turning puce.

'I want him in here and on tape before today is over.'

'He's a witness, not a suspect.'

'We don't know he's not a suspect. It could have been a bloody lover's tiff or something. He found his policeman boyfriend in some queer cruising area with some other bloke and stabbed him. It happens.'

'I don't believe he's our suspect.'

Parker looked at Jack with mounting anger enflaming his eyes. Growling, he said, 'I'm the S.I.O. on this case and I get to decide who is and who isn't a suspect. Now take Armstrong and get over to the kid's flat. I expect him back here within the hour.'

With that he turned to the window and gazed out signalling that Jack was dismissed and that any further conversation on the matter was over.

Jack got up and left the office to look for Armstrong. He found him in the canteen half way through a sandwich.

'I heard T.C.P. was giving you a hard time.'

'Bad news travels fast.'

'He was shouting so loud I reckon everyone in the station heard him. He's a dying breed, Jack. You can't speak to people like that. I don't know how the old bastard gets away with it.'

'He's a boss and we're the workers. He says jump and we just have to ask how high.'

'So, what's it all about and what's the plan?' Dave said, changing the conversation.

'We have to go and bring in a witness. A young lad who turns out to be Wilson's boyfriend.'

Armstrong raised his eyebrows and the questions quickly followed.

'Who is he? How did we trace him? How old is he? He's not under age, for Christ's sake?'

Jack promised to fill him in on everything as they drove and asked him if he had the keys to the unmarked police car. He didn't want to risk his own car left unattended in Benwell again.

Five minutes later they had driven out of the police car park on the short drive to Drew Sterling's flat.

Jack filled Armstrong in on how he had traced Drew and what he had been told of their relationship and the possible reasons why Wilson had been where he was on the night that he was murdered.

Dave was driving and listened intently to his friend, only interrupting to ask the odd question.

It was as they turned into Benwell that Armstrong voiced what they had both been thinking.

'Jack, you know the press are going to go to town on this. Seeing gay conspiracies and police cover ups. It can only cause distractions and cloud the investigation. Maybe even divert us from finding Wilson's killer. And when that bitch Harmon gets in on the act she'll milk it for all it's worth, especially after Parker's denials at the press conference.'

Jack decided not to mention the requests from Harmon that had been regularly appearing on his desk.

'Fuck Liz Harmon,' Jack muttered.

'No thanks... not whilst there's still dogs on the streets.' Armstrong laughed as he nosed the car into Drew's street and, directed by Jack, parked up in front of his gate.

Getting out of the police car they were conscious of several youths watching from a distance. In Benwell, the locals could spot an unmarked cop car at two hundred yards. Within minutes the word will have spread.

DEATH RATTLE

Watch out, watch out! There's Bizzies about!

Slade recalled a tale his father had told him of when he had been a panda car driver in the seventies and drove a Ford Escort Popular. He had returned after taking a report to find the car turned upside down on its roof. It took four burly cops to right it before he could get back to the station and start his damage report. Jack looked at their vehicle and hoped that it would be intact when they returned.

He was doubly pleased that he hadn't brought his BMW.

They approached the front door to the flat and Slade knocked heavily on the flaking blue paint. After a short time he saw a tell-tale shadow cross the small spy hole set in the wood and knew that Drew was looking out at him. After a few moments the door was opened by the clearly nervous youth who flashed glances from Slade to Armstrong.

'We need to come in and talk to you, Drew.'

Hesitantly the door was opened fully and both men stepped into the flat.

Jack explained that Drew had to attend the police station on the orders of the Superintendent and tried to reassure him that everything would be alright.

Drew protested and Jack had to use plenty of coaxing to get him to agree to go with them to the nick and give a statement concerning his involvement with his dead boyfriend.

Reluctantly, Drew picked up his jacket and house keys and walked sullenly to the door with the two detectives. Before he stepped out into the street, he turned and fixed Jack with a glare.

He said nothing, but the look spoke a thousand words.

You said this wouldn't happen. I trusted you. You lied to me.

At the station Drew was placed in an interview room. The sparse room had a table bolted to the floor and three small office chairs. The walls were a light grey colour and appeared to be lined with some kind of soundproof material. Set into one wall was a black microphone below which was a recessed glass fronted cupboard housing a black twin deck cassette recorder.

109

Drew began to lose track of time but thought it must have been between ten and fifteen minutes that he had been sitting alone before the door was opened and in came Slade and Armstrong.

Jack tried an engaging smile. It was not returned.

During the tape-recorded interview Drew was told that he was considered as a 'Voluntary Attender' and not a suspect so was at no time under arrest. Although he had been given the option of having a solicitor present he had declined.

The interview was little more than a rehash of what Jack had been told in the pub but he knew that getting it down on tape would give the feeling of some progress, generate some further actions and ultimately keep Parker off his back.

Apart from giving his name, Armstrong sat silently throughout the interview but was listening intently to every word, occasionally jotting down some fact that he would want to check further into.

Drew was open and frank concerning his relationship with Darren Wilson and reiterated the events leading up to Johnny's disappearance.

When Drew talked of Johnny and his friend's involvement in the rent boy scene, Armstrong did not react, but the world he was hearing about was not one that he or many of the other detectives had ever had much dealings with. It was going to be a difficult one for officers to infiltrate.

One thing was for sure. The revelations were certainly going to spin the investigation off into a different direction.

After the interview, the drive back to Drew's flat was in silence. Since they had left the station Drew had hardly exchanged a word with Slade. The atmosphere in the car was a lead weight pressing down on Jack who was keenly aware of Drew's feeling of betrayal. Jack felt guilty but knew in his heart that it was the correct decision to bring in the frightened youth.

There was an additional problem. There was no doubt that the visit of police officers to his flat had not gone unnoticed. Talking to the cops in Benwell was the big taboo. So far as the locals were concerned the worst thing you could do was to get labelled as 'a grass.' The repercussions would be swift and windows would be shattered.

Jack hoped that with a bit luck having seen Drew being taken away the locals would think that Drew had been arrested as a suspect, rather than helping as a witness.

Armstrong drove the car skilfully through the early afternoon traffic passing several motor dealers on Scotswood Road and turned up past the Cruddas Park tower blocks.

As they turned into Drew's street it seemed the same group of youths were hanging about but you could never be sure. From a distance, they all looked the same dressed in their street uniform of 'snide' trainers, tracksuit bottoms and hoodies.

Armstrong pulled the car into the kerb and all three got out. Without a word or a backward glance Drew walked the short path to his door and Jack got out of the car and followed him.

Drew seemed to hesitate at the door and as Jack caught up with him he instantly saw the reason why.

The wooden frame beside the mortise lock was splintered and the door was very slightly ajar.

The flat had been burgled.

CHAPTER 24

Entering cautiously Jack climbed silently up the stairs keeping to the edge of the steps which were less likely to squeak and announce his presence. It was almost certain that any intruder had long gone but Jack did not believe in taking chances.

He felt his fist clench involuntary and every sense was highly tuned to any sound of movement inside the flat as reaching the landing he moved along towards the front room.

Pushing the door quietly open with his foot Jack peered in.

It was empty.

The front room had been ransacked and every drawer was turned out with the contents strewn around. Papers littered the floor and a small flat screen television was lying on its side but the screen was not broken.

Jack moved to check out the bedrooms and saw that the second smaller bedroom had been similarly ransacked. Jack turned to Drew's room and studied the scene. It had also been hurriedly searched with drawers of a bedside cabinet tipped onto the floor. Amongst the detritus and drawer contents Slade spotted a five pound note and several pound coins lying where they had been tipped.

He sensed Armstrong at his shoulder and muttered, 'There's cash lying on the floor.'

Dave shrugged and glanced around him wordlessly taking in the scene of mayhem.

He turned to Slade. 'I know that look on your face, Jack. What's up?'

'My first thought was the group that had been hanging about in the street when we left. But look – every room ransacked, but cash left untouched. This wasn't your local teenage 'scrote' burglar.

'They were after something specific?'

'I'd put money on it.'

'But what?'

'Now that's where your guess is as good as mine. Then of course there's the other question... did they find it?'

Although he had been told by Armstrong to stay outside and wait, Drew suddenly appeared on the landing. The colour drained from his face as he took in the scene.

Jack spoke softly. 'We think they were looking for something. Have you any idea what?'

'What have I got... other that the TV and DVD?'

Jack considered this and looked around the room. The TV and DVD remained amongst the mess littering the room.

'It's obvious they were searching for something. If not something of yours, did Johnny leave anything with you?'

Drew seemed to consider this and Jack persisted. 'Drew, you have to tell me. Did he ask you to look after something for him?'

'No! Nothing! And he never left anything or I would have noticed it by now.'

Jack frowned. 'Can you see anything missing?'

Drew started to shake his head, but stopped abruptly, before hurrying through to the small bedroom. Scanning the contents of a set of drawers, he turned back to Jack.

'My laptop's gone.'

'Anything else?'

'Yes! All my discs and memory sticks.'

'What's on them?'

Drew grew sheepish.

'Don't hold anything back from me, Drew.'

'Just some copy movies.'

Jack couldn't help but smile. 'I can assure you copyright movies are the least of my concerns at the moment. Anything else?'

Drew shook his head and Jack found himself staring at Drew's eyes, trying to see any indications that he knew more than he was letting on. There were none.

What Jack did see again was the fear.

Armstrong broke the silence. 'I'll get on to control room. I'll ask Uniform to up patrols in the street in case they decide to come back. I wouldn't mind having a chat with them.'

At the suggestion that the intruders might come back, Drew's eyes widened.

Jack scanned the room, taking in every detail of the mess surrounding him.

'Dave, do me a favour. Go speak to those lads on the corner. See if they saw anything.'

Armstrong grunted a half laugh. 'Jack, they probably did it. Even if they didn't, this is the West End. They won't give a cop the time of day in case they get accused of being your snout. We don't have Jehovah's Witnesses in this area. We have Jehovah's Bystanders. Even that lot won't refer to themselves as witnesses in the West End.'

Slade smiled across at his friend. 'Just covering bases, Dave. If we don't do it T.C.P. will ask why not.'

Dave nodded and reluctantly left the flat to question the 'potential witnesses'.

Jack then turned to Drew, who was numbly picking up some discarded papers.

'Leave that for the moment. I'm going to get forensics down here. They'll dust for any prints. If you can just check around and see if anything else has been taken... but don't touch anything. I'll get on to the council and get the door repaired.'

'That other detective said they might be back,' Drew uttered quietly.

'I don't think there's much chance of that happening,' Jack lied.

He knew that if it was connected with the murder and the intruders hadn't found what they were after then they could expect a return visit, but didn't want to spook the teenager more than he was already.

Drew seemed lost in his own flat, turning away and wandering back into the front room. Slade stared after him. He had seen enough victims of crime in the past to know that the he was in shock. His home had been burgled and it takes a while to get over the knowledge that your sanctuary has been violated.

Jack took the police radio clipped to his belt and called up control room.

It was four o'clock and Liz Harmon sat at her desk in her city centre office.

She idly twirled a pen between her fingers as she stared out the window at the rain beating down on the people rushing about on the street below.

Her article on the murder had been put to bed for the

late edition, but with few minor additions it was little more than a rehash of the story to date. Going over the events in her mind she felt sure that there was something still to be uncovered.

At the press conference that prick Superintendent Parker had been lying about the gay angle. Who did he think he was fooling?

Like a shark at a shipwreck Harmon could scent the blood of a story from a mile off and she was getting a strong whiff of scandal in this one. Better still... a possible cover up.

It wasn't the first time she had covered the story of a murder in the Gardens. *Everyone and his granny knew it was a gay meeting place. Was the dead police officer a closet case?* She would bet a month's bar expenses on it. And a month of her bar bills was not a small wager.

But there was still something else.

Could there be young kids in the mix? Nothing sold papers better than a bit of scandal involving underage boys, especially if it implicated teachers, vicars or scout masters. The addition of a police officer was guaranteed to up the paper's circulation.

But who to ask?

She was sure that wimp Spence at HQ had stopped taking her calls. She knew that there had already been some gossip about how far their friendship went. Was he worried about the investigation into the information leak or was he more worried that his wife would find out he was shagging away from home?

She smiled to herself.

Keep trying to shut me out you weedy little bastard and she just might.

When she next left a message she would remind him that she had his home telephone number if he thought it might be easier to contact him there.

That should get a reaction.

She stopped twirling the pen and glanced at the open book on her desk displaying Spence's contact numbers.

Sod it!

She picked up the phone and dialled his mobile.

The rain had turned to snow as Jack battled through the Christmas shoppers and made his way towards the city centre. The snow wasn't lying deep but what there was turning to slush making the pavements slippery and difficult to negotiate.

Reaching the Civic Centre he climbed the steps and, bypassing reception, made his way towards Jamie's office, where he was met by the young outreach worker. There was that smile again.

'I didn't expect to see you again so soon. As I told you when you rang I've heard nothing so far that helps you, I'm afraid.'

'Well, there's been a bit of a development from our side and I was hoping that you might be able to assist.'

'Go on,' Jamie said, waving him to one of the chairs. 'How can I help?'

Jack considered this for a moment, before continuing. 'You've said part of your work is to visit the cruising areas. In particular, the Gardens?'

Jamie nodded. 'Sometimes I feel I'm spending half my working life there.'

'You must meet with many of the young lads who frequent the area?'

'Yes. But if you're fishing for names forget it. I told you last time confidentiality is paramount. If I start talking to the police my credibility goes down the toilet and months of work building relationships gets flushed away with it.'

'I'm dealing with a murder here.'

'Which is why I'm speaking with you at all. In my world policemen don't have the best of reputations for community relations.'

'You could prevent another death.'

'I'm doing that with the free condoms I give out. I have to weigh up how many lives might be lost by alienating my clients through talking to you.'

Jack sat back and studied Jamie. The face looking back at him was friendly enough, but Slade knew that taking his current line he was going to come up against the same brick wall that was continuing to dog the investigation.

It was clear that the "them and us" attitude between cops and the gay community was born of a mutual distrust. There were clearly some barriers to overcome.

However, from first speaking with Jamie, Jack had a feeling that he was someone to trust. He wanted to take him into his confidence, but knew that if anything he revealed found its way into the media it could seriously screw with the investigation. It would also have everyone from TCP to ACC spitting blood and fire.

Jack made a decision.

'Listen. If I tell you some things, I ask that you treat them with strictest confidence. If details of the investigation get out it might hamper the search for the killer... and maybe put another young lad's life at risk.'

'I can't make any promises, but go on.'

'The papers are speculating about a gay link between the murder of a police officer in the Gardens and whether the officer might have been gay.' Jamie did not respond, but sat back in his chair.

Jack continued. 'I can tell you the officer was gay... but that was not the reason he was in the area. He was trying to trace a young man who is missing and we believe also spent some time there. We are becoming very anxious about the youth and think his disappearance is connected with the murder of our officer.'

Jack reached back into the document case and pulled out an Information System photograph of Johnny Lee that he had obtained from police files.

'His name is Johnny Lee. Do you know him?'

Jamie tried to maintain a poker face, but Jack spotted the slight flicker of recognition as he studied the photograph.

Jack pressed on. 'We have some serious concerns for this boy. I'm guessing you have had some dealings with him?'

The silence seemed to go on for several moments. This time it was Jamie's turn to make a decision and it was clear that it was a difficult one.

He shuffled uncomfortably before he spoke. 'Yes. I know Johnny. When he was a lot younger he used to come to the youth group. As he got older, I used to spot him around the bars or several times cruising down in the Gardens area.'

'Was he a rent boy?'

'That's not a term we tend to use these days.'

'So what do you use?'

'Sex worker.'

'So, was Johnny a sex worker?'

'Let's say, I don't think that there's much doubt he chose his partners by the size of their wallet, rather than by looks or age.'

'When did he stop coming to the youth group?'

'A couple of years ago. I couldn't say exactly.'

'Why did he stop coming?'

Again, Jamie shifted in his seat. 'We had to ask him to stop.'

There was a long pause whilst the unasked question hung in the air. Slade waited until Jamie continued.

'There were a couple of issues …concerning some of the younger boys.'

'Was Johnny into younger boys?'

'Oh! God no! That wasn't the problem. It's just some of the boys told staff that Johnny had tried to persuade them to go with him to parties with the promise that they would be able to make some easy money.'

'What sort of parties?'

'For a policeman, you can come across as very naïve.'

'I just like people to come out with things direct instead of talking in riddles.'

'From the little snippets we were told we believed that Johnny was trying to recruit some of the younger prettier boys to be sex workers. Johnny was always an enterprising young man and I think he saw his future in management, as opposed to working the shop floor.'

'A pimp you mean?'

'I see what you mean by direct.' He smiled.

'So what happened?'

'We can't keep the young ones locked up, but we still try to protect them from the more seedy side of the 'scene'… so we asked Johnny to stop coming. He did try turning up a couple of times, but we made it clear that he was 'persona non grata.' For a while he started hanging about outside at the end of meetings, so workers would go out with the boys as they left. After a couple of weeks he got the hint and even that stopped.'

'And that was the last time you spoke to him?'

'No. As I said I would sometimes bump into him down in the Gardens or in the bars. He was always chatty, but never gave away much about what he was up to.'

'Was he out looking for customers?'

'A bit of that. I think he was also looking for young lads who were new to the scene. The occasional runaway or any young lad he might be able to recruit. Fresh meat for the punters, if you like. You often get young lads hanging round by the train station and on the fringes of the gay scene.'

'So when did you last see Johnny?'

'It's got to be about three maybe four weeks ago. I can't be sure.'

'How did he seem?'

'Johnny was Johnny... always cocky and sure of himself.' Jamie frowned. 'Do you really think something serious has happened to him?'

'We don't know for sure. It's possible, but it's also possible that he may have just disappeared out the area for a time.'

'But you don't think that, do you?'

Jamie caught Jack's eye and had his answer.

Slade thanked Jamie for all his information and once again asked him to not divulge any of their conversation. Jamie asked Jack for a similar commitment. As the detective got up to leave Jamie asked him to wait a few moments.

Leaving the office, he returned a few minute later with a list showing a number of bars in the town centre. 'I've put a tick next to the gay bars that Johnny usually frequented.'

Jack thanked him and as they strolled back to the reception area he handed Jamie his card.

'If you see Johnny or hear anything about him, or anything at all that could be relevant to the enquiry, I would appreciate a call.'

Jamie nodded and Jack headed out into the street where the snow had stopped falling and patches of cobalt blue were breaking through the clouds as the sky slowly cleared.

Maybe it was an omen and like the skies the enquiry would start to become clearer. The more he dug the more his instincts were telling him that the murder of Darren Wilson was not some random homophobic attack or robbery. He was becoming more convinced that it was intrinsically linked to the disappearance of Johnny Lee.

Jack decided to keep his latest visit to Jamie to himself,

DAVID JEWELL

conscious that he had told him more than he should have. He hoped that the outreach worker really could be trusted.

Feeling a little bit happier he made his way back to the station for the late briefing.

At the nick, they went through the results of the enquiries to date. Repeat visits to previous robbery victims in the Gardens had yielded no further clues. Although there were eleven such reports it was suspected that the unreported attacks were probably many times higher.

All eleven victims claimed that they were taking a short cut to the quayside and had just been in the wrong place at the wrong time.

Every one of them denied being in the area for anything other than a legitimate reason, including three who had previous cautions for gross indecency.

Two had been in drag at the time.

DEATH RATTLE

CHAPTER 25

Next morning following the briefing the detectives had been allocated various enquiries and the office was unusually quiet. Jack was sitting at his desk checking back through the results of the previous days actions to see if anything had been missed when Armstrong knocked on the door and entered clutching a piece of paper.

'There's a request from some guy asking you to ring him. He wouldn't leave a message and said that he would only speak to you. He said it might be important.'

Jack took the piece of paper and saw Jamie's name and a mobile telephone number. He took the paper, thanked Armstrong and reached for the phone on his desk.

Jamie answered on the second ring and wasted no time in getting to the point.

'I've been asking around. No-one at all has seen Johnny Lee for at least two or three weeks. He hasn't been into his usual bars and no-one has spotted him at any of the cruising areas. It's as if he has just vanished.'

'That fits in with enquiries our end. Have you managed to find out if he had a regular partner? Or even some sugar daddy who might have taken him away somewhere on holiday?'

There was a slight pause, before Jamie said quietly. 'Can we meet? Not here... and definitely not at the police station. I prefer to talk face to face, rather than over the phone.'

'OK. It's your call. Name the place.'

Opened in 1937, the Tyneside Cinema was originally the Bijou News-Reel Cinema, where in the days prior to television people could call in to view newsreel film of events across the country or abroad. The brain child of a local entrepreneur Dixon Scott it is an eclectic mix of Art Deco with a heavy Arabic and Asian influence; the result of Scott's extensive travels throughout the Middle and Far East. The decline of cinema audiences had led to the venue's closure some years back, but following an extensive renovation project it

121

reopened in 2008, complete with cinema screens and a relaxing café.

Slade climbed the stairs to the café passing a large glass display case where an old cinema projector took pride of place next to cinema reels, film baskets and cuttings of films.

Set into the wall was a looped black and white film of famous historic events and as Jack passed he glanced across at original newsreel of the Hindenburg disaster.

Entering the café, he spotted Jamie sitting at a table farthest away from the till and behind him was an art deco style display board with photographs of movie stars from a bygone age. Jack sat down opposite him just as a waiter arrived to take their order.

'So why here?' Jack asked as the waiter left to prepare their drinks.

'I love movies and used to come here as a kid. For me, this place is as much a part of the city's history as the Tyne Bridge.'

'So what was so important that you couldn't just tell me over the phone?'

'It mightn't be anything.'

'I don't believe that you dragged me out and we're sitting here 'cause they make a good latte.'

Jamie leant forward his voice barely over a whisper. 'I spoke to a young lad at the Gardens last night and asked after Johnny. He told me that Johnny had tried to persuade him to go to a party at some big house in Northumberland. Said it would be well worth his while and he would meet some *generous* people.'

'And did he go?'

'It was going to be an 'all-nighter' and the lad was only fifteen. He told Johnny that he had to be at a family christening the next day and cried off.'

The waiter arrived with two coffees and set them down, before hurrying away to take another order.

Jamie glanced around to ensure that no-one was close enough to hear.

'The truth was there have been lots of rumours about private parties. Plenty of drink… and drugs. Some suggestions that young boys were made to do things they weren't all together happy with. They ended up well paid but were warned to keep their mouths shut and it was made clear what would happen to them if they didn't.'

'How often are these parties supposed to happen?'

'Apparently they're every few weeks. The thing is the party the young fifteen year old was invited to was about three weeks ago and no-one seems to have seen Johnny since.'

Three weeks ago would put it around the time of Johnny's late night visit to Drew's flat.

'So, where was the party held?'

'He didn't get to find out. Johnny just told him it was somewhere out past the airport.'

Newcastle International Airport was about ten miles north west of the city, on the border of Northumberland.

Once past the airport house prices rose considerably and many well off owners bought into the exclusive Darras Hall Estate in Ponteland, which boasted properties from several hundred thousand pounds to sprawling mansions costing in the millions.

In addition, there were other more secluded houses on the outskirts of the village and then beyond, were several dozen square miles of open countryside and isolated farmhouses.

'That doesn't narrow it down much.'

'He didn't get to hear much more.'

'Are you going to tell me the kid's name?'

'You know I can't. I'd get the sack if I breached client confidentiality.'

He knew that if it came down to it Jamie could be forced to tell. This was a murder enquiry. Jack decided to let it ride... for now.

'No other description? A name for who was holding the party? Who else would be there? Anything you can give me to go on?'

Jamie hesitated, before saying, 'I don't know where the party was, but I did hear there was someone other than Johnny trying to recruit young boys to attend.'

Jamie seemed to mentally weigh something up.

'Are you going to tell me or will your secret die with you?'

'I don't know his real name, but everyone knows him as Weasel.'

'You'd recognise him?'

'I've seen him a few times, but he tends to keep out of the way if we are doing any kind of outreach work in the area.'

'First impressions?'

'Not the sort you would take home to mum. Weedy... a bit scruffy looking. Always looks shifty.'

'So how do I get to meet him?'

'I'm not sure you can. All the young lads know him, but I don't think any of them would want to speak to the police. They don't like speaking to your lot in the first place in case they get accused of being a grass. Besides, despite his weedy looks there's a bit of malevolence about Weasel. It makes people wary about crossing him.'

'So how do I go about finding him?'

'He gets in the bars, but other than that...' Jamie's voice trailed off.

Jack's mind was ticking over rapidly. The Northumbria I.S. Information System did hold details of nicknames and aliases, but he wondered if Weasel would be amongst them.

'OK. I'll try to find out what I can from our files. Which bars does he frequent?'

'Any of them where young guys get in. He likes them young, but to be honest the sort of lads he wants to recruit are probably too young to get into the usual gay venues.'

'So come on, Jamie. Help me out here.'

Jamie slid a piece of paper across the table. It looked like it had been torn from some magazine guide and on it were listed a number of bars and clubs in the city centre.

'The bars are the place to start. That's a copy of the list of the gay bars that I gave you. I've underlined the ones where I hear the weasel gets in. The ones that attract the young lads. That one circled is where older boys might go who are after making some easy pocket money. Whether anyone will speak to you... well I wouldn't hold my breath on that one.'

Jamie drained his coffee.

'I have to get back. I've probably said much more than I should. I could probably get the sack if you mention anything.'

'So why tell me.'

'I'm not sure. Maybe I sense we're both on the same

side. Maybe I think cops and the gay community should work closer. Maybe I'm worried about Johnny. Or maybe I just don't really like this Weasel character and all he stands for. Getting rid of some abusive shit like him would be in both of our interests.'

'You do know that I might have to get back to you about the fifteen year old kid and the party.'

'I'm not stupid. I know that. But you know that if you did I might just deny I ever said anything.'

'Your word against mine?'

'You may have noticed that your gang doesn't rate so highly in the telling the truth stakes as they used to.'

Jack couldn't suppress a smile. 'So let's try not to let it get to that stage.'

Jamie nodded. 'Agreed.' Then, before Jack could say anything else, Jamie stood up to leave. He paused for a second and looked Jack directly in the eyes.

'If something has happened to Johnny or any of the other young lads this Weasel has picked up, promise me you'll make sure that he gets what's coming to him.'

Slade held his gaze. 'You have my word.'

Jamie nodded again, turned and without another word strode off towards the door.

Slade looked down and could see he hadn't even touched his own coffee.

Abandoning his drink, he headed out the café, down the several flights of stairs and out into the crisp winter air. He wished they had met in a bar as, on days like this, he felt more in need of a large Glenmorangie than a coffee.

Putting the thought at the back of his mind, he quickened his step and headed back towards the warmth of the nick.

It was almost eight o'clock in the evening and although there was no rain, the clear sky meant a heavy frost had already formed on the pavements throughout the City centre.

Slade pulled the collar of his overcoat tighter against the bitter chill wind and stepped into a doorway to get some shelter. This area on the fringe of the town centre was where the gay establishments were to be found. Taking out the list that he had been given by Jamie he ran a gloved finger down it to the one that was circled.

The bar he had been searching for was on a corner terrace. Small and inconsequential it appeared no different from the dozens of other bars dotted around the city apart from the rainbow flag fluttering above the entrance.

Jack watched from the street opposite as a smartly suited middle-aged business man entered the bar accompanied by a boy of about eighteen. The youth was wearing loose fitting grey tracksuit bottoms with a matching fleece top, and they made an incongruous couple as the older man held the door open for his younger companion.

Jack waited a couple of minutes and then crossed the road and went inside the pub.

A bar ran almost the length of one side and was lined with several tall bar stools. The rest of the room was taken up by a dozen wooden tables seated at which was an eclectic mix of customers.

The business man and his young companion were seated at a far table opposite the bar and appeared in animated conversation, the younger man laughing at what he clearly thought were the appropriate moments.

At the next table sat two women in their thirties, both of whom were wearing denim jeans. One of them was slightly built, with medium length light brown hair and drinking some kind of cocktail. The second was of quite stocky build, wearing a dark blue baggy T shirt and clutching a pint of lager. She had short collar length mousy hair and both her arms were heavily tattooed.

You can always tell the quality of a West End lass by whether her tattoos are spelled correctly.

In the corner nearest the door sat two men aged in their sixties nursing pints of dark beer and talking together. From their corner, they were able to take in everything and everyone around them. With their rubbery faces and drink enlarged noses they reminded Jack of Statler and Waldorf, the two old men on the Muppet show.

A barman sat behind the bar on a tall stool that matched those in front of the bar. In his mid-fifties with very short greying hair, and a lived-in face, he looked every inch the no nonsense landlord who had probably spent a lifetime in the trade. He was short and so obese that Jack feared for the stool bearing his weight. However, underneath the rolls of fat Jack detected thick set arms used to hauling heavy casks of beer, and Jack imagined that he wasn't the sort to mess with.

Still if you wanted to attract a young clientele, or even an older type seeking younger, he would not be your first choice to greet the customers.

They must save the good-looking staff for the weekends.

As Slade entered, the barman's keen eyes swivelled, locking on to him and, as he moved towards the bar, Jack felt every other person in the room was also checking him out: assessing how he fitted in to the mismatch of clientele.

Reaching the bar counter, Jack drew one of the stools towards him and ordered a pint of John Smiths.

Without speaking the barman slowly eased himself down from his perch and filled a pint glass with the dark frothy brew. Slade passed over a five pound note and, after ringing it into the till, Mister Affable handed Jack his change.

As he bent down to restock a fridge, Jack asked him, 'Does it get busy in here later?'

Drawing himself up to his full five feet three inches, the barman turned and studied Jack for a few moments. 'That depends on what you're looking for,' he replied. 'Workers call in from half five until eight or eight thirty, the young 'uns don't usually come out 'til nine thirty or ten.'

He fixed Jack with a long hard stare. 'So what is it you're after... officer?'

Jack tried hard not to show he was rattled. 'What makes you think I'm the Polis?'

The barman smirked, picked up a small towel and began polishing a pint glass.

'You heard of *Gaydar*? Well, we also have *Copdar*.'

He paused from polishing the glass. 'Add to that thirty years in the pub trade and forty years of being gay. You can smell... trouble. Besides, you haven't denied it yet... and you're not going to... are you?'

Jack smiled down into his pint. 'So why does the polis always mean trouble?'

'A bizzie in a gay bar. You don't come across to me as a sad closet case, so it has to be trouble.'

He continued rubbing away at an imaginary stubborn

mark on the glass.

'So... again, what are you after... officer?'

Slade weighed up his options and decided not to waste time.

'I'm after information about someone.'

'And you've already tried Google?'

Jack ignored the sarcasm. 'I'm told he comes in here a lot.'

'That should narrow it down. We get all sorts in here. Gay, straight, closet, drag and just plain curious.'

The barman turned away, walking the length of the bar to serve a customer. He returned a few minutes later to continue with his glass cleaning.

'So, who are you looking for? We don't get many serial killers popping in for a pint... well not too many.'

'Someone called Weasel. You heard of him?'

Jack noticed a slight hesitation. 'Lots of punters get in here. I don't know all their names.'

'I'm not asking about all of them. Just the one.' The barman looked away and busied himself wiping down the bar counter, avoiding Jack's gaze.

'Doesn't ring a bell.'

Jack turned and looked at the incongruous mix of people drinking at the various tables. A couple had been glancing across at Jack and the barman, sensing trouble.

'Maybe I should start asking some of the customers. They might know who he is.'

Angrily, the barman snapped, 'Howay man! What's your problem?'

'My problem is I don't believe that you've never heard of him, and I'm starting to think that I should stop here the rest of the night and ask everyone who comes in if they would like to help their local constabulary with an enquiry. Who knows? Maybe eventually Weasel himself might come in. In the meantime, I wouldn't take bets on this being one of your better nights when it comes to takings. You're not exactly overrun with orders. Do you want to risk losing what few customers you have?'

If the barman had even a hint of humour remaining, it was wiped away in an instant. 'You won't find him in here.'

'Why's that?'

'He's barred.'

'What for?'

The barman put down the glass and looked stone-faced at Slade. 'I assume this is about chickens?'

Slade was conscious of a change in the atmosphere.

'Chickens?'

'Under age boys. Chickens... young cock. If it is, you can forget it. Everyone who gets in here is street legal. No ID. No entry.'

'Is that what he's in to? Chickens?'

'He's into them all right. But as well as the usual interest, he's also in to how much he can make from them.'

One of the two old men had got up from his table and was impatiently tapping his empty glass at the far end of the bar. The barman stalked off to serve him, before quickly returning.

'What do you mean by make from them?' Slade asked.

'The chickens he finds all end up rent.' The anger in his tone turned to disgust, adding, 'He also likes to sample the quality of his merchandise. Especially the very young ones.'

'And that's why he's barred?'

'He started bringing them in here. One of the kids couldn't have been more than fourteen. Dark haired bairn with a Scottish accent. I told him to get him out the bar and not bother coming back. That sort of thing loses licences and I don't need the crap. I have quite a good set up here, so I don't want to screw things up because of the likes of some fucking chicken hawk.'

As the barman turned to restock one of the fridges, Slade let the information sink in. Both Johnny and Weasel were into recruiting young boys for rent.

Were they working together or were they rivals? Could Johnny have been taking business away from Weasel?

Could he be taking away some of Weasel's rent boys to work for him? Either scenario could be a good reason to fall out. Where big money was involved either could be a motive for murder.

The Barman returned and Jack turned his thoughts back to him. 'So where does he find them? These young boys?'

The barman gave him a quizzical look. 'Is that what you're into?'

Jack looked shocked.

The barman shrugged. 'Howay man, you never can tell. I've told you, we get all sorts in here. Teachers, lawyers... the polis. Mind you, it's not so busy now there's the internet. It's all 'dial a fuck' these days. Why trawl bars all night when a casual shag is just a click on a phone app away?' He shook his head resignedly. 'It's playing hell with the pub trade.'

'So is that how he finds them?'

'The very young 'uns don't have some of these apps. The Scots kid he had his hooks into looked like a runaway. You'd be surprised how young some of these street kids are. Then there's the care homes. Mostly the young ones are just out to make some extra pocket money and before long they get sucked in to a heavier scene... if you pardon the pun.'

'So, if this Weasel guy is barred from here, where can I find him?'

The barman glanced across at the businessman and young 'trackie' bottoms who had both clocked Slade and, smelling cop, had finished their drinks and were getting up to leave.

'You're beginning to scare my customers.'

'So give me a starter for ten with Weasel.'

The barman seemed to weigh up giving information against the loss of more of his customers if Slade hung around much longer. Reaching a decision, he leant closer to Jack and spoke quietly.

'His real name's Donkin. You could try the Central Station or any of the amusement arcades during the daytime. At night you could try the late night cafes where runaways hang around.'

'What's my best bet?'

'Probably one of the cruising areas like the Gardens down by the castle. Anywhere rent and their punters hang out that's where you'll find the bastard.'

Straightening up to signal that the conversation was at an end, he walked off to the far end of the bar and began washing some used glasses. Jack had all the information he was getting.

Draining his glass, Jack started to leave when he realised there was something else he needed to know and walked back across to the barman.

'You never told me *your* name?'

The barman seemed to consider this for a second.

'Aye. You're right,' he replied, before turning back to polishing another glass. 'You should be a fucking detective,' he muttered to himself as Jack turned and walked out.

CHAPTER 26

Back at the nick and a quick C.I.S. check on 'Donkin' threw up a couple of possibilities.

The first was a scruffy looking alcoholic who had been picked up several times for drunk and disorderly. He didn't fit the bill.

When Slade pulled up the second record onto the screen he knew he'd found his man.

William George Donkin had a couple of cautions as a juvenile for shoplifting and some minor convictions for theft and damage. He'd been given a three month suspended sentence some years ago for a burglary. A names check confirmed his nickname as Weasel.

Amongst the previous arrests one stood out. An adult caution for gross indecency five years previously when he'd been detained with an eighteen year old boy called Dean Masters in a toilet in the city centre. Since then there was very little other than a drunk and disorderly and a couple of traffic offences. Either Donkin had turned his back on a life of crime or he was being a dammed sight more careful. Jack's money was on the latter.

He moved the curser to a box at the bottom of the screen and typed in PH. A colour photograph of Donkin from the arrest five years previous flashed up on the screen.

At last Jack could see an image of the man that he had been seeking and whom he was sure held some clues to the disappearance of Johnny Lee, and maybe even to the murder of Darren Wilson.

From between the greasy brown hair, black hooded eyes stared out at him. The sallow thin features made it clear how Donkin had earned his nickname and, as he scowled back at the camera lens, he had a face that even a mother would find hard to love.

'With a mug like that he should learn to walk on his hands and talk out of his arse,' Jack mused to himself.

Although taken five years earlier, Jack doubted whether he'd changed much. It would take a bloody good plastic surgeon to improve on that.

Jack printed off the photograph. Now he had a face to

match the name.

Checking out "marks" on the computer, he saw that Donkin, AKA Weasel, had several tattoos. Some were blue self-inflicted marks on his hands, which he had probably done when younger, but another photograph showed an elaborate design of a tiger emblazoned down the length of his left arm.

Typing IN into the space at the bottom of the screen, Slade began to scan through any current intelligence or recent sightings of Donkin.

Bingo! There was a routine stop/check fed into the system by a British transport officer in which Donkin had been moved on from Newcastle Central Station when spotted loitering by the public toilets.

Probably looking out for new boys for his business.

At the time he had not been alone.

He was in the company of Johnny Lee.

Looking back through the intelligence, there were a few other sightings down in the Gardens area, including a second with Johnny.

Donkin had given a home address in the Jesmond area, and although Jack had no reason to believe it was false, he knew that it would be unlikely he would get a reply at the door. Even if he did, Donkin didn't look the sort to invite him in for a cuppa.

The reality was that he had nothing whatsoever to drag Donkin in for, and a couple of sighting connecting him with Johnny was a big fat zero when it came to linking him to Johnny's disappearance, let alone the murder in the Gardens.

He looked at his watch. It was now after ten o'clock. If he wanted to speak to Weasel, it would have to be an encounter on the street. And that meant another visit to the bars, cafes and cruising areas in the town centre. Might as well start with the scene of the crime.

Snatching up his coat, he headed for the door.

Jack hesitated on the cobbled road and looked down at the entrance to the Gardens. He checked his watch. From what he had been told, at this time under normal circumstances the gay cruising area would be busy. He felt sure that the recent murder and subsequent police activity would have driven many of the usual visitors away to find pastures new, but that there would be some "die hards" that were creatures of habit.

Making his way out from the shadow of the towering Castle Keep he looked up. The damp night air shrouding the street lights seeming to give the ancient fortress a threatening air. He shivered but wasn't sure if that was just from the damp night air.

It is said that one of the most powerful drives in human nature is the desire for sex. It must be an irresistible urge to make a lone person venture down into this netherworld during the hours of darkness.

Approaching the steps leading down to the overgrown secluded area, he remembered that first night that he had been called down to examine the body of Darren Wilson. Though only a few days had passed it seemed so long ago.

On that occasion he had felt no trace of fear, but tonight was different. There was an air of menace about the place and he couldn't help but feel apprehensive.

Was this a good idea?

Probably not... but...

Down the steps and turning to his right he followed the darkened path along past where the body had been discovered and made his way further into the Gardens. A discarded piece of blue police tape still tied to a branch fluttered on the evening breeze.

The undergrowth on either side showed signs of disturbance, betraying evidence that the whole area had been scoured. It had been clearly combed through by Area Support Group officers carrying out their fingertip searches.

He cautiously pressed on.

Tonight was the first time seventeen years old Jason had visited the area. He had heard about the Gardens in casual conversation and had Googled it to find out more. That just made him all the more curious. At first he had been too scared to dare coming down, but eventually desire overcame his fear and he had decided to risk it.

The uneven path and overgrown vegetation was unwelcoming and the whole ambiance was making him uncomfortable and a little frightened.

When he saw the boy similar in age to himself standing alone in the distance, he was at first wary. He stood still for a while, before carefully approaching him. The stranger was slightly taller that Jason. About five eleven, he was clean shaven, wearing fashionable tracksuit bottoms and expensive looking trainers. The boy turned to look at him and Jason's heart began to beat a little faster.

When he was just a few feet from him, Jason's heart began thumping faster still as he heard the rustle behind him. Whirling around quickly he saw the two other boys emerging from where they had been concealed in the undergrowth.

Twisting forward Jason saw that the boy in the tracksuit bottoms was now smiling, and he caught the glint of a knife in his right hand.

Jason was trapped and for the first time in his short life he felt abject terror.

Standing rigid with fear he cursed himself for ever coming down to the place.

The two figures from the bushes had closed up behind him, and the boy with the knife was slowly approaching from the front. Jason thought that he might start crying.

'Hello, boys. Is there a problem?'

The deep voice had come from somewhere behind the boy with the knife causing all four of them to jump with surprise.

As Jason stared off into the darkness beyond, the figure of a tall man seemed to materialise from the gloom. The boy with the knife had rotated around at the sound of the voice and now stood facing the man.

Jack Slade had clocked the knife as soon as the boy had turned. He was careful to keep at least an arm's length from the vicious looking blade.

If the youth had been taken by surprise, he was in no mood to show it. 'Fuckin' hell! There's plenty of the queer bastards out tonight.'

Jack didn't respond, but kept his eyes constantly on the youth; mindful of the knife held out in front of him.

'So faggot! What have you got in your pockets?'

Jack remained silent.

The latest potential victim held the promise of much better pickings, although his size and demeanour suggested he might not prove such an easy target.

Jason appeared to have been forgotten as the two other muggers moved closer to back up their pal against this

135

possible threat.

Jack gave them a quick appraisal.

Both were aged about seventeen, and although one was slim and almost six foot tall, the other was considerably shorter and stockier.

The Little and Large of the city centre muggers world.

The knife wielding lad had moved closer, causing Jack to instinctively step back, keeping his distance from the weapon.

The lad glanced at his two back ups, a smile spreading across his face, before turning back to look at Jack.

'My dad says that all dirty puffs should have their balls sliced off.'

Raising the knife, he glanced back to see if his two friends were finding this just as amusing.

The glance over his shoulder only took a second.

That was all Jack needed.

He took a long step forward with his left foot, closing the gap between them, and grabbing the boy's wrist with his left hand, Jack swung hard with his right foot.

The blow struck the target full on and the youth let out a piercing wail and bent double, clutching at his groin.

As he fell forward, Jack twisted his wrist sharply, causing him to drop the knife and then, bringing up his left knee, connected with the youth's face, breaking his nose and sending a spray of blood out across the pathway.

The boy fell to the ground, groaning as Jack regained his breath. 'You can go home and tell your dad that you've been chinned by a puff.'

The taller of the other two youths was first to recover and was already moving forward as his friend lay crumpled on the ground in a foetal position. With the flat of his foot, Jack shoved the injured youth into the tall boy's path, causing him to stumble. A quick left hand jab and he joined his now whimpering pal on the ground. The third youth had by now taken in the rapidly changed situation and reacted instinctively.

He ran. He ran as fast as he could and never looked back.

Jack looked down at his trousers. *Fuck!* They were smeared with blood from the nose of his knife wielding attacker.

He looked around for their first intended target. *Double Fuck!*

Their potential victim, the young lad, was nowhere to be seen, having taken his opportunity to flee. Looking down at the two would be muggers, Jack considered just slipping away into the night; leaving them where they lay, writhing in pain.

He knew without doubt that if he arrested them, he would be in for a grilling about what he was doing off duty at night in the Gardens. Add to that the fact that his witness, the young lad, had pissed off and tracing him would be a nightmare.

As soon as he nicked them, the two robbery suspects would be crying police brutality, and any solicitor would be itching to play the excessive force card.

It would be yet another complaint to add to his prior collection.

Except that he knew that he couldn't just walk away. Whilst there was every likelihood that these two were just low level criminal shite who were trying their hand at robbery and "queer bashing", there was another possibility.

They could be responsible for Darren Wilson's murder. Maybe that had also been a knifepoint robbery gone wrong.

If they were responsible for the murder then they would be absolutely feckless to return to the scene of the crime so soon.

But there's no cure for stupid.

Even if not responsible for the killing then they could still be witnesses. Jack reluctantly reached into his pocket for his mobile.

Back at the nick the Custody officer made little attempt to disguise his displeasure at the prisoners that he had been presented with.

'They're both known to us. West end shite coming down town for a bit of sport and thieving. However, I think when any brief gets here he'll be asking who mugged who. The one with the black eye and bruising to his face is Tyson Campbell. I've asked for the police surgeon to attend and check him out. The other one is his cousin Rocky Dixon. What is it about the West End that they give their kids names best suited to Rottweilers? The world's gone fucking mad.'

'What about the Rocky lad. Will he be fit for interview?'

'You must be joking. I'm not even waiting for the Police Surgeon for him. I've requested an ambulance. From the looks of him, he'll have bollocks the size of tennis balls.'

Jack nodded. 'Has he made a complaint yet?'

'Give him time. He's got other things on his mind at the minute. Since he came in, his hands have never let go of his balls. I reckon he's not feeling them... he's trying to fucking count them.'

Jack shrugged. 'His choice. He had a knife. I'd rather be a defendant in court than the primary exhibit in a murder trial.'

'It'll not be me that you need to convince, Jack. Anyway you'll have plenty of time to get your act together. They've both been drinking and stink of weed. They'll not be fit for interview until after an eight hour lie down.'

'Since they're not going to be ready until morning, do you want me to leave a statement?'

'Aye. And what I'd also like is for you to arrange a couple of detectives to come in first thing tomorrow and crack on with interviews.'

Jack nodded. 'I'll also set someone checking the CCTV from the area to see if we can trace that kid they tried to rob.'

'You can sort that out with the uniform shift sergeant. If I was you, I'd head home and try to get back in early tomorrow. You best be alert. I suspect that you might have a few questions to answer yourself.'

As Jack left the custody suite, he heard the desk sergeant muttering under his breath. 'That's at least one cop tied up all night babysitting some scrote at the hospital'

Jack looked away down at the cell complex.

At least there's not much chance of him running away.

He kept the thought to himself.

The next morning Jack arrived early and made sure that he briefed the couple of detectives well before they went in to the interview.

It was decided that because of his involvement, that the interview would be conducted by two cops from the local C.I.D. Because of the Gardens connection, Jack had arranged for the interview to be remotely monitored by two of the H.MET. interview advisors.

As expected the prisoner was crying police brutality, but was advised to wait until he was released before making his complaint to the duty inspector.

The interview began along expected lines, with a solicitor present and Tyson Campbell answering 'No reply' to every question asked.

That all changed at the first mention of the murder of Darren Wilson at the same location.

'He was killed with a knife similar to the one recovered from your mate, Rocky. We are going to have it forensically tested.'

Young Tyson suddenly became much more animated. 'What! Murder! That's nowt to do with me. You're not gonna fucking stitch me up for that.'

After that it was difficult to shut him up.

Twenty five minutes later Jack was sitting with a cup of coffee in his office, listening to the two grinning detectives recounting details of the interview.

'The little bastard wouldn't stop talking. He's coughed to about a dozen robberies in the area of the Gardens. Seventy per cent of them haven't even been reported. Dropped his mate Rocky right in it and named the third lad that pissed off and did a runner. He's shitting himself that we're going to stitch him up for the Darren Wilson case. Seems to think we can tamper with the evidence and somehow put Wilson's blood on Rocky's knife.'

'He's been watching too many conspiracy programmes on Netflix,' Jack said.

'The good news is that it doesn't look like Tyson Campbell is thinking about making a complaint. He'll be happy not to end up on a charge sheet for Darren Wilson's murder. The bad news is that his pal, Rocky, is a different matter. He's being detained in hospital, so we can't speak to him. He's having problems pissing and his bollocks are swollen and have turned black.'

'What about the one who did the runner?'

When we're finished here we're heading off to pick up the last of the Three Stooges and see what he has to say.'

The two detectives exchanged glances.

Jack looked from one to the other, sensing a problem.

'So what else is there to tell me?'

'For one thing that detective from Complaints, Burton, has been down sniffing around and checking through the custody record. The good news is that he's gone away.'

'So what's the bad news?'

'He's gone away because they're not your suspects, boss. They all have perfect alibis. At the time of Darren Wilson's murder all three were banged up at Etal Lane after a fight outside a pub in the West End.'

Bollocks!

It was back to square one.

The rest of the day passed without any major developments. City Centre C.I.D. had agreed to take over the previous night's incident and had tracked down the third offender. All three were being bailed until Rocky Dixon could be fit for interview and CCTV enquiries were underway to trace the young witness who had fled the scene.

Jack went on with the Wilson enquiry, but was becoming concerned that leads were drying up. At the end of shift, Jack shied away from going with the team for a drink and instead headed home.

He was feeling quite shattered and needed to get a couple of hours' rest.

He needed some.

He had decided on a plan for later that night.

DEATH RATTLE

CHAPTER 27

The city at night takes on a different aspect. By day the streets teem with hundreds of shoppers and workers going about their daily business, flitting past each other with a purpose or destination in mind.

Later, when the shops close and the workers go off to their suburban homes a different crowd emerges to fill the vacuum. Newcastle upon Tyne had long established itself as a party city. The high student population from the two universities and various colleges had meant that the city's reputation had been spread far and wide through the country.

Traditionally there had just been the one Newcastle University with a good reputation for medical training and research that singled it out as one of the leading institutions for doctors in the making. Later the University of Northumbria had arisen like a phoenix from the ashes of the former Newcastle polytechnic, but was regarded by many as a distant second to its longer established rival.

Jack smiled at the urban legend that claimed whilst searching for a suitable title for their new educational establishment the organisers had hit upon the grand title of 'City University of Newcastle on Tyne.' That was until someone had pointed out the unfortunate acronym.

With the party people came the recreational drugs. Not that there hadn't been drugs before it just seemed to Jack that there was much more now including what was described as "Legal Highs". The means for "Getting off your head" was now not only more readily available but seemed to be more socially acceptable to the younger generation.

Slade felt old as crowds of young girls and boys passed him by in groups; some looking for homeward taxis having probably been drinking since leaving work or college. Others, the more nocturnal, appeared to be just at the start of their night and after the bars would probably head for the nightclubs to extend the evening's partying into the early hours.

So much for a recession. There seemed no shortage of cash when it came to drinking.

Looking up, he could see the striking edifice of The

Centre of Life rising above the city. Linked to Newcastle University, it was recognised as one of the country's leading areas in genetic research. Not everyone was a fan of the modern construction, with some of the more vocal describing the glass bricked construction on one side as looking more like a sixties public toilet block.

Despite it being a bitterly cold night, the streets were busy and as Slade watched the drunks staggering out into the road in front of the night time traffic he wondered how some of them didn't end up as bloodied mascots on the bonnets.

Jack was reminded of the article he had read concerning the Darwin Awards given out each year to people who have accidentally killed themselves by doing something so utterly stupid that they do the world a favour by removing themselves from the gene pool.

He didn't know too much about genetics but it seemed to him that playing dodgems at midnight in the middle of a busy city road, after consuming copious amounts of cheap alcohol should at least deserve an honourable mention.

He waited for the pedestrian lights to change and crossed the road to one of several all-night cafes catering for the revellers.

He stood outside each one in turn studying the occupants, until inside a small dingy fast food joint he saw a skinny greasy haired man sitting at a table in the window giving him a good view of the city street outside. Jack didn't need to check the C.I.S. photograph in his inside pocket. The tattoo of the tiger down the man's left arm told him what he wanted to know.

Jack had found his man.

Entering the café, Slade went up to the counter, ordered himself a large coffee and found himself a seat from where he had a good view of not only Weasel Donkin, but the street and the free late-night cabaret taking place outside.

A police transit pulled up and two officers, a man and a woman, got out and stood on the pavement. Their presence seemed to calm down some of the loudest of the drunks but it wasn't long before a couple of them, men aged in their early twenties, gravitated towards the female officer to try out their drunken chat up lines.

Though she had no doubt heard them a thousand times

before, she smiled with good grace and their macho pride sated they continued on their way.

After a few minutes the cops climbed back into their van and moved off to find some other location to briefly fly the flag. It made it seem there were more police around than there really were because the drunks only saw the uniform and not the person wearing it. Jack smiled to himself that if they met up with the same drunks then the poor female officer would have to endure the chat up lines for the thousand and first time.

He turned his attention back to the man he had come to find. During the police van's brief stop outside Weasel had kept his head down, studying the tattered burger menu as if his life depended on it. Now they had gone he was once again watching the people going backwards and forwards in front of the café window.

Weasel was wearing black denim jeans and despite the freezing cold night a blue short sleeved shirt that proudly displayed the tiger tattoo climbing his arm. A black worn leather jacket was draped over the back of his chair.

As Donkin casually checked out each passer-by outside he reminded Jack of a cat stalking birds. Suddenly he seemed more alert and Jack followed his gaze to see the reason why.

A young boy had paused to glance through the window.

With a mop of dark hair framing a very young looking face he could have been no more than fifteen. Wearing scruffy blue denim jeans and a crumpled black hooded sweat top with some sports logo on the front, he was carrying a small black rucksack by the straps.

As the boy turned and began to walk away Donkin shot up from out of his seat and leaving behind his drink, set off in pursuit.

Jack was about to follow but saw that the boy had stopped and Donkin was engaging him in conversation.

Donkin was only gone a few minutes before he returned with the boy and made his way back inside. In the short time he was away two lads aged about nineteen had sat down at his table. Despite his slight frame, the hard glare from the tattooed Donkin convinced them to find another and Weasel reclaimed his seat with the young boy taking a chair opposite.

Jamie had been right. For such a slightly built man he

certainly had the ability to exude an air of menace.

Weasel seemed to be working overtime to put the teenage boy at ease. A cup of hot chocolate appeared along with a cheeseburger and, before long, the teen was telling a story to Donkin, who was nodding with apparent concern at appropriate intervals.

Occasionally Slade would notice middle aged men come into the café and glance around. Often their eyes would settle on the fifteen year old with a hungry look. If they stared too long they would be rewarded with a laser like glare from Donkin and would rapidly look away or leave. Like the tiger on his arm, Donkin was jealously guarding his 'meat.'

When the boy had finished his burger, Donkin said something quietly into his ear. The boy nodded and both made their way to the door to join the flow of people in the street outside.

Jack followed, watching them pause at the street corner as Donkin attempted to hail a taxi. He decided to make his move.

'William Donkin?'

Taken off guard, the weedy man quickly recovered. 'Depends who's asking?'

'D.I. Slade. Northumbria Police. Can I have a word?'

The boy had been looking up at Donkin, but at the mention of police, he took on the appearance of a rabbit caught in headlights.

Donkin's eyes narrowed. 'What about?'

As Donkin turned to face Slade, the rabbit suddenly bolted.

The flash of anger on Donkin's face betrayed his mood at having lost his prize.

Jack glanced after the boy, who quickly disappeared around a corner and was lost to sight. 'Your friend seems to have left in a hurry. Hope it wasn't something I said?'

Jack made a mental note to check the CCTV at the nick later and see if he could get a still image of the young lad.

'Did your friend have a name?'

Donkin let out a snort. 'No friend of mine. Just some kid asking directions to the train station. I was helping him out.'

'I bet you were,' Jack said evenly.

'So what the fuck do you want?' Donkin snapped.

He seemed to exude a confidence that was at odds with his slight frame. Jack often saw this arrogance in criminals who were no strangers to the inside of a police station, but with Weasel it was even more so. It was as if he felt he had nothing to fear from the police at all.

'You can tell me what you know about a young lad called Johnny Lee.'

Donkin seemed to consider this for a while, before shrugging. 'Doesn't ring a bell. Mind you I know lots of people. Can't always remember their names. Know what I mean?'

'Funny that. Because you're shown on our system as being sighted with him on two occasions in the city centre.'

Donkin didn't flinch. 'Like I say, I know loads of people. Probably know a few Johnny's. Can't say I know the one you're asking after.'

'Let me refresh your memory. He hangs around the same bars and cafes as you. He seems to be interested in the same type of young lads as you as well. You might even attend the same parties.'

A worried look flashed across Weasel's face, but was quickly quelled. 'What's that supposed to mean?'

'It means that I'd like you to come down the station and answer a few questions.'

'Well, unless you've got anything to arrest me on that's not going to happen. Like I told you, that kid was just asking directions and I don't know any Johnny Lee, so if that's all you want to know then I've got things to do. Nice talking to you detective... what was your name again?'

'Slade. Inspector Slade'

'Slade?' Donkin gave him one last twisted smirk, before walking off in the direction in which the boy had left.

Jack called after the retreating figure. 'Try to remember the name. I've got a feeling you're going to hear it a few more times in the next couple of weeks.'

CHAPTER 28

The following morning Jack regretted his late night off duty excursion. By the time he had returned home it was the early hours of the morning leaving only time for a few hours restless sleep before having to get up to make it in for the briefing.

When the alarm jolted him from his bed at seven in the morning he felt that he hadn't been asleep for any length of time. Even two strong cups of filter coffee did little to dispel his sluggishness and lethargy.

Not that the visit hadn't proved fruitful; he had actually come face to face with Donkin. But where did he fit into the picture? Was he directly connected to Johnny's disappearance or was Johnny simply on his toes because some drug induced paranoia was causing him to believe that someone was wanting to kill him? Had he decided to move town to pastures new?

Did Johnny even have anything to do with the murder of Darren Wilson or was the whole thing just a wild goose chase distracting Jack from tracking down the real killer?

It was no longer raining thank God. Leaving the car behind the chill winter morning air did its work and once at his office after a second cup of coffee he was ready to face whatever the day was to throw at him.

What it threw at him was Parker who had decided to sit in on that morning's briefing and took a chair at the back next to Burton.

Jack filled the assembled detectives in on the information he had obtained about Weasel Donkin and his possible link to Johnny, which made him a periphery figure in the investigation.

Parker did not seem so sure of the importance of the link and when asked directly by T.C.P. Jack had to admit that any concrete links to the murder were at best tenuous.

Parker gave a grunt. 'So Wilson knew Sterling, who knew Lee, who was sighted with this Donkin character a couple of times. It sounds like we've got one of those six degrees of separation scenarios here. We could end up wasting valuable resources on a load of bollocks.'

'I'll admit that it's a stretch, sir, but it's a lead, and

we're getting short of them by the day.'

'I don't think I buy it,' Parker said.

'If we don't follow up every lead and hindsight shows we missed something important then the press will have a field day.'

It was clear that Parker didn't put much weight into there being a connection, but at the mention of the press, his face darkened. In such a high profile investigation, he was well aware of the implications of ignoring even the flimsiest of connections.

'Okay. Action it. But if it turns out to be a waste of cash, it's down to you.'

Like every other aspect of the case, muggins was being set up as the fall guy.

Jack noticed Burton scribbling down some notes and wondered if he had more faith in a link, or was he just making damn sure that the top brass were warned well in advance of any possible rent boy connection. Command Block would want to be given a head start in case any damage limitation was required.

Jack still had a gut feeling that the gay scene was going to provide further leads in the search for Wilson's murderer. First Jack had to convince a particular person to help him and knew that wasn't going to be an easy sell.

Briefing concluded, Jack told Armstrong that he needed to see someone and would be gone about an hour. Armstrong assured him that he would ring on his mobile should anything urgent turn up before he got back.

Thirty minutes later, Slade was sitting opposite Jamie clutching the obligatory coffee.

Jamie had been updated about Jack's visit to the late night café and his confrontation with Donkin. The detective now sat back in his chair, waiting to see what, if anything, Jamie had to say.

He didn't have long to wait.

'I'm pleased that you've tracked him down, but I'm guessing you're not just here to keep me up to speed with your enquiries.'

Slade smiled. 'You'd be right.'

'Look, instead of dancing around, why don't you ask me what you want? You know I won't compromise any of our

clients, but believe me I do want to help, so save us both a lot
of time. Ask away. If I can answer without breaking any
professional code then I will.'

Smart guy, thought Jack.

'I want to go with you and meet up with some of the
kids that you deal with… especially any that frequent the
Gardens.'

Jamie shook his head, 'Forget it. It just isn't going to
happen. Never mind my personal views, I've already told you
as an organisation we can't compromise client confidentiality.
Taking a detective down to a cruising area would destroy any
trust between us and the people we're here to help.'

Jack started to try to give assurances, but it was clear
that Jamie wasn't going to budge.

'I could just send detectives down into the Gardens to
talk to them without your co-operation.'

Jamie couldn't suppress a smile. 'You could try. But
from what I hear, within minutes of the first officer appearing,
the place would clear and you could spend the whole night and
never see another soul. I understand that you had a similar
problem last week with some uniform officers. Word gets
back and people cruising can spot the polis at a hundred
yards.'

'I'm not going to convince you, am I?'

'To take you down the Gardens? No chance.'

'Someone was killed down there. Stabbed to death in
what might be a homophobic attack. We're on the same side
here.'

'We might want the same result, but we're not on the
same side. Gay people have been treated so bad by the police
in the past that having any faith in cops is almost impossible.'

'So, what can I do to get them to trust the police?'

Jamie gave the question a great deal of consideration,
before saying, 'Listen, I stand by what I said. The Gardens is
never going to work. Sending cops down there would just
drive everyone away. However, what we do have are a couple
of groups that meet here in the office twice a week. One group
is for adults and one a youth group. I'll speak to my bosses
and we'll try to sell your coming along as some kind of
community relations. Speak to the groups and if they get to
trust you they might tell you things or pass things on to me to

tell you.'

'When could you fix it up?'

The adults meet on Wednesday, but there's a youth group that meets tonight. If my boss will agree then you can come along. The group starts arriving at seven so if you get here for about seven thirty. That'll give me time to warn them, so if anyone wants to leave or spend time in one of the other rooms then they can do so before you get here.'

'You're not painting a picture of me getting a warm welcome.'

Jamie offered a shrug. 'I would definitely not get your hopes up about that.'

It had been clear that this would be the best he was going to get, so Jack reluctantly agreed to try Jamie's suggested softly-softly approach, as opposed to flooding the Gardens with heavy footed detectives.

It wouldn't do to embark on too many clandestine jobs, thought Jack, remembering his previous night's visit to the bars.

There had, as yet, been no comeback from that confrontation and Jack wasn't expecting one, but Donkin wouldn't be the first to scream harassment when a cop got too close to his operations.

With that in mind, Jack would put the visit to the MESMAC youth group down as an action and allocate it to himself.

When Slade returned to the office, he found Dave Armstrong at the coffee machine. On seeing his boss, the sergeant poured a second mug and handed it to Jack.

'Anything been happening while I was away?'

'Nothing new. Burton's been hanging around like a bad smell. Asked me what you were doing and I told him that you were on some enquiry. He looked pissed when I couldn't tell him where or when you would be back. I take it there's some history with you two.'

'I'll tell you some day.'

'So, are you going to tell me what you've been up to?'

'I've been to that gay organisation MESMAC again. I'm meeting up with their youth group tonight. See what if

149

anything I can find out.'

'Want me along?'

'They're wary of one cop. Two might be considered as over egging the cake.'

'Do you think that our murder victim was into kids?'

'No. To be honest with you, I can't even be sure that this whole gay angle is not taking us off on a tangent, but at the moment we've got next to nothing to go on. At the very least some of these young guys might frequent the murder scene. We'll see what tonight turns up.'

There was little advance in enquiries that day, and information coming in had slowed down to a trickle so Jack kept looking at his watch, fighting off the urge to go early to the meeting. He managed to find plenty of paperwork to work through and at seven thirty exactly was heading up the steps towards Jamie's office.

He was greeted at the door by Jamie, who showed him into a room and introduced him to a small group of teenagers as a police officer from the city centre, who was trying to build links to the community. The murder in the Gardens was never mentioned but it was unlikely that they hadn't guessed the true reason for the surprise visit.

The gathering consisted of about a dozen young people mostly boys but with two girls sitting together at the back. It seemed that sometimes even minority groups have subgroups in them.

The group was of varying ages ranging from about fourteen to seventeen and an eclectic mix. There were obvious street wise kids in scruffy tracksuit bottoms and hoodies, others in expensive looking fashionable tops and everything in between. The only consistency was that the clothing was named brands... even the tatty stuff.

All of them stared warily at Jack when Jamie asked them if they had any questions to ask.

There was a long silence before one of the boys spoke. 'Why do policemen always harass and arrest gay people? We're not doing anything wrong.'

The speaker was a tall handsome boy of about sixteen with blonde hair that was short at the sides, but stood up straight at the front, reminding Jack of some pop duo twins he had seen once on television. He was wearing a T shirt with the slogan, *I'm gay. Get over it!* When he spoke up several other members of the group began nodding in agreement.

'I'm always being stop checked coming back from the club,' added another boy, wearing a dark hoodie, emblazoned with a sports logo across the front. 'One night I got stopped twice by two different bizzies.'

Looking at him, Jack thought to himself, *if I saw him dressed like that, hood up, wandering the streets in the middle of the night, I would stop and check him as well.*

'What are you doing coming back from the club at night? You're only seventeen. You shouldn't be drinking. He'll arrest you for that,' a girl's voice shouted from the back.

'He'd have to prove it first,' the boy countered, to laughs from some of the others.

Jack chose his words wisely. 'You're not getting stopped for being gay. Maybe there's been crime in the area and you fit the description of someone seen. If you're not committing crime then you've nothing to fear,' Jack said, although it was clear from some of their expressions that they were not convinced.

Over the next twenty minutes, Slade listened to a catalogue of complaints, some personal, but most second or third hand and possibly exaggerated in the recounting.

Then the lad in the hoodie piped up. 'So if they're just after car thieves and burglars why do they hassle people down in the Gardens? There's not any cars or houses down there to get screwed.'

'No, but there are plenty of boys who wouldn't mind,' another lad added, causing a ripple of laughter.

Jack managed a smile and glanced across at Jamie, who caught his eye.

'Right, if no one has any further questions then can someone make Inspector Slade a cup of coffee and we'll get on with the social?'

The blonde boy with the gravity defying hair asked Jack how he liked his coffee and wandered off towards the coffee machine.

Walking over, Jamie asked, 'What do you think of our little group?'

'A tough audience. One or two have some issues.'

'They're teenagers. Issues are part of the job description. You're probably the first police officer they've had contact with in anything other than a confrontational situation. Be thankful they even spoke to you. I mentioned that you were coming and at least two left before you arrived. With these ones left you at least have a chance to break down some barriers.'

The blonde boy returned with the coffee and Jack thanked him and tried to engage him in conversation. His name was Josh and he came from a middle class family from the Woolsington area, a moneyed suburb not too far from the airport. His father was a doctor and his mother a teacher. He was polite and his refined accent was quite a contrast to the rough Geordie that some of the other boys spoke.

His nickname amongst the group was 'Posh Josh', but it was clear that despite their differences he was still regarded by the others as part of the gang. It seemed that their shared sexuality in a straight dominated world was the glue that bound them all together. He was accepted by his parents and appeared to be well adjusted and accepting of his sexuality, as it appeared were all the others. Jack liked him and found him mature and easy to chat with.

The boy in the hoodie was called Darren or 'Daz' by the others and was quite a different kettle of fish. He was very wary of Slade and, at first, any attempt at conversation was met with grunts and one word answers. Jack persisted and once they established a common ground in a shared love of cars, the boy began to relax.

'Now the 320i is canny. It's got a bit of poke. But you should get yourself an M3. Now that's a fast motor.'

Slade said that he didn't want to fork out the running costs, but legalities of paying for insurance premiums didn't seem to have entered Daz's head when it came to such things. As the conversation drifted, the boy began to open up and Slade got to hear a little about his background.

The product of a broken home, he had spent the last five years in care and had recently moved into a one bedroom studio flat provided by the social services. Although staff were on hand at the complex twenty four hours a day, he was expected to cater and look after himself as a first step to totally

152

independent living.

Jack knew the place that he was staying in, having attended during a missing person enquiry a year or so before and they were able to talk about the area and the people. At almost eighteen, Daz was the oldest of the group in terms of age, but lacked a lot of the social skills of some of the others, dyslexia having hindered his reading and writing skills.

Over the next couple of hours, most of the group took the chance to speak to Jack and by the end of the night he had warmed to a few, if not all of them. Some of the stories that they told both shocked and saddened him.

There was the usual talk of bullying at school, but often it wasn't only the other kids. Sometimes a homophobic teacher would go out of his way to upset or frustrate a pupil that they suspected of being different.

One of the boys, confused and frightened had come out to his parents, only to find himself thrown out onto the street at sixteen with nowhere to live. Several admitted to bouts of self-harm and one even told the story of a close teenage friend who, unable to cope with aggression and cyber bullying, had taken his own life with an overdose.

If even half the stories weren't exaggerated it was a sad endorsement of some sections of society.

Jack found himself becoming angry at what some of these kids had gone through at such an early age and, at times, his heart went out to them. By the end of the night, he had a greater insight into why so many gay people felt side-lined by society, but it wasn't helping him to move further forward with his enquiries.

During his chats, he had mentioned to several of them about Johnny Lee, but no-one seemed to know of him, or if they did weren't going to admit it.

At the end of the meeting as the youth group put away chairs and tidied up, Jack went across to speak with Jamie and thank him for facilitating the evening's events.

In between bidding good night to his charges as they left, Jamie enquired whether any information had been forthcoming, and seemed genuinely saddened that it had not.

'Give them time. They need to know they can trust you. It has taken me weeks, if not longer, but they now do come and tell me things they have heard on the street. If they ask me to I'll pass on any information.'

With a final thank you, Jack stepped out into the crisp night air, intending to head straight home and try to catch up on some lost sleep. The sky was clear and he had to watch his step on the untreated pavements, slippery with black ice.

Cutting through Grainger Town, the historic heart of the city, he turned south down Grey Street, passing the grade 1 listed Theatre Royal, with its classic columns and impressive portico. Crowds of well-dressed theatregoers were streaming from inside, huddled against the bitter wind and heading towards nearby wine bars or hailing taxis for their journey home.

Had he not been concentrating so hard on the theatre crowd and the icy path, he might have noticed the dark shape that had been huddled in the darkness of a nearby shop doorway, watching him as he left the MESMAC offices.

He might have noticed the figure ease out of the doorway and, increasing pace, begin to fall into step behind him.

As it was, the first Jack knew he was being followed, was towards the bottom of the street when he was alerted by a loud crunch as the dark figure stepped on a sheet of ice, cracking it under his weight.

Jack whirled around and almost lost his footing as he turned to confront the person behind him.

DEATH RATTLE

CHAPTER 29

Daz looked almost as startled as Jack as they stood facing each other.

'You were asking about Johnny Lee. Can I speak to you... off the record, like? I wanted to tell you something and you didn't seem to mind when we were talking about me going to the club under age.'

'Well, I can't promise anything, but I'm not bothered about minor things. Johnny's missing and I just want to make sure that he's alright.' Jack gave a conspirational smile, and said, 'So long as you don't cough to any major crime I think we're going to be alright.'

Daz seemed nervous and was moving his weight from one foot to the other.

'Do you want to go somewhere for a coffee?'

'If I'm seen with you people'll think I'm a grass.'

'So what do you want to tell me?'

Daz seemed to think about this for a moment, before he finally spoke up. 'Johnny and me... we were supposed to meet up in town a few weeks ago. He was looking for somewhere to stay and I said I'd sneak him into my flat until he could find somewhere else. I used to see him a few times when I first came out on the scene. He was one of my first proper boyfriends and we were together for a few weeks. Even after that we used to see each other occasionally. Just fuck buddies. You know?'

Slade managed a noncommittal shrug.

'He was dead good to me when I was younger. Showed me around the scene. Sort of took me under his wing.'

'Did he ever try to introduce you to older guys? Invite you to parties?

Daz looked down, avoiding Jack's eyes. 'You know about them?'

'Yes,' Jack said, 'but why don't you tell me what you know?'

'This is off the record? Yes?'

'Yes.'

'Johnny told me about the parties. Said they were a bit of a laugh and there was plenty of booze and smokes. Other

155

stuff if you wanted it. I only ever did a bit of weed. He said if
you kept your mouth shut and were nice to these blokes you
could earn some good money. I went with him a couple of
times. It was canny.'

'So who was at these parties?'

'We were told not to ask names. So Johnny and I made
up nicknames for some of the blokes. There was one with a
wig that Johnny used to call "syrup" and another camp one
what spoke dead posh and we called him "The Princess". But
Johnny told me who was OK to go with and who to steer clear
of. Who was into rough stuff – you know?'

Jack nodded. 'So I take it you were expected to earn
your stay?'

Daz looked a bit sheepish and returned to his mantra.
'Off the record?'

'Off the record,' Jack repeated.

'Usually they just wanted to give you a blow job.
Sometimes they would get you to do it to them. One guy was
in his seventies. Johnny said he recognised him and he used to
be a teacher at one of those posh schools in Jesmond or
Gosforth. He just liked to talk to you for a bit. Then he'd
ask... dead polite like... if he could wank you off. Always
gave a good tip. I spoke to him afterwards and he seemed a
really nice bloke.'

'Did they ever try to force you to do anything you
didn't want to do?'

'One of them... we called him Ginger on account of his
hair... he got really pissed off once 'cause he wanted to shag
me and I wasn't up for it. Not with him. I didn't mind when
Johnny did it a few times, but we're mates. You know? That's
different.'

'So what happened with this man when you refused?'

'Johnny came over and spoke to him and they went off
to one of the rooms and he left me alone.'

'Did you go to very many of the parties?'

'Four or five. It was quite good really. We each got
fifty quid just for going. If you was good and did what the
punters asked they would give you tips. One night I came
home with just over four hundred quid.'

'How many lads would be there?'

'It depends. Usually about half a dozen or more.'

'And punters?'

'Normally about ten or twelve blokes.

'So how old were the other lads?'

'Usually sixteen seventeen. There was one looked dead young about fourteen. He was a right little queen. Prepared to do owt. A lot of the older ones liked him. It was good money, but you just had to make sure you never told anyone about any of the punters.'

'So why are you telling me this now?'

'Johnny would never just go away without telling me. He was really good to me. I know something bad has happened to him. I want you to find him.'

Slade promised him that he would try his best to do so, but he had a nagging feeling that when, and if, he did, there wasn't going to be a happy ending.

Jack knew that there was no way that Daz would put pen to paper and no point in even asking. Giving him one of his cards with the contact details on, he made the boy promise to contact him should he hear anything else, or find out any more about the parties or who attended.

As he made to leave, Jack told him to tell no one about what they had talked about.

'You're kidding? Down our way there's only one thing worse than a puff... and that's a grass.'

With that, he turned and headed off in the opposite direction.

It hadn't been such a wasted night after all.

CHAPTER 30

The following morning, after the usual morning meeting, Jack raised the issue with Parker about putting more resources into tracing Johnny Lee. He was becoming more and more convinced that finding what had happened to him would lead to discovering why and by whom Darren Wilson was murdered.

Parker remained unconvinced, but strangely enough, Burton seemed to agree with Jack that it was a possible route to go down. Parker grunted a couple of times, but he wasn't about to go against anything that HQ Professional Standards thought was a good idea. Somewhat reluctantly, he agreed that Jack should try to get Donkin in and speak to him.

Jack felt sure that Burton would push to be present when Donkin was interviewed, or worse, insist that he go with them to pick him up. However, he gave no indications that he wanted to do so. Since there was a strong possibility that a complaint of harassment might come from it, Slade could understand his reasoning.

If there's a chance of any shit flying Burton was making sure he was the right side of the fan.

Slade went through to the incident room and, finding Armstrong checking through the results of the morning actions, called across to him. 'I've got some car keys. Grab your coat. We're off to pay a visit.'

Slade was halfway to the police yard before Dave caught up with him. 'The actions are drying up. Please tell me you've got a lead.'

As they located an unmarked police car, Jack told him about the parties and what he had found out from Daz the night before. He also told him about the previous off duty encounter with Donkin in the late night café.

'And just F.Y.I. I might have forgotten to mention that last bit to Parker and Burton.'

'Bloody hell, Jack. You're playing some risky cards close to your chest. If either of them find out you've been withholding info they'll sauté your balls for an entrée... and you don't want to know what they'll do for the main course.'

'Well, I won't tell them if you don't.'

Smiling, Jack slipped the car into first and pulled out the station yard, heading for the address in Jesmond shown on Donkin's I.S. record.

Fifteen minutes later, they turned off Osbourne Road in Jesmond with its multitudinous student bars and turned down a tree lined street onto one of several long terraces of red brick houses. This was bedsit land; most of the once grand houses had been turned into multi occupancy student rental or divided into smaller flats.

It was a residents only parking area, so Armstrong put the police vehicle log book in the windscreen along with a "Police Business" sign hoping to keep the council run parking enforcement officers at bay… but not convinced that it would.

They located number fourteen, which was a three-storey house with a dormer attic room perched at the top. The building had a slight air of neglect, with dusty sash windows and the postage stamp garden at the front looked like it hadn't seen a lawnmower in several years. Despite this, they both knew that the area carried a rental premium because of the proximity to the city centre.

Dave looked at the rusting intercom with a line of bell pushes, none of which had any name under it. He pressed the one for apartment fourteen 'C' and waited. There was no reply and when after several rings there were no signs of life they turned to go.

They were heading to the car when Jack spotted a red Audi A4 pull up in the street and a figure begin to emerge from the driver's side. He recognised him immediately. It was Donkin.

Almost as soon as he began walking towards his apartment he spotted the two police officers standing near his gate. He seemed to hesitate for a second but then continued towards them.

'Hello again, mister…'

'Inspector… Slade.'

'Yeah. Slade. Who's your boyfriend?'

'My colleague is Detective Sergeant Armstrong. We'd like you to come with us to the station to answer a few questions.'

'I'd like to get inside the knickers of the cute blonde student in the flat opposite. I've got about as much of a chance of that as you have of me going to the nick with you.'

'It might be in your best interests,' Armstrong said.

Donkin looked from one to the other, before speaking. 'I very much doubt that.'

'We want to speak to you about a missing person. We think you might know something about him.'

'Is this that Johnny character you were going on about? I've already told you I don't know who he is.'

Jack decided to try to rattle him. 'I'm told you may have met him at some parties you both go to.'

For a brief instant, Donkin's eyes widened, but he quickly recovered. 'I'm not really one for parties. More of a pint and game of pool man me. So, unless you're going to arrest me for something, I've got things to do.' Smirking, he added, 'And I take it you're not going to do that?'

The two detectives remained silent.

'I thought not.'

Donkin moved past the two police officers and, as he made his way towards his front door, Slade spoke up.

'Nice car you have there. Drive it in the city centre a lot?'

Donkin hesitated and turned. 'That's not some kind of threat is it? It sounds like harassment to me.'

Slade walked slowly up to Donkin and, leaning in close, whispered quietly. 'Listen, you think you're a clever little shit, but I know about your little soirées. If I find out something's happened to Johnny Lee and you're involved a bit of harassment will be the least of your worries.'

Then, taking a business card from his pocket, he flicked it into Donkin's face then, walking away, called over his shoulder. 'Speak to your brief. I expect to hear from you by four this afternoon. Don't make me come looking for you.'

Armstrong followed Jack back to the car. 'He'll never call.'

'Did you see his face when I mentioned the parties? He'll call alright. He is going to want to know just how much we've found out.'

The call came just before a quarter to four. The front office rang the incident room to say a Mister Donkin was at the front counter with his solicitor to see Detective Inspector Slade.

Less than ten minutes later seated opposite Donkin in one of the interview rooms Slade and Armstrong set the tape recorder going and introduced themselves. They read through his rights and entitlements whilst Donkin's solicitor Steve Thompson listened intently.

The two detectives knew the legal rep, Thompson, well, having dealt with him on numerous occasions. He was a senior partner in one of the leading firms in the North East, specialising in criminal matters and was usually the first port of call for many of the better class of villains.

Thompson wasn't well liked by many of the detectives; partly because he seemed just a little too pally with his clients, but mainly because he was good at his job and as wily as a fox.

'Before we begin,' Thompson said, 'I'd like to make it clear that my client is here as a voluntary attender and is doing so as he wishes to assist the police in what we understand to be a missing person enquiry. Should your questioning deviate from that in any way we reserve the right to terminate this interview. I hope that I make myself clear.'

'Perfectly,' Slade said. 'As you know, we are investigating the disappearance of a young man called Johnny Lee. We believe that your client may have been an associate of the missing person.'

Donkin looked to his solicitor and received a sharp nod before he began speaking. 'I think I know the lad you're on about, but I don't know him well and only spoke to him a couple of times. If he's missing I don't know where he is.'

'How do you know him?'

'I've seen him around and about.'

'Where?'

'Town. The bars.'

'Which bars?'

'I don't remember.'

'You frequent the gay bars in Newcastle city centre?

Donkin shrugged,' I go in lots of bars. Gay. Straight. Who cares these days?'

'Did you ever meet him in an area called the Gardens?'

Donkin looked towards Thompson who nodded.

'I might have. I sometimes cut through to go to the pubs down on the Quayside.'

'Did you know that the Gardens is what's known as a cruising area? A meeting place for gay people?'

Donkin gave a shrug. 'I might have heard something like that, but as I say I just use it to cut down to the quayside.'

'Did you know that Johnny Lee was working as a sex worker in that area?'

'I wouldn't know anything about that. Like I said I hardly knew the lad.'

'So you wouldn't be in the Gardens trying to talk to the rent boys who frequent the area?'

Thompson interrupted. 'Officer, if you are suggesting that my client was loitering in the area for immoral purposes I may have to stop this interview.'

'Never crossed my mind,' Jack feigned innocence.

'That's not really my scene,' Donkin said, smiling to himself.

'It's just we've spoken to a witness who says that you go to the Gardens in order to speak to the sex workers and other young lads who frequent the area.'

Donkin shook his head. 'Not me. You've got me mixed up with someone else.'

Thompson opened his mouth to speak, but Jack continued. 'The witness says that you are known to pick up young boys in the Gardens…'

Thompson raised his voice above Slade. 'Inspector, I think we're about done here.'

'… that you invite them to parties where they get sexually abused by older men in return for money.'

Thompson's face was reddening fast and he rose to his feet. 'Right. We're finished. Mister Donkin has nothing more to say and this interview is concluded.'

As Thompson and Donkin both made for the door, Jack couldn't resist one last dig. 'I know you're not clever enough to be the main man. You're just the oily rag, but I'm going to find out who's the engine driver and when I do I'll make it abundantly clear that I got to him through you. Think about that one, Mister Donkin.'

Even as his solicitor ushered him out, Slade caught Donkin's eye and recognised anger, but also, for the first time,

DEATH RATTLE

Jack could see a look of doubt in his eyes... and something else. *Fear.*

CHAPTER 31

Jack watched Donkin and his solicitor from a second floor window as they stood outside the police station speaking briefly, before shaking hands and moving off in opposite directions.

His eyes followed Donkin as he made his way along the road towards where Jack knew he had parked his red Audi. He waited for some minutes until the vehicle appeared, driven by Donkin and turned right to head off towards the city centre. He couldn't resist a little smile when moments later the unmarked car driven by Armstrong appeared and, keeping a couple of vehicles in between, fell in behind the Audi.

Dave had been reluctant to carry out Jack's plan and had voiced his concerns.

'Unauthorised surveillance? If Parker finds out he'll go ape shit.'

'Like I've said before... I won't tell him if you don't.'

'Keep saying that and you'll get us both shot full of shit... if not worse. Besides, anything we uncover will probably be thrown out at court.'

'It's a risk we'll take. So far as anyone's concerned you weren't following him. You were just driving in the same direction and happened to see where he goes. Look, I'm not expecting anything evidential. I just want to know where he runs to when he's rattled. Let's just call it intelligence gathering.'

'I'll call it crazy.'

'Just humour me,' was Slade's parting shot as he threw across the keys to the spare unmarked car. Dave caught them effortlessly.

As he watched the car with Armstrong disappearing after Donkin, Slade hoped that he had made the right decision.

Donkin's Audi took a fairly direct route across town and turned off the central motorway towards the East End of the city. Keeping his target in sight, Armstrong followed him through the Byker area, where he pulled onto the forecourt of a car sales room and came to a halt.

The unmarked police car behind quickly hit a left and doing a quick U-turn in a side street pulled up in a line of cars, sufficiently hidden, but with a line of sight to where Donkin had parked.

The sign above the tidy freshly painted single storey building read NGA Motors. There was a plate glass showroom and the front parking area was dotted with numerous vehicles with signboards on their windscreen displaying prices and boasting "Finance Available". A few vehicles appeared relatively new, but there were several off to the side with signs declaring, "Trade-Ins to Clear".

As Donkin got out of the car, he was approached by a figure who emerged from what looked like a reception-come-office. Tall and stocky, the man had a domed shaven head that glistened in the sunlight as he strode across the car park. He was wearing a short sleeved shirt with collar and tie. The shirt struggled in vain to contain his bulging frame. If he was trying to give an impression of a businessman to the world, the tattooed muscled arms of a bodybuilder were telling a different story.

At first the meeting seemed to be amicable, but Donkin appeared to say something that made the bigger man become quite animated. He began looking around suspiciously and pointed a stubby finger at the chest of the much smaller Donkin.

He didn't seem a happy bunny.

Donkin himself began looking around at passing vehicles and parked cars, but Armstrong had parked in a line of cars out of direct sight and was not easily visible.

Bit late to wonder if you were followed. Dave smiled to himself.

You were right, Jack. Squeeze the bastard hard enough and he'll run to his protector.

The large man then strode off into the office building, leaving Donkin standing alone and looking somewhat lost. He seemed to gather himself, before glancing around again and then returned to his car.

He pulled out into traffic and didn't notice the police vehicle discretely pull out after him, keeping once again at least two cars between them.

On this occasion, Donkin headed straight back to his

Jesmond apartment, where he parked up and hurriedly let himself in.

Armstrong sat outside, some distance away. It looked like his target wasn't coming back out anytime soon, so after giving it fifteen minutes he headed back to the nick to update Slade.

Dave was sitting opposite Jack in the Inspector's office and being grilled by his friend on the result of his unauthorised tail of Donkin.

'So, do we know who the man mountain car dealer is or his connection with our weaselled pimp?' Jack asked.

'Not yet, but I've asked the front office downstairs to run a check on the address of the dealership, NGA Motors, see who's the keyholder, and whether he owns the property or leases it. We can do a cross check and see if we can link him to Donkin.'

Jack looked thoughtful. 'I'm thinking slightly out the box here, but how about asking one of the 'tecs or one of the uniform, preferably someone who looks the least like a cop, to drive across town and make some enquiries about buying a second hand motor. See what he can pick up.'

'Will do. And I know just the person. Cowan downstairs. Very bright, but about ten stone wet through and wears specs. Looks more like a fucking vicar than a cop. There is no way he'll get made.'

'We obviously spooked Weasel and I think where he ran to is going to prove significant.'

'It certainly seemed that big bastard didn't want to be seen with him. I don't see those two sitting down for a nice chinwag over a pint.'

'Which makes me even more interested in the connection. Get things moving with Cowan and we'll see what we come up with.'

'Any other developments while I was away.'

'A beat cop picked up the boy that Donkin had been chatting to in the café the other night. Found him sleeping rough behind the coach station in Churchill Street.'

'Not far from the café you saw him in with Donkin. What did he have to say?'

'Not a lot. Just says he was offered a hot drink and a burger by Donkin who he'd never met before. Looks like I moved in too soon before anything else got put on the menu.'

'Where's he now?'

'Social Services have him and are taking him back to Berwick from where he was reported missing. Apparently he didn't look too unhappy to be heading back. Seems the bright lights of the big city didn't prove as welcoming as he'd first thought.'

Just at that point a uniformed officer appeared at the office door clutching several pages of computer printout and Slade beckoned him in.

'Sir, sorry to interrupt, but the sergeant said this was urgent.' He nodded at Armstrong. 'Here's the results of the background checks on NGA Motors that you wanted.'

Dave thanked him for being so prompt and scanned the documents, before looking up at Jack.

'Keyholder is down as a Neil Allen. Long history of convictions. Older ones are for violence, including when a juvenile. Not much for the past few years. Spent some time as a bouncer at various bars and clubs, but as of four years ago seems to have dropped off the radar. Nothing since then.'

'Bouncer?' Slade said. 'There could be a drugs connection.'

'He wouldn't be the first doorman whose real job was to control the influx of drugs into a club. Backhanders from dealers or even a percentage cut of the deals. It's a good way to make your money through drugs without getting your hands too dirty.'

'Could be how he got the cash to start up a business.'

'I can't see a prig with his history and previous record stepping away from a lucrative drugs income unless something better came along.'

'Me neither. What about the garage business? Any indication of car ringing?'

Ringing was stealing vehicles and changing their identity for selling on to unsuspecting customers. Often it involved the swapping of identities from written off vehicles onto stolen cars, but with increasing checks on write offs through the PNC system, it was now proving more profitable and less risky to simply strip down stolen cars for their parts.

Often with vehicles, especially the high-end value makes, the sum of their parts could easily outstrip the value of the vehicle as a whole.

'I'll check with the Stolen Motor Vehicle Squad and see if they have any information on NGA Motors. I've a contact in S.M.V. so it shouldn't take long. In the meantime, I'll get one of the squad to run background checks on Neil Allen. See if anything turns up on associates and see if we can find a link to Donkin.'

'That would be very nice,' Jack said.

'I'm sure it would, but I saw Allen's reaction to Donkin at the garage, so I'm not holding out much hope on that one, Jack. He didn't look happy at the possibility of them being seen together.'

Armstrong gave a boyish grin. 'In fact he looked decidedly pissed off.'

CHAPTER 32

The next day was typical of the investigation to date. One step forward and two back.

Despite extensive searches through the CIS system there were no known links between Weasel Donkin and the motor dealer Neil Allen.

Whilst the Stolen Motor Vehicle Squad did have an interest in NGA Motors, which was strongly suspected of dealing in stolen vehicle parts, there was never anything concrete and certainly nothing to justify being able to obtain a search warrant with which to turn over the premises.

Neil Allen lived in a decent area, drove a nearly new high end BMW and did not appear to be short of cash, but any suggestion of dishonesty against him was based on innuendo and suspicion about his previous reputation and current affluent lifestyle. He would of course put that down to his thriving car sales and repair business.

Slade had Cowan visit the garage, posing as a potential purchaser. Although Cowan looked nothing like your typical cop, it was clear that Allen was on his guard. Maybe it was the recent visit by Donkin that was making him extra cautious, or maybe it was true that career criminals had a sixth sense and could smell a cop.

Whichever it was, Allen was very wary of engaging in any small talk and it was clear that Cowan was going to get no further forward with him. He didn't think Allen made him as a cop, but he sensed there was a palpable distrust.

Cowan did report back that there was a large tiled showroom with some very clean looking second hand cars, but out back there was an additional repair garage that could be used for stripping down cars.

He could not see anything to suggest that Allen was into car ringing and there was certainly nothing that would justify a warrant. There was nothing whatsoever to suggest that NGA Motors was anything other than a legitimate car dealership. There was nothing that they could pass on to interest the S.M.V. Squad.

With regards to Johnny Lee's disappearance, there was also no good news on that front and Jack could count on one hand the number of actionable information messages that had been received.

On the plus side, an address had been found for Johnny Lee in a new build block of apartments just off Welbeck Road in Walker to the east of the city. Slade travelled over with Armstrong to see what, if anything, a search would reveal. Although they had no keys they were prepared to force entry and took along a heavy metal 'Enforcer' door opener.

The block was a four-storey building of sixteen flats and, despite being a stone's throw from some of the deprived areas of the city, still had a newly built look with no signs of graffiti.

Dave rang the entry buzzer for flat five, but wasn't expecting a reply, so was a little taken aback when the voice of what sounded like a young man responded. When Armstrong identified himself as a cop the occupant sounded suspicious.

'What's it about?

'We're trying to trace a missing person. Can you buzz us in so we can speak to you?'

There was a slight pause, before he got a reply. 'I'll come down.'

Questions were already flashing through Slade's mind. *Had Johnny Lee been living with someone? Had he sub-let the flat before taking off somewhere?*

After a couple of minutes, a young male appeared at the foot of the steps. He looked about seventeen and had a spiked haircut dyed blonde. A metal ring pierced his bottom lip and a wispy moustache of downy hair covered the top one. Jack guessed that was intended to make him look older, but it had the reverse effect. He was wearing a black T shirt and faded denim jeans with rips in the knees.

The young man appeared wary and asked to see their warrant cards, before letting them in. Satisfied, he opened the metal door and led them up a flight of stairs to the first floor.

'Can't be too careful around here. Last week I came down one morning and found some junkie sleeping under the stairwell. He must've buzzed all the flats until someone let him in. We're told not to let anyone in if we don't know them, but some people don't listen. I rang the management company and he was gone before I got back that afternoon.'

DEATH RATTLE

Slade and Armstrong were shown into a small studio flat which smelled of fresh paint. The room was clean and tidy and a tall bookshelf displayed a number of Blu Rays and DVDs, as well as a selection of books, mostly novels, but a few on movies and film.

The youth gave his name as Ben Grey, but when Slade told him what it was about he said he had only been at the flat less than two weeks. The flat was empty when he had arrived, but the management company provided every new tenant with fresh carpets.

'Not the best quality, but a bit of a bonus. To tell you the truth, I think it's just a form of sound insulation to stop the other tenants complaining about noise.'

Armstrong showed him a photograph of Johnny Lee, but Ben couldn't remember ever seeing him. He told them that some bits of post had arrived in that name. He had contacted the management, but they just told him they had no forwarding address and if it was junk mail just to bin it.

'So I did.'

Content, but disappointed that they were no further forward, they both thanked him and left him with a contact card.

'If anything else comes to mind just give me a call on that number,' Slade said.

As they left, Ben suggested that they should contact the management company direct just in case they might know more. He gave the company name as Triple 'M' Development.

Slade knew the company. Mike Martin Management and Development Ltd was owned by the rags to riches entrepreneur who gave the company its name. Mike Martin had made his fortune on the back of the property market and, in only a few years, had rapidly become the largest property development agency in the North East.

His rapid rise in fortune came with the push for what the Government liked to call affordable housing projects. Cheap, but functional housing, which seemed to oil the wheels for property developers, whilst at the same time salving the social consciences of the local politicians and councillors.

They decided to action the company for a visit, but from what Ben Grey had said, they didn't hold out much hope of any leads.

Back at the nick, enquiries into Johnny showed no trace of any bank or building society accounts and, although an aunt had been traced to an address in North Northumberland, she said she had not had any contact with him since the death of his mother.

It seemed that Johnny Lee had just vanished off the face of the earth.

Beat officers and community support officers in the area of the gay scene had all been briefed concerning any information about Johnny Lee and the alleged gay parties, but no-one on the scene claimed to know anything... or if they did, they weren't talking.

On a more positive note, Drew Sterling, the former partner of the murdered officer, had been back on and left a message for Jack. He had found an old contact number for Johnny and had tried ringing it, but it was discontinued.

A detective had been tasked with getting the necessary authorisations to obtain mobile phone records from the line supplier, with a view to tracing any associates through any telephone numbers it had called. Jack hoped this might throw up a clue as to who was holding the boy sex parties.

There was some reticence as to how much information would be gleaned, because Drew mentioned that Johnny had at least two phones and changed his mobiles more often than some people change their shirts.

To add to the problem, usually they were throw-aways and unlikely to be registered.

With other leads drying up, Slade was beginning to fear that they were now grasping at straws. He was getting increasing telephone calls from Parker, who Jack had no doubt was in turn under the close scrutiny of Command Block.

Burton was still a constant presence at every briefing, but tended to remain at the back of the room, soaking up the information, but never contributing to the direction of the enquiry. He was starting to feel a bit like an annoying fly on the wall.

Armstrong said he was more like a bad smell that won't go away.

Liz Harmon had also been constantly leaving messages

for Jack, but he had refused to answer them and had told front office staff to refer any enquiries to Northumbria Police Press Office.

On one occasion, Harmon managed to come through on Jack's personal mobile. Annoyed, he had refused to answer any of her questions, demanding to know how she had obtained his private number. She had avoided answering and instead asked about any updates on enquiries in the gay scene. Even on the phone, Jack could sense her smirking as she spoke.

Jack had vented his anger at Dave. 'She has better snouts in the force than we have with the prigs. If I ever get definitive proof she's getting info from that prick, Spence, I'll happily choke the life out of the bastard.'

His friend stared at him and was in no doubt that Jack would happily carry out the threat with gusto.

'This is going to interest you, Jack,' Dave said, anxious to change the subject. 'I've been trawling through the CIS records for Donkin and accessing the HI screens.

The HI screens of the force computer related to Historic Intelligence. Old sightings and information that drops off the records when they are no longer deemed current, but like all computer generated data, they are never ever fully deleted.

'I was hoping for maybe a sighting or something that might connect Donkin to these alleged parties. Maybe even a lead on whoever might be behind them.'

Both he and Slade knew that Donkin was no more than a facilitator when it came to the parties. His role appeared to be picking up suitable boys. Up market events at country houses involving posh sounding men appeared to be out of his league. What they needed to do was track down the organiser.

'So, did you come up with anything?'

'Nowt... at first... but then I found something just as interesting.'

'Well, don't let your secret die with you, eh?' Jack prompted impatiently.

'There's several associates listed on the computer; a couple were people he had been arrested with as a juvenile, but most related to people he had been sighted with over time. I've been cross-checking the names against CIS. I didn't hold out much hope and nothing seemed to strike a chord, until I came to a Dean Masters.'

'That name rings a bell.'

'It should do. He was the eighteen year old who had been with Donkin in the toilet when he had been arrested for gross indecency. Well, at the time of his arrest the kid gave his employment as a barman, so I checked into that and turns out he worked on the gay scene.'

'How does that help us?'

'At first I nearly missed it because Masters only had the one arrest with Donkin in the public toilet. But he does feature on another record I found. Nothing to do with convictions.'

Dave smiled like the cat with the cream.

'Come on. Spit it out!'

'Dean Masters is listed as a missing person *and has been for over four years.*'

Slade's eyes widened. Quickly, he tapped away on his keyboard and the relevant records came up on the screen. 'And you say there's been no trace of him since? No sightings. No contact with family?'

'Sod all. It's as if Dean Masters disappeared off the face of the earth. I've dug out the computer record for the Misper. I've also sent down for the paper based record, but haven't received it yet.'

'Disappeared... just like Johnny Lee,' Slade said to himself, his mind racing.

'He was reported missing by another barman at the pub he worked in. Apparently, they had arranged to meet one Saturday night for a meal at one of those little Italian pasta joints down Pudding Chare, but he never showed.'

'Do you know which bar he was working at?'

'A gay bar. Pinochio's. It's not there anymore. It closed a couple of years ago. But would you like to take a guess at who else worked there?'

'Not our friend, Mister Donkin?'

'You've got it in one. That's obviously where they know each other from.'

Slade let this new information sink in. 'Two people, both known to Donkin and both missing without a trace. Can we try to trace any other staff that worked there at the same time? See what that throws up.'

'I'll get on to licencing and pull details of the

management.'

Jack sat back in his chair, considering where this new line of enquiry might lead, when Dave interrupted his thoughts.

'There's more, Jack.'

Slade knew from the tone of his voice that it was going to be controversial.

'The meal had been put off to the Saturday from the Friday. Masters had cried off on the Friday because he had a prior commitment.'

'Let me guess. He had been invited to a party.'

Armstrong nodded. 'Apparently at some posh house up in Northumberland.'

CHAPTER 33

Jack took the new information straight to Parker.

Looking up from some papers on his desk, Parker rewarded Jack with one of his best scowls. 'We're meant to be investigating a murder and now you've got your detective sergeant looking at old missing person cases. While he's pissing his time away doing that, I'm getting major flak from Command Block complaining about a lack of progress in the murder enquiry.'

This wasn't the reaction that Jack was hoping for. 'I think it's all connected, boss. The murder, the missing rent boy, Johnny Lee, and now this Dean Masters is also missing.'

'Well, I'm not convinced. We get hundreds of these missing persons reported every month. The bloody children's homes have so many that they have a stash of misper forms to fill in before the cops arrive.'

'But most of those come back within a day or two. Johnny Lee has been missing for about three weeks now... and this Masters kid about four years.'

Parker shook his head, still unconvinced. 'I think it's a distraction, Jack.'

'Well, we haven't got a lot to lose. Most of the other actions are drying up.' Angrily shaking his head, Parker opened his mouth to launch a tirade, but Jack jumped in to deliver the clincher.

'If Harmon or any other press get hold of it and link the mispers to the murder we need to show we're ahead of the game. We need to be on top of every lead before the likes of Harmon.'

When it came to his boss, Jack knew which buttons to push. Even if Parker didn't want to tie up any resources on Lee and Masters, he wanted even less to be answering tough questions from the press or Command Block.

Parker closed his mouth and sat back, mulling over Jack's annoyingly astute observation. Finally, he let out a sigh, and reluctantly said, 'Alright, Jack... but you keep me informed if anything turns up. Anything. You hear me?'

His glare lingered a moment, but then he looked back down at his papers, which Jack took this as his usual cue to leave.

That afternoon Jamie Heatherington from MESMAC telephoned Jack to update him on his feedback from his contacts within the scene.

It was much the same as before and confirmed some of Jack's fears. No-one had heard from or seen Johnny Lee since the night he had attended Drew's flat.

Whilst there was a good chance that Johnny was so scared that he had just done a runner, there was the distinct possibility that whoever he was running from had caught up with him. That was the scenario that most concerned Jack.

Jamie's news didn't get any better. He had heard second hand that Harmon had embarked on her own enquiries concerning the gay scene. She had been seen visiting various bars trying to establish a link between Darren Wilson and anyone frequenting the scene. She was digging for her dirt.

Slade was banking on her having as much success as the police.

Firstly, he knew that their murder victim didn't visit the bars. He was quite closeted and the bars were a bit too close to where he worked, with too great a chance of him being recognised, either by customers or fellow cops.

Secondly, as Jack had already discovered, the gay scene was a closed shop. Any outsiders asking questions were unlikely to be trusted and he was betting that press were probably ranked only just behind the cops on that score.

There was however the distinct possibility that the lure of cash might loosen some tongues. Even if someone only told Harmon what questions the police had been asking, it might lead her to hearing about Johnny Lee.

That might be just the spur to get her digging further into Lee's associates and from there get to Drew Sterling.

After that, she might make the connection with Darren Wilson. It was a long shot, but not beyond possibility. Jack told Jamie of the second missing boy from several years before.

'His name was Dean Masters. Does it mean anything to you?'

'I don't recognise the name, but you're going back well

before my time. Besides, if he wasn't cruising any of the usual haunts it's doubtful any of the outreach workers would come across him.'

'He has one arrest for cottaging, but obviously it's going back several years.

'Again, it's probably before any of the current staff. I can certainly ask around, but I'm not hopeful.'

'He used to work in a gay bar called Pinocchio's. It's closed now, but someone on the scene must have known him.'

'Come on, Jack! How old do you think I am?' He laughed. 'I was probably still at school when that place was on the go.'

'You have contacts that I don't have.'

'Alright…' Jamie conceded, 'I'll ask around. It's before my time, but as you say, if he was a barman then people on the scene might remember him.'

'If you hear anything at all please let me know.'

Jamie paused and, in the silence, Jack sensed that there was more.

'Jack, you've got to understand something about the scene. It's very fluid and people come and go. Often they're only known by a first name and then, depending on their circumstances, that might not even be their real name.' Jamie's tone turned very serious.

'Many kids on the scene have been disowned by their families. They often disappear for whatever reasons. They move away… sometimes abroad. They meet someone and stop coming to the scene. Sometimes they get sick. The scene is so transient that often people don't notice. Someone could disappear and, unless they had family or a close friend, no-one would notice… and even if they did they might not care.'

Slade knew what Jamie was struggling to say. He had considered it himself. They had only just heard about Dean Masters and there's nothing to say Johnny was only the second young guy to go missing. It wasn't something that Jack wanted to dwell on, but it was something that he could not and would not dismiss.

For all they knew, there could be half a dozen or more people that had similarly just disappeared.

The headlines of the early edition of the evening paper declared, "Cop Murder. Police Probe Newcastle Gay Scene Connection".

It came as no surprise, as it was something that was being alluded to from day one. Nevertheless, it produced the usual backlash from headquarters about leaks to the press.

Jack spoke to Parker and suggested that it might work to their advantage and could throw up some new leads. He reminded him that Darren Wilson was not someone who frequented the scene, so it was unlikely that Harmon would find out much from there.

'This article is just a rehash of previous reports and, other than the headline, includes no further inside information.'

Parker asked if the enquiry team had any positive new leads and Jack told him that copies of the phone records from Johnny Lee's mobile had been obtained.

'Sergeant Armstrong has got one of the team going through the print out to get a picture of which numbers Johnny had been ringing and who had been calling him.'

Jack was trying to sound positive, but knew that most of the numbers were turning out to be unregistered mobiles, and short of ringing them and asking who was on the other end, there seemed no way of ascertaining who was using them.

'A detective is cross checking the numbers against all telephone calls into the control room to spot any possible matches.'

A computer data file was kept of all numbers reporting incidents, so as to identify frequent hoaxers. Through this data trail and cross check, it might be possible to trace names for many of the people who had received calls from Johnny.

This had already led to some further actions, but Slade was aware that so far none of the people contacted had seen Johnny Lee for several weeks. Several of those contacted had immediately hung up at the mention of police and were in line for home visits, where an address could be traced.

However, there was one particular number that Johnny had rung more than half a dozen times in the three days leading up to his disappearance. Although it was also unregistered, it was considered a promising lead as the calls were made just before his disappearance. One of the other detectives had been allocated a separate enquiry to obtain records of any calls made to or from that particular number.

Simply calling the number would be more time effective, but would alert the person on the other end of their interest. The owner clearly didn't want to be located as the phone was yet another disposable and might be just thrown away.

Phone records and cross checks were proving a long and labour intensive task, but one that it was hoped would provide some good leads.

And God knows, we're not over burdened with those.

It was gone four in the afternoon and the sun had already set on the still bustling city streets. The blackness of the winter afternoon outside the office windows matched Jack's mood. He had gone over the latest results from actions and was coming to the sickening conclusion that each one led to a dead end.

When an enquiry first kicks off, there is an energy about it that drives everyone on the team. It's like an electric current – almost tangible – as officers rush around, chasing down leads and, like the branches of a tree, each result can throw up a new line of enquiry. However, when the branch fails to produce fruit, and leads dry up, then the energy inevitably starts to fade.

If no leads are being generated then after a while the enquiry is scaled down and officers reassigned. At worst, the case is consigned to Headquarters as a cold case, awaiting some future lead to free it from its cardboard coffin in the archives.

Jack was beginning to worry that this might happen with the brutal murder of Darren Wilson. There were lots of theories to do with Johnny Lee, and maybe other missing persons, but nothing firm. Some in the squad were leaning towards the theory that Darren Wilson had just been unlucky. Someone who had simply been in the wrong place at the wrong time, and the initial gay mugging theory was gaining momentum.

Have we been following completely the wrong track?

It would certainly explain away why every lead they followed was drawing a blank. But, despite this, Slade felt that there was much more to it than just a robbery gone wrong.

His thoughts were interrupted by a knock on his office door. Dave entered, without waiting for a reply, and Jack could see a worried look on his face.

'What's up?'

Without a word, he dropped into a chair opposite Slade.

'We've got the results of the check on the telephone number in Johnny Lee's mobile.'

'The number that he was in contact with several times before he went AWOL?'

'Yeah. No user yet for the number. It's yet another unregistered throwaway, so to get further information, we had the provider give us a list of numbers that the phone has been ringing.'

Slade didn't know where this was leading, but the look on his friend's face did not bode well.

'Most of these in turn were registered, so we're making a comprehensive list to follow up as actions.' He hesitated, struggling to find the words. 'Jack, you need to see this before it goes upstairs. This particular telephone number stood out as one I recognised.'

He handed the list to Slade and Jack's eyes were drawn immediately to the mobile number highlighted. He recognised it at once. He couldn't fail to.

It was his own.

CHAPTER 34

The telephone number that had been in such frequent contact
with Johnny in the days leading up to his disappearance had
also been used to call Jack's personal number only a couple of
days ago.

'I have no idea who that was,' Jack said, mentally
cataloguing all his calls over the previous few days. 'I must
have made and received dozens.'

'You only got one call from this number and it lasted
less than ninety seconds.'

'I don't remember.'

'Check your own phone log. See if it jogs your
memory. What about that Jamie Heatherington character?'
Armstrong suggested. 'He's a part of the Gay scene. He also
has frequent connections with rent boys. Have you... have we
been getting played? Does this Jamie character know more
than he's letting on? Maybe he's been pumping you for
information, rather than the other way around.'

His office suddenly felt considerably hotter than it did a
few moments earlier. He thought of all the things that he and
Jamie had discussed. If Jamie was involved then Jack was
going to have a lot of awkward questions to answer.

'It might be an idea to pull out all the stops and find out
who owns that mobile before Professional Standards in the
form of Burton starts salivating,' Armstrong said, his own
concerns written all over his face.

Quite suddenly, Slade reached a conclusion. 'No. Jamie
is genuine. I would have sensed if he was lying. But there's
one way to be sure.'

He reached for his mobile and scrolled down for
Jamie's number. 'How many times did the phone call me?
Give me some times and dates.'

'Just the once and the date and time are here on the
log.'

'Well, it's not going to be him then. We've spoken
quite a few times.'

Jack found what he was searching for. 'Look here.
Jamie's number is different. It wasn't him.'

Dave glanced at the mobile display on the phone as

Jack stared the mysterious telephone number.

'Jack, it still could be him. Maybe he used an office phone or a spare for that call.'

'This number. There's something familiar in the fact that it ends treble seven. I know that I've seen it before.'

'Whoever it was there wasn't much conversation. Try to think, Jack. Who have you been talking to for such a short length of time?'

'There's no one... unless...'

Suddenly he jumped up and, crossing the room, began going through the papers in his trays, post it notes, and any messages left on his desk. He then checked the rubbish bin, while Armstrong looked on, perplexed.

'Boss, what are you looking for?'

'A telephone number. I wasn't talking with someone. They were talking to me. I think you were right the first time. I'll just ring it.'

'But, Jack you said...' His voice trailed off as Jack was already punching numbers into the desk phone.

Slade listened as the number rang. Once, twice three times. It was picked up before the fourth ring and he immediately recognised the voice on the other end.

It was Liz Harmon. She put on her best silky smooth voice. To Slade, she sounded like a snake.

'Well, Inspector Slade. Thank you for finally returning my calls. I was beginning to think that you were ignoring me.' Her friendly greeting was dripping with sarcasm. 'I was hoping that we could meet and have a chat about the Darren Wilson case. Off the record, of course. Maybe over a drink. Just name the place.'

'How does my office in twenty minutes sound?'

'Well, that's cutting it a bit fine. I was thinking more like...'

'Take it or leave it.'

There was a slight pause on the other end of the line. 'Twenty minutes it is then. I take it that...'

But Jack had already hung up.

Exactly twenty minutes later, Liz Harmon was sitting opposite Jack in his office, with Armstrong leaning against the metal filing cabinet, quietly surveying the scene.

Harmon looked across at the silent Armstrong, before turning her attention back to Jack.

'I must admit, I was hoping for a more relaxing chat over a gin and tonic. This seems a bit... formal.'

'It's not a social meeting, Miss Harmon. It's more business.'

She held Jack's eyes, trying to get some idea of what this was about. She didn't like the way events were progressing, but any nerves were well hidden. She didn't respond and waited for him to continue.

'I'll get straight to the point,' Jack said. 'What exactly is your connection with Johnny Lee?'

There was a flicker of recognition, before she slowly repeated the name, as if trying to place it.

'Johnny Lee? I can't say that it rings a bell. Now let me see...'

'Just cut the crap. We know you were in contact with him and you both exchanged numerous calls, so don't waste my time.'

'Tell me, Inspector, has this anything to do with your murder enquiry?'

'Why don't you let me be the judge of that? I don't know if you think you're playing some game here, but I can assure you that if you withhold any evidence from me that is crucial to my enquiries you won't be writing the front page story. You'll end up as part of it.'

'If... and only if I have had contact with this Johnny Lee, you know that my sources are confidential. I think you'll be hard pressed to get any conviction on that.'

'Maybe not. But I'll have a dammed good try. In the meantime, I'll make sure you're so bloody toxic that no-one in any force will so much as look in your direction, let alone talk to you. Do you honestly think that your editor will employ a crime reporter that can't report on crime?'

'Look, Inspector, I came here in good faith to talk to you about your enquiry.' She began to get up from her chair. 'If you don't want to talk then I suggest...'

'Sit down.'

The steel edge to Jack's tone was enough to find Harmon dropping back into the chair.

184

Slade turned to Armstrong, who was failing to hide his amusement. 'Sergeant, what does it say in the definition for perverting the course of justice?'

'Any act that interferes with an investigation or causes it to head in the wrong direction may tend to pervert the course of justice.'

'And what punishment does it carry.'

'A maximum of life imprisonment.'

Harmon shifted uncomfortable in the chair. 'You're bluffing.'

Jack's words were like bullets. 'Try me.'

'I think my editor might have a few stories to run if you try to go down that track.'

'He can try running them from the cell next to yours, if I think he's withholding the same evidence.'

'That'll not do your career much good,' Armstrong added, allowing himself a wry smile.

Harmon glanced across at Armstrong and back to Slade. She had gone a little pale and appeared to be considering her options.

When she spoke, her voice no longer carried the usual arrogance. 'Well, why don't we talk about a trade? I'll give you what I know and you feed me a little to keep me in my editor's good books.'

'I don't think that you're in a position to bargain. Maybe I'm not making myself clear. We believe that Johnny Lee is connected to the murder of a police officer. Lee has now done a runner. We need to speak to him. If I think you're holding back from us then that's attempting to pervert the course of justice. You'll find yourself banged up in the cells and looking at heavy time.'

'Well, suppose I do know something about Johnny Lee?'

'Then you tell us and you leave.'

Jack could see that she was about to crumble.

'Can we make a deal here?' Harmon's tone was near pleading, desperate to regain some ground.

'I've told you the deal. Tell me everything you know and you walk. That's the only deal that you're getting. You can take it or leave it.'

'I was thinking more…'

Jack moved forward, so that his face was inches from hers.

'I'm not pissing around here.' He shot a quick glance at Armstrong. 'Sergeant…'

'Yes, boss.'

'Tell the custody sergeant that we have one coming in for perverting the course of…'

'Alright! Alright. I do know Johnny Lee. He rang the paper about two months ago. Said he had a big story. Said it would rival anything in the Sunday papers.'

'Go on.'

'He was touting a claim about parties. Ones involving several young boys and important people. People with loads of cash to throw about and particular tastes to indulge in.'

'Sex parties?'

'Yes. There was mention of several young lads. Some may or may not be under age. Johnny said that he could get me names.'

'And what was he after in return?'

'What's anyone after these days?'

'Money?'

'What else? It's always money.'

'And did you oblige?'

'Silly sod believed what he'd read in the magazines about million pound payments for juicy gossip. Well, that might be with the big celeb mags, but we're talking about a provincial newspaper here. He was living in cloud cuckoo land.'

'So, with no cash on the table, what did you tell him?'

'I asked him to get me names, dates, that sort of thing. I wanted to make sure he was genuine. That it wasn't some fantasy to try to con some cash out of the paper.'

'And was he genuine?'

'Well, he said that he wouldn't be named as a source, but could point me in the right direction. I told him that we couldn't run any story without proof, so he asked what sort of proof I needed.'

'What did you tell him?'

'I told him photographs would be good. It might even get him the cash he was after. That seemed to cheer him up a bit.'

'So you strung him along.'

'I told you... I needed to know the strength of the story.'

'What happened?'

'Nothing for a few weeks. Then just over three weeks ago, he got back to me. Said he had what I wanted. Names and even some photographs. Laughed that some of them were the *not safe for work* kind.'

'How had he obtained the photographs?'

'He said he'd thought about one of those miniature hidden cameras, but the boys were all searched and he was frightened what would happen if it was found. So, the next party he attended, he managed to sneak into an office and found a memory stick in a drawer. He said he was nearly caught.'

'Have you copies of the photographs?'

'We arranged to meet. He told me about one of his contacts who procured the boys, but when I asked to see the photographs, he became very cagey. He wanted to see cash on the table first. I said I would see what I could do, but told him that the sort of money he was asking was out of the question.'

'How did he take to that?'

'How do you think? He got really pissed off. Became aggressive. Said he had taken real risks to get the photos and if they found out he would be dead. I tried to calm him down, but he went off it, saying he would go elsewhere. I tried to reason with him, but he stormed off.'

'Did you see him again?'

'I tried to ring him, but he would just hang up on me.'

'And you never heard from him again?'

'I assume that you've done your homework and checked telephone records, so you know that he rang me again.'

'To say what?'

'To say that I'd screwed him over. He was hysterical. High as a kite on smack or something. I couldn't get much sense out of him. He claimed that I'd dropped him in it and people were after him and wanted me to give him some money, so he could leave the area. He was talking nonsense.'

Jack felt anger rising like bile in the throat, but managed to keep it in check as Harmon continued her story.

'I told him that I couldn't give him any money, but asked him to meet me. He just hung up and I never heard from him again. I put it down to some drug fuelled fantasy, or maybe the whole thing was a scam. I did try ringing him... several times... but it just went to voicemail, so after a while I just gave up.'

'Why did he think that you'd screwed him over?' Armstrong asked.

Harmon shifted her gaze between the two men. 'After he stormed off, I made some enquiries of my own. I started asking around about the parties and some of the people that he had described to me. Maybe he heard, got spooked and did a runner.'

'You really think so? Or do you think that maybe someone else heard about your enquiries? Maybe that someone wasn't happy with young Johnny talking to a reporter and decided to have words with him about it. That's why he felt you'd screwed him over.'

'He talked about heading to London. Selling his story to the big papers.'

'He never ran off to London and you know it. I wouldn't be surprised if he never made it out of the North East. You pushed him into getting incriminating photographs and he lifted a memory stick with some on. Did you not think that something like that going missing wouldn't be noticed? They must have realised that it was one of the boys who had taken it. You asking around alerted them to Johnny. You used that boy and then you abandoned him. So Johnny tried to do a runner. Maybe he succeeded... but maybe he didn't.'

'What's that supposed to mean?'

'Come on! You're not that naïve. They had a leak. Leaks need to be plugged... one way or another.'

Jack let the message sink in, but doubted that the likes of Harmon would take responsibility for what may or may not have befallen Johnny Lee. To her, the story was always more important. Johnny Lee would just be collateral damage.

'No. I honestly believe he's just made himself scarce. He'll turn up when and if he gets a buyer for his story.'

'Except, I'm guessing that you were hoping to get in first. Tell me who did he say was holding these parties? And don't say he didn't give you a name. You were digging close enough to spook someone into action. Hold anything back and, if I find out that there was a chance we could have got to Johnny alive... I'll burn you.'

Harmon only hesitated for a moment. 'He told me his contact was a man called Donkin. He fixed up the boys off the street.'

Slade and Armstrong exchanged glances.

'Goes by the nickname of Weasel?' Jack asked quietly.

'That's him. Turns out all the boys for rent have had dealings with him at one time or another.'

'And who holds these... parties?'

Harmon shrugged. 'I didn't get that far up the food chain.'

Jack noticed her eyes flickered to one side. She was lying. He let it go... for now. 'Did you confront Donkin?'

'I got nowhere.'

'I take that as a yes.'

She nodded. 'He wouldn't even speak to me. Bit of a scary man, when confronted.'

'So, why don't you tell me what you're holding back?'

'I don't know what you mean.' Again, the eyes flickered.

Jack was finding it harder and harder to control his anger.

'Yes, you do. Who is the real organiser of the parties?'

Harmon sat silently. Considering her next move; weighing up what she could say and what she could hold back.

Without warning, Slade slammed his hand down on the desk, causing both Harmon and Armstrong to jump.

'Make no mistake. A young lad is in danger. It might already be too late, and the way I see it, a lot of this mess stemmed from you stirring the shit.'

'Johnny didn't give me a name. I don't think he even knew one. But, he had an app on his phone. It tracks where you've been. He had it running the night he got the photos.'

'So what did you do?'

'Before we had the bust up, we met up one night and retraced his route to a house in Northumberland. One of those rambling Georgian stone built places way out past Ponteland. We couldn't get too near to it. The entrance was blocked by big wrought iron gates and the house was well back in its own grounds.'

'So, what did you find out about the owner?'

'I checked the electoral role. It belongs to Mike Martin.'

'The property developer?'

'The very same.'

And also the owner of the property where Johnny had lived, Jack thought.

'And did you approach him?'

'With what? There was no evidence. I took the story to the editor, but without some back up there was no way he would run it and risk the paper being sued. I was told to keep on it. Firm it up. That was why we needed photographs.'

Harmon again shifted uncomfortably.

'What else are you not telling us?'

'I went back to the house myself, during the day, to get a photograph of the outside. Then if I traced any of the other young lads from the party they could identify the house. It would maybe give me some corroboration.'

'And what happened?'

'I saw cameras mounted in the trees near the gate. Infrared. I hadn't noticed them the first time because the light was fading.'

'So not only did you take Johnny back to the scene of the parties, but you probably managed to get him seen outside with you on camera.'

The gravity of the situation was starting to show on Harmon's face.

Jack kept his voice steady, even though he wanted to scream out at her stupidity. 'So, Johnny rings you up, upset and claiming you've dropped him in it. Well, you had dropped him... right in it. Then he disappears and no-one's seen him since. Well, thanks to you and your incompetent meddling we might have another murder on our hands. I hope you're bloody well pleased with yourself.'

'I couldn't have known...'

'We're talking about people here that have a lot to lose. Of course you knew. You just chose to ignore it.'

Jack needed to wrap this conversation up. He wasn't sure how much more of her presence he could take before he would completely lose his shit with her. The arrogance of this woman, who was so intent on getting her story, that she had no care for the possible ramifications for others.

Through gritted teeth, he said, 'Is there anything else that you know and are not telling us?'

'You know about as much as me. Look, I've told you all I can. I don't suppose there's a chance of an inside line on how things are progressing?'

Jack's stare was both incredulous and fuming. 'Do you not think you've done enough damage? You're lucky you're not getting dumped in the cells. My sergeant will show you out. I suggest you leave quickly before I change my mind.'

He spun his chair around to hide his overflowing fury and glared at the wall.

Armstrong straightened up and indicated to the door.

Harmon seemed about to say something, but decided against it and meekly followed Armstrong out of the room.

After a couple of minutes, Armstrong returned. 'You almost had me convinced by the perverting justice line.'

'I was tempted to do it just to wipe that smug smile off that face of hers.'

'CPS would never wear it.'

'You know it. I know it. Just so long as she didn't know it.'

'So, where do we go from here?'

Jack got up and walked to the window, where he stood for a while in silence.

'I have a bad feeling about this one, Dave. I'm convinced that things didn't work out as he planned for young Johnny.'

CHAPTER 35

Mike Martin. Property developer. At one point several years ago in the running as a possible buyer for one of the local football teams. A man on the upward curve. Before Jack went to the top brass with such a high profile suspect, he decided to do some digging of his own.

A check through the C.I. records gave him a little background.

Martin had started from humble beginnings on a Benwell estate. There was a chequered history as a juvenile, with a couple of cautions for theft recorded against him, but no convictions.

Between eighteen and twenty one there were also a number of arrests for assault... but again no convictions. It seems that the victims always dropped the charges or suddenly remembered that the offender looked nothing like Martin after all. He certainly had led a charmed life.

No-one was sure where he got his first few thousand from. His story was that it was a loan from a nameless friend who recognised his potential. Most people believed it came from some other less reputable source. There had been whispers about drugs, but once again nothing seemed to stick.

He used the money as a deposit on his first property, a run-down house in the West End of the city. After renovating and reselling it, he ploughed his profit into the next venture and continued in the same vein, living in each property as he restored them and so avoiding any Capital Gains tax.

There were still the occasional arrests for theft or violence, but nothing seemed to come to anything. It seems the victims were either frightened off by Martin's associates or bought off with cash.

As he moved up in the world, he got his hands less dirty, both with his building projects and with his meting out violence. He preferred to surround himself with friends from his old neighbourhood... people he knew and trusted. Ones who could be relied upon to do any dirty work for him.

As the business expanded, he moved into the new build sector. There were a number of whispered stories about how rival building sites would suffer losses of building materials, whereas his sites always remained untouched.

This had clearly given him an idea and he developed a side-line in building site security. Although he at first met with some resistance, it became less stressful for the other builders to invest their cash in Triple M Security Services. It appeared that those that didn't suffered more than their fair share of thefts of materials and the occasional fire.

If other builders put on their own security the thefts seemed to continue; either because the low paid guards turned a blind eye, or were intimidated until they decided to take up other employment. It was not unheard of for stubborn security guards to be followed home or meet with an accident whilst off duty.

There was never anything to link the unfortunate events to Mike Martin, but it always seemed to work to his advantage.

Before long, Triple M Security Services had most of the contracts for building sites in the Tyneside area. Those he didn't have weren't worth having.

Martin never married, but was always seen about town in the best bars and restaurants with an assortment of beautiful young women on his arm.

The house he owned in Northumberland, the one that Harmon had attended, had been quite run down when he purchased it. A former mine owner's house, it had been passed down to his daughter, a spinster, but the expensive upkeep had gradually eroded whatever inheritance she had been left. Over time, it fell into disrepair. When the old lady died, Martin made his move and was able to pick it up for a song. Using his building company, he lost no time in restoring it to former glory.

Recently, Martin had begun to dabble in local politics and there were rumours that he had considered standing as the local M.P., but the local Conservative party were wary about backing the candidacy of an unknown and were quite happy with their current choice.

Still, in a few years' time...

Martin was certainly very well connected and Jack wondered if his posh friends stopped to consider where his money came from when they attended his political soirees and helped themselves to canapés and Champagne.

Did they even care?

What Jack also wondered was whether any of his wealthy friends attended his other parties.

Now, that would be a turn up for the books.

Jack looked up as Dave entered, jacket over one arm and a wide grin spread across his face.

'There's been a further development on tracing the frequent numbers from Harmon's phone. This one should bring a smile to your face.'

'I could do with it. I've just been reading about our Mister Martin and he seems like he'll be a tough cookie to crack.'

Dave's grin did not falter. He wasn't giving up his moment of triumph. 'It seems your new best friend, Liz Harmon, has been in frequent telephone contact with a certain police officer... other than you of course.'

Jack raised his eyebrows. 'Come on then. Make me smile.'

'Chief Inspector Spence in Criminal Intelligence.'

Slade let out a humourless laugh. 'Got the bastard.'

'Not yet, but he's got some explaining to do.'

'He's definitely the leak?'

'That's who I'd put my money on. Burton obviously thinks the same and has already got him sweating up at Professional Standards. Burton may be a twat, but he has his uses. If I know him, Spence is already spilling his guts in an effort to save his pension.'

Jack managed a smile. 'Well, all that shit a couple of years ago in the Met about selling stories to the press, it's my guess that Chief Inspector Spence's New Year's resolution will be to try to stay out of prison.'

'And with her top snout out of the picture, Harmon will be spitting blood.'

'Serves her bloody right. Because of her some poor kid's on the run... or worse.'

'So, what's our next move, Jack?'

'I think we should pay a visit to Mister Martin. Let's see what he's got to say for himself.'

Armstrong frowned. 'Do you think that's a good idea, Jack?'

'Maybe not. You got a better one?

DEATH RATTLE

Armstrong let out a long sigh and pulled on his jacket.

The trip out past Ponteland took more than half an hour, before Slade and Armstrong pulled the unmarked police car up outside a large Georgian manor house set in its own grounds. It looked just as Harmon had described it.

'Wish I was a few quid behind him,' Dave said as they stopped outside two sturdy wrought iron gates.

Jack got out and approached a small intercom set to the left of the entrance. He buzzed and, after a few seconds, a voice answered.

'Who is it?'

'Detective Inspector Slade and Sergeant Armstrong to see Mister Martin. We have an appointment.'

There was a loud buzz and the whirr of machinery as the heavy gates began to swing slowly open.

Jack returned to the vehicle and Armstrong negotiated the tree lined driveway up to a large turning circle in front of the house. A curved set of steps led up to a large portico, supported by two Doric columns either side of a double width entrance door.

As they approached the door, it was opened by a smartly dressed man in a dark suit, who looked to be in his early twenties. 'Mister Martin is expecting you both. Please come in.'

Slade got the distinct impression that this ostentatious display of ceremony was for their benefit and designed to put them ill at ease. If he was totally honest, it was having the desired effect. Money can buy you lots of friends and, if the rich furnishings around him were anything to go by, Martin certainly had plenty to throw around.

They were shown through to a large room, decorated with reproductions of classical art and decked out with a mixture of antique and modern furnishings.

Seated on a plush sofa was Martin, who Jack immediately recognised from photographs he had researched in the archives.

Mike Martin was in his fifties, but there was no sign of the middle-age spread that usually accompanies men of that age when they have the money to afford rich food and expensive drink. He was tanned and gym-fit.

When he smiled, he displayed even white teeth that a Hollywood actor would be proud of. He looked like the epitome of a successful entrepreneur. The only things that hinted at his tough upbringing was a two-inch scar on his left cheek and the cold eyes. Despite the laughter lines around them, they had a dark depth that seemed to bore their way into you.

Martin stood up to greet them and appeared every inch the affable host. 'Please take a seat. Can I get you a drink... or is it the old *not while I'm on duty* line?'

Jack nodded towards Armstrong. 'He's driving. He'll have a coke. I'll have a malt if you have it. No ice.'

'I have a very nice aged Jura if that would suit.'

'That sounds very nice.'

Martin nodded to the hired help, who disappeared, returning a few seconds later with two drinks. Jack took the glass of whisky with a smile.

Armstrong seemed considerably less impressed with his coke.

'So, how can I help you, Inspector Slade?'

'We're making some enquiries into a missing person and are hoping that you may be able to assist,' Jack said, studying the man opposite him for any reaction.

Martin smiled and gave a short nod for Slade to continue.

'His name is Johnny Lee. Do you know him?'

'I can't say the name rings a bell. Is there some reason I should know this... Johnny Lee?'

'We believe he may have attended a number of parties at your home.'

If Martin was rattled he gave no indication. 'Well... it's possible. I host a lot of parties. I'm a businessman. They're mainly corporate functions; it comes with the territory. Networking, and all that.'

'I don't think Johnny Lee was connected to business.'

'Was he employed as catering staff? If so, I'm afraid that I wouldn't have a clue. I leave all that to my P.A. He will of course have kept records of catering companies used, but I wouldn't think that he will have details of individual employees. Besides, I believe many of these companies bring in help on an ad-hoc basis.'

'Our information is that he was a guest at a private party.'

Martin looked thoughtful, but shook his head.

'I'd love to help, but the name means nothing. Guests bring friends or partners and I don't always know everyone who attends. You know how it is at these things.'

'No. I don't, please tell me.'

'Mister Slade, I'm…'

'It's Inspector Slade.'

'Sorry, Inspector Slade, I'm beginning to think that I'm supposed to be connected to this Johnny Lee character. Now, I don't know what, if anything, this man may or may not have done to bring him to the attention of the police, but I can assure you that I know nothing about it.'

'We believe that he attended a party at your home on or about 25th of November. Can you confirm that you held a party on that date?'

'I can check my diary and will certainly get back to you, but as I've already stated I wouldn't be able to confirm whether your young man attended.'

'Could you give us details of any people that attended?'

'Look… Inspector Slade, I don't know what this is about, but I certainly would not want my guests to be upset. It could be bad for my business. Now, of course I want to assist you, but I'm unsure of what exactly your agenda is.'

'There's no agenda. As I said, just an enquiry into a missing person.'

'Inspector, this has been very interesting and I'm sorry if I haven't been able to assist you. I will speak to my guests and see if they're able to provide you with anything else, but I'm not prepared to give out personal information to you in some kind of fishing exercise. Now, if you'll excuse me, I do have an important video conference that I must attend. My assistant will show you out.'

Martin stood and held out his hand.

The two detectives got to their feet. Armstrong shook the outstretched hand, but Jack was already heading for the door.

Dave followed his boss outside onto the gravelled driveway and unlocked the car. As he got in, Jack paused and looked back at the imposing house.

Dave followed his gaze. 'He's come a long way from a petty thief to lord of the manor, hasn't he?'

'He has that,' Jack said, climbing in. 'But no matter how much you polish a turd it's still just shit underneath.'

Armstrong started the ignition and headed towards the electric gates that had already been opened to usher them out.

'I don't think we achieved much there,' Dave muttered, glancing out at the fields and hedgerows, covered with a sprinkling of snow, as he accelerated along the narrow country roads, past the old police headquarters and towards Ponteland village.

'Oh, I don't know,' Jack said. 'He confirmed he had a party around about the time Johnny went missing. He was very evasive when I asked for a list of the other guests and he didn't deny outright that Johnny was there.'

Jack glanced across at his friend and smiled. 'And more importantly, he referred to Johnny as *your young man*. I don't recall mentioning his age. Did you?'

DEATH RATTLE

CHAPTER 36

Back at the nick, Jack was trawling through the records for any associates of Mike Martin, anxious to find someone or something to link him to any other of the players in the enquiry.

So far, he had drawn a blank. It was interesting that Triple M Development owned the property where Johnny had been living, but that was easily explained as a coincidence; the company owned property all over the city.

What he had really been hoping for was to find a link between Martin and Donkin, but despite all his digging there was nothing to be found. Whilst Jack was going through the records he received a call from Jamie.

'I just wanted to give you the heads up. Last night your pal Harmon was doing the rounds of all the bars on the scene again and asking a lot of questions.'

Doesn't she ever give up? Slade thought.

'She was particularly interested in anything the police were asking to do with missing persons and whether anyone knew boys who had suddenly disappeared. She was also mentioning Johnny Lee and asking who he usually hung around with.'

It was inevitable after their conversation that Harmon would now be aware of the significance of Johnny Lee in the enquiry.

The afternoon's edition of the local newspaper had the murder back on the front page again, but this time hinting strongly that the investigation was floundering. It stopped short of old clichés like 'the police are baffled', but the implications was all there.

It was clear from the latest article that Harmon was putting some store in the hunt for any other missing persons, but so far there was no indication that she had turned up details of any. Slade was relieved to see that there was no mention of the missing Dean Masters. The only other consolation was that Harmon was also going to struggle for any inside information now that her source, Spence, was on gardening leave, pending an internal enquiry.

Of course, it wasn't only the reporter struggling, and

Jack's mood wasn't about to improve when shortly afterwards his door opened and Superintendent Parker entered.

'Have you seen the latest garbage from that bloody crime reporter?'

'Well, at least we now know who her source was,' Slade said.

'Aye. Well, Burton turned the heat up on Spence and he's spilling his guts. He's admitted giving information to Harmon, but denies that any money changed hands. He's given us access to his bank accounts and there's no evidence of any unauthorised deposits, so he may be telling the truth.' Parker loudly cleared his throat. 'Looks like he was getting paid in other ways.'

'He was screwing her?'

Parker nodded.

Jack let out a snort. 'You'd have to pay me to screw that dragon. Spence must be crapping himself. He could be looking at time for this.'

'I'm not so sure. Because no cash changed hands, it may be that Command Block just want the whole thing to go away. No bad publicity. A quick early retirement and everything hushed up.'

Parker waved his hand. 'Anyway, what about the Wilson murder? Any new leads?

Come to all the bloody briefings and you would be up to speed, thought Slade, but said, 'We've had uniforms down the bars asking about any missing persons that suddenly disappeared from the scene but, to be honest, the way things work people come and go all the time and it's just too hard to keep track of anyone. One of the lads is going through records of historic missing persons who fit the profile, but there's not much to go on and there's nothing turned up about Dean Masters.'

'So, more brick walls?'

'Well, at least by doing the enquiries we're ahead of the curve. Imagine the press coverage if Harmon had uncovered about the missing boys before us. I don't suppose HQ would be so happy with those headlines.'

Parker grunted, but reluctantly agreed.

DEATH RATTLE

In the street outside Drew's home, Jack noticed a build up of litter, cans and broken bottles in the gutters. It seemed that even the council road sweepers might avoid this area.

Getting out of the unmarked car, Jack took out a leather document case and walked up to the door to the flat, knocking sharply. A greying net curtain to the upstairs bay window fluttered and Jack spotted the nervous face of Drew peering out. He gave him what he hoped was his most reassuring smile and waited.

A couple of minutes later, the door opened, but there was no greeting and Drew turned and walked back up the steep staircase to his lounge. Jack followed in silence.

Drew dropped down onto a faux leather settee, avoiding eye contact with Slade.

It was Jack who broke the silence. 'How've you been?'

'I've been better.'

As Jack sat down on a chair opposite, he could feel the resentment in Drew's voice. He was clearly still smarting from having been forced to attend Forth Banks nick to give his statement.

'I'm sorry that you got dragged down to the station, but believe me, if I could have avoided it I would.'

Drew looked across at him, but simply shrugged without replying.

'I know this must be hard for you, but...'

'Do you? I keep expecting Darren to walk through the door smiling, but it isn't going to happen.'

His voice trailed off and he stared down into his lap, lost.

Jack had no choice but to press on. 'I need you to look at a photograph. Tell me if you recognise someone.'

Drew did not reply or look up, so Jack removed a large photograph from the case and held it out under Drew's gaze.

It was the old photograph from the C.I.S. records of William Donkin.

The young man sighed then took the photo. He studied it for a time, before saying, 'I don't think I've seen him before.' He looked up at Jack. 'Does he have something to do with Darren's murder?'

'I honestly don't know. We're just covering bases here. To be honest, we still have no idea why anyone should have targeted Darren or even if he was targeted. This still could be just a random mugging gone wrong, in which case, it will be even more difficult to solve.'

Drew nodded slowly and handed the photograph back to Jack. 'So you're saying that you might never find out who killed Darren?'

Slade didn't respond and just stared at the photo.

Drew had just voiced what many of the cops working on the investigation were starting to believe.

Dave Armstrong was walking towards the incident room, carrying a stack of printouts, when he spotted Jack appear at the top of the stairs. He caught his eye and nodded towards the papers.

'Boss, I think we may have found the connection that we've been looking for. Although there's no direct link between Donkin and Martin, I dug a bit further and have found something. Remember Neil Allen, the car dealer that Donkin ran to after we interviewed him?'

'The one with the dealership in Byker?'

'That's the one. Would you like to guess which property developer owns the lease to the building where Neil Allen has his garage based?'

'Mike Martin?'

'Give that man a coconut.'

'A bit of a tenuous link, but a start.'

'Do you think we should pay Mister Allen another visit?'

'It's tempting, but I think we should keep our powder dry on this one. Neil Allen hasn't got a clue that we're interested in him or that we have any inkling of his link to Donkin. Let's keep it that way for now.'

Jack's phone began to ring and, answering it, he heard the voice of the front office receptionist.

'Inspector, I have a call for you. He's given his name as Drew Sterling. He says that it's urgent.'

'OK. Put him through.'

Drew's voice was trembling and his words tumbled out almost incoherently. He was teetering on hysteria and it took Slade some time to calm him down.

'Just take your time. You're alright. Just slow down and tell me what's wrong.'

'That man you showed me. The one in the photograph. I've seen him. Today. He was outside my flat.'

Twenty minutes later, Jack was sitting in Drew's front room, whilst Dave stood by the window, listening, and occasionally glancing out at the street from behind the blinds.

'You're sure it was him?' Slade asked. 'You couldn't be mistaken?'

'It was him. I recognised him. He looked a little older than the photograph, but it was definitely him.'

'There's no way that he could know about this flat or about you.'

'Maybe he knows Johnny stopped here. Maybe he's looking for him, just like you. Do you think it was him who broke in?'

Slade had considered the possibility. Burglary was not beyond the Weasel, but why would he risk coming to the flat and being seen, when he knew that he was already a suspect and firmly in their sights? Was it an act of desperation, worried that Drew knew something that would lead back to him?

On the way over, Armstrong had suggested that the most obvious explanation was that Drew was mistaken. He had seen someone who looked like the photograph and became so spooked that he convinced himself it was Donkin. Or maybe it was just the actions of someone who was lonely and grieving?

Jack hadn't been so sure. But now that he had seen the look in Drew's eyes, he had no doubt that his witness was convinced that he had seen Donkin.

'Listen, I don't want to take any chances. I'm arranging for an alarm to be fitted in your flat. It's a panic switch and links directly back to the Control Room. Set it off and uniformed officers will be here within minutes.'

Although Drew was clearly terrified, the stark reality was that there was nowhere else for him to go. He would have to take what Jack was offering and make the most of it. It wasn't like on the television where the police would allocate a personal guard for your property or put you up in a safe house. In the real world, it was monetary cost that dictated much of police procedure. An alarm was the cheapest option.

As an additional measure to reassure him, Jack gave Drew his mobile number and told him to phone if he saw the man again.

There was nothing else to be done, so to calm Drew down, the two detectives waited with him until a SOCO specialist turned up with the panic alarm, and then left him with the officer as he explained to Drew how the system worked.

As Jack slid the key into the ignition, Armstrong asked, 'You don't think he's making it up... do you?'

'I'm certain that he's not. Donkin was there outside the flat.'

'Why so sure?'

'Drew said that it was the man in the photograph... only a bit older. I didn't tell him that the photo was five years old.'

DEATH RATTLE

CHAPTER 37

As they headed back to the city, they went over the recent events.

'Look, Jack, we both know that we can't put surveillance on Donkin twenty four hours a day. There's no way that the superintendent would give that authority on what we have and, either way, HQ wouldn't wear the cost. You seem to have more faith in the kid than I do, but I'm worried he's just getting a bit paranoid.'

Slade gripped the wheel and accelerated past a slow moving car, before cutting back in a little too sharply. Dave observed the manoeuvre, but did not comment.

'It's Donkin who's spooked,' Jack said. 'He's after something and believes that Drew has it. Whoever turned over the flat last week was looking for something. If he went back it's 'cause he hasn't got it yet.'

'If Johnny was telling Harmon the truth then *it* has got to be the memory stick with photographs on.'

'So, who is on the photographs and where did Johnny hide the memory stick?'

'Maybe they've already got them.'

'So, why keep going back to Drew's?'

'Frighten him? Keep him quiet?'

They sat for a while in silence, each lost in thought, until Armstrong finally spoke up. 'We're just guessing at the moment, Jack. The only one who seems to know is Donkin and I'm not convinced that it was him at the flat.'

'So, let's go and ask him,' Slade said evenly.

'Who? Donkin?'

'Why not?'

'I can think of plenty of reasons. Complaint forms for harassment being top of the list.'

'My dad used to say it was only coppers that were doing the job properly who got complaints,' Jack said and, instead of turning towards Forth Bank, headed for the Central Motorway East, where he picked up the signs for Jesmond. Ten minutes later they were outside Donkin's address and Slade was banging loudly on the door with his open hand.

An upstairs window flew open and the thin face of

Donkin looked down at them. 'What do you want?'

'We want to know what you were doing earlier today in Benwell,' Jack shouted up at him.

'I don't know what you're on about. I've been here all day. My brief says that I don't have to talk to you, so why don't you just fuck off and leave me alone?'

'You wouldn't like to come down here and repeat that would you, Mister Donkin?'

'This is fucking harassment.'

'If I find out that you were involved in harming Johnny Lee in any way, I'll not harass you... I'll fucking haunt you.'

'You'll be hearing from my brief,' Donkin yelled, before slamming down the sash of the window.

Jack turned and made his way back to the car, with Dave hurrying to keep up behind him.

'What was the point of that? All we've achieved there is a probable complaint. You saw what that brief, Thompson, was like. I think you made a mistake there, Jack.'

'Maybe,' Slade said, without breaking step. 'But, he knows now that he was seen, so maybe he'll be a little less anxious to go back again to Drew's.'

Back at the station, they went through into the late briefing and discussed the actions for the day and the results of the enquiries.

The detective who had been probing the disappearance of Dean Masters had managed to trace the barman who had reported him missing, and two officers had been to see him at his home address.

Mark Little was in his late twenties, medium build, with short dyed blonde hair in a crew cut. Initially, he had seemed quite nervous to be questioned by the detectives, but once convinced that it was not some homophobic witch hunt, but genuine concern for his former flat mate, he had been more forthcoming.

Little told them he had been sharing a flat with Dean at the time of his disappearance and, although not partners, when pressed he admitted that they had been in a casual sexual relationship. One night, Masters had left work after his shift and was never seen again.

After a couple of days, convinced something had happened to him, Little had contacted the police to report his flatmate missing.

Jack listened in silence to the detective's update and when he had finished, asked him, 'Why didn't he report him missing straight away?'

'It wasn't the first time Dean had been on a bender or got fixed up with some other young guy and stayed away for a few days.'

Dean's personal belongings had been boxed up, but he never came back for them. They were still at the flat, so the detectives had collected them and took them back to the nick, where they prepared a full inventory, before entering the items into the exhibits book.

There was nothing in them to shed any light on what had happened to Masters.

Jack wondered if Mark Little himself could have had anything to do with Dean having gone missing, but the detectives didn't believe so. Slade accepted their judgement.

Nodding, Jack said, 'OK, but still check him out fully. Any convictions. Any suggestion of violence. If you haven't already done it then let's have a full I.S. search on historic intelligence. We need to cover all bases.'

It seemed as if both Johnny Lee and Dean Masters had simply vanished without trace.

Later, when the briefing was over, Jack was making his way to his office when T.C.P. appeared. His face was red and he seemed about to burst.

'Jack... my office. Now!'

Jack followed Parker into his office and had hardly closed the door before he exploded.

'I've had that solicitor, Thompson, on. He's wanting to make an official complaint that you've been harassing his client, despite the other day being told specifically not to approach him.'

If anything, T.C.P. was a deeper shade of purple than normal. Jack wondered when he'd last had his blood pressure checked.

'Donkin claims you've been to his house, making

allegations and embarrassing him in front of his neighbours. He says you actually told him you were going to harass him.'

'Haunt him.'

'What?'

'Haunt him. I said I would haunt him.'

Parker fixed Slade with what he considered his hardest stare. A vein pulsed on the side of his head.

'If you're taking the piss you'd better change your attitude. This enquiry is being scrutinised from the very top. Some people have already suggested you may be out of your depth.'

I'm willing to bet that Mister Burton will be somewhere on that list.

'Well, Donkin's solicitor is coming in today with his client to make an official complaint, alleging harassment and abuse of authority concerning your threats.' Parker gulped in a breath. 'It's being suggested that your conduct is based on homophobia and a deep rooted hatred of gay people.'

'That's bollocks,' Jack snapped, raising his voice for the first time.

'Donkin is claiming that you began harassing him in a café next to the gay bars in the city.'

'This is a load of crap. He's shitting himself and trying to put us off track.'

'Is he telling the truth? Were you out at night around the gay bars?'

'I was making some enquiries in relation to possible missing boys.'

'I don't recall you mentioning these enquiries. Are they recorded in your pocket book?'

'They didn't come to anything.'

'So why were you down there on your own? Is he telling the truth about you stopping him at this café and harassing him about being gay?'

'No, I did not harass him about being gay.'

'But you were at this café at night. Jesus Christ, Jack! The last time you went off piste making your own enquiries in town, some teenager ended up in hospital with melon sized bollocks. Was this even a part of the enquiry? Was it actioned? Was it authorised?'

Parker sank back into his chair, gasping for breath.

'I've got Headquarters breathing down my neck, not to mention the press and that bitch, Harmon, ringing up every day, and you're going around like some maverick. What the fuck is going on here?'

'I was out for the night and saw him with a young runaway, so spoke to him.'

'And you often spend your nights drinking in late night gay cafes do you? You're playing with fire, Jack, and if you start to burn don't expect me to be on hand with the fucking extinguisher. As of now, Donkin is off limits. If anyone does need to speak with him, it will only be with my say so... and it will not be you who does it. Do I make myself clear?'

'Perfectly.'

'So, get on with what you're being paid to do and no more unauthorised visits to bars, cafes or anywhere else for that matter. We're two weeks into the investigation and there's no sign of any real suspect. Just vague connections to queers and pimps and, to be honest, everything you've uncovered so far just seems to put the organisation in a bad light.'

'I didn't realise that this was about protecting the force's reputation. I thought it was about finding a killer.'

The vein began pulsing in Parker's neck again. 'You're skating on thin ice, Jack. Unless you have something solid, keep away from Donkin.'

'Come on, boss. Donkin's a piece of shit and he's up to his neck in this enquiry. This is his way of getting us off his back.'

'Well, it's worked. Thompson's been on direct to Professional Standards. You're to stay away from him. No-one goes near him without my say so. Got it?'

'Donkin knows a lot more than he's telling.'

'You're not listening, Jack. This isn't just from me. It's direct from Command Block. It's a done deal.'

The phone on Parker's desk began to ring and he swiped it up, barking, 'Yes?'

As Slade turned to leave, Parker called after him, 'Just for once take the gypsies warning, Jack. You're not irreplaceable.'

Yet another clue that he was being set up to be the fall guy when the proverbial hit the fan.

Parker put his hand over the receiver and added, 'And I

want a report on my desk in an hour, covering what you were doing in the bars that night.'

Jack slammed the door behind him.

Once outside, Jack reflected on the latest turn of events. What he'd done was intended to spook Donkin and the threat of a complaint was always to be expected. Screaming harassment is often the first port of call for a villain under pressure. But his enquiries had been legitimate. Donkin was a lead and it seemed obvious to Jack that the gay scene was part of the investigation.

Jack couldn't help but feel that Parker's reaction was a little over the top.

There was no doubt that Parker was under pressure to get a result on the Darren Wilson murder, but the more Jack's hands were tied, the less likely a positive result would be forthcoming.

Slade's thoughts turned to the photographs. The boy that he had met at MESMAC had suggested that there were important people at the party. Could one of those people be a Police Superintendent? Did Parker have a personal interest in the enquiry? Slade recalled that Parker had been at the crime scene pretty damn quickly.

Stop it, Jack. You're starting to get paranoid.
And yet...

DEATH RATTLE

CHAPTER 38

Before Jack packed up for the evening, he checked through his in tray, which only ever seemed to get deeper. With a sigh, he stood up to leave, when he received a call from the front office.

'Sorry, sir, but a message came in about an hour ago. You were in with the Superintendent. It was just to inform you of an alarm call to an address that you were interested in.'

The alarm had been activated at Drew's flat, but although officers attended within a couple of minutes there had been nothing to see. Jack picked up his radio and, by inputting the officer's collar number, was able to speak directly to him for an update. He was told that Drew had claimed again to see the man from the photograph, hanging around outside. An immediate search of the area had turned up nothing.

The uniform cop at the scene thought that Drew appeared genuine, and had obviously seen something that had frightened him, but they thought there was a strong possibility that he was just spooked.

Slade tried to work out the timing. Donkin could have had time to drive over to Drew's flat and have been seen outside. But why? To spook him into leaving the flat? Would Donkin be so brazen as to do so after being warned off?

If he had, he was cool as a bloody cucumber. Or maybe he knew that Slade was about to have his wings clipped.

Slade thought again about Parker.

Either way, any repeat visit to Donkin was now a non-starter. The desk officer in the front office had tipped Slade off that Donkin and his solicitor were downstairs at that very minute, speaking with a uniform inspector and filing a complaint of harassment.

Jack could be a bit gung-ho at times, but he wasn't stupid.

He decided to drive across town to speak to Drew and check things out for himself. Armstrong was out on an enquiry in the unmarked car, so Jack grabbed the keys for his BMW and made for the door.

Twenty minutes later, and for the third time that day, he

found himself outside the flat. He was careful to manoeuvre around all the broken glass.

The uniform cops had left long before he arrived and, when Slade knocked at the door, he saw the upstairs curtains twitch. The door opened with palpable trepidation.

Drew was pacing and trembling and Jack had a great deal of difficulty in persuading him that the alarm would keep him safe. Jack suspected that the frightened youth could possibly be mistaken on this occasion. He kept thinking that even Donkin wasn't so foolish as to make a repeat visit so soon.

Unless he was ordered to?

Drew was more concerned with the police response to the alarm.

'It took them ages to get here,' Drew said, his voice cracking. 'What if he got in the flat? Who the hell is he and what does he want from me?'

Slade had checked the computer log and knew that it had only been two minutes between the alarm activation and officers attending the scene. To Drew, it had seemed like hours.

If Drew was right in his identification, and Jack still wasn't convinced this time, why did Donkin keep coming back? Did the photographs Johnny claimed he had taken really exist? If so, then obviously he was looking for the memory stick or any copies of the contents. An extensive search of the flat had turned up nothing.

He again pressed Drew as to whether Johnny had left anything with him, but Drew was adamant that there was nothing and, reluctantly, Jack believed him.

'Did Johnny mention anything about any photographs?'

'No. What photographs?' Drew asked, clearly confused.

Jack was convinced that Drew knew nothing further, but was equally concerned that he was at risk. Whoever was after the photographs might not be so easily convinced that Drew knew nothing about them.

Slade pulled out his mobile and rang through to Parker's office extension. It was answered on the second ring. Jack was clearly the last person Parker wanted to speak to.

'That solicitor has just left. I have some complaint

forms to serve on you.'

Slade changed the subject, briefly explaining the circumstances and stressing that there had possibility been a further visit from Donkin.

'You don't sound too convinced, Jack. It's more likely the kid's just being paranoid. Either way, you stay away from Donkin. You're already up to your neck in shit.'

'Well, what about leaving a cop here with the lad? If Donkin does come back, we can nick him.'

'A cop to stop with him? For how long? And whose budget will that come out of? Uniform are stretched as it is with all the cutbacks, and strange as it seems, I don't get allocated a fucking babysitting budget. Get the alarm reset and tell him we'll get the local panda car to keep an eye out.'

'That's not going to be good enough. I think that if we leave him he's going to do a runner.'

'Well that's all you've got. Take it or leave it.' With that, he hung up.

Slade turned to Drew, who was clearly on the verge of breaking down. The past couple of weeks had taken their toll and Jack wondered if Drew would ever be able to put these events behind him.

He was deeply concerned for the lad's welfare, but the professional side of him was even more concerned about losing his witness. If he couldn't secure somewhere safe for Drew, he was sure that he would end up just making a bolt for it. He had to keep him on side. Slade was convinced that Drew was a key part of the investigation.

'Have you anywhere else you could go? Family? Friends? Just for a couple of nights.'

'I don't have any family and most of my friends are in bedsits or small flats,' he replied, sullenly. 'You said I would be safe.'

'Look, I should take another statement from you. Let's get the alarm reset and head down to the nick. We'll get you a coffee and try to sort out some friend that you can stay with, even if it's just one night. Uniform patrols will keep an eye on your flat.'

Out of being left along in his flat, spending some time at a police station was the lesser of two evils for Drew, so he reluctantly agreed and headed out with Jack to his car.

The drive in to the city was quiet, with both lost in their own thoughts concerning the recent events and Jack turning over in his mind what his next move should be.

Glancing across at Drew, Jack could see that he was still trembling and that his eyes were watery. He had calmed down a little, but he was still clearly terrified.

There were many times in life, when faced with difficult decisions, Slade knew that to take one direction was the right move and would keep him on track. This was the less complicated route... the safe, well-worn path. Usually, self-preservation dictated that this was the way that caused him the least grief.

But Jack knew that there were other times when he chose to follow his heart and not his head. Times when, as Parker put it, he would veer off piste. And do what his colleagues would warn him was likely to bring a shit storm down on his head.

Yet his gut would tell him that was the way to go. Jump and be damned. Jack usually knew the right move to make. But, on far too many occasions, he did the exact opposite.

This was one of those times, and a voice in his head was screaming at him not to do it.

There was something that kept nagging Jack. Every time he made *the right move,* Donkin, or whoever he worked for, were always one step ahead.

There was something else. Drew hadn't had any problems with Donkin *until* he had told Jack about Johnny's overnight visit to his flat.

The burglary at Drew's flat could have been a simple one off. After all, for some of the kids in the West End, committing burglary was as natural as puberty. A coming of age ritual. However, it was a bit of a coincidence that it happened at the very time Drew was at the station giving a statement.

Over the years, Jack had grown cynical about coincidences. They made him uneasy.

All these thoughts were flashing through his mind as he approached the turn off for Forth banks. Jack knew that he was literally at a crossroads. Turn right and he would be at the nick and Drew would be someone else's problem for a time.

To carry on ahead would take him to the Tyne Bridge,

214

the south side of the river and towards his own apartment.

He glanced across at Drew, ashen, and tried to imagine the fear that the lad was experiencing.

The traffic cleared.

He carried on straight ahead towards the Tyne Bridge and calmly explained to Drew his plan.

At first Drew was wary and suspicious about Slade's suggestion. But he certainly didn't want to return alone to his flat and, with nowhere else to go, his options were limited.

Jack suggested that he could stay at his Quayside apartment overnight and then, in the morning, he would ring around and try to find a friend of Drew's with whom he could stay for a few days, until they could come up with somewhere more secure.

Jack radioed in to book off duty and informed control that Drew had left his flat to stop with a friend, but could be contacted through him if required. That was enough to satisfy the radio despatcher.

Pulling up outside the apartment block, Jack guided Drew to the entrance and they took the lift to the seventh floor.

Showing Drew into the lounge, Jack telephoned out for a couple of pizzas and, when the take-away food eventually arrived, both tucked in. Although Jack was famished after a long day, Drew only managed about half his of his meal, slowly picking over it over a couple of hours.

Fixed up with a spare toothbrush and towel, Drew was shown to the spare room and, as he scanned his new surroundings, Slade assured him that the next day he would find somewhere safe where no one could harm him.

Drew went off to his room and Jack returned to the lounge, where he fixed himself a large Glenmorangie. Unable to settle down, he lay back on the couch and mulled over everything that had happened. Things that already seemed to have been moving fast now appeared to be charging ahead at a steadily increasing pace.

There were still many worrying questions to be answered.

Soon, the malt whisky began to take effect, his eyes became heavy and, still fully dressed, Slade fell into a restless sleep.

215

CHAPTER 39

The following morning, Jack awoke with a start. It took a few seconds to recall why he was asleep in his front room. Mulling over the events of the previous night, he went into the kitchen and set the filter coffee machine away, before having a hot shower.

A couple of strong coffees later and suitably refreshed, he tapped lightly on the door of the spare room and a dishevelled Drew emerged still fully dressed. Jack guessed that he had lain on top of the bed and he didn't look like he'd had much sleep. While Drew showered, Slade fixed a light breakfast of scrambled eggs on toast for his unexpected house guest and himself.

When Drew re-appeared, he looked a little more refreshed. He also seemed a little calmer. Drew claimed that he wasn't hungry, but Jack insisted, and despite what he had asserted, he managed to clear his plate.

Since first awakening, Jack had gone over the situation a hundred times in his head and believed that he had formulated a strategy to keep Drew safe. It was obvious that even with the police alarm, there was no way that Drew was going to agree to return to his own flat.

Although Drew was a crucial witness, Detective Superintendent Parker remained unconvinced that he was in any danger, and had made it very clear that the force was not going to foot the bill for putting him into protective custody. There was no way Jack could risk his witness doing a runner… or worse, falling into Donkin's hands.

Although far from ideal, Jack proposed that until he could think of somewhere else, Drew should stay at his flat for a few days. If he was able to come up with somewhere else, preferably out of the city, then Slade would arrange for his transport, and a new attack alarm could be fitted wherever he ended up.

Jack was well aware that he was embarking upon a risky proposal, but felt, in the present situation, that he was the only one who believed that the young man was truly in danger. The decision was to keep Drew's location to himself until he could convince those leading the enquiry that their witness was at risk.

It may be that Jack himself was becoming paranoid, but it concerned him that he was always lagging behind in the enquiry. Maybe it was time to start playing his cards closer to his chest.

It was certain that if T.C.P. found out what he was doing then it would make life very difficult for Jack and, with Burton hanging around like some dark suited vulture, he didn't want to risk it.

He glanced up at the humorous quotation hanging on his kitchen wall.

Semper in merda sum; solo altitudo variat.
I'm always in the shit. It's only the depth that varies.

After breakfast, Jack explained his plan to Drew.

'Will you be stopping here with me?' Drew asked, hesitantly.

'You know that's not possible. I need to go into work today but you'll be safe here for a few days. No-one will be looking for you here. There's everything you need and I'm just at the other end of a phone. I'll get a couple of T shirts and joggers from my room. Put the clothes you have through the washing machine today and if all's quiet tomorrow we can head back to your place and get yourself a change of clothes.'

Drew seemed uncertain, but it was far more preferable to returning to his own flat. Reluctantly, he agreed to Jack's scheme. After breakfast, leaving Drew alone in the flat, Jack headed into work and the morning briefing.

T.C.P. did not attend because he was at headquarters, but the word was that he intended coming back for mid-day, for a chat with Jack.

The morning passed uneventfully, with Jack sorting through any urgent paperwork and checking through the results of the previous day's actions.

Mark Little, the flat mate of the missing Dean Masters, had now been eliminated from enquiries into the Wilson murder. He had been on a week break in Blackpool at the time of the death and this had been confirmed through hotel records and CCTV. He was, however, still on the back burner as a suspect for his old flat mate until Dean finally surfaced.

If he ever did.

A copy of the paper based missing person report for

Masters had been obtained from the archives and copies made of the attached photograph. It showed an eighteen year, clean shaven boy with dark hair, blue eyes and a cheeky grin. There were no tattoos, but under marks/scars was noted, 'chocolate coloured birthmark below the left nipple'.

A number of other missing persons who fitted the profile had been identified. All were male, of teen age or early twenties and a few had links to the gay scene… although some were more tenuous than others. Several were clearly street wise and had previously had contacts with the police.

In addition, a detective had been allocated to make enquires with the various internet groups who liaise between people who have chosen to make a new life and the relatives that they had left behind. So far that had also drawn a blank.

Jack tried to contact Jamie, but he was out of town in meetings all day. The person he spoke to at MESMAC said that he would be back in the office the next day.

Just after mid-day, Jack was summoned to see Parker in his office and served with his complaint forms. The allegations were of harassment and abuse of authority. Jack was left in no doubt that any further contact with Donkin was prohibited.

Jack took the pale blue coloured forms and left with dire warnings ringing in his ears.

Returning to his desk, Jack started on yet another pile of paperwork when, after only ten minutes, he was disturbed by a knock on the door and Armstrong entered.

'You got served your Bluies, I see.'

Bluies, was the slang term used by cops for complaint notification forms, which had traditionally been printed on blue paper.

'Shit happens.' Jack said. 'I guess you didn't get any.'

'A privilege of your rank, Jack,' Armstrong said, smiling. 'The bosses obviously consider that I was just along for the ride. Besides, it's you who seems to have got under Donkin's skin.'

'I'm still convinced that slimy bastard is one of the main players in our enquiry.'

'Well, it looks like they've given him a get out of jail free card.'

'For now,' Slade said, quietly.

That afternoon, after what had seemed a long and fruitless day, Slade headed home. As he entered the apartment, his nostrils noted some pleasant cooking smells. Drew was busying himself in the kitchen over a couple of pans on the hobs.

Jack opened a bottle of red from the wine rack and they ate a spaghetti bolognaise. Although the sauce was clearly a jar from his cupboard, the meal was tasty and most welcome, and Jack was reminded that food always tastes nicer when someone else cooks it.

Something that had been missing in Jack's life for a while. Following dinner, Jack clicked on the television and began channel hopping, trying to find something that would take Drew's mind off his current situation. He had little success.

Admitting defeat, Jack made small talk, quizzing Drew about his life, family and his relationship with Darren Wilson.

It was clear that they had been a very close couple and Darren's death was not something Drew would easily put behind him. There were no words of consolation that Jack could find to say, so he changed the subject, talking about anything that came to mind... except the murder.

When eventually they had headed off to their beds, Jack lay on his bed, with the last glass of wine from the bottle resting on his chest. As he ran through events, he thought he could hear soft crying from the spare room.

Early the following morning, showered and ready to face the day, Jack took Drew out to the car. There was a good hour before he was due at the briefing, which gave him ample time to drive across to Drew's flat, stock up on a few changes of clothes, drop him back off at the apartment and still make it into work on time.

They had considered Drew staying and Jack going alone, but that would've taken up too much time. Drew knew exactly what he needed and where it would be.

As they crossed the car park, neither had noticed the dark shape standing in the shadows beside the Millenium Bridge. They didn't see the figure raise the lens and point it in their direction, whilst carefully adjusting the focus on the zoom.

They didn't hear the rapid click click click of the camera as multiple photos recorded them leaving the flat and climbing into the car.

Nor did they see the face of Liz Harmon, as she lowered the camera and allowed herself a self-satisfied smile.

With Slade still not returning her calls, she had arrived early, hoping to doorstep him and see if he was more amenable when not at the station. She hadn't expected this.

Depending on who the young man was, it might prove a better story altogether.

CHAPTER 40

Jack had an uneasy feeling as he pulled out of the car park. Call it that gut instinct again. Call it a sixth sense. He couldn't put his finger on it, but decided to act on it just the same.

Instead of taking the Central Motorway after crossing the river, he took a left and drove into the town centre. With one eye on the rear view mirror, he took the one way system around past Central Station, all the time heading west towards Benwell and Drew's flat.

Twice at traffic islands, he employed anti surveillance techniques that he had been taught during advanced driving courses and did a full three hundred and sixty circle, or on occasions, heading back in the direction from which he had come.

At one point, he was sure that he saw a small black Nissan some distance behind, but had lost it when he doubled back through the Rye Hill area. After several minutes, he was confident that he wasn't being followed, so taking a course through the West End, headed for Drew's street.

Although he had done everything to shake off any possible pursuers, a niggling doubt remained, but despite frequent checks of the rear view, nothing was evident.

Liz Harmon was furious. She had tried to follow Slade, but he had been making so many twists and turns that she couldn't continue without making it obvious and being spotted. With little traffic on the roads, she had held back further and further until she had totally lost him. She drove around for a while without any luck, so gave up and headed to the office.

On the plus side, if the detective was prepared to go to such lengths to throw off any pursuers, then he definitely didn't want to be seen with the boy.

That in itself was interesting.

After picking up several changes of clothing, Jack dropped Drew back at the Quayside apartment then headed into work.

As soon as he entered his office he saw two more new messages waiting for him from Liz Harmon. He had no desire to speak with her and not the faintest intention of returning her calls. He threw them into the bin.

After the morning briefing, Jack's extension buzzed. He picked it up to be greeted by the unwelcome voice of Harmon. 'You've not been returning my calls.'

'I've already told you not to ring this number. I suggest that you contact the Northumbria Police Press Office for any information. They are handling all press enquiries.'

'There's something I would like to discuss with you. Not over the phone. I thought we could meet up and…'

'You're not listening to me, Miss Harmon. Contact the press office.'

'I have some information that you might find interesting.'

'I'll put you through to the incident room. You can tell them any information you have and it will be recorded and acted on.'

'I really would like to speak to you personally. One to one. It would be in your own interests.'

'Well, that's not going to happen. I have nothing further to say to you, so if you don't mind, I'm very busy.'

With that Jack hung up.

Sounds like she's after a replacement informant now that Spence was no longer available.

The rest of the day was spent doing routine enquires and catching up on outstanding paperwork, including signing overtime forms. Everyone below the rank of inspector could claim overtime, but those of inspector and above were considered salaried and could not.

This meant that during a murder enquiry, many of the junior cops could earn considerably more than their bosses.

At mid-day, Jack telephoned his apartment and, using the previously agreed code, rang three times, rang off and then rang again.

Drew answered almost immediately. His morning had been uneventful and he had spent it watching television. Slade told him that he would be back shortly after six o'clock.

As Jamie Heatherington had been unavailable the previous day, Jack decided to call in at MESMAC and see if he had any further information. It proved a wasted journey, because other than confirmation that no-one had seen or heard from Johnny for several weeks, there was nothing else to tell.

Feeling the morning's efforts had been a bit of a waste, Slade made his way on foot back through the city centre and back to the nick to check on progress.

As he approached the front entrance, Jack spotted a figure in the distance leaving. He couldn't be sure, but from the way she moved, he could have sworn that it was Harmon.

Perhaps she had been in with some information after all.

The very second that he walked into the incident room, Jack could feel the strange oppressive atmosphere. The hubbub of conversation died as he entered, and he noticed that the other officers suddenly became very busy, heads down in whatever papers were strewn around their desks.

No-one wanted to catch his eye.

Slade sensed that there was a cauldron of shit bubbling and guessed it was about to hit the fan. He had a feeling it would be heading in his direction.

At that moment Armstrong appeared and hurried across to him. 'I don't know what's going on, Jack, but T.C.P. is going around with a face like thunder and demanding to know where you are. He's got that twat Burton from the rubber heelers in with him.'

As Jack glanced across at Parker's office, the door was suddenly flung open and the Superintendent glared around the room. Slade heard his name barked, before Parker turned on his heel and strode back into his lair.

Shrugging, Jack strode across the incident room and followed, glancing around to see if he could glean any clue as to what was going on.

Everyone avoided his eye.

The inside of Parker's office was even more claustrophobic and oppressive than normal.

'Door!' was the monosyllabic command as soon as he entered, and Jack noted that he hadn't been offered the opportunity to sit down. He closed the door and, looking around the office, saw Burton sitting in the corner, watching proceedings with interest.

Parker dropped into his chair and nodded towards Burton. Jack thought he detected the faintest smile playing on Burton's lips.

That was definitely a bad sign.

Parker cleared his throat and appeared to be trying not to explode.

'I need to ask you about your relationship with one of the witnesses in the case... the young man, Drew Sterling.'

Jack looked from Parker to Burton and back.

'There is no... relationship. He's a witness in the case.'

'Just a witness? There is no other relationship?'

'No. What do you mean *other relationship*? What's this all about?'

Burton remained silent and sphinx-like in the corner.

'There's been an allegation.'

'Allegation? About what?'

'Look! Stop pissing about, Jack. What is your connection to this Andrew Sterling character?'

'I've told you. He's a witness.'

Parker cleared his throat again, as if not sure how to proceed.

'There has been a report that you are involved in a close association with that lad. It has been suggested that the relationship may be of a sexual nature.'

Jack held Parkers eyes for several seconds, scarcely believing what he was hearing, before growling, 'Bollocks!'

Parker glanced again to Burton and Jack spotted an almost imperceptible nod from him, before the Superintendent continued. 'Where exactly is this person now?'

Jack was taken off guard and hesitated.

Parker snatched a pen off his desk and jabbed it at Jack. 'For God's sake, answer the bloody question.'

Jack knew from his own interview techniques that a good interrogator asks questions to which he already knows the answer, to ascertain whether or not the subject is lying. Any untruths are used to undermine the interviewee's credibility. It's what is referred to in interview parlance as 'the provable lie'.

'We know that he's not at his own flat. We've checked. So, where is he?'

Jack weighed up his options. If they knew he was at Slade's apartment and he lied that would give credence to the false allegation. He made up his mind. 'He's at my flat. Now, what's this about?'

224

Burton couldn't suppress a smile and glanced down at the carpet.

Parker threw his pen down onto the desk with enough force to send it bouncing back into the air and onto the floor.

'I don't bloody believe this! You've compromised the whole bloody enquiry.'

Parker opened his desk and took out three photographs, which he threw down onto the desk, facing Slade. They were high quality prints taken with a zoom and were a view of the street outside his apartment. The images were sharp and clearly showed Drew and Jack leaving the flat.

'He wouldn't stay at his place and the enquiry wouldn't splash for protective custody. I did what I thought was best.'

Parker stood up, sending his chair clattering into the wall. He glared at Jack. 'For fuck sake, what are you thinking about? I've had the heads up from Harmon. She wants some kind of a scoop or she's running with a story of the cop and the gay teenage boy.'

He strode away from his desk and stared out of the window, in an effort to calm down. Without turning around, he growled at Jack, 'Are you screwing him?'

Jack chose his words carefully and struggled to maintain an even tone. 'I am not... as you say... screwing him. Nor am I in any relationship whatsoever with him, other than that he's a witness in the case.'

Parker wheeled around. 'So, why the hell is he staying in your flat?'

'I've already told you. His flat was ransacked and no longer secure. He was about to do a runner. You made it crystal clear that there's no way the job was forking out for a safe house. I decided to provide one.'

'Don't you try to drop this at my feet. I don't fucking believe you. You may or may not be screwing him, but you've done a bloody good job screwing up your position as lead investigator in the murder. You've dropped the force in the shit and you may have undermined the whole fucking case. I know you sail close to the wind at times Slade, but I never thought even you were that bloody stupid.'

Parker dropped back into his chair and Jack was aware that Burton was now staring at him. There was a long oppressive silence, while Parker tried to catch his breath.

DAVID JEWELL

'He's in your flat now?'

Jack nodded.

Parker barked, 'I want you back at your flat.' Then, turning to Burton, said, 'You go with him. Pick up the kid and get him back here. Make sure there's no press hanging about. I want him interviewed and I want it done in the video suite. Let's get his version of what he's doing at Slade's flat.'

Looking at Jack, he made no attempt to disguise his utter contempt. 'You were on thin ice as it was. How could you be so bloody irresponsible?'

Parker looked down at his desk and continued, 'Well, you've really fucked up this time. It comes from the top. You're out. You're off the case and I wouldn't be surprised if, after the rubber heelers are through, you'll be lucky to get a job as security at Tesco.'

Jack opened his mouth to respond, but Burton interrupted. 'I'm sure that you understand that because of the nature of the allegations, you will have to be suspended, pending a full internal enquiry. Can you please hand over your warrant card and station key?'

'Suspended? For what? I was doing my job!'

Jack detected a slight smirk on Burton's face and he very nearly opted to wipe it off with his fist. Anger was bubbling over and getting extremely difficult to control. Restraining himself, he took out his warrant card and holder and slammed it down on the desk in front of Parker.

'And your box key, please.' This time the smirk was more noticeable.

The bastard is thoroughly enjoying this.

Jack dropped his police station key on the desk and stared at his tormentor.

'So, what happens now?'

Parker picked up the warrant card and key, placed them in a drawer in his desk and locked it. 'You will be escorted from the station. Go with Inspector Burton to your flat, where he can pick up Sterling. After that, you are to have no contact whatsoever with any serving officers or police staff. You are not allowed any entry to police premises and you should have no further contact with anyone connected to this case... and that especially includes Drew Sterling.

As Slade left Parker's office, escorted by Burton, he

could feel everyone's eyes on him. No one looked at him directly, but he knew that from their peripheral vision, they would be watching. No one he passed on the way out of the station spoke and it was only Dave who tried to make any form of eye contact.

Jack avoided his gaze. He knew he was damaged goods. Toxic. The last thing he wanted was to risk his friend any further contamination.

Besides, if what Jack was thinking turned out to be true, he might be the only friend he had left in the force.

Outside, in the station yard, Burton steered them towards a brand new high end Audi.

It seems HQ staff don't get the pleasure of driving dented pool cars with abandoned chip papers and the smell of stale prisoner.

Burton opened the rear door for Jack. Not out of politeness, but to ensure Slade knew his place. The back seat of any police car usually meant detainee. Jack played his role well and climbed in, but not without a fake smile and 'thank you', as if he was talking to a chauffeur. He got no response. It was clear that Burton regarded Jack as tainted and any attempt to engage him in conversation was to be met with deathly silence.

Might as well just sit back and enjoy the ride. It gave him time to think.

Clearly Harmon had arranged for Jack to be watched, or had even been watching him herself. She must have almost wet herself with excitement when he emerged with Drew Stirling. Jack didn't agree with Parker that Harmon would print any allegations of a sexual relationship with the lad. In the current litigious society, she would want her facts carved in stone before she would risk being sued.

Then again, she wouldn't have to. Readers would pick up on the subtext and what they didn't know they would just make up.

The worry was that Slade had been careless. If a reporter had been staking out his home then it could be equally true of someone else. Had Donkin been watching? Had he followed them to the apartment? As the Audi approached the Quayside apartment, Jack had an empty feeling in the pit of his stomach.

By the time they pulled up outside, Slade had run through all the possible scenarios and wondered whether Drew would go willingly with the officers. If they couldn't persuade him, then they couldn't force him. They had nothing to arrest him for.

As soon as the car stopped, Jack wound the rear window down and reached out to open the door from the outside, to avoid the child lock. This drew a sharp look from Burton. He wanted Slade to know his place.

Escorted by Burton, Jack entered the block and headed for the lift. Pressing the button for the seventh floor, the two men ascended in silence.

At his door, Jack turned the key in the lock and, opening it, called out Drew's name. There was no reply. Jack had that sinking feeling again. He hurried through into the lounge, the kitchen and then checked both bedrooms.

The apartment was empty.

Drew was gone.

DEATH RATTLE

CHAPTER 41

'Where is he, Slade?' Burton was not in the mood for pleasantries. 'If you've been pulling our plonkers about this you'll be in deeper shit than you can imagine.'

Jack didn't even bother to respond. Paying him no attention, he began to check around for signs of a struggle. Nothing seemed out of place.

Had Drew left willingly or had he been tricked into leaving?

A check of the spare room revealed that Drew's overnight bag and changes of clothing were lying by the side of the bed and his toothbrush was on the bedside table. What set Jack's heart racing was the mobile phone lying on top of a set of drawers.

There was no way that Drew would leave his phone, even if he had decided to leave in a hurry.

Slade paused to get his breath and began to check every room thoroughly, in cupboards and under beds. All the while, he could vaguely hear Burton in the background muttering empty threats.

There was no sign of a struggle, but there was also no sign of the teenager.

It was as if Drew had simply vanished into thin air.

Burton growled. 'Has the kid done a runner?'

'I don't know, but what I do know is that you whingeing like a spoilt brat isn't going to find him. We need to start doing some house to house. Check if anyone…'

Burton cut him short, 'You are not doing anything. You're off the case. The kid has obviously decided to make himself scarce. That's if he was ever here.'

'That's his bag you dickhead!'

'Remember who you're talking to, Slade.'

'You know,' Jack said, fixing him with a cold stare, 'this is starting to make things a bit clearer in my mind. The more this goes on the more I'm becoming convinced that the problem isn't with me. It's with you.'

'What's that supposed to mean?'

'Every move I make someone is always one step ahead. I bring in Sterling. His house gets screwed. We take his

229

statement and Donkin appears outside. I move him here and someone gets to him.'

'So what are you trying to say?'

'This investigation is leaking like a sieve. It has been from the beginning. No-one, except me, knew that the kid was here. I tell you and suddenly he disappears.'

'You're being stupid. If a reporter can stake out your flat anyone could have followed you here.'

'I made sure I wasn't followed. No-one knew Drew was here until I told you and Parker. Someone close to this case is taking some risks to make sure Sterling doesn't talk. And my money's on you.'

Fifteen minutes later, Slade was back in Parker's office, along with Burton, who had definitely lost his smile from earlier on.

Parker's voice echoed around the room. 'What do you mean... gone?'

T.C.P. had barely calmed down from earlier and now a witness was missing and, to make it worse, Slade was back in front of his desk. Like a bad bloody penny. 'This is all down to you, Slade. Burton says that control room are circulating the kid's photo as we speak. He's certain that Sterling is on his toes. We had him safe in his flat, with a police radio alarm, until you took him to your place... for whatever reason.'

'I think there's a high probability that he's not decided to run... I think someone took him. He must know something or, at least whoever it was, is convinced that he does. If that's the case, then he might be in danger.'

'Don't be so bloody melodramatic. He's pissed off because you left him alone. When you look around your apartment you'll probably find he's nicked something. You just won't admit you were a bloody fool for taking him there in the first place.'

'He hasn't nicked anything. He didn't even take his own stuff. Someone has taken him.'

'Who took him?' Parker yelled.

'Ask Burton.'

'Now you're moving into fantasy land. You're trying to conjure up a conspiracy to cover up your cock ups. Well, I won't have it. Burton never left the station, until he went out with you.'

'He has a mobile.'

'Give it a rest, Slade. I've already had that bitch, Harmon, back on the blower. She's going to run her article in her local rag about you and the kid and wants to know if I have any comments.'

'Maybe we should be less worried about Harmon and more about our missing witness. If Sterling turns up dead then you'll have the nationals digging up shit. We'll have the whole front page to ourselves.'

Parker glowered at Jack and, if looks could kill, then Slade would have been struck down where he stood.

'There is no *we* about this, Jack. You're out of it. Just piss off home and let us get on with our investigation. Get one of the woodentops to escort you out. Expect a call to come in to headquarters for a full interview. It'll be an internal enquiry. You'd better bring your Federation rep.'

A few minutes later and Jack was being escorted from the station once more.

As he stepped out into the winter afternoon, a sharp blast of icy wind charged up Forth Bank, causing him to shiver.

Whoever is behind this must have a great deal to lose if they're prepared to go to these lengths.

Later, it was barely gone five o'clock and already dark. Jack sat alone in his apartment, looking out at the cold black river, meandering past on the ebbing tide. He turned his attention to his wallet and keys, lying on the glass topped coffee table.

He felt naked, knowing that his warrant card and badge were not lying next to them.

He was out of the loop and with no access to the force computers, or up to date intelligence on the case. A dark cloud hung over him.

Glancing across at the bottle of Glenmorangie, he considered drowning his sorrows. There was still half a bottle and at least it would bring him some sleep, and a rest from the swirling thoughts in his head.

What it won't do, is bring back Drew Sterling.

No matter how he dressed it up, Parker was right. Jack

231

had left him alone at the apartment. Alone and vulnerable. Ultimately, Jack would blame himself if anything happened to him. He needed to right this wrong… whatever it took.

Well, if I'm not part of the gang now then I'm not tied to playing by the rules. It could be time to start playing dirty.

Ignoring the siren call of the bottle of malt, Jack changed from his suit into blue jeans and a dark hoodie. Taking his leather jacket and a pair of warm gloves, Jack again checked his watch. He might have a long wait, but there was someone he needed to speak to. Someone who he was sure held the answer to all of this and probably knew exactly where Drew was.

It was now a question of convincing him to talk.

Going to the sink and taking an empty plastic coke bottle he filled it with water from the tap.

Wary that he would now be under surveillance as he left the apartment, he cautiously checked around, before making his way to the parked car. There was no sign of anybody hanging around. No figures standing in doorways or in the shadows.

Protected against the biting wind whistling down the Tyne, Jack went to the boot and pulled out a green plastic petrol can. Giving it a shake around he could hear the contents sloshing about inside.

Unscrewing the cap he emptied most of the small amount of fuel into the cars petrol tank, leaving just a very small amount inside the can.

Lifting the empty can to his nose, the acrid smell of petrol still coming from the container filled his nostrils. Taking the bottle of water he had filled from the tap, he poured the contents into the petrol can. Again he took a whiff and, although mainly water the contents still stank strongly of petrol.

The decision had been made and his face hardened.

It was time to get some answers.

DEATH RATTLE

CHAPTER 42

It was freezing, standing out in the North East wind. The sort of icy wind that takes bites out of any exposed flesh. The snow had now turned to wet slush and Jack felt his feet turning numb. Stamping them several times to restore circulation, he pulled the hoodie tighter in a vain attempt to stave off the cold.

Waiting in the deserted residential street in Jesmond, he regretted having left the warm interior of his car parked enticingly nearby, to stand in the shadows, looking up at the brightly lit top floor apartment.

Though he had parked the car in a line of similar vehicles, he was worried that it still stood out; the ice free windscreen noticeable next to all the other frozen ones. It was a necessary risk. He needed the car to hand and, unlike on all the television cop shows, people sitting in parked cars always attract attention. The last thing he wanted was for some passer-by to get suspicious and ring the police.

He was also pretty sure that many of the local cops might recognise his car. If so, it would only take a passing patrol car and a curious cop and his plan would go to rat shit.

Slade wondered if Burton was sly enough to add Jack's registration number to the Automatic Number Plate Recognition System, so as to keep a surreptitious track of his movements, but doubted that he would have thought that far ahead.

He never thought that he would be hopeful for unobservant plods. They might miss him. The A.N.P.R wouldn't.

He checked his watch. Seven fifteen.

Jack had been standing across from the apartment for over an hour and the occasional shadows flitting across the blinds confirmed that his quarry was at home. Donkin would have to leave sometime if he was staying true to form and still doing his nightly trawl of the bars. Rubbing gloved hands together for warmth, Slade hoped that it was soon.

Just when he was beginning to think he was in danger of losing a couple of toes to frostbite, the lights in the upstairs apartment went out, and a couple of minutes later, the front door opened and out stepped Donkin.

Jack watched him stroll casually down the short garden path out onto the icy pavement, and make his way towards his Audi.

Showtime.

Like a crocodile that had been lying on the river bottom waiting for the right moment to leap out, Jack sprang to life and, within seconds, was up behind his prey.

Donkin was taking a key fob from his jacket when he became aware of the crunch of footsteps on the icy pavement. Whirling around, he stared wide-eyed at the dark figure coming up behind him. Then, as he recognized Slade, the shock evaporated and was replaced by a sly smirk.

'What the fuck do you want?'

'You and I need to talk.'

'Go fuck yourself.'

Donkin turned his attention back to the car and pressed the key fob to unlock the doors.

Before he could get into his car, Jack took hold of his arm and, in one deft movement, Donkin found himself forced forward, bent over with his face pressed against the frost covered roof.

'What the hell are you doing? Are you fucking crazy? What...'

The rest of his sentence was cut off as Donkin gasped in pain, his arm twisted double and forced further up his back. Slade's other arm was around his throat and Donkin felt himself dragged backwards, with a searing pain in his shoulder muscles.

'Shut up or I'll break your arm!'

It took a few moments for Donkin to catch his breath, by which time, he was being pushed up against another vehicle and felt both wrists forced behind his back.

The cold steel of quick cuffs cut into his wrists as he was bundled into the car.

The seatbelt was fixed, pulled tight and, with his hands behind his back, he was pinned painfully to the seat. The engine was fired up and the car pulled away from the curb and heading rapidly away from his apartment.

It had taken less than a minute.

Donkin rediscovered his voice and began a tirade of insults. He could see Slade occasionally staring at him in the

234

rear view mirror, but his abuse was met with a wall of silence from the stern faced detective.

'You're fucked this time, Slade. As soon as we get to the bizzie station, I want to see an Inspector. I want to make a complaint.'

Slade's cold eyes glared back at him. His lack of response seemed to fire his prisoner up even more and Jack was subjected to another barrage of expletives that would make a squaddie blush.

The car splashed through the slush of the side roads and out onto a main road.

'You shouldn't even be talking to me. You're suspended.'

'Really? So who have you been talking to?'

Donkin hesitated. Aware that he had made an error by revealing something that he shouldn't have known, and he fell uncharacteristically silent.

'Aye. Best save your voice for later. You've got some talking to do.'

As the car flashed through the darkened early evening streets, Donkin shuffled uncomfortably, the rigid handcuffs cutting into his wrists.

His anger and discomfort had distracted him, so it was some time before he noticed they were not heading to Forth Banks, but that Jack had deviated and they were heading in the opposite direction on the Central Motorway and out towards the airport road.

Not heading into the city centre, but away from it.

'Where are we going?'

Jack didn't respond. Eyes fixed straight ahead, he drove on, passing several semi-detached houses. With a week to go until Christmas, they were adorned with a multitude of coloured flashing lights and decorated trees filled bay windows.

Donkin had fallen quiet, his head darting right and left, trying to get his bearings.

It was only when Jack was a few miles from Newcastle International Airport that he suddenly swung the car off the main road onto one of the narrow country lanes that criss-cross the area.

Speeding down a country lane lined with snow covered

trees, Donkin was bounced around in his seat as Jack skilfully threw the vehicle around the twisting bends.

Suddenly, Donkin was thrown forward, as Jack slammed on the brakes and turned right, into what was no more than a single lane track. Had he not been securely strapped in he would have been thrown into the front of the car. As it was he, he would be feeling the after effects of whiplash for some time to come.

The BMW continued to bump a short distance over the uneven surface, before finally coming to a rest in the middle of the dirt trail, well out of sight of any road.

Jack switched off the ignition and turned in his seat to face Donkin. The silence was deafening.

A realisation began to dawn on Donkin. He was in deep shit.

His initial confusion was rapidly giving way to fear. It caused a strange tremor in his voice. 'Where the fuck are we?'

Wordlessly climbing out the car, Jack opened the passenger door and pulled Donkin roughly from his seat. Donkin had no desire to leave the warmth of the car, but the handcuffs chaffing at his wrists made any resistance useless. He found himself dragged unceremoniously out and his feet kicked from under him. He landed heavily on the frozen ground.

'What are you doing? Why are we here?'

'I told you, we're going to talk.' Slade's voice was as cold as the night as he went to the boot of the car and removed the plastic petrol can.

Donkin's eyes widened as he saw the small container.

Wordlessly, Jack unscrewed the cap and fixed his captive with a steady gaze as he drew closer.

Donkin could smell the petrol vapours that still lingered in the container. 'What the fuck are you doing?' His voice rose even further.

Jack remained silent and, with a flourish, began throwing the water from the can across the figure on the ground. Some landed on the earth melting the snow, but the rest soaked through Donkin's clothes, filling his nostrils with the acrid smell of residual petrol fumes.

All his previous bravado deserted him.

'You can't do this! You're the fucking Polis, for

236

Christ's sake!'

Discarding the now empty can, Jack retrieved a lighter from his pocket and finally broke his silence. 'No. I'm not a polis anymore. Don't you remember? You saw to that.'

Jack flicked the lighter in the damp night air. Once. Twice. Finally, it sprang to life at the third attempt. He smiled. 'What do you know... third time lucky.'

Donkin was unable to take his eyes off the dancing flame. It was both beautiful and terrible.

Jack took a step forward and, as he did so, his captive kicked his legs and frantically shuffled himself backwards, desperate to maintain some distance between them. The man's fear was more pungent than the petrol fumes. A new smell stung the nostrils; urine, as Donkin lost control of his bladder and a dark stain began to spread across the crotch of his jeans. He began to whimper.

In contrast, Jack's voice was cold and steady. 'I need some answers... and I want them now.'

'What do you want to know for Christ's sake?'

The flickering flame threw shadows across his face as Slade moved in closer. 'You can start by telling me where Drew Sterling is.'

His wide, terrified eyes never left the flickering flame. 'I don't know. Please, please... for fuck's sake, put it out. I'll tell you whatever you want to know.'

And he did.

Donkin confirmed Jack's fears that Drew had been tricked into leaving his apartment.

'I was told that you were keeping him at your flat.'

'How did you get my address?' Slade snarled.

'One of your lot spilled it.'

'Who?'

'I don't know his name.'

Jack swilled the petrol can around in front of him.

'If I knew I'd tell you, for fuck's sake.'

'So, who picked him up from my flat? It couldn't have been you. Drew knows what you look like. There's no way he would have let you anywhere near him. So, who was it?'

'Please. Oh God! He'll kill me if I tell you.'

Jack glanced down at the petrol container.

'It may have escaped your mind... but *I'll* kill you, if

237

you don't.'

'Neil Allen. Neil Allen. He took the kid. He went over to your apartment and, as someone entered using the door code, he just followed them in. At first, he couldn't get an answer at your door, so shouted through that he was a cop from Forth Banks. He managed to convince the kid that you had arranged for the safe house and he'd been sent to take him there.'

Jack thought of the thick set thug and could only imagine how terrified the lad would have been when he realised that he had been duped. Jack felt a deep pang of guilt for having left him alone.

'Where has Allen taken him?'

'I don't know. He never said. Maybe to his garage.'

Jack took out the lighter and held it close. Donkin whimpered and shrank away.

'If you don't want to end up barbequed then you're going to tell me everything you know from the beginning.'

Donkin's story had begun five years earlier. He already had a reputation as a fixer, for those who had particular preferences when it came to sex, so it was not a surprise when he had been approached by Neil Allen to procure boys for some exclusive parties.

'He wanted half a dozen. Some were camp and others bits of rough, but they all had to be young and good looking. They also had to be willing and were to be made well aware that talking to anyone about the guests was not an option. Not if they wanted to remain healthy.'

'So, who was holding the parties?'

Donkin hesitated, so Slade took out his lighter again and immediately refocused Donkin's attention.

He shivered on the ground and Jack was unsure whether it was from the cold or he was going into shock. He decided to play a hunch.

'Don't lie to me. I know about Martin's involvement.'

Donkin looked startled.

'If Martin thinks I told you, my life won't be worth living.'

He didn't know it, but Donkin had just corroborated all

of Slade's suspicions. Martin was definitely the main man.

'And the parties are held at Martin's Northumberland house? Answer!'

Donkin nodded. 'Only for a small number of special guests.'

'What does Martin get out of it?'

'Connections. Power over the people who attend. He's on the way up. There's talk of him getting into politics.'

'So, we're talking blackmail?'

'Not in the usual way. Not money, but sway, influence. I'm sure anyone would be crazy to refuse Martin a favour if they'd attended one of the parties.'

'Especially if there was some photographic back up,' Slade muttered. 'So who are these guests?'

'I never got to attend, but I heard rumours. An M.P., quite a few wealthy businessmen, even an Arab executive for one of the large oil companies.'

Donkin looked away from the flame for a second, avoiding Jack's eyes.

'What are you not telling me?'

Donkin hesitated. The lighter flickered again and moved closer.

'I heard that one of the guests was a bizzie. That's who feeds Martin information. That's how he knew about the kid being holed up in your flat.'

Another one of his suspicions confirmed. The reason that someone was always one step ahead of him. He thought of Burton. He wondered again about Parker. They were the only two that were aware of everything, almost as soon as Jack discovered it.

But which one?

'Does he have a name, this cop?'

'I don't know his name.'

Jack's thoughts turned to Burton and his smug grin. 'Ever heard the name Mark Burton?'

Donkin shook his head.

'What about Parker?'

'I told you. I don't know his name.'

'What does he look like?'

'I've never seen him.'

'So where did Johnny Lee fit into all this?'

'I picked Johnny up a few years ago, hanging around the Gardens. He was really cute in those days. Any boys hanging around that area were always on the make for some extra pocket money. And then there were the runaways. They hang around the bus station and train station. They're easy pickings.'

Once he began talking, Donkin couldn't seem to stop. 'I would pick up the runaways down by the station. You could spot them a mile off. Sometimes they would be begging for small change. I would buy 'em a burger and coffee... offer them a place to crash for a few nights.'

Slade listened as Donkin continued. 'Teenage boys aren't as naïve as people think. If you offer them a bed, free booze and the odd bit of weed, they aren't so stupid as not to realise they have to provide something in return.'

'Go on.'

'At first, I don't pressurise them too much, but after a bit they're more than willing. Getting a blowjob in a warm bed is better than freezing your balls off on a cold street. After a few nights, I'd get them really pissed or high and after that I could just do whatever I wanted. Quite a few had been there before... sometimes it was why they'd left home in the first place.'

Jack was trying to hold back his anger and wished it was real petrol in the can.

'After they got used to the idea, I'd let slip how much money they could make if they just did a few favours for some friends of mine. Once the big money started coming in, they couldn't get enough of it.'

'And that's how you picked up Johnny Lee?'

'Johnny was at it long before he met me. He'd been giving blow jobs to his stepfather since he was about twelve. Getting screwed by the older lads by thirteen. Back in those days, he was giving it away, but once he found out how much cash he could make he took to it like a dog at broth. All the punters loved young Johnny.'

'So where is he now?'

Donkin hesitated and once again avoided Jack's eyes. 'Don't know. Fucked off. London probably. He could make twice as much in the smoke. Some of those rich Arabs love young white boys. Younger the better.'

240

'You're lying.'

'No. The smoke. That's where he'll be now.'

'You're lying. Do you want to die?'

'Please. I'll be dead if I tell you.'

Jack clicked on the lighter. 'You'll be dead sooner if you don't.'

'Alright! Alright, for fuck's sake! He got used to the money. But he was getting older. The punters prefer them young and pretty. When they get to eighteen or nineteen some of them start to get past their sell by date. Especially if they start to develop a habit... and Johnny had a habit.'

'So, what happened to him?'

'He started looking to the future. A time when a hairless body and tight arse were no longer going to support him.'

'Which means?'

Donkin hesitated again and Jack flicked the lighter.

'He tried to get clever. Started putting together a pension plan.'

'This pension plan wouldn't involve a little bit of blackmail of his own, by any chance?'

'At one of the parties, someone got into Martin's office. The next day, he found that a memory stick with photos on of a previous party was missing.'

Slade couldn't hide the urgency from his voice. 'So Johnny definitely had incriminating photos?'

Jack wondered if Burton or Parker featured in them.

'Martin found out that Johnny was planning on going to some reporter on the local rag. Harmon, the one that does all the crime stuff. She was starting to ask around and her and Johnny were clocked together outside Martin's house.'

Slade's heart began to sink as he realised his worst scenario had probably played out.

'What happened to Johnny?'

'Neil Allen and I took him up to the big house. I thought maybe they were just going to rough him up a bit. Put the frighteners on him. I just left him with Allen and Martin. Honest to God. I never saw him after that.'

'You knew what they would do to him. Knowing that, you still took him... and now they've got Drew Sterling.'

Donkin looked away and did not reply.

'Why do they want Sterling?'

'No-one knows what Johnny did with the memory stick or whether he made copies. Martin thinks he had to have left them with Sterling.'

Jack threw down the petrol can in disgust. 'If anything happens to that kid, you're going to wish I'd lit that petrol.'

As Jack reversed the car back down the narrow track, he passed the cowering figure, lying in a urine soaked heap on the frozen dirt.

Though now out of the handcuffs, Donkin was not yet free from the nightmare that he had just been through and was shivering with fear and the cold. Jack thought of the misery that he had caused to young boys he had bullied and to those whose lives he had ruined.

He felt no trace of sympathy. His only thoughts were of finding Drew before he too became a Home Office statistic in the homicide table. Swinging the car around on a wider section of the lane, he drove off without a backward glance at the trembling wreck of a man whimpering and sobbing on the cold snowy ground.

Jack was finding it hard to think straight. Martin could count on some powerful friends and they in turn would have equally powerful people that they could call upon. Contacts in the government, in business and finance. More worrying to Jack, contacts in the police.

That was why he had kept hitting obstacles at every turn. Why someone always seemed one step ahead of him. As soon as Jack uncovered some little piece of information, someone was there to thwart him before he could develop it.

And that someone had to be a member of the Murder Incident team. It all pointed to Burton or Parker.

It seemed that friends were something Jack was short of at the moment.

Who could he turn to? Who could he trust?

DEATH RATTLE

CHAPTER 43

As Dave Armstrong got out of his car, he juggled the shopping bags, trying not to drop them, whilst kicking the door shut. His feet crunching on the frozen ground, he made his way up the path of his semi-detached home and performed the same balancing act with the shopping as he unlocked the door. Just as he was about to enter, a voice from behind made him jump, almost dropping everything.

'Late night shopping?'

A tall figure had emerged from the darkness to the side of the house and was approaching.

'Jack? What the hell are you doing here?'

'Invite me in and I'll tell you.'

Armstrong glanced around, concerned. 'I didn't see your car when I pulled up.'

'You know me, Dave. Always discreet. It's parked a couple of streets away.'

Armstrong surveyed the road, checking for any eagle eyes, before ushering Jack into the house. He didn't try to hide his concerns.

'You shouldn't be here, Jack. You're suspended. We've all been given the lecture from Burton and T.C.P. Anyone seen with you is off the case and back on the streets, wearing a pointy hat. If anyone saw you come in, we'll both be in the shit.'

'Why don't you just get me a drink? It's freezing out there.'

Armstrong gave way, to allow Jack through the hallway. Before closing the door, he had a final look around the street. It was dark and deserted.

Slade headed into the kitchen and put the kettle on.

Following him and dropping his shopping on the workbench, Dave watched as his friend took a couple of mugs off a rack and spooned coffee into them.

'We've been told to report any sightings of you or your car to the incident room.'

'Sounds like Burton and Parker are getting a bit paranoid to me.'

'What have you done with Donkin?'

243

'Ah! I see. That's why you're so wound up.'

After the stunt you've just pulled, people are beginning to think you've lost it, Jack.'

Jack feigned innocence, 'What stunt might that be?'

'You were seen, man. Clocked forcing Donkin into your car. A neighbour got your registration number. It's been circulated force wide. You're in it over your head, Jack.'

'No change there then.'

'You've always been a chancer, Jack, but at least you always managed to stay within the law. You always used to say bend the rules but never break them. Tonight was different. You've turned a new page now.'

Jack tried to look unconcerned and merely shrugged his shoulders. 'A kid's life is at stake.'

'That doesn't warrant kidnapping. What have you done with him?'

'He's alright. Shit scared and probably half way to London now.'

'Well, if he makes a complaint...' His voice tailed off and there was a moment of quiet.

Slade poured boiling water on top of the coffee.

'You might want something stronger with that, Jack?'

'That would be nice, but the way my luck is, I don't want to risk being breathalysed.'

Dave couldn't resist a wry smile. 'I guess this hasn't been your best week on the job. In view of the circumstances, you don't mind if I partake?' He dug out a half empty bottle of whisky from a cupboard and tipped a generous measure into a glass.

Dave pulled two bar stools up to the breakfast bar and placed the whisky next to the coffee Jack had made him.

'So, what's with grabbing Donkin in the street, Jack?'

'Someone in the incident room is involved in this up to his neck and Donkin knew more than he was saying.'

'The leak. You think it's one of our team?'

'I wondered about Parker, but the more I think about it, Burton comes to mind. He's always there in the background, saying nothing, but scribbling away in his little book.'

Armstrong shook his head. 'Nah, Parker's too much of a company man. As for Burton, I know there's history between you two and I know he's a back stabbing shit... but rent boys and murder? Don't you think it's you that's getting a bit paranoid?'

'Look at the facts. He gets himself parachuted into the investigation and from then on the whole thing has been leaking like a sieve.'

'I still don't buy it, Jack. I think your dislike of him is clouding your judgement.'

Dave took a sip of whisky and stared at his friend. 'So, why are you here, Jack? I take it that this isn't just a social call?'

'I need some help from inside and I'm running short of friends at the moment.'

'What sort of help?'

'Access to the C.I. for some computer checks.'

'Are you for real? It's all traceable. Don't you think you've dropped me in it enough just by coming here? For all we know, there's a surveillance team watching this place as we speak.'

Suddenly Armstrong's phone burst into life, causing them both to start.

Jack glanced at his watch. It was gone eleven.

'Expecting anyone?'

Dave looked at his phone. 'Number's withheld. Looks like work. I'd better take it.'

Holding the phone to his ear, Dave glanced across to his friend as he answered, 'Dave Armstrong.'

As Jack watched, his friends face changed and took on a look of concern. 'OK... yes... give me twenty minutes.'

He hung up and stared silently at Jack.

'Don't tell me. I'm now wanted for abduction.'

Something in the way Dave was looking at him made Jack's concern ratchet up a level.

'Well? Come on, what's up? What's Donkin saying?'

'He's not saying anything, Jack. That was control room. Donkin's dead.'

The blood had drained from Slade's face.

'Jack, you're wanted for murder.'

CHAPTER 44

The coffee was left to go cold as Jack sat nursing a large whisky. It wasn't his usual single malt... a cheap blend, but beggars can't be choosers.

'Christ, Jack. What the fuck have you done this time?'

'I swear he was OK when I left him.'

'Donkin called in on the treble nine system and said you'd kidnapped him. Took him out to some woods by the airport, threatened to kill him and tried to torch him with petrol. He told the call taker that he was terrified you might be coming back to finish the job. A unit was despatched to pick him up, but when they got there he was dead.'

'How?'

'Skull caved in. He'd named you in the phone call before he was killed. It's all on tape.'

'It makes no sense. He was alive when I left him.'

Jack's confusion grew with his alarm. He tried to rationalise events. 'No. After I left, he must have called someone. They came and decided he had become a liability. They probably told him to ring in naming me and then topped him. Getting me framed for it was a happy bonus. What's the betting his mobile phone isn't at the scene? Whoever did this wouldn't want us interrogating his call records.'

'You're going to find it hard to convince a jury.'

Jack fixed him with an enquiring look. 'Have I convinced you?'

Armstrong hesitated before answering. 'I think topping bad guys is a bit rich... even for you.'

'I didn't kill him, Dave.'

'Who do you think did?'

Jack thought for a moment. 'He told me some things, but I'm sure he knew a lot more than he was saying. I think Martin couldn't have him talking and decided to shut his mouth permanently.'

Dave looked towards his mobile phone lying on the coffee table, before turning back to his friend. 'You know I can't just let you walk away, Jack? I mean, we're not talking a fucking parking ticket here. We're talking murder.'

'You know I didn't do it.'

'Shit, Jack! I don't know what to think anymore.'

'Dave! You have to trust me on this one. I need you to do me a favour. Go in to work as they've asked. I need you to use your supervisor's access to do a C.I. data trail. We know that Darren Wilson was researching Lee in the lead up to his murder. But my guess is that someone else was doing so, even before Johnny went missing. I need you to confirm for me who that person was.' Jack paused for a moment, gathering his thoughts. 'I'm leaning towards Burton.'

'You have got to be kidding. You're asking me to illegally access the computer records of a Professional Standards inspector?'

'If we can prove that Burton was checking on Lee for a while we have a link.'

'If you're so sure it's Burton come in with me. Give yourself up.'

'I'm being stitched up here. I don't think I'll stand much of a chance.'

Armstrong spent the next five minutes trying to get Jack to ring in and take his chances with Professional Standards, but it became increasingly evident that was not going to happen.

'You said it yourself, I'm going to find it hard to convince a jury.'

They sat for a long time in silence. It was finally broken by Slade. 'Well, it's make your mind up time. Are you going to help me or not?'

'Jack, you stand no chance. Give yourself up. By now your vehicle's been added to the ANPR system. As soon as you go mobile they'll get a hit.'

This was something Jack had already considered.

All Automatic Number Plate Recognition cameras passively read the numbers of any vehicles that pass and immediately flag up any stolen or suspect vehicles.

A lesser known fact is that all the information is downloaded onto what is known as A.N.P.R. Back Office. Should a serious crime occur, it is possible to feed in an offender's registration number and retrospectively interrogate the system to ascertain where and when *any* suspect vehicle has been.

This is an invaluable aid to crime investigation and, in

the past, had been used to track murder suspects from the scene of the crime to their current location, leading to their quick arrest.

In this case, Jack knew it could lead to his downfall.

'Have you got another car I can borrow?'

'For fuck's sake, you don't ask much do you, Jack?'

They looked each other in the eyes.

'Do you believe I'm innocent, Dave?'

'It's not that I don't believe you're... Oh, sod it.' His resolve seemed to crumble. 'There's my brother's Peugeot in the garage. The wheel bearing sounds like a stuck record, so it's off road until it gets through the MOT. I'm sure at the minute a fixed penalty for no M.O.T is the least of your problems.'

'What about Parker and Burton?'

'I'll have to tell them you've been here. They'll probably track your car to here through A.N.P.R. anyway. Unless they ask about the spare car, I'll play dumb. It's not registered to me and I've never looked at in a month, so I can say the keys were in it and I didn't notice it had gone from the garage.'

Armstrong sighed then pleaded, 'If they catch me out lying for you I'm fucked. They'll drop me lower than whale shit.'

Jack tried to sound reassuring, 'I'm not asking you to lie for me, Dave. Just to be a bit economical with the truth.'

'I'll give you five minutes before I ring. If you get caught, don't drop me in it. I'll deny everything.'

Dave reached into a drawer and took out a mobile phone.

'Take this. It's a cheap one I use on holidays abroad when I leave the iPhone at home. Nobody has the number, so if anyone other than me rings you on it then ditch it.'

Jack took the keys and thanked his friend, before leaving.

'Don't thank me yet, Jack!' Dave called after him and offered a grim smile.

Slade slowly eased the small hatchback into the evening traffic and headed west away from the city.

The stakes had been upped. It was now he who had become the hunted. Whoever topped Donkin had been given the added bonus of putting him in the frame for his murder.

Jack was well aware that it was his own reckless behaviour that had landed him in this situation.

Unless he could prove who the killer was, he would be banged up on remand and in no position to prove his innocence.

The prospect of being locked away with half of Newcastle's criminals, many of whom were languishing in their cells because of him, was not one he relished.

From what Armstrong had said, the bosses were still treating Drew's disappearance as him having run off. With no evident signs of a struggle, Parker was of the opinion that he had decided not to be a witness and so made himself scarce.

Jack now knew for sure that this was not the case and the lad's life was probably at risk.

There was no doubt where Jack's priorities lay... and no doubt what his next move would have to be.

The drive out to Ponteland was uneventful and, other than passing one patrol car parked on a slip road off the dual carriageway towards the airport, Slade saw no signs of any police activity.

Turning right in the centre of the village, he again took the road that passed by the old headquarters and headed out into the countryside beyond.

After driving for several miles along the narrow twisting road, Jack glanced to his right and saw Mike Martin's house standing back from the carriageway, behind the imposing gates. He made no attempt to slow down, but continued driving almost a quarter mile, before he spotted a narrow lane. Turning in, he pulled to a stop.

The icy air exposed his breath and, although warmth had not been his primary intention for bringing the leather gloves, he was doubly glad of them. He looked up at the clear night sky which, with the lack of city light pollution, glimmered with thousands of stars.

He took a deep breath. Now was not the time for star-gazing. There was a job to be done and a boy's life might depend on it.

He looked back down the road, towards where he had passed Martin's house. The narrow single carriage road was bordered on both sides by hedges and the odd wooden fence or gate to the farmers' fields beyond.

The jog back to the house took longer than expected. A couple of times, Slade saw the glimmer of approaching headlights and, with the advance warning, was able to tuck behind the hedgerow to avoid being seen. A walker at night on these roads, so far from a town or village, was certain to cause interest, and he didn't want to attract any unwelcome attention. It was not beyond possibility that a passing motorist would consider it strange enough to call the local police, which would leave Slade with a lot of explaining to do.

Eventually, he arrived at the gates. For the final hundred yards, he had kept low behind the boundary wall, wary of the presence of CCTV cameras. A sign adjacent to the gates showed a sketch of a Rottweiler and the slogan, 'Go Ahead Make My Day.'

Jack couldn't recall any evidence of guard dogs during his last visit and hoped that it was just to deter any casual passer-by. Nevertheless, he made a mental note to be extra cautious.

The house was as he remembered it and every stone of the restored building oozed wealth. The main house was approached by a long driveway lined on both sides by tall trees. The last stretch was open and formed the large turning circle set in carefully manicured lawns. In the centre was a reproduction Georgian fountain in grey stone, which was now floodlit, although the fountain itself was not in operation.

Looking around, he spotted two cameras against the trees on either side of the driveway. Both seemed to be fixed and covering a view of the gates and house approach. Jack looked for a likely point of entry, but if he wanted to avoid detection this was not it.

He edged away from the gates and made his way down the boundary wall, to the side of the building. Using an overhanging branch, he was able, with some difficulty, to haul himself up onto the wall, and peering over, surveyed the side and rear of the building.

The rear was extensive lawns and an outdoor swimming

pool, with an additional two security cameras, which afforded no concealment. To the side of the house was an open run of about twenty yards between the boundary wall and the side of the building, with only a few ornamental bushes for cover. It wasn't what Jack would have wished for, but was clearly the best option. It would have to do.

During his skirting of the property, Jack had noticed that apart from the security lights, there was no other lighting evident inside the house, with all the rooms in darkness. It was just after midnight, but the place had an abandoned air about it. There was no sign of the smartly dressed assistant from his first visit, no sign of Martin or of anyone else. Slade also noted with not a little relief that there was no indications of any dogs... Rottweiler or otherwise.

Easing himself over the wall, Jack silently dropped down into the garden beyond.

Sprinting across the grass to the side of the house, he looked for any possible points of access, but peering through a side window, he could see only a darkened room beyond. The book-lined walls suggested it to be a small library and Jack noticed a tell-tale red pinprick of light flashing from high on one of the walls. It looked like an alarm was set.

Slade made his way along the perimeter of the building, looking through any available window, whilst staying out of sight of any of the security cameras. It didn't take long for him to realise that the house was deserted and all the alarms set.

He considered forcing an entry, but with the level of security the likelihood of prompt arrival of a private protection company or even the police made such a move foolhardy. He would have no time to search and, assuming he could get away before they arrived, his car was half a mile away and might easily be detected before he could get to it.

It seemed his only chance of finding Drew unharmed had just vanished.

CHAPTER 45

Slade made his way back to the car and headed back towards the city. He was tired, but knew that he still could not relax and was running on adrenaline. It was late and he would need to stop at some point to recharge his batteries or he would start making mistakes.

Just after the airport, he passed a large public house with a Travelodge attached. He couldn't risk checking in in case his details had been circulated, but he could park up in the car park, which was not barrier controlled. He hoped that there was no night time security patrol and that one more car amongst another thirty or so would go undetected.

Pulling between two cars he switched off the engine. Checking the boot, he found an old rug and some random tools. He picked up a small jemmy. That might come in useful later. Getting back into the warmth of the car, he pulled the rug over him and tried to get comfortable.

Although his mind was still racing, the lack of sleep had caught up with him and he quickly dozed off.

The following morning, he awoke very early and it was still dark. His watch showed just after six o'clock. He was cold and there was a hard frost on the car windows from the icy cloudless night before, which hopefully had helped stop any casual passer-by from noticing the overnight sleeping figure in the car. As he began to move, his neck felt stiff and he tried to stretch inside the car to get his muscles working again.

Going over everything that had happened the previous day, he wondered if he had missed anything and whether there was any further lead to follow in order to find Drew.

Jack was now convinced that Drew's flat had been burgled for the missing photographs. It had never been just a random house entry by local kids, as Burton had suggested.

No one had taken an interest in Drew prior to his first meeting with Jack following Darren's funeral. That meeting had changed everything.

Obviously until Jack had introduced Drew's name into the enquiry nobody even knew of his existence. Everything backed up what Donkin said about someone within the enquiry leaking his details.

Drew became part of the enquiry and his flat gets burgled. Whoever arranged the break in knew that the flat was empty... because Drew was at the police station.

Finally, Drew is abducted from Jack's flat... a very risky crime to commit, but easier if you knew that Slade was at the police station and that Drew was alone.

And who knew? Parker and Burton. Now they had Drew. They clearly haven't got the photographs, but think Drew knows where they are. If he does know and they find them then it would be too dangerous to hang on to him. If he doesn't know where they are then he'll still know from their questioning what they're after. Either way, he now knows too much and it would be too risky to leave him alive.

He's as good as dead.

Jack wondered about his next move.

Johnny had stayed at the flat the night before he disappeared. It seemed a good chance that, despite the search of the flat, the memory stick or photos would still be there.

Jack started up the engine, cleared the screen of ice and headed for the West End and Drew's flat.

Although the police hunting Jack were not aware of which car he was now driving, it was still best to take no chances. Parking it several streets away, he cautiously made his way on foot to a vantage point from where he could check out the flat unseen. He had no intention of walking into the arms of some bored probationer constable left guarding the place in case Drew turned up.

There were no cops in sight. Probationer or otherwise.

Jack made his way to the front of the flat. There was a new mortise lock on the wooden door.

Taking the small jemmy from inside his jacket, Jack placed the pointed wedge in the jamb next to the lock. Glancing around, he checked that the street was deserted. In this area, if you hadn't got a job to go to then six thirty in the morning was a world that you didn't frequent.

Jack leant his weight against the metal bar and the wooden door frame gave with a resounding crack.

He remained still and waited.

No one appeared. No faces peered out from behind nets or blinds. This was an area to keep your nose out of other people's business. Don't get involved was the Benwell mantra.

Despite his situation, Jack couldn't help but smile to himself.

I'm wanted for murder. Might as well add a burglary to my growing list of offences.

He pushed back the door and entered.

Inside, the layout of the flat was as Jack remembered and, despite the dark, Jack was able to make his way around by the light of the street lights, which shone in from the road outside.

Conscious of the damaged front door, Jack began his search, with one ear listening for anyone curious who might approach the insecure flat.

During attachment to the drug squad, he had taken advantage of a POLSA or Police Search Advisors course and now put his training to great use.

Ignoring the bedrooms, he concentrated on the front room, where Drew had allowed Johnny to spend the night. He pulled out drawers and, using a small Mag-lite that he kept on his belt, checked behind them. He lifted the cushions on the chairs and sofa, sliding his hand into the lining to check if anything had been secreted down the sides. He found thirty three pence in assorted coins, but nothing else.

He checked in all the CD and DVD cases. He ran his hand along the tops of doors and door frames. He even peeled back the corners of the carpets.

Nothing.

Acutely aware that, with the damaged front door, the longer he carried on his search the more chance of being discovered, he moved to the kitchen. Another room Johnny would have had easy access to.

He checked on top of the cupboards, but found nothing. There were a few tins of food in the cupboards and he quickly found one of those fake bean tins that unscrewed to reveal a hidden container. It too was empty.

He checked inside jars of coffee and powdered milk. He even checked the fridge and contents of the freezer compartment for hidden packets.

Still nothing.

He stood back and whispered a few expletives out of

pure frustration.

As he scanned the room, his impatience growing, something caught his eye at floor level.

The kick board of the kitchen units didn't follow the line of the tiles.

Maybe it was crap kitchen fitting or maybe something else.

Dropping down to his hands and knees, Jack tried to pull back the white chipboard. Using the sharp edge of his jemmy, he inserted it between the small gap and pushed against the boards.

The flimsy wood parted and Slade peered behind. He saw a small piece of red plastic about five centimetres long.

Reaching in, he picked it up and brought it into the light of his small torch.

It was a computer memory stick.

He glanced around for a computer to plug it in to, but could see none and recalled Drew saying that his was taken during the burglary.

He needed to find a computer to view its contents. He couldn't go back to his flat. Burton would be stupid not to have Jack's apartment watched.

It's likely that Dave Armstrong would have similar surveillance on his house as, by now, the bosses would be aware of Jack's visit.

His options were running out.

Who can I turn to that won't immediately turn me into the police?

CHAPTER 46

Newcastle City Centre was one of the last places Jack wanted to visit. He was well known to every cop in the city and with patrols cops, PCSOs and a city-wide CCTV system, the chances of being spotted were far too high. But it was where he needed to be.

He timed his arrival carefully. He arrived just before start of business, when the streets were full of people going to work in offices and shops. Hopefully, half the cops were having breakfast and others filling in reports of overnight crimes or processing enquiries from night shift arrests. The fewer available for patrol the better for him on this occasion.

Jack hung around beside the Civic Centre, near the entrance that Jamie was most likely to take. Trying to look as inconspicuous as possible, he prayed that Jamie would be at work today and not away again at some conference. He had only been waiting about fifteen minutes when his prayers were answered. Hopefully, his luck was turning. Up until now, if it wasn't for bad luck, he would have had no luck at all.

Waiting until Jamie had entered the building and passed through reception, Jack hurried up behind him. 'Jamie.'

The outreach worker was startled, but relaxed when he saw it was Jack. 'What are you doing here so early?'

'Can we go to your office and I'll explain?'

Jamie frowned, but together they made their way up the stairs to the offices. Once inside Jamie's office, Jack felt a little less exposed and took a few deep breaths.

On the contrary, Jamie grew a little more concerned as he took in Jack's unshaven and dishevelled appearance.

'You don't look so good this morning. Is everything alright?'

Without telling Jamie the full story, Jack explained that, as the result of his enquiries, he was currently enjoying a period of rest from work.

'Suspended? But what's all this got to do with me?'

'I need your help. All I want is access to a computer to view a memory stick.'

'Don't you have your own computer? Why don't you just go and…'

'Trust me on this one. The less you know the better.'

Jamie glanced at the memory stick in Jack's hand.

'Should I ask what's on it?'

The look on Jack's face gave him his answer. Jamie absently scratched at the back of his neck and then sighed. 'OK. But, I can't allow you to use a MESMAC computer, without knowing what's on the stick, in case it's infected.'

He reached into a drawer and pulled out a laptop. 'It's getting on a bit and I'm about to replace it. Depending on what's on your stick, it could be getting changed sooner, rather than later.'

'Thanks. I owe you one. There's one other thing that you could do for me.'

'I might regret this as well, but go on.'

'I could murder a cup of coffee.'

Jamie managed a smile. 'That, I can manage.'

While Jamie headed off to make coffees, Jack switched on the laptop and plugged the memory stick into the port on the side.

After a tortuous moment of the laptop thinking about it, a slideshow of photographs finally popped up. They all seemed to have been taken from a fixed camera and were high resolution.

All were of a similar nature and most involved an adult male with one, or sometimes two, teenage boys in various positions and states of undress. As Jack flicked through, he saw that in some cases the age of the boys could be as young as fourteen or fifteen and it didn't take a genius to realise that the participants were unaware that they were part of a recorded sex show.

As Slade clicked the mouse, changing images flickered before him and he was able to recognise a few of the adult faces. One was actually a barrister, with whom he had clashed in court on several occasions. Another, he knew as a councillor from the West End and one he thought he had seen before, hosting a show on local television.

One particular set of photographs caught his eye. In the first, a teenager, aged about eighteen, was lying back on a bed. He looked almost white in contrast with the dark blue sheets. He stared defiantly at the camera with bright blue eyes and Jack could see a hint of down on the top lip of the otherwise hairless face. The boy was naked and the rest of his body appeared equally hairless, apart from his shock of dark head hair and a small triangular tuft below his pierced naval.

From the identifying marks section of the Missing Persons report and the chocolate coloured birthmark below the left nipple, Jack had no doubt that this was his second missing boy, Dean Masters.

The following photographs showed the same boy in various different poses with different men.

However, it was the latter photographs in the file which caused Jack a sharp intake of breath.

In these, a blonde boy of about sixteen had been joined by an older man, who looked to be in his late thirties. The first couple of shots showed the boy lying back, arms behind his head, whilst others were more explicit.

Slade recognised the boy immediately from his I.S. record.

It was Johnny Lee.

Other pictures showed the roles reversed, but were no less graphic.

In these photographs, the man's face was clearly visible to the camera.

The tanned face was clean shaven and, though not overweight, he was starting to show the signs of a man who enjoyed good living and spent too many days sitting behind a desk.

Jack knew this to be true, because he recognised him.

So engrossed was he in the photographs, that he hadn't noticed Jamie had returned with the coffee and was standing, looking over his shoulder.

'Shit! I'm so pleased I didn't let you view that on the works computer. You owe me a laptop, because that's going to the tip in pieces as soon as you log off.'

"Recognise anyone?'

Jamie looked closer at the screen. 'I recognise the lad as Johnny Lee. Who's the older guy?'

'It would be better if you forget that you've seen it.' Jack looked around the office. 'Can I use your printer?'

Jamie nodded.

Flicking through the images, Jack carefully selected a compilation of images, and as he jabbed at the keyboard, the wireless printer cut through the disquiet, whirring into life.

Before leaving, he borrowed two memory sticks from Jamie and made copies of the original. Placing them in separate envelops, he addressed them and handed them to Jamie.

'If anything happens to me, I want you to give a copy to Sergeant Dave Armstrong at Forth Banks nick.' After a moment's thought, he added, 'And if you hear that anything's happened to him, post the second to Liz Harmon at the address on the envelope.'

That done, Jack pulled up his hood, thanked him again for all his help, left the office and headed back onto the cold December streets.

CHAPTER 47

Darras Hall in Ponteland is one of the up market suburbs of Tyneside. Each of the detached houses is set in a minimum of a quarter acre and the neatly trimmed lawns and precise topiary contrasts strongly with the tough inner-city council estates, where Jack usually made his house calls. A firm favourite with social climbers and the *Nouveau rich,* it was where those who had the cash lived… and those who wanted people to believe they had cash attempted to survive. The *fur coat and no knickers type*, his father used to call them.

Jack glanced at the brown envelope, lying on the passenger seat that contained the printouts that he had made at Jamie's office. Maybe, if the people in them had kept their own knickers on one young boy, probably two and now maybe three, would still be alive.

Jack looked back to the road and glanced across at the house names, as he slowly cruised along. No house numbers for the residents of this avenue. Green Larches was set some distance back from the road, behind sandstone gateposts, leading onto a wide driveway.

Jack swung a left, between the pillars and the vehicle tyres crunched over gravel as he slowly pulled up in front of the large detached house, set among immaculately trimmed lawns.

Two matching stone urns, festooned with trailing plants, stood at either side of an imposing door. He studied the elegant façade and wondered how far up the social pyramid he would have to scale to afford a place like this.

Jack picked up the envelope from the seat and clambered out of the car.

Walking up to the door, he noticed a brass bell push, but ignoring it, took hold of the heavy metal knocker and banged on it three times. A real policeman's knock.

After the shit I've been through recently, I deserve a bit of satisfaction.

After only a couple of minutes, the door was answered by a slim woman, the wrong side of forty, wearing designer jeans and blouse. She looked every bit as manicured as the lawns and had the look of someone relying too heavily on surgery, botox or both. Stern eyes looked out from above an aquiline nose.

All the better to look down on you.

As if reading his mind, she gave Jack the sort of look she reserved for something the gardener brought in on his shoe.

Jack certainly didn't look at his best. Hair unkempt, unshaven and clothes crumpled and dirty from the previous night's escapades. Not the usual caller to Green Larches.

When she said, 'Can I help you?' She clearly intended to do the exact opposite.

'Good morning. Is your husband in?'

'Is he expecting you?'

'No. But if you tell him that I'm from work I'm sure he'll see me and it's very important.'

Jack gave her his best false smile.

She seemed to be considering whether to close the door on this scruffy looking individual, before calling for her husband, when a voice from inside called out, 'Who is it, darling?' and a familiar figure appeared in the doorway behind her.

Assistant Chief Constable William Curtis was clearly shocked to see Jack, but quickly recovered his composure, turning to his wife and quietly saying, 'Go inside and leave this to me, darling.'

She seemed to sense trouble, and it was only after a few moments of hesitation, she retreated into the house.

'Can I come in, Mister Curtis?'

'No, you cannot. What the bloody hell do you want coming to my home?'

Curtis barked in a voice used to intimidating people, but not so loud as to disturb any neighbours who might be within earshot. There were standards to uphold in Darras Hall.

The senior officer was glaring at Slade, making no effort to conceal his distaste.

'I've got nothing to say to the likes of you. Now leave, before you find yourself in more trouble than you are already.'

Curtis momentarily shot a sideways glance to his right and Jack spotted the small red button mounted on the wall.

'If that's a panic alarm then I'd rather you didn't press it just yet.'

Jack produced the brown envelope from behind his back, 'At least not until you've seen what I have in here.' As he spoke, Jack placed a foot in the jamb of the door.

Curtis looked at the foot preventing him from closing the door and then scowled at the package Jack was holding. 'And what the hell's that?' he snapped, eyeing the package suspiciously.

This time, Jack detected a slight tremor in his voice. In his hesitation, Jack took the opportunity to ease past him and into the hallway. 'Have you somewhere we can talk?'

Curtis's wife was hovering in the background.

'Private would be best,' Jack said, quietly.

The Assistant Chief Constable seemed about to break into a further protest, but with his eyes fixed on the envelope, the words stuck in his throat. He was losing confidence and with it, control of the situation.

'This had better be good,' he muttered, with as much bluster as he could summon, and strode off down the hallway.

I very much doubt you're going to think so, Jack mused, as he followed behind.

'Come into the drawing room.'

Only the people with plenty of cash have drawing rooms, thought Slade, crossing the hallway.

As Jack followed in Curtis's wake, he noticed a photo-portrait of the senior officer with his wife and two children; a girl of around twelve and a boy aged about thirteen.

About the same age as Johnny Lee was when he was lured into prostitution.

At the end of the corridor, Slade was ushered into a large room. To one end, was an ornate mahogany desk, topped with gold edged green leather, and one wall was dominated by a bookcase as tall as it was wide and crammed with hardbacks, many of which were law books and biographies of prominent political figures, past and present.

Neatly spaced on the other walls, were several paintings by a local artist, featuring Northumbrian scenes, such as Alnwick Castle, Bamburgh beach and several of the Newcastle area, featuring the Tyne Bridge.

Jack realised that he had prints of two of them in his own apartment.

The room reeked of money. Wealth smells like new

carpets and fresh polish, Jack thought, and, without asking, he plonked himself down onto the deep leather sofa.

His reluctant host appeared about to protest, but then thought better of it.

In the corner of the room, standing sentry, was an antique grandfather clock. The pendulum slowly swinging back and forth, was the only movement in the room, as the two men gazed in silence at each other.

'Well? What is this about?' Curtis demanded, standing over Jack, in an attempt to regain some of his authority.

So far as Jack was concerned, that boat had long sailed... and was about to be well and truly torpedoed.

Without a word, Jack placed the envelope onto the coffee table. He continued to stare into the senior officer's eyes, until Curtis looked down at the envelope.

Curtis seemed hesitant to touch the small package, as if fearing, like a cross to a vampire, it could scorch his skin.

'Go on. Open it,' Jack said.

He noted that the tremor in the other man's voice was now replicated in his hand.

Picking up the envelope, Curtis stared at it for several seconds, before tearing it open and taking out the contents.

Jack had heard about colour visibly draining from a face. Now he saw it at first hand.

As he sifted through the photographs, the tanned face took on a grey pallor. Quite suddenly, he threw them back down on the table and glared at Jack.

Slade wondered if looking through the photographs for Curtis was like looking in a mirror.

For in each one, he could see his own face staring back at him.

Curtis sank down into a leather armchair chair.

Slade stood up and strolled across to an impressive display of crystal glasses and a well-stocked drinks cabinet. Taking two heavy whisky glasses, he selected a particularly rare thirty year old Macallan and poured two hefty measures. He handed one to his dumbstruck boss and took a long satisfying swing from the other.

As he savoured the whisky, he said, 'You look like you could do with a drink.'

'Where did you get the photographs?'

'I think you can guess that.'

The shrunken and pathetic figure hunched in the chair bore no resemblance to the haughty Curtis that everyone had come to know and despise.

Clearing his throat, Curtis said, 'so, what do you want? Is it money?'

'Is that what Johnny Lee wanted?' Jack asked.

Curtis did not answer, but stared down into his glass.

'That is him in the photos, isn't it?'

Curtis looked up for a second and nodded slowly, before returning to stare at the amber liquid.

'Was Johnny trying to blackmail you?'

'He said if I didn't pay up, he would go to the papers. He said he had a reporter that was interested, but thought I might want first refusal on the photos.'

'It wouldn't have stopped at a one-off payment though, would it?'

'I think he was considering more of a regular long term arrangement.'

'How did you meet him?'

'A party.'

'One of the parties thrown by Mike Martin?'

Curtis did not reply, but gave a slight nod.

Jack shook his head, 'You've been keeping some strange company. How does an Assistant Chief Constable end up invited to a party thrown by the likes of Martin?'

Curtis swirled his glass and sank the malt down in one.

'We're in the same lodge.'

Curtis looked as if he might not have the strength to get up from his chair, so Jack went to the cabinet and brought across the bottle. He poured another large one for Curtis and a smaller one for himself.

It looks like he needs it more than me.

Jack watched his boss swig down another mouthful, before speaking. 'You never considered it might be a set up? You weren't worried about the rumours about how Martin got the cash to start his empire building?'

'I know what you're suggesting, but Mike said any drugs talk was all wild speculation. I certainly never saw any evidence of drugs... even at the parties.'

'Still, the senior police officer and the dodgy property

developer... That would make a good story in itself.'

'I swear, so far as I knew, he was a successful businessman, who made his money through property development and was on the fringes of politics.'

'So, how did Johnny Lee fit in?'

Mike used to throw big parties. Lots of people there. Important people. As much booze as you could handle. Sometimes, he laid on entertainment. Girls you know.'

'Drugs?'

'No. I've told you, I never saw any evidence of that. I wouldn't touch the stuff,' he said, taking another slug of whisky, 'but Mike had a knack of knowing what you could be tempted by.'

'And, I guess, that's why Johnny appeared?'

'He knew I wasn't interested in any of the girls at the parties, and then one night he introduced me to Johnny. He seemed a nice lad. Mike told him to look after me. Johnny must've been about sixteen then, although he said that he was eighteen and acted a lot older.'

His speech was beginning to waver and Jack couldn't tell if it was emotion or the whisky kicking in. He allowed him to continue.

'I swear, I never intended anything to happen. I got too pissed to drive one night. Mike said I should stop over. Sleep it off. The wife was away at her mother's and the kids at boarding school, so I thought what the hell.'

He took another slug of the whisky.

'I was in one of the guest rooms. I had just got into bed and was about to crash when Johnny came in. He didn't say anything. Just stripped off and climbed into bed. I didn't realise then that he was just doing what he was told. I saw him several times again after that. We would sometimes go to a little riverside holiday cottage that Mike owned and I'd tell the wife I was away at a conference.'

Curtis was staring off into space.

'So, when did it turn sour?'

'I had being seeing Johnny for about a month. We were at the cottage one night when Mike just turned up. Apologised for the intrusion, but asked to speak to me alone.'

'And asked for a favour?'

'Just a small thing at first. He wanted a P.N.C. check on

a car. He said he was having problems with a business partner. I told him at first that it wasn't possible. But then he said I owed him favours. I knew he meant. Johnny. So, I did the check. It came back as a hire car and I thought nothing of it at the time.'

'But?'

'It turned out to have been hired to the National Crime Agency. Through contacts, I later found out they were looking at Martin in relation to suspected drug distribution.'

'So, what did you do?'

'What could I do? There was already a check of the P.N.C. logged in my name. If I said anything, it would only take one data trail check and it would come straight back to me.'

Curtis stared into his whisky flavoured oracle.

'I went back to Mike. I confronted him. I told him I couldn't have anything to do with drugs.'

'And what did he say?'

'He said, "But sixteen year old rent boys were O.K." It was obvious what he meant. If I said anything, everything would come out.' Curtis raised his head and his eyes were damp and bloodshot. 'I know it was stupid but…' His words seemed to trail away into the whisky glass.

'So, what did you give him?'

'Lists of vehicles hired by N.C.A. We didn't always know what they were working on at the time, but up at H.Q. Crime Department, we got to hear quite a bit. We had to be kept in the loop to ensure we didn't accidently blow any of their ops.'

'And you passed this to Martin?'

He nodded, dutifully.

'What went wrong in the end?'

'Johnny was such a sweet boy when I first met him. Full of energy and great fun to be with. Then he started shoving powder up his nose. I always suspected he might smoke a bit of weed, but this was different. He started to get a habit. He became… difficult. That's when I tried to distance myself from him. I told you, I wanted nothing to do with drugs.'

Curtis drained his glass. Jack walked across and poured him another.

'We argued. I said I could get him help. A drugs programme. He screamed at me and said I was acting like I was his dad and stormed off. I never saw him for over two weeks.'

'Then what?'

'Out of the blue, he rang up and wanted to meet. When I saw him, he looked bad. He told me that at one of the parties he'd sneaked into Martin's office and had taken a memory stick. He said that he had photographs. Not just of me. Of others who had been at the parties. Johnny told me it was his insurance. He asked for money and started rambling on about journalists and front page stories. I tried to calm him down, but he was definitely off his head on something. I couldn't reason with him. Then he stormed off again.'

'What did you do?'

'I didn't know what to do. I panicked.'

'And you went to Mike Martin?'

'I didn't know who to turn to.'

'You told him about Johnny? About Johnny's insurance?'

'I swear to you, Slade. I didn't know what he would do. I thought he might just frighten him off a bit.'

'You really thought Martin would let some young smack head screw up his thriving business and political ambition by dropping him in the crap? You must have known what he would do.'

There was no reply.

'So, Johnny Lee had to disappear?'

Curtis leaned forward and put his head in his hands. Tears splashed onto the highly polished coffee table. 'I never meant for any of this to happen. It just all got out of hand.'

Staring back at the once powerful and arrogant man, Slade felt no pity.

'So, what happens now?' Curtis managed, in between stifled sobs.

'It seems like Johnny Lee's retirement plans have pretty much screwed up yours. I take it Burton was put into the enquiry to feed everything back to you?'

He was rewarded with a nod.

'And you fed everything back to Martin. Does Burton know about your connection to your pal, Mike?'

'God no. Burton's a ruthless bastard, but he's not bent.'

Jack fixed the crumpled figure with a cold stare. 'Well, there's more at stake here than just your career.'

Curtis looked up from his empty glass.

'You know Drew Sterling was abducted from my apartment. You know, because when Burton telephoned you to keep you updated on where he was, it was you who passed it on to Martin.'

Curtis avoided looking at him.

'I thought they were just going to scare him.'

'Really? Like they *just scared* Johnny?'

No reply.

'Where have they taken Sterling? I've checked Martin's Ponteland house and it's locked up and empty.'

'I don't know.'

Jack leaned in close, so that their faces were almost touching.

'You're lying. Where is he? Or do you want another boy's murder on your conscience? Johnny didn't deserve to die... and neither does Drew Sterling.'

Releasing a trembling sigh, Curtis said, 'None of this was supposed to happen.'

Jack grabbed him by the shirt collar and snarled at him, 'Well, stop it now. Where is he?'

'He probably guessed that you'd go to the big house. Maybe even bring other cops along with you.'

'So, where else would he go?'

'The cottage. The one where Johnny and I used to stay.'

'Where?'

'Just outside Wylam. Down next to the river.'

'Give me the address.'

As Curtis wrote down the address and handed it to Jack, he seemed to recover some of his composure.

'I don't suppose you and I could come to some... arrangement?'

Curtis's mouth clamped shut under Jack's icy glare. Even at this late stage, the man's arrogance allowed him a tiny thread of hope that he might be able to salvage something from the wreckage that was once his career.

Curtis could see from Jack's eyes that there was to be no last minute salvation. No deal to be struck. No get out of jail free card.

'You're coming with me. I want you to point out the cottage.'

Several seconds of silence passed. Jack could hear the loud ticking of the antique clock in the corner, as his boss slowly dragged himself from the chair and muttered quietly, 'I'll get my coat.'

As Slade watched the hunched figure amble towards the door, he considered following him, as he would do any other person he took into custody, but couldn't see the point. He wasn't likely to try to flee. Where could he go? For him, there was no escape.

Jack sat listening to the gentle steady tick of the clock and thought about how fast things had moved in the past twenty four hours.

A sudden loud bang snapped him back to the present.

Jack leaped from his seat and out into the corridor. Seeing another door slightly ajar, he wrenched it open and entered a small study.

Slumped in a plush leather chair, was William Curtis, or rather what was left of him. He was only recognisable to Slade from the clothes he had been wearing minutes before.

Lying beside him on the floor was a double barrelled shotgun, which he had dropped, as the force of both barrels, discharged simultaneously, removed his face and the majority of his head.

Blood and brain matter plastered the ceiling of the small office, splattered over the Christmas decorations, and slowly dripped from the light fittings to join the pools of crimson soaking the cream coloured carpet. What first appeared to Jack to be a piece of broken crockery caused him to shudder, as he recognised it to be a section of human skull, with some hair still attached.

As he took in the gory scene before him, Slade became aware of someone pushing past him into the room. What started as a gasp, became a low moan and escalated to a screaming wail, as Anne Curtis came to the realisation that the gory mess on the chair used to be her husband.

Jack struggled to pull her back, but eventually shock took hold and she allowed herself to be led out, back to the drawing room, where she collapsed in a heap on the sofa.

He offered her his half glass of whisky, but she knocked it to the floor.

Slade went to the desk and, picking up the telephone, dialled three nines.

After getting through to the operator, Jack spoke rapidly, before replacing the handset and turning to look at the former wife and now widow, Curtis. She stared blankly back at him, as if unable to comprehend what was happening.

Suddenly, recalling the photographs, Jack grabbed them from the desk and shoved them back into the envelope.

If the sight of her husband's body in the office hadn't totally destroyed Anne Curtis then the sight of his body in the photographs would.

Jack wondered if it was because of his wife and family that he had blown his brains out. By doing so, he had ensured that he died in service and not convicted of any crime, and had preserved for his wife a widow's pension.

Probably the least selfish thing he had done throughout this whole sorry debacle.

It seemed that William Curtis had found his alternative pension plan after all.

He'd signed it in blood, all over his study ceiling.

DEATH RATTLE

CHAPTER 48

Slade estimated that the first police car would arrive at the scene within three to four minutes. He aimed to be long gone by then. He didn't want to wait around and spend the next several hours explaining his actions. His priority was to get to Drew.

As he turned out of the drive and drove down the leafy road, putting as much distance between him and the bloody carnage behind as possible, he glanced in his rear view mirror, just in time to see a patrol car in the distance driving at speed with the flashing blue roof lights and glaring headlamps. Turning back to the road ahead, he concentrated on working out the quickest route down to the A69 and on to Wylam village, and what might await him there.

He hoped for Drew's sake that he wouldn't be too late and drove as fast as he could, whilst still keeping an eye out for any police patrol vehicles. The last thing that he needed was to be stopped for speeding.

He hoped that Anne Curtis had not had the presence of mind to take down his registration plate before the gunshot. He was fairly sure that afterwards she was in no state to do anything.

Even looking at the best scenario, he was up to his neck in trouble. He was suspended. He had ignored orders to stay out of the enquiry, had broken into Drew's flat and was a suspect in Donkin's murder.

Now, to top it all, he was probably the prime suspect in the death of an Assistant Chief Constable.

But, what worried him most, was that Drew was missing, and for all Jack knew he was already dead... and it was all down to Jack. If he hadn't got Drew involved then none of this might ever have happened.

On the plus side, he had the photographs of Curtis together with the missing boy.

They told their own story and were the key to why Darren Wilson had ended up murdered. Together with a data trail on what the senior officer had been looking at, it might be enough to connect him with Martin, but with Curtis now dead, it was looking thin.

The whole investigation had turned into one great momentous fuck up.

He still had no positive evidence that Johnny or even the other missing person, Dean Masters, were dead.

He thought again of Drew. He had promised him that he would be safe if he cooperated.

It was now up to Jack to try to keep his word.

The mobile phone given to him by Dave Armstrong started to ring. Jack didn't want to risk being stopped by a patrol officer for using a mobile whilst driving, but had no time to pull over.

Screw it. What's another ticket when you're wanted for murder?

Snatching up the phone, he pressed the accept button.

'Jack... you there?'

He recognised his friend's voice on the other end.

'What have you got for me, Dave?'

'You were right about Darren Wilson checking records on Johnny Lee. You were also right about someone else checking Johnny out earlier. After the kid disappeared, the same person did a data trail on Johnny's record. He would have seen from the result that Wilson had taken a keen interest.'

'It was taking an interest in the disappearance of Johnny that had led to Wilson's murder. He couldn't be allowed to dig deeper,' Jack said.

'Yes, but it wasn't who you thought it was searching the records.' Armstrong paused for effect. 'But, you'll never guess who.'

'A.C.C William Curtis.'

'How the hell...'

'I've just been chatting with him. If I was you, I'd check the incident logs for the Command area covering Ponteland. You'll find them of interest. I can't talk just now, I'm driving. I'll ring you later.'

Jack hung up and pressed down harder on the accelerator.

The address Slade had been given was a neat stone built cottage on the outskirts of the village. What it lacked in size, it made up for in seclusion, with the nearest building almost a half a mile away. Situated central to a large plot, a long sloping garden led down to the north side of the River Tyne. The cottage was in a good state of repair and had retained the quaintness of a nineteenth century building, with roof tiles of dark grey slate and window frames of wood, rather than PVC plastic.

Jack had found it easily enough. He drove some distance past, before finding somewhere to park up and walking back.

As he approached, he noticed that all the curtains at the front of the cottage were closed, although a glimmer of light through a crack suggested that someone was at home.

There was none of the security of the large house outside Ponteland. Jack surmised that not many people would know about the small holiday retreat and that it was probably rarely used by Martin.

Using what little cover there was in the garden, Jack cautiously approached the building. He could hear no noise from inside, but with curtains drawn and lights on inside, he had a gut feeling that this was where he would find Drew.

Alive or dead.

At the side of the cottage was a small window, with a chink in the curtain, through which Jack was able to peer inside. Beyond, was a small room and, although there was no light on in this room, Jack could make out a bed and a dressing table. The door to the bedroom was closed.

Jack listened. There were no sounds of movement within.

Pulling the small jemmy out of his jacket, he slipped it between the wooden window frame next to the latch and began to apply pressure. At first there was little give, but the paint flaked and he saw that he was making an indent in the wood. He applied more pressure.

Crack!

With a sudden noise of splitting wood, the lock gave and the window sprang open a fraction.

Alarmed by the noise, several small birds shot out of a nearby bush and flew up into a tree some distance away.

Jack waited to see if anyone had been alerted by the noise, but could hear no raised voices or sounds of hurried movements from within. He prayed that being at the side and some distance from the main room that no-one had heard the noise.

After a few moments that seemed like hours Slade slowly eased the window open and cautiously climbed inside.

The room was larger than he had expected and thankfully carpeted allowing him to move silently across to the door.

He listened and then opened it a fraction. There were no sounds of any life but the lights were on in the hallway beyond.

He slipped out of the room and moved towards what he took to be the main lounge.

He listened again. Silence.

Turning the door handle, he opened the door slightly. He could see a figure seated in an old wing back chair, but from behind only the top of his head was visible. Even so, he knew that it was Martin.

Slade opened the door and walked in.

Martin stood up quickly and turned to face him.

'Inspector Slade. I thought I had heard a noise from outside. Don't you believe in knocking or are police officers so used to just forcing their way in?'

'I thought I'd like to surprise you.'

'Well, you've certainly done that. Are you alone? It's just that my friends tell me that you've got yourself into a little trouble with your old pals in the police force.'

'I'm looking for a friend of mine.'

'Yes, my friends also told me that you're looking for a different missing boy now.

'I'm looking for both actually. Drew Sterling and Johnny Lee.'

'Oh, young Johnny Lee. I asked around after your last visit. I was told by some contacts of mine that he'd run off to London to make his fortune.'

'I doubt that. My contacts tell me, contrary to what you claimed at our last meeting, that you knew him very well.

Martin smiled. 'Well, if I did, he hasn't sent me a postcard.'

'I heard he was working as a rent boy for you.'

'Which fantasist have you been listening to? But now

274

you mention it, maybe he did do a little PR work for me with clients. A little tough nut if I remember. I had to let him go in the end.'

'According to our mutual friend, William Curtis, you had him selling himself. He was just a kid, for fuck's sake.'

Martin broke into a wide smile. 'I see someone has been telling tales. I don't suppose it makes a difference now.'

Martin stood, facing Slade and seemed to be enjoying the situation.

'Please, Inspector, don't be so naïve. I didn't corrupt our young Johnny. He had been whoring himself since he was in short trousers. I believe one of his mother's boyfriends taught him the ropes and he loved it. I'm a businessman. I just showed him how to make some money at it. The punters like them fresh. The fresher and younger the better... and of course, the better, the more expensive.'

'You hawked him around like a piece of meat to your sick perverted pals.'

'There you go being naïve again. The Arabs have a saying, *Women for duty. Boys for pleasure*. Don't tell me you've never considered it.'

'You are one sick bastard.' Jack wanted to grab him by the throat and throttle the life out of him right there and then.

'Come on, Inspector Slade. You must have thought about it at least once. Everyone has... just some of us have the courage to try it.'

Jack was well aware of the arrogance of the man, but was still amazed that he seemed totally unfazed by the situation he found himself in. He was deliberately taunting Jack, and actually enjoying himself.

'Most of the boys' customers are married men. Closet cases, who are too scared to expose their true nature.'

'Like your pal, Curtis.'

'Oh, yes. Your boss, Curtis, had his own tastes. He's not alone. Did you know that just over a decade ago it was illegal to have anal sex with a woman... even if you were married to her? It carried a sentence of life imprisonment, no less. They had to change the law because... if you pardon the pun... every bugger was doing it.'

He chuckled at his own joke, but Jack remained stone-faced.

'It's actually quite fashionable to screw boys these days. The TV helps. If you watch the soaps, it's almost compulsory.' He smiled again at Jack, who was finding it ever more difficult not to launch himself at the man.

'Supply and demand. It's what drives any business. Drink, drugs... boys. I can supply and believe me there's no end of demand.'

When he spoke, Jack's voice was calm, with no betrayal of the inner tension he was suppressing. 'What have you done with Drew Sterling?'

'I thought he might have something belonging to me. Turns out he didn't, but I had some fun finding out. He's really quite pretty. You should have tried him yourself when you had him overnight in your apartment. He likes men in uniform, I believe.'

There was something disconcerting about how Martin continued to act. Jack felt the anger rising and took a step forward.

The blow came from behind. Sudden and unexpected, it felt like his head had exploded and Jack dropped to his knees. He turned in time to look up at a burly tattooed thug. He recognised him from his mug shot as the garage manager, Neil Allen.

Before Jack could speak, a kick to the stomach drove the air from his lungs and he found himself gasping.

He was dragged roughly to his feet as a muscular arm wrapped itself around his neck and began to squeeze, until he felt like he was about to pass out.

At the last moment, the grip slackened and he was able to finally gasp for air, but there was no strength left in him to break free.

Hauled across the room, he was dumped unceremoniously onto the floor. He saw Martin standing over him, with that wide grin across his face. As Jack lay on the ground gulping in mouthfuls of air, he was aware of Allen drawing back his foot, as if in slow motion, but couldn't sum up the energy to avoid the blow.

A violent kick struck his head, followed by a sickening crunch.

Then everything went black.

DEATH RATTLE

CHAPTER 49

Slade felt cold water splash over his face.

A bass drum was banging inside his head, as he struggled to take in his surroundings. At first, he couldn't remember where he was, but then slowly the realisation came back to him.

Painfully, he tried to open his eyes. One wouldn't open and the other was watering. He tried to blink it clear and attempted to focus through his one open eye.

He was in the same room as before, but was now seated upright on a wooden dining chair. He tried to move, but his hands were bound tightly behind his back. He dropped his head again and noticed that heavy duty polythene sheeting had been placed on the floor.

A sudden dread knotted his stomach. The sheeting was to protect the carpet from whatever was about to happen.

Attempting to get the circulation going in his hands, he felt what appeared to be plastic cable ties cutting into his wrist. Too tight to get any movement. Running his tongue around his lips, there was the faintly metallic tang of blood in his mouth.

There was a movement to his right and a face moved into his line of vision.

Mike Martin was looking down at him with a crooked grin.

'We thought we'd lost you there, Mister Slade. How are you feeling?'

At that very moment, Jack didn't think he could say anything. The right side of his face was badly swollen and his left eye refused to open. His nose was throbbing and enflamed and he could feel a mixture of blood and water running down his face and onto the sheeting.

He tensed his jaw in an effort to block out the pain. His brain franticly began working through his options for some way out of his predicament.

Going through his options didn't take long. There weren't any that he could think of.

The imposing figure of Neil Allen was to his right and Jack surmised that he must have been standing concealed

277

DAVID JEWELL

behind the door when he had entered the lounge. No wonder Martin had been so relaxed and confident.

Martin drew closer, so that his face was only inches from Jack's. 'Now it's my time to ask some questions. You've been on the afternoon news, Jack. That's some drama you've caused at your late boss's home. Since you found out all about him then I'm guessing that you have… or know where I can find some property of mine. A memory stick.'

Jack looked up at the leering face. 'I don't know what you're on about.'

Martin gave a momentary sideways glance at Allen and Jack's head exploded again in a brilliant white light. When the light faded, he could feel that one of his teeth felt slack and a trickle of blood was oozing from his mouth.

'You're going to tell me sooner or later. Our friend, Mister Allen, is probably hoping it will be later. He really enjoys his little chats with people.'

Martin gave another smirk. 'He particularly enjoyed his chat with young Mister Sterling.'

Jack struggled to form the words, slurring, 'If you've hurt that kid, I'll…'

'You're hardly in a position to start issuing threats. By all accounts, you've been a bit of a bad lad. What did you do to your old boss? The public are being told not to approach you. *Dangerous,* they're saying on the news. Oh, then there's the matter of the murder of poor Mister Donkin. Yes, it seems you've been a very bad boy. Nobody will be the least surprised if you disappear.'

'We both know that I never touched Donkin.'

'Not quite true. You were actually seen by witnesses dragging Donkin away. After you dumped him, he phoned me and told me what had happened. Mister Allen here had to go and rescue him.'

Martin broke into a wide grin. He was enjoying himself.

'He showed Neil where you had pulled your little petrol stunt. There were some tyre tracks on the grass. I'm sure that they are going to match the treads on your car. Of course, Donkin swore to me on his life that he hadn't told you anything.'

Martin gave a twisted smile. 'That was a most

278

unfortunate thing for him to say. Swore on his life, he did. One of the things people like you and I have in common is, that in our line of work, we can tell when someone's lying. I can't have people like Donkin gossiping. Little bits of tittle tattle can ruin a man's reputation.'

The throbbing in Jack's head was intensifying.

'So, I'm afraid that Mister Donkin met with an accident. What with people seeing you drive him off and with your tyre marks at the scene, your colleagues seem to have added two and two together and got twenty-two.'

Martin broke into a broad smile. 'You can always count on plod to jump to conclusions. It appears you're wanted for murder.'

Jack opened his mouth to speak and, with each pained word, produced speckles of blood flying from his wounded mouth. 'I suppose it was Allen responsible for Darren Wilson as well?'

'He was another person who couldn't keep his nose out of other people's business.'

'Where's Drew Sterling?'

Martin smiled again and glanced across at Allen. With a perfunctory nod, the thug left the room and returned a few moments later, dragging with him the boy, wearing nothing but a pair of boxer shorts.

At first, Jack didn't recognise him, but as soon as he did, a wave of relief came over him.

Drew looked how Jack felt. His face was bruised and swollen, with dark welts patterning his body. There were splashes of blood on his chest and some had run down an arm and covered his hand. His nose was swollen and had clearly been bleeding. As he was thrown onto the floor, he turned to look up at Jack and his eyes held a haunted look. Jack tried not to envisage the torment that he had been through.

But at least he was still alive.

Slade's relief was short lived.

Allen placed a leather case onto a side table and turned to Jack, a twisted leer on his face.

'Ah now! This is the bit Neil enjoys the most,' Martin said with a grin. 'You obviously know where my property is, so I would suggest that you to tell me sooner, rather than later.'

Jack thought of Jamie Hetherington and the copy memory sticks he had left with him. Slade now feared that he had put him in danger as well. He hoped that he wouldn't reveal anything about Jamie... no matter what was about to happen to him.

'Come on, Inspector. You might be able to hold out for a while...' He turned to look down at Drew. '...but what about your young friend here? You don't want his pain on your conscience, do you? Neil is very persuasive.'

Allen opened the case to reveal a strange assortment of tools. A hammer, a mallet, a set of pliers, some kind of small vice, an assortment of knives and, what appeared to be, a long screwdriver with the end filed to a sharpened point.

Jack pulled desperately at the plastic cable tie, but there was no give at all.

'Tell me where the memory stick is and whether you have made any copies. You can save young Drew here a lot of needless pain.'

Allen moved across to the shivering, almost naked figure on the floor and Drew Sterling was dragged unceremoniously across to the table, on which Allen had laid out the contents of the bag.

Allen picked up the vice-like implement and, taking Drew's right hand, forced it down on the table. Then, placing the vice below his thumb, he slowly twisted the butterfly wing and tightened the screw. Drew cried out in agony as the screw began to exert pressure on his fingernail.

'You have no doubt heard of the thumb screw. It's very effective. Most people think that the pain is from pressure on the nail.' He smiled. 'They'd be wrong. The real pain is when the screw is released and the blood flows back into the thumb, causing it to swell. That's when the real agony bites.'

The thumb screw was released and Drew let out an ear-ringing scream.

'Young Johnny never got to experience that particular pain. Neil was a bit over zealous with the preliminaries and he died from internal bleeding, before we got properly started. It caused me no end of problems, because he never got around to telling me where he had hidden my property. I'm hoping that you can maybe help me there.'

He turned to the quivering figure of Drew, who was

lying on the sheeting and had begun quietly sobbing.

'We actually went easier on this one. Neil is saving him for later. He likes the fresh ones. Likes it when they struggle a bit. You don't know what you missed, Jack, when you had him all to yourself in your nice cosy flat.'

His face was so close that Jack could smell red wine on his breath. 'After we've finished, I've promised Neil that he can play all he wants with your little chicken friend.'

Jack renewed his struggle, but was no closer to freeing himself. He tried to think clearly. To say something that might save Drew from the ordeal. Finally, he managed, 'People know where I am.'

Martin hesitated. 'I doubt that, Jack. I've heard you're running short of friends.'

'Don't be so sure. I wouldn't be so stupid as to come here alone.'

For a moment, Jack saw the shadow of a doubt cross his tormentors face. Martin looked across to Allen.

'Just check around outside. See where he's parked and make sure that he came alone. While you're there, search his car for the memory stick.'

Allen nodded and, selecting one of the larger knives from the table, headed out the door.

'You're only putting off the inevitable. Just tell me what I want and things will be so less painful for both of you.'

So intent was his focus on Jack, that he didn't notice the slight movement behind him, as Drew struggled painfully to his feet.

Jack thought fast. 'How do you know that I haven't already posted copies of the photographs to the press?'

The smile left Martin's face and he moved closer, glaring at Jack.

Behind him, Drew reached out with a shaking and bloodstained hand for the sharpened screwdriver. Summoning up all the strength left in his ravaged body, he swung it up and brought it down hard just above Martin's collar bone.

The honed point slid easily through the soft flesh of his neck and Martin's face contorted. He gasped and yelled out in pain and, half turning, saw Drew standing behind him.

With an animal cry of pain, he grabbed for the sharpened tool and pulled it free from his neck and from the weak grip of the terrified Drew.

That was a mistake.

Jack stared in fascination at what happened next.

A jet of blood shot out in a pulsating stream from the neck wound. At first, Martin seemed unable to comprehend what was happening. Then, dropping the screwdriver, he began franticly pressing down on the dark red fountain, but this just sent the spray out in different directions, as he desperately attempted to stop the flow.

The blood was beginning to pool on the polythene sheeting all around him and Martin whirled back around to face Jack. There was desperation in his eyes.

If Martin was appealing for help, he had chosen the wrong person.

Jack looked on, shocked but unfeelingly, as Martin sank to his knees, the life literally draining from him.

With a last desperate look at Slade, Martin slumped to the sheeting in a crumpled bloodied heap.

The flow of blood had slowed down from the wound, but still came in short regular spurts, as his body twitched and a large pool of blood spread slowly across the plastic sheeting.

Finally he stopped, and eyes so recently wild with terror now stared blankly up at the ceiling.

Drew lay paralysed on the floor, hypnotised by the bloody maelstrom he had instigated.

Jack needed to get his attention. 'Drew! Drew! Listen to me. You have to get me loose.'

Drew looked across to Jack as if seeing him for the first time.

'Come on, Drew. Quickly, before Allen gets back.'

Slowly Drew moved along the floor, sliding his bare feet through the pool of gore, as he made his way towards Jack.

'Get something sharp from the bag.'

Drew paused for a second, turned to the bag and took out a small knife with a four inch blade. He stumbled across to the chair and, in a pain-addled daze, began to saw at the bonds, until with a sudden snap, Jack was free.

Slade rubbed at his wrists and his hands felt on fire as the blood began once again to course through his veins.

Their ordeal was not yet over, with Allen able to return

at any moment.

Every inch of Jack's body ached with the effort, but now he was free he stretched to try to get blood flowing to his muscles.

Then, glancing around for a suitable weapon, he snatched up the hammer from the assorted tools.

Then there was the sound of footsteps approaching down the hall.

Jack stumbled, wincing, to the hinged side of the door, where Allen himself had earlier been concealed. Leaning back against the wall, he felt weak and was trying to blank out the throbbing pain from his face and chest.

He knew that he was running on adrenaline and prayed that he would have the strength to finish this.

The door swung open and Allen sauntered in, still carrying the large knife.

He stopped and his mouth dropped open as he tried to take in the scene before him.

Drew was still on the floor, awkwardly in a foetal position, and beside him, the body of Martin lay in a dark pool of blood, which was already starting to congeal.

Turning to the chair upon which Jack had been seated, Allen realised that it was now empty. This seemed to suddenly register and he wheeled around to see Jack behind the door.

Allen began to raise his knife.

He was too late.

Jack swung the hammer wildly aiming for Allen's head, but instead, caught the bodybuilder a heavy blow on the top of his left arm, below his shoulder.

There was the loud crack of splintering bone and Allen dropped the blade.

Letting out a loud piercing shriek, he instinctively grabbed at the injury with his other arm.

This left him vulnerable and facing Jack squarely.

Drawing back his foot and with every ounce of strength left that his battered body could muster, Jack let fly with a kick which connected with his opponent's groin.

It may not have featured in the police manual of self-defence, but as moves go, it was extremely effective. It might just become Slade's signature move.

With a strange high pitched squeal, Allen pitched

forward and dropped to the floor like a sack of potatoes, where he lay in a heap, writhing and whimpering.

Jack resisted the urge to deliver a further kick. He probably knew he couldn't summon up the energy. Besides, there was no fight left in the convulsed figure lying at his feet. Jack had seen the results of injuries like that before.

In less than an hour, Allen would have a scrotum to match a certain teenager currently recovering in the local hospital.

Stumbling to the corner of the room, Jack retrieved his discarded sweat top and walked sluggishly across to Drew. Gently, he put it over the shivering boy. It was too large for him, but that went some way to cover him. Carefully raising Drew to his feet, he guided him out of the room, away from the carnage and into the hallway.

A telephone rested on a small glass table by the wall and, as Jack lifted the receiver, he realised that he was leaving wet smears of blood on everything he touched.

Ignoring the mess, Slade punched in the treble nine and asked the operator for the police control room.

His voice sounded croaky as he spoke and it was only when he had finished that he allowed himself the luxury of collapsing into a chair.

He watched as little droplets of blood from an open cut on his face dripped steadily onto the cream carpet.

His first instinct was to somehow avoid the carpet becoming further stained. Then he thought, *Fuck it. Martin's hardly likely to complain.*

DEATH RATTLE

CHAPTER 50

Over the following week, a search team using ground penetrating radar located Johnny Lee's body, or rather what was left of it, buried in a shallow grave, within the grounds of the small cottage.

When exhumed, the soil stained and badly decomposed body was placed in an undertaker's zip up body bag and transported from the scene in a black transit van.

Because of the state of decomposition, the corpse couldn't be accepted at the hospital mortuary, but instead was taken to a small brick building at the edge of a local cemetery, usually reserved for any bodies fished out from the river.

The last ignominy was that, even in death, no-one wanted Johnny Lee.

With no close family, Johnny would lie alone and unclaimed to await a post mortem.

Another grisly task for Doctor Paul Clifford.

A second body was also located nearby and a check of dental records identified it as the missing barman, Dean Masters. Jack could only guess what transgression he had been guilty of to end with him being dumped in a shallow unmarked grave.

Slade was only thankful that Drew had not suffered the same fate.

One of the team suggested it had been a bit of a risk to bury the bodies in the grounds of the cottage, but then no one was looking for just another couple of missing boys. That had been the problem from the start.

They were the real lost boys.

Johnny Lee and Dean Masters had become non-persons. No family, few friends and even fewer people to mourn their passing. Jack thought back to the boys he had met that night at the MESMAC offices and wondered how many hundreds of other lost boys were out there.

On the fringes of society... who would miss them if one day they simply disappeared?

The following week, Johnny's funeral was held in the smaller East Side chapel at the Newcastle Crematorium. Parker attended, representing the force, as was often the protocol for funerals of murder victims. The main body of mourners consisted of Jack, Dave Armstrong, several members of the Homicide Investigation Team and, a couple of rows from the back, sat Mark Burton.

Jamie Hetherington had turned up and was standing at the back of the chapel, next to Drew Sterling, who had his head lowered, shielding his red and swollen eyes. The bruises had gone, but he still looked only a shade of his former self and Jack wondered how long it would take, if ever, for him to get over his ordeal.

The only relatives of Johnny who were eventually traced were a middle aged aunt and uncle living in Northumberland. They couldn't be bothered to turn up, but had agreed that Johnny Lee was to be cremated; a decision, Jack suspected, based solely on economic grounds.

Short service over, the small group made their way slowly to the chapel exit, where the minister stood to shake the small congregation's hands as they left.

Outside, Jack approached Drew to offer him a lift home, but the boy merely shook his head and walked away across the car park, towards the crematorium entrance.

Jamie spoke briefly to Jack, before making his way to the car park. There wasn't much to say.

Dave said quietly, 'I'll get the car,' and walked off towards the parked vehicles.

As Jack watched Jamie and Drew walking away, Parker approached with Burton in his wake.

'Jack, I've had word from Professional Standards. Seems the Chief feels that, under the circumstances, it would be best if the internal enquiry into your actions should be dropped. Command Block want a line drawn under this. They would like us to get our heads together and make sure we're singing off the same hymn sheet when it comes to any press release.'

He looked uncomfortable and cleared his throat. 'So, you'll be wanting this back.'

He held out an open padded bag and Slade saw that it contained his warrant card in its black leather holder and a station key.

He stared at them for what seemed an age. Then, reaching out, silently took the bag and slipped it into the pocket of his overcoat.

'So, Jack. No hard feelings? Parker said. 'We got a good result, in the end.'

Slade held his gaze for a few seconds, before wordlessly pushing past between them, and crossing the car park to join Dave.

As he walked away, he felt the first spits of rain falling and and quickly getting heavier.

Looking up, he saw black gathering clouds coming down from the North.

That's where the movies get it right. It always rains at funerals.

FIN

ABOUT THE AUTHOR

David Jewell is a North East based award winning writer and the Producer and Director of the UK Television series, Write On. His recent documentary programme, 'From Pit To Parliament' featuring the controversial politician, Ronnie Campbell, was Nominated for a Royal Television Society Award in 2020.

With thirty one years police experience, rising to the rank of Inspector, he has worked at the sharp end of some of the toughest areas in the North East, receiving several commendations.

His writing captures the voices and attitudes of a tough working class Northern city, and often the black humour of those characters who police it.

In his debut novel 'The Death Rattle', he introduces Detective Inspector Jack Slade and brings a new dark and gritty realism to the crime writing genre.

Lightning Source UK Ltd.
Milton Keynes UK
UKHW010745220820
368657UK00001B/200